# An Alternative History of Britain

# An Alternative History of Britain

## The Wars of the Roses 1455–85

Timothy Venning

Pen & Sword
**MILITARY**

First published in Great Britain in 2013 by
Pen & Sword Military
an imprint of
Pen & Sword Books Ltd
47 Church Street
Barnsley
South Yorkshire
S70 2AS

Copyright © Timothy Venning 2013

ISBN 978-1-78159-127-7

A CIP catalogue record for this book is available from the British Library.

Typeset in 11pt Ehrhardt by
Mac Style, Beverley, E. Yorkshire

Printed and bound in the UK by MPG Printgroup, UK

Pen & Sword Books Ltd incorporates the Imprints of Pen & Sword Aviation,
Pen & Sword Family History, Pen & Sword Maritime, Pen & Sword Military,
Pen & Sword Discovery, Wharncliffe Local History, Wharncliffe True Crime,
Wharncliffe Transport, Pen & Sword Select, Pen & Sword Military Classics,
Leo Cooper, The Praetorian Press, Remember When, Seaforth Publishing
and Frontline Publishing.

For a complete list of Pen & Sword titles please contact
PEN & SWORD BOOKS LIMITED
47 Church Street, Barnsley, South Yorkshire, S70 2AS, England
E-mail: enquiries@pen-and-sword.co.uk
Website: www.pen-and-sword.co.uk

# Contents

# Acknowledgements

With thanks as usual to my editors at Pen and Sword – Phil Sidnell for his support for the 'Alternative History' series and Ting Baker for her painstaking work on the text.

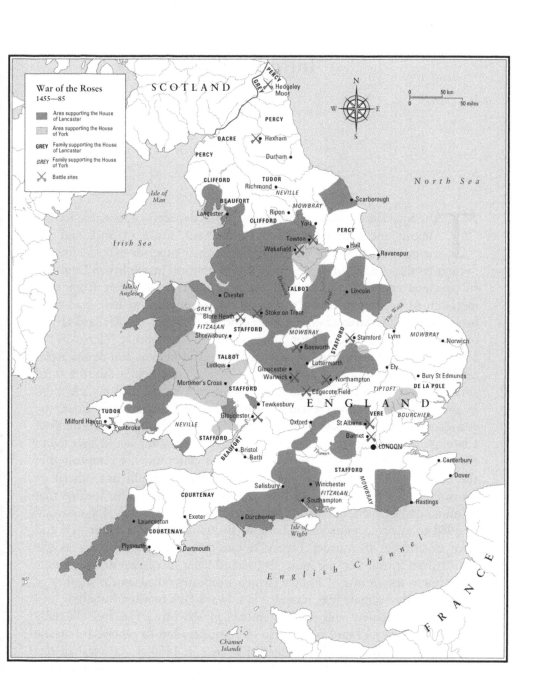

War of the Roses
1455—85

- Area supporting the House of Lancaster
- Area supporting the House of York
- **GREY** Family supporting the House of Lancaster
- *GREY* Family supporting the House of York
- ✗ Battle sites

SCOTLAND

PERCY
GREY
Hedgeley Moor

PERCY

DACRE
Hexham

PERCY
Durham

North Sea

TUDOR
Richmond
NEVILLE

CLIFFORD

BEAUFORT
Lancaster
Ripon
MOWBRAY
Scarborough

CLIFFORD
York
PERCY

Towton
Hull

Wakefield
Ravenspur

Isle of Man

Irish Sea

Isle of Anglesey
Chester
TALBOT
Lincoln

GREY
Blore Heath
Stoke on Trent
Derwent
Dun
Trent
The Wash

FITZALAN
Shrewsbury
STAFFORD
MOWBRAY
STAFFORD
Stamford
Lynn
MOWBRAY
Norwich

TALBOT
Bosworth

Ludlow
Lutterworth
Ely
Bury St Edmunds

Mortimer's Cross
Gloucester
Warwick
Northampton
TIPTOFT
DE LA POLE

STAFFORD
Edgecote Field
E N G L A N D

Tewkesbury
VERE
BOURCHIER

TUDOR
Milford Haven
NEVILLE
Gloucester
Oxford
St Albans

Pembroke
STAFFORD
Barnet

BEAUFORT
Bristol
Bath
Thames
LONDON

Canterbury

STAFFORD
Dover

COURTENAY
Salisbury
Winchester
MOWBRAY

FITZALAN
Southampton
Hastings

Launceston
Exeter
Dorchester

COURTENAY
Isle of Wight

Plymouth
Dartmouth

E n g l i s h   C h a n n e l

F R A N C E

Channel Islands

N
W E
S

0   50 km
0   50 miles

# Introduction

The final thirty years of the 'Plantagenet' dynasty – a surname for the family incidentally invented by Richard, Duke of York and his supporters in the 1450s to emphasize their superior dynastic lineage to their rivals – was an unprecedented era of political instability in England. In previous centuries the smooth (or not) transfer of power from each monarch to his son or brother, usually his own choice as heir, had been broken only once when childless and autocratic 32-year-old Richard II was overthrown in an invasion by his cousin Henry of Bolingbroke (Henry IV) in 1399. Henry had claimed to be Richard's rightful heir, as son of the next-senior male offspring of Edward III to leave a male heir, Edward's third surviving son Duke John of Lancaster (John 'of Gaunt'). But his 'election' by an assembly of nobles excluded the rights of Edmund Mortimer, the grandson – daughter's son – of Edward III's second son, Duke Lionel of Clarence, who was only a child at the time so his accession would have led to the instability of a regency. Indeed, Edmund's claim was not even tested at the election; the 'Salic Law' theory that a woman could not inherit or transmit rights to a throne did not apply in England. The feeling that Edmund had been cheated by the illegal usurpation of Henry's 'Lancastrian' line led to assorted plots and rebellions in his name under Henry IV and later an attempt to murder Henry V, but then these faded away as the Lancastrian throne became more secure and led a successful war to pursue its rights to the throne of France (which ironically relied on the legality of succession via a female line, namely via Edward III's mother, Isabella).

But the incapacity and misjudgements of the unwarlike and allegedly unworldly Henry VI and his coterie of favourites led to renewed dynastic challenges after the humiliating loss of France in 1450–3. As we shall see, this was largely stimulated by the exclusion of powerful nobles from decision-making at court and the fruits of office by Henry's clique, led by the junior Lancastrian line of Beaufort, and was thus politically opportunistic. Dynastic luck and the shifting sands of politics resulted in the current heir of Edmund Mortimer's line, his sister Anne's son Duke Richard of York, being the leader of the politico-military 'opposition' to Henry VI's disastrous governance in the 1440s and early 1450s, excluded from power and seemingly under threat of elimination like the King's late uncle Duke Humphrey of Gloucester. Thus a mixture of ambition and self-preservation determined his struggle for influence with the King's favourites in 1450–5, a political bid for power over an increasingly feeble and once catatonic King rather than a dynastic challenge, although his role as a potential heir also implied the latter. It was as much a case of 'storming the closet', as eighteenth-century politics called a bid by frustrated 'opposition' figures to force their admission to office (and perks) on a reluctant king, as a dynastic coup.

The drastic way in which York secured this, on the battlefield at St Albans in 1455, and his choice to physically eliminate the King's closest advisers in the process, then turned it into a vendetta between his 'party', led by his family and the Nevilles, and the King and Queen's court faction led by the Beauforts and Percies. But York's initial sights were set on the heirship to the King, in place of his infant son who was soon being claimed to be a bastard by the 'Yorkists', rather than a direct claim on the throne. The latter was only made after York and his allies had been driven into exile and stripped of their lands by the Queen's faction in 1459, fought their way back to power in 1460, and seized the King. Even then most of his own supporters were opposed to his claim to be rightful king, which had to be halted – and Henry's deposition only followed the next round of the vendetta, when the Queen's men attacked and killed York and other nobles at Wakefield in December 1460 but York's son Edward (IV) successfully fought back. Edward IV's disputed 'election' was then followed by victory on the battlefield of Towton, the elimination of more of Henry's allies, and eventually the capture of Henry and the flight of Queen Margaret to France. Seemingly routed for good, Henry's faction then had an unexpected stroke of luck as Edward quarrelled with his cousin and chief backer Richard Neville, Earl of Warwick, who killed his chief rivals and arrested the King in 1469, backed down from deposing him, but was driven out of England by Edward in 1470 and in retaliation invaded to restore Henry VI. The unlikely alliance of Warwick with Queen Margaret, the woman responsible for the deaths of his father and brother, was then overthrown by the returning Edward in March to May 1471 – but Edward died aged forty in 1483 and his son Edward V was then deposed as a 'bastard' by his brother Richard (III). Richard, the most controversial monarch in English history, then faced the implacable hostility of many of his late brother's loyalists, who lined up with a seemingly insignificant Beaufort scion (Henry Tudor) and other diehard 'Lancastrians' to overthrow him in August 1485.

The Crown thus changed hands unexpectedly six times in 1461–85 – and nearly did so again in a Yorkist invasion in 1487. Kings were deposed, murdered (or not), died in suspicious circumstances, or were killed in battle, the senior nobility were destroyed by deaths in battle and political executions, and high politics seemed dominated by unsavoury and violent blood-feuds. Not surprisingly, this era has provided a rich field for writers since the days of Shakespeare, and is still a favourite for romantic historical fiction (usually centred on Richard III) in modern times. Recent contributors have included Rosemary Hawley Jarman, Josephine Tey, Sharon Penman, and Philippa Gregory, and TV programmes include a 'Trial of Richard III' on Channel Four. Was he really a child-murdering psychopath, a self-preserving political strategist who went too far, or an honourable and misjudged figure 'smeared' by Tudor 'spin-doctors'? The influence of fiction on the popular conception of the period indeed includes the very concept of a 'War of the Roses' – not a contemporary term, but thought up by Sir Walter Scott in his novel *Anne of Geierstein* in 1829. The first serious historical novel about the period, *Last of the Barons* by Edward Bulwer Lytton in 1843, introduced the concept of 'Warwick the Kingmaker' and of Edward IV as a smooth-talking lecher (whose secret betrothal/ marriage c.1462 is still a topic of controversy).

In reality, the idea of a 'White Rose' (York) and a 'Red Rose' (Lancaster) faction, which Shakespeare peddled in the 1590s, comes from the retrospective viewpoint of post-1485 chroniclers, who celebrated the marriage of Henry Tudor and Edward IV's daughter Elizabeth as uniting the two heraldic roses of their families. As the 'Plantagenet' surname was a propaganda invention of 1450s Yorkists who revived the personal sobriquet of Henry II's father Geoffrey, so the notion of a self-proclaimed 'Tudor' dynasty is inaccurate – Henry VII usually called himself 'Richmond' after his earldom. But what is not at issue is that a remarkable degree of political instability – some of it self-generating – and changes of fortune saw control of power shift with the results of political alliances, chancy battles, kingly mental breakdown, and sudden royal deaths (natural or not). The issue arises – how easily could things have turned out differently? What if York had been able to secure political power in the 1450s without removing Henry VI or his son, or he had not been killed by the Queen's men in 1460? What if Edward IV had never broken with Warwick, been deposed or killed by him in 1469–70, or had failed to regain power in 1471? What if Edward had not unexpectedly died in 1483, his son's advisers had fought off the challenge of Duke Richard of Gloucester, or Richard had won the battle of Bosworth? This study seeks to explore some of these very real possibilities.

*Chapter One*

# Before 1453: Henry's Degree of Culpability. Holy or Incompetent?

The intense turbulence and political reversals of the period from Henry VI's first outbreak of mental incapacity – a period of catatonic stupor when he was unable to speak or move unaided – threw up a series of unstable governments, although the problem of domestic strife long predated his breakdown in 1453. The country was afflicted by private warfare between rival great families, itself a sign of their confidence that they could take advantage of an absence of firm government, with the skirmish between Percies and Nevilles at Heworth Moor in Yorkshire the first serious inter-magnate clash of many. The aftermath of the humiliating loss of the King's last lands in France in 1450–3, leading to anger from those who had suffered from the restored Valois' confiscations of the lands Henry V and VI had granted them there or deplored the poor English military commitment and leadership, was tied in with resentment of the monopoly of patronage by a small faction around Henry VI in the 1440s. The most powerful magnate minister of this period and royal 'favourite', Michael de la Pole, Duke of Suffolk, was also held responsible for a lack of serious military commitment to Normandy and blunders such as the failed 'appeasement' that saw the surrender of Maine in 1448, and was impeached by Parliament and murdered in flight during the popular outbreak of 1450. But his political allies, led by the Beauforts under Edmund, Duke of Somerset, remained at the centre of a 'court party' who had strong personal support from the increasingly forceful young Queen Margaret (herself the symbol of Suffolk's failed rapprochement with Charles VII in 1444, the occasion of her marriage to Henry) and the partisan King. Edmund bore as much responsibility as Suffolk for the disasters in France, having been an unsuccessful governor of Maine in the early 1440s and overall commander in Normandy at the time of its reconquest in 1449–50 (where his inaction and willingness to surrender were controversial). He and his late elder brother John, Marquis of Somerset, had diverted scarce English royal resources to their governorship of Maine at the time when the Duke of York had been struggling to hold back the Valois advance in 1442–3, and John's Loire valley expedition of 1443 had been a costly failure. (Their uncle Cardinal Beaufort was the principal private financer of the defence of France, and funded their campaigns; he was also more inclined to compromise in the failed Anglo-French peace-talks than York's 'hard-line' ally, Duke Humphrey of Gloucester.) This seems to have soured relations between York and the Beauforts, adding to their dynastic rivalry as potential heirs to the childless King Henry.

It should be noted that there was a marked similarity to the situation of the early 1320s and 1380s in official patronage in the 1440s, with a concentration of the grants of offices and lands on one small faction of senior courtiers – and with other figures, who were to be prominent in the violent 'reaction' (as in 1326 and 1387), excluded.[1] Suffolk, like his ancestor Michael de la Pole in 1385–6 and the Despensers in the early 1320s, seemed to have an unnatural grip on patronage and on the King's favour. The King was personally alienated from and feared his 'excluded' close relative and potential successors, Duke Humphrey (to 1447) and then the Duke of York, as Edward II had feared the intentions of his Lancaster cousins Earls Thomas and Henry and as Richard II had feared John 'of Gaunt' and his son Henry of Bolingbroke. In all these cases, it was the King's 'natural' advisers, his close relatives, who were excluded from influence and the benefits of patronage – although Henry VI did not go as far as Edward II, who executed Earl Thomas in 1322, and Richard II who was accused of plotting to kill Gaunt in 1385–6 and again in 1398 and did kill his uncle Thomas of Gloucester in 1397. It was Suffolk and the Beauforts who were blamed for Duke Humphrey's sudden death while under arrest in 1447, though the King had arrested and ruined him first.[2] The Duke could be regarded as a 'martyr' of Beaufort intrigue, one in a long line of 'honest' senior royal relatives ruined by jealous court rivals such as Thomas of Lancaster and Thomas of Gloucester. (His arrest and suspicious demise also warned York, already a prickly character insistent on his 'rights', of what could happen to him if he let his guard slip.)

The idea of the Beauforts and Suffolk as a 'peace party' at odds with the 'hard-line' York in the 1440s is, however, too simplistic – John and Edmund both fought hard, if incompetently, to defend their lands in Maine and Edmund did not have the troops, money, or local Norman support to mount a vigorous defence of Normandy in 1450 (though his passivity was still worthy of criticism). John and Suffolk had both fought in France back in Henry V's reign and had been captured by the French, the former at Baugé

(1421) and the latter at Jargeau (1429), and were not inexperienced civilian courtiers; and Suffolk's eagerness to negotiate and to surrender Maine in the mid-1440s was the King's personal – naïve – policy not his alone. Arguably both Suffolk and Edmund Beaufort were 'defeatist' – the first as a negotiator to hand Maine over without a fight, the latter in his somnolence in Normandy in 1449–50 – out of hard experience of French military strength, and York lacked their experience of defeat and captivity. For that matter, York had been as ruthless and militarily dilatory as John Beaufort in insisting that he had his 'requests' for extensive legal power over his command in France granted before he sailed there, thus delaying a vital campaign (1436).[3] His attempt to induce the Council to give him full vice regal powers then delayed his sailing until it was too late for him to co-ordinate his march in Normandy with Duke Humphrey's 'push' southwards from Calais. In 1443, in a similar manner, John Beaufort did not sail for Normandy until August due to haggling over his powers and his rewards (the latter to include a dukedom); he thus arrived too late for his planned march to the Loire and on to Bordeaux to drive Charles VII's army back in Gascony.[4] Was York really so much more zealous and war-ready than his rivals in the crucial period of 1435–50? The latter were not unfairly traduced by him, however; the demands that John Beaufort made of the government in 1443 were outrageously venal, his brother Edmund was keen to secure his personal safety not that of Normandy as he surrendered Rouen in October 1449, and Suffolk undermined the King's finances in the 1440s by his wasteful administration.[5]

The fact that Charles VII pressed so relentlessly for the return of Maine in 1444–8, invaded it when the English broke their agreed surrender date in January 1448, and then raised more troops to attacked Normandy within a year-and-a-half shows that if anyone was cozening the 'war-averse' Henry in the 1440s it was him, not a 'treacherous' Suffolk. The fault equally lay with Henry for assuming that handing over Maine would satisfy him for years rather than being regarded with contempt as a sign of weakness. The blame for the ignominious debacle in Maine in 1446–8 was, however, laid on Suffolk by York as early as 1447–9,[6] and was extended when the King's chief negotiator (and ex-Treasurer) Bishop Moleyns of Chichester, hapless facilitator of the surrender, accused him 'in extremis' as he was about to be lynched by angry soldiers in Portsmouth.[7]

The disaster in Normandy that followed was duly blamed on Suffolk by a furious Parliament in winter 1449–50 and he was impeached, pardoned by the King but exiled, and was seized and executed as he fled at sea by vigilantes.[8] The charges against Suffolk had included a paranoid but believable claim that he had betrothed his son to Margaret Beaufort, future mother of Henry VII and daughter of the late Marquis of Somerset, so that her claim to the throne could be used to make this couple Henry's heirs.[9] The principal loser if this had occurred would have been York – so had York or his allies invented or backed up the charge? The hand of York might be seen behind the disgrace and death of Henry's trusted minister Suffolk, at least in Beaufort eyes, and the events of early 1450 could thus add to the King's alienation from the Duke.

Marginalized senior royal relatives took the lead in the forcible removal of previous kings' 'evil counsellors': Edward II's estranged wife and elder son were the leaders of the revolution of 1326–7; Richard's uncle Gloucester and cousin Henry of Bolingbroke were among the 'Appellants' in 1387; Henry removed Richard in 1399; and York was accused of suspicious encouragement to rebels in 1450 and defied the King in arms in 1451–2. So was it plausible for courtiers or the King to believe that York was aiming to emulate Henry of Bolingbroke? Or did the fact that a second arrested Duke of Gloucester had died mysteriously in custody in royal hands in fifty years (1397 and 1447) exacerbate the problem that Humphrey's arrest had been meant to solve, i.e. removing or intimidating the King's untrustworthy heirs? It is more likely that Humphrey died naturally than that he was poisoned, but that was not how contemporaries saw it[10] – and arguably it lessened the chances that York would ever permit himself to be taken alive by the King's officials. Was Humphrey dead more dangerous than Humphrey alive, in increasing the chance of York defying the King with armed force? Was the real 'first act' in the slide to civil war the Duke's arrest in 1447, neither the fall of Normandy nor the Cade rebellion?

Crucially for the future, Somerset – a personal foe of York by 1450, as shown by their repeated claims against each other – inherited Suffolk's role as Henry VI's most powerful magnate courtier after 1450 and was regarded as close to the Queen (he was rumoured to be the father of her son).[11] His faction, in which the semi-royal Dukes of Buckingham and Exeter were prominent, continued to monopolize office and favour and exclude York despite the threat posed by the latter's vast estates in the north and the Welsh Marches. Genealogy and family tradition mattered a great deal in fifteenth century noble politics, and Buckingham was the heir in the female (Bourchier) line of the executed Duke Thomas of Gloucester and Exeter was the head of the Holland descendants of Richard II's loyal half-brothers, enemies of the 'usurper' Henry of Bolingbroke. Both had a distant claim on the throne, and could be plausibly elevated to heirship if York was disinherited and the Beaufort claim was disallowed through illegitimacy – or the Beauforts could call on their alliance in joint enmity to the heirship 'front-runner' York. There was, in effect, an alliance of the junior royal lines against the next line to Henry's, that of York, with Somerset representing the family of John 'of Gaunt' by his third marriage.

York united the lines of Edward III's second and fourth sons, Lionel and Edmund. He had inherited his mother, Anne Mortimer's, extensive Marcher lands – and her claim to the throne via Edward III's second surviving son, Lionel. Richard II had recognized the March line as his heirs, and its descent via the female line was not an insuperable legal problem – after all, the English kings claimed the French throne by that means. This genealogical seniority to the House of Lancaster (descended from John 'of Gaunt', the third surviving son of Edward III) made York more of a threat than his father Richard, Earl of Cambridge (descended from the fourth son, Edmund of Langley) had been. The latter had already been executed in 1415 for plotting to murder Henry V before the Agincourt campaign. To add to the danger, York had made a name for himself as a reasonably successful military commander in Normandy in the early 1440s (unlike his successor, Somerset's older brother John Beaufort) and had opposed Suffolk's unsuccessful governorship and policy there. He was a magnet for returned captains and soldiers disgruntled at the inadequate support they had received from Suffolk's regime at home in the final years of Henry V's Continental empire. The popular anger at this 'betrayal' and its focus on Suffolk and his cronies as the villains was shown in Parliament and the Cade revolt in 1449–50. 'Cade' claimed to be from York's Mortimer family,[12] so was he an ally of the Duke?

The alienation of York, sent out of England by Suffolk's government to carry out the (usually titular) titular governance of Ireland in person in 1449, from the dominant faction at court thus continued after Suffolk's death. Far from solving the conflicts by removing the perceived chief 'evil counsellor' attacked in Parliament in 1450, the politically dangerous monopolizer of Royal patronage, Suffolk's death only led to new problems. There were allegations at court that the exiled York had been behind the popular outbreaks of 1450, and that they were aimed at removing the childless Henry from the throne in his favour. (The Cade rebels denied this.[13]) Whether or not this finally alienated the threatened Queen from York, the Duke was not trusted with any major office or role at court after his return from Ireland. Indeed, amidst the continuing factional confrontations York's leading supporter Sir William Oldhall (in trouble at court as a leader of Parliamentary action against the Suffolk regime) was ostentatiously dragged out of sanctuary at St Martin's-le-Grand in London by Somerset's men in a blatant sign of official ill-will to the Duke.[14] A first military confrontation between York's armed supporters and the King occurred at Dartford in March 1452, though on this occasion the greater numbers of the royal faction's troops enabled the mediating senior clerics to persuade York into a formal submission.[15]

The tension between court/magnate factions over the correct policy towards France was inevitable, and the disgrace of the loss of both Normandy and Aquitaine in 1450–3 led to Suffolk's enemies blaming him for incompetence or even deliberate sabotage of the English war-effort. His attempt to win a long truce with Charles VII by the Anjou marriage and the 'goodwill' abandonment of undefendable Maine in 1445–8 had been exploited by the French who had returned to the attack as soon as it was convenient – as was probably inevitable. But as far as Suffolk was concerned, the alternative was a financially exhaustive and politically risky long-term war where failure could see overwhelming public demands for York's recall from Ireland to take command. Retrenchment at court would, however, have enabled more troops to be sent to Somerset's army in Normandy, giving him a better chance of holding out – and in 1448–50 court prodigality continued unabated. This was a major mistake by Suffolk, though cutting back would alienate his avaricious clients and threaten his power as well. The political storm that broke in 1449 was at a lower level than magnate criticism, being centred on Parliament in the first instance (with demands to sack and prosecute the 'corrupt' ministers reminiscent of the 'Good Parliament' in 1376)[16] and then a violent popular outbreak. Indeed, Henry arguably made matters worse by not giving in and dismissing Suffolk at the first Parliamentary demands in July 1449, at a time when he still held Normandy and the blackmailing MPs were prepared to fund a new army if he sacked Suffolk – which would have helped to raise a larger army than was actually gathered in winter 1449–50. This might have held onto Normandy, at least in the short term – long-term defence of the 'open' frontier and the walled towns against Charles VII's large army and artillery was unlikely. Instead, Henry dismissed Parliament and had no money to pay for reinforcing Normandy in autumn 1449,[17] and the French invasion proceeded with only a small English expedition – under a minor captain, Sir Thomas Kyriell, not the capable and popular York – to try to halt it. The King's failed gamble on dismissing Parliament to save his chief minister, then having to call a new one in less favourable circumstances later, is reminiscent of Charles I's actions with the 'Short Parliament' in 1640. To that extent, Henry bore major responsibility for the debacle in Normandy in 1449–50 – as he did for vainly writing admiring letters to his hostile uncle Charles VII in the mid-1440s assuring his goodwill and promising to hand over Maine by a certain date when he could not be sure this would be practicable.[18] (What if his local garrison-commanders refused to do it?) In reality, Henry was as guilty as Suffolk of naivety and incompetence in his French policy of the 1440s, and his extravagant expenditure at court made his ability to raise armies less possible.

The Cade revolt, as in 1381, focussed on Kent and led to a march on London and 'lynch-law' by the armed protesters in the streets. (Henry, unlike Richard II in 1381, hid in the Midlands.) The extent of the anger and violence seems to have been unexpected, and probably Suffolk was too preoccupied with the danger from dissident magnates of royal blood which the Crown had faced in 1387–8 and 1399 – a problem seemingly warded off by sending York to Ireland. The popular anger was bound to focus on Suffolk, given his visible monopoly of patronage and policy. But this raises the question of why an adult king had allowed one minister such a free rein, and thus Henry's culpability for the crisis. Already in the 1440s the evidence of popular rumour, recorded in the chronicles of Harding and Capgrave, spoke of Henry being scorned by his most outspoken subjects as a simpleton.[19] The probability is that he was easily led by unscrupulous courtiers into giving them excessive grants rather than judiciously buying support from a wider 'constituency'. The likely fate for a king who had such an 'unbalanced' use of patronage had been seen in the fall of the over-rewarded and recklessly greedy Despensers in 1326 and of Suffolk's ancestor Michael de la Pole in 1386, if not the grants Richard II had made to his favourites (a somewhat wider circle) in 1397–9. Henry thus neglected his first duty as a political leader – and his generous grants to his favourite projects, such as King's College Cambridge, can also be seen in the light of reckless favouritism rather than of piety alone.[20] The land-grants that Henry had been making since his effective majority (1437) were subject to a sweeping review and cancellation by Parliament in the early 1450s, an indictment of nationwide perceptions of their fair distribution of assets among the landed gentry and nobles. Like Edward II and Richard II, the King was perceived to be the tool of a greedy and politically disastrous faction. But it is clear that Edward and Richard both asserted themselves after their political 'defeats' (1310 and 1387–8) in angry retaliation against those who had constrained them. The executions of ex-rebel Thomas of Lancaster in 1322 and of some of the 'Lords Appellant' in 1397 were the King's work, though encouraged by their 'ultra' supporters. In Henry's case, his personal role in the 'reaction' in the 1450s is absent – at least from the time of his mental collapse in 1453. This helped to save his reputation in subsequent decades and he became known posthumously as a saintly fool not a villain, though it should be pointed out that any 'evidence' of this attitude in post-1485 works may have been influenced by his nephew Henry VII's propaganda efforts to have him canonized.[21]

Henry VI's unwillingness to see the necessity of balancing grants among different factions at court was coupled with an undoubted political reliance on one group of lords. The latter were confident enough of his support (or his indifference to injustice) to abuse their power and manipulate local politics for their own benefit. Significantly, the major disturbances of 1449–50 broke out in areas under the dominance of Henry's favourite ministers, the beneficiaries of his lavish patronage – Suffolk in East Anglia, Lord Treasurer Fiennes in Kent and Sussex, and Bishop Ayscough in Wiltshire. All of these men, Suffolk in particular, had a collection of offices and grants of royal lands in their regions unprecedented for generations; the last such political 'monopolists' had been the favourites of another weak king, Edward II's Despenser allies, who met a similarly grisly fate at the hands of their enemies when overthrown. Their local leadership of society had been delegated to their clients in their absence at court, and the latter were abusing the processes of government and justice without any prospect that the King would intervene.

As in 1326, 1387, and 1399, the King was seen to be partisan and not carrying out his duty to see justice imposed, and the victims ended up by taking revenge themselves; this 'anarchy' of local armed feuding was underway well before the explosion of anger caused by the loss of Maine and Normandy in 1448–50 and so had other causes. It also preceded the return of soldiers from the evacuated lands in France and so was not due to unemployed soldiers or ruffianly retainers used to having their way by force; the infamous and long-running feud of the Courtenays and Bonvilles in Devon was descending into armed clashes as early as 1440–1.

Henry's lack of discrimination or common sense in his lavish generosity with grants of Crown lands and local offices were complained of at the time in the 1440s, and were later indicted by Lord Chief Justice Fortescue as an example of how not to run a just and successful government.[22] To that extent the monopoly of royal favour and receipt of grants by the Suffolk-Beaufort faction in the 1440s was both a reason for and a result of the young King's naïve ineptitude, and it reflected his insecurity about his potential heirs – Humphrey and then York – who were the main political 'alternatives' as his senior advisers. The early death of Henry's elder uncle John, Duke of Bedford, aged forty-six, in September 1435 was thus a political disaster as he had 'held the ring' between Humphrey and the Beauforts in their power-struggles since 1422. Had he been alive in the 1440s he might have been still in office as lieutenant of Normandy (his regency there would have lapsed on Henry's 'majority' in 1437) and so been unable to rein in the King's extravagance and reliance on venal courtiers. But if he had been back in England Suffolk's and the Beauforts' misrule would have been less likely, and so a violent Parliamentary 'purge' and popular revolt in 1450 have been averted. Would this have lessened Henry's estrangement from York? (It would also have meant that Bedford's widow, Jacquetta of St Pol, would have been unavailable to marry Sir Richard Woodville, meaning that York's controversial daughter-in-law-to-be, Elizabeth Woodville, was never born.)

Henry VI was not the first king to act with injustice and suspicion towards his relatives, and ambitious courtiers were always ready to accuse a monarch's kin of treason with the hope of obtaining their confiscated lands and offices. But it is symptomatic that those kings who listened to and acted on such stories were the ones who were later accused of bad governance and placed under restraint or overthrown – Henry III, Edward II and Richard II. Even Henry V had accused his stepmother, Joan of Navarre, of witchcraft on uncertain evidence, imprisoned her, and seized her property (the main reason for the prosecution?), but she was allowed respectable accommodation while in disgrace – Leeds Castle – and eventually exonerated. Duke Humphrey's second wife, Eleanor Cobham, similarly accused of plotting to kill the King, was condemned, divorced, and deported to the Isle of Man for life – possibly due to a Beaufort plot to ensure that she did not give Humphrey any heirs to challenge them for the succession.[23] Humphrey was not guiltless in his alienation from the King in the early 1440s, having been threatening Cardinal Beaufort with violence and/or political ruin for two decades and had been conspicuous for his petulant disloyalty to Bedford in the 1420s. He had been opposing the King's conciliatory French policy noisily in recent years. But proceeding to the extreme of arresting him was politically unwise. Crucially, Humphrey had had no children either by Eleanor or by his first wife, Jacqueline of Holland. Due to the papal ruling confirming the latter's disputed first marriage (regarded as void by her and Humphrey) in 1428,[24] Humphrey's children by her would have been bastardized, but any children Humphrey had had by Eleanor would have been next in line for the throne in 1447–53 and the Suffolk faction would duly have feared them not York as the 'reversionary interest'.

**Henry's responsibility for the disasters of 1440s – not a 'holy fool'?**
Henry used to be regarded as ultra-pious even before his illness in 1453, influenced by his prudish religiosity and his foundation of King's College Cambridge; thus the blame for the disastrous policies of the 1440s could be placed on an unscrupulous Suffolk whose greed, incompetence, and acquisition of offices and lands were listed in the hostile 1450 Parliament. Even that implied that Henry was too open to the influence of unscrupulous advisers, while absolving him from the active part in ministerial misrule laid

against Richard II. The requirement of Parliament after Suffolk's fall that all royal grants of Crown lands during his adult reign be 'resumed', i.e. cancelled,[25] need not imply that he had committed these controversial alienations to 'unworthy' favourites as a conscious policy. Excessive generosity also marked his attitude towards his educational projects. But has his later 'simpleton' reputation after his 1453 breakdown been 'back-dated' to the period before his illness? It is now thought by historians such as Bertram Wolffe that he played a more active role in the diversion of influence and patronage to the Suffolk faction than was once thought. The records show that he made his rash of lavish grants to 1440s courtiers and their clients in person, many being politically unwise, and was requested to reverse some at the time. The King was in full possession of his faculties, and showed signs of spendthrift habits. His favouritism was notable. At the very least he showed a degree of political incompetence in his lack of even-handedness, and was over-willing to lavish power and influence on a small group of congenial advisers.[26] Like Edward II and Richard II, he had no concept of the political need for 'balance' or for wooing powerful nobles whom his personal friends disliked.

The contrast with his father, his uncle Bedford, and paternal grandfather is notable. So is his complete lack of interest in taking up the family cause of fighting for his French Crown – though he was a crowned sovereign of France, unlike his ancestors. His response to the rising disasters after 1429 is marked, and in contrast to what was normally expected of an English king – and would have been expected of him, as he had had the usual 'knightly' military training in arms under the veteran Earl of Warwick as a teenager. He was no pacifist at this stage, being prepared to endorse a large-scale military campaign by his court favourite Somerset to the Loire in 1443 to secure his lands though after that he naively put faith in the good will of his uncle (and new uncle-in-law) Charles VII in 1444–8. In this crucial period he also showed no interest in 'negotiating from strength', not building up his forces ready for a potential military clash if the 'peace-policy' failed as Charles was doing. It is probable that he entirely misread Charles' intentions, putting his faith naively in a projected meeting between them set for 1446–7, which never took place – and where his politically shrewd and unscrupulous counterpart would have run rings round him. Instead he instituted a secret negotiation with Charles via his episcopal diplomats, led by Bishops Moleyns and Ayscough, and in modern parlance 'left out of the loop' his experienced commanders in France (e.g. York) who would have been hostile but at least knew the local military situation. He even privately promised to hand over Maine in December 1445 without any clear guarantees of an end to French claims on Normandy in return.[27] The entire concept of a 'reverse dowry' – land being given by the husband to his wife's family, not the other way around – on his marriage in 1445 was unusual, though evidently judged worthwhile to secure a truce after the failure of the Somerset offensive in 1443.

But Henry and his bishops did not appreciate that the whole lesson of French revival since 1429 was the ultimate power of military force – Duke Philip had stayed with his English allies until the tide of battle decisively turned and Bedford was dying, then shamelessly violated his oath to Henry as King of France. Negotiating from weakness would earn Charles' contempt not his respect, and in due course he resumed the war and took over Maine – and then Normandy – once his new army was ready. Henry was inflexible on refusing to give up the claim to France, which Charles had made clear in the Gravelines talks of 1439 was his 'sine qua non', but hopeless at accepting the political and military implications of what that refusal entailed. At least after Somerset's failure and death in 1443–4, he had no senior semi-royal commander adequate to the task of fighting and loyal to his policies apart from possibly Somerset's younger brother Edmund (a competent local commander in the south of Normandy). Henry reportedly wept at the 'betrayal' by his greatest vassal Duke Philip in 1435 and he hesitated over handing over Maine after 1445, possibly for fear that his furious local commanders would refuse to carry it out. In the event, the latter were still uncertain of government intentions and without direction when Charles invaded in March 1448, and had to negotiate their surrender on their own initiative to stop a massacre. But Henry neither sought to fight in person nor put trust in his most competent and vigorous commander, York. The latter, like equally 'persona non grata' Duke Humphrey before 1447, was studiously ignored on his return to England for the 1445 Parliament, was neither given an extension of his governorship nor superseded in Normandy for many vital months, and was eventually sent off to Ireland in semi-disgrace. In fact, Ireland was a logical field to use his military skills, and he had a 'stake' there due to inheriting Mortimer lands. But did his absence from England in 1450 enable enemies (Somerset?) to undermine him at court more easily? If he had been in England and helping Henry against the Cade rebels, would he have lost the King's trust as he did?

York could have been expected to be hostile to Henry's timid policy towards Charles VII, not least as his years in Normandy and his many military 'contacts' warned him of a continuing French 'build-up'. As he saw matters – accurately – Charles was only playing for time in the mid-1440s, not seeking a permanent settlement that left England with Normandy. As seen from court, England could not afford the level of military spending that would raise enough troops to dissuade Charles from attacking. (It would also require undesirable cuts to the King and his new Queen's spending, risking their wrath with those who suggested this.) But there is no evidence that the King – or his more forceful 'pro-peace' ministers, led by Suffolk – ever sought to explain their rationale to York or to win him round. On the contrary, York was treated with suspicion as the politically dangerous leader of the 'opposition' to war and ministers alike – increasing the risk of the feared clash occurring? Crucially, securing enough troops and money from the political 'nation' in Parliament for a more vigorous policy in France after 1444 would have required a degree of honesty and seeking collaboration with elite across the nation that the government clearly avoided for its own security. As seen by Parliament's demands in July 1449, the MPs would have wanted Suffolk to be sacked.

Logically, raising funds would need a Parliament, on a wider basis than the carefully-controlled and partisan one that met in February 1447, with the resulting danger of demands for reform of abuses. There would be a danger to the monopoly of power and patronage by Suffolk and the Beauforts, and their allies such as Lord Fiennes – either Humphrey or, once he was dead, York could be expected to demand more influence and patronage (if not Suffolk's instant dismissal) in return for any co-operation. Disputed offices and lands would have to be returned to Suffolk's opponents in the localities – which would build up the 'client-base' of men he feared.

It is probable that York's enemies actively blackened his name to the timid King, building him up as a potential rebel. Denied access to court after his return in 1445, York was left to brood in what amounted to disgrace despite the supposed honour of his command in Ireland – with his political allies denied lands or office, which mattered a great deal to a proud magnate in an era when a lord was supposed to secure patronage for his clients. This obviously increased the risks of a 'backlash' from the affronted Duke, as it had done for similarly alienated royal magnates Duke Thomas of Gloucester and Henry of Bolingbroke towards Richard II with the 1387 revolt. Suffolk (and after his return from Normandy on its loss in 1450 Edmund Beaufort) had the political experience and skill to appreciate this if the naïve King did not. It would seem that the lust of the Suffolk clique, allied to the Beauforts, for monopolizing office and land-grants in the 1440s added to the King's fear of Humphrey and York as potential rebels to repeat the disastrous political confrontation of the 1380s. But would York have been feared by the King anyway, without the use of his name made by the Cade rebels in 1450? Was he, as presumed rival heir, an inevitable target for Somerset (or the Queen)? Or was this the 'turning-point' for his reputation? The French disaster from 1448–50, for which Suffolk was publicly blamed, added humiliation to political frustration and rising disorder and produced a massive explosion of public hatred in the risings of winter 1449–50 (many, significantly, in areas of court favourites' political dominance).

Demands were made in 1450 that Henry replace these men with the group of senior lords of royal blood who were unjustly denied influence, headed by the Dukes of York, Buckingham (descendant of Edward III's youngest son), and Norfolk and Exeter (descendants of Edward I's youngest sons).[28] This was similar to the charges of favouritism that could be levelled at Edward II and Richard II (and to a degree against Henry III), none of whom were to be remembered as saintly simpletons not responsible for the chaos their favouritism unleashed. In their cases, it was their victims – Simon de Montfort in 1265, Thomas of Lancaster in 1322, and the Earl of Arundel in 1397 – who acquired a popular 'cult' as 'martyrs'. Henry's mental breakdown thus did his subsequent and posthumous reputation a lot of good, though it helped that he could never be plausibly charged with unsavoury homosexual practices as were Edward and Richard. He could even be suggested as a possible saint by his nephew Henry VII once he had been dead for two decades and memories of his incompetence were fading; arguably the continuance of political faction after his overthrow in 1461, leading to his successor's removal in 1470, aided his reputation by showing that national unity had not returned under his replacement after his deposition (as it did, after a few years' serious turbulence, after 1327 and 1399). As suggested above, Henry VII also promoted the idea that his uncle had not been personally responsible for the disasters of the 1450s as he sought to have him canonized.

*Chapter Two*

# The Yorkist Reaction: From Control in 1453 to Deposition in 1461. Inevitable?

## (i) The opportunities offered by the King's madness. The road to St Albans, 1452–5

The onset of the King's mysterious mental collapse in early August 1453 was completely unexpected and caused a radical reversal of politics, rather than being an 'inevitable' follow-up to his problems in the late 1440s. He had given no previous sign of serious ill-health, as opposed to being rash, extravagant, unmilitary, and easily manipulated by his advisers. Despite the evidence of scurrilous public remarks about his being weak-minded, there had been no serious attempt to depose him after the overseas humiliations and poor domestic government of the late 1440s. Indeed, the nebulous 'Mortimer' claims during the Cade revolt and hints that York was the rightful king were subsequently denounced in terms of outrage – in reasonably representative meetings of Lords and Commons after 1450. One MP in 1451 – York's ex-attorney Yonge – had formally proposed York as heir. York had been abroad then – but it was logical for his foes to think he had approved, and York's tenants had been involved in rioting.[1] The loss of Normandy and Aquitaine in 1450–2 was met by a determined effort on the part of the political elite to regain them, rather than just a search for a scapegoat – and in any case Suffolk's violent death had served to satisfy the latter demand though it probably also emboldened would-be anti-court vigilantes. In 1452 the veteran royal commander Shrewsbury led an expedition to regain Bordeaux, and the subsequent Parliament at Reading (March 1453) made massive financial grants to the King for a 'follow-up' expedition of 20,000 archers. Tonnage and poundage were granted to Henry for life, only the second such grant since 1399. The archers – England's best military weapon against the numerically superior French – were to be given four months' notice to assemble at the ports and then be paid for six months' service overseas.[2] This would enable an

Agincourt-size expedition, and Henry was expected to lead it in person – as hoped for in the *Book of Noblesse* by his general Sir John Fastolf's secretary, William Worcester.[3] Despite Henry's past failure to fight or to pay an expedition adequately, there was evident goodwill among the political 'nation' for a new beginning and a major effort to reverse recent disasters. Many MPs can perhaps be written off as 'trusties' carefully selected by pro-court patrons, as there were complaints about the Commons being full of Royal Household men; the same cannot be said of the peers, almost all of whom attended.[4] If Henry had led his nobles to war, would it have rallied malcontents behind the King as in 1415 – or shown his lack of leadership skills?

At this point, it was York, not Henry or Somerset, who seemed politically isolated. He had behaved – with some excuse – like a man under threat of destruction by his ill-wishers at court in early 1452, issuing a belligerent manifesto from his headquarters at Ludlow Castle on 9 January claiming that the King's mistrust was due to the influence of his enemies and then summoning his supporters to join him in a march on London. He complained that his advice to Henry at an interview at Westminster on 6 October 1450 to do justice on those accused of misrule by the Commons (i.e. York's enemies, headed by Somerset) had been ignored to the resultant damage of the realm, and that he was to be accused of treason and his family disinherited.[5] When he sent these letters and then marched on London in February he was aware of Henry's refusal to back down, which the royal letters patent of 17 February calling on all loyal subjects to rally to the King in arms confirmed.[6] He was thus guilty of fully intentional defiance of his sovereign by armed intimidation on this occasion, though the subsequent royalist claim in 1459 that he had previously forced his way into Henry's presence past his guards at Westminster in September 1450 cannot be proven.[7] Luckily for the King, York's supporters at their rendezvous on Dartford Heath (10–20,000?) were outnumbered by Henry's, by three to one according to Abbot Wheathampstead of St Albans.[8] He had to submit to coming to the King's camp, where he vainly presented a list of charges against Somerset to Henry,[9] and a few days later swore an oath of allegiance to him at St Paul's Cathedral and promised never again to raise an army against the King.[10] So far, York had been the aggressor, though some of his charges against Somerset (over the attack on Fougères, which provoked Charles VII's final invasion and the surrender of Rouen) were based on truth.

It was, however, symptomatic that there was no politic generosity towards York by the supposedly holy King. He had used a progress through York's Marcher lands in 1452 not to display forgiveness to his errant subjects but hold judicial tribunals for ex-rebels and require miscreants to appear before him wearing halters to beg pardon – not even staying with York when he visited the Duke's principal residence at Ludlow, an evident snub.[11] He also endeavoured to hand over a disputed part of the Despenser inheritance in Glamorgan from York's nephew and ally, the (Neville) Earl of Warwick who held it by fully legal warship, to rival claimant Somerset. Warwick was refusing to obey and holding onto the disputed castles, while in the north another armed magnate dispute saw his relation Sir John Neville fighting the pro-Beaufort Percy cadet, Lord Egremont.[12] It was while on progress in the West Country, rather than preparing for his promised expedition, that Henry suffered his mental collapse. His recent official references to his wife's uncle Charles VII had been unusually bitter, suggesting that the King was in a belligerent and vengeful mood towards France, and the royal ally Cardinal Kemp (a 1440s peacemaker) vigorously denounced French cunning and treachery in the 1440s as he issued official prayers for military success.[13] A planned expedition for 1453–4 thus seems genuine, rather than an excuse to raise an army to attack the Duke of York. Possibly, if Henry's health had not declined he would have been resentful enough at his French uncle's duplicity to lead a campaign in Normandy in 1454, though his character and total lack of martial ability would indicate that he would have had to rely heavily on his senior commanders – including York? Any such expedition would have been a blow to his future hagiography as a holy peacemaker, as played up by Shakespeare in his plays, but as of 1453 he had no reputation as a would-be saint and it is logical that he would have seen his 'betrayal' by the French as justifying the war. The shock of actually witnessing battle in person at St Albans in 1455 may have given him another mental breakdown, but is no indication that this would have happened in a stressful situation if he was leading his army in France. A sudden shock while on 'active service' had, however, driven his grandfather Charles VI of France insane in 1392, so it cannot be ruled out.[14]

If Henry genuinely intended to lead an expedition there was no sign of its imminence as he suffered his sudden illness in Wiltshire, and his collapse paralyzed the government – which depended ultimately on personal leadership by the sovereign. The timetable of events was such that Shrewsbury's defeat and death at Castillon and the second loss of Bordeaux meant that any expedition would now have to reconquer the city again – but this was perfectly feasible with such a large army. The King's illness may have prevented a campaign to reconquer Aquitaine in 1454, presumably led by the experienced Somerset as the latter's faction (and apparently the Queen) irrevocably distrusted York. The government and the well-armed peers would then have been concentrating on France not on civil strife, and the sense of national unity in a 1415-style patriotic war have reacted to Henry's benefit. But there must still be a possibility that the rising tide of Neville vs Percy armed clashes in Yorkshire (with a pitched inter-family battle at Heworth on 24 August) would have distracted Somerset into a domestic expedition of revenge against his faction's enemies.

The King's first mental collapse in 1453 led to him spending months in a catatonic state, unable to speak or move and being kept in seclusion away from the London area (mostly at Clarendon near Salisbury, where the illness began in August 1453). At the time, shock at the news of the final English defeat in Aquitaine at Castillon was supposed to be the likeliest cause.[15] Losing the last of his ancestral Continental possessions but for Calais was a profound humiliation, and could have stimulated a depressive stupor. The main symptoms of his illness were complete loss of awareness and movement – by contrast, his maternal grandfather Charles VI's mental illness had involved delusions and bouts of violence.[16] As the next legal adult heir, York assumed the regency as 'King's Lieutenant' to open the next Parliament by request of the Council as it became apparent that feuding great lords (particularly in the north) were taking advantage of the lapse in personal royal rule to wage private war. Rather than seeking reconciliation with his foes and broadening his support as the government was paralyzed, he was still issuing bitter complaints about Somerset.[17] Ironically, the birth of a son to Henry and Margaret in the interim, in October, meant that York was no longer heir apparent and so would not take the throne if Henry died – which may have induced his fearful enemies, led by Somerset, to go along with granting him regency powers. To make matters worse, Archbishop and Lord Chancellor Kemp died on 22 March so there was no official licensed to operate the Great Seal and legalize administrative measures – and the catatonic Henry could not appoint or approve a successor. York had not endeared himself to Parliament by his vindictive arrest of its Speaker, Thomas Thorpe, a personal foe, but there was no other option but to grant him the power to run the government if chaos was to be avoided. On the 27th he was named as 'Protector' of the realm – like Duke Humphrey, military leader and first among equals on the Council but not Regent.[18]

York led the Council – minus the arrested Somerset – until Henry was demonstrably capable again in early 1455. His monopoly of power meant the inevitable dismissal of his rivals from office to secure control for his nominees, but he made no attempt to come to an agreement with Somerset and used his power to place the latter in the Tower.[19] This escalated the already toxic distrust of Beauforts and allies for the York faction, and once Henry regained his senses they arranged the dismissal of York's appointees (led by his brother-in-law the Lord Chancellor, the Earl of Salisbury) and a formal absolution of Somerset from all charges.[20] Somerset's ally Exeter, who had been arrested by York in summer 1454 for assembling an armed force in Yorkshire and claiming that he should be both Duke of Lancaster (as a descendant of Elizabeth, the daughter of John 'of Gaunt') and the rightful Protector during Henry's incapacity, was released from custody and the accusations made against him declared groundless.[21] This was legally dubious, as Exeter had been defying the legally appointed Protector by armed revolt and so was as guilty as York had been in 1452. Exeter was a close ally of the Percies, and had been disputing the inheritance of some of Elizabeth of Lancaster's estates with the pro-York Lord Cromwell, whose daughter was married to Salisbury's son.[22] York and Somerset were bound over to keep the peace until their disputes were to be resolved in June.[23]

The Duke's withdrawal from court under threat of prosecution returned matters to the uneasy stand-off of 1452, with York unable to answer summonses to court for fear of arrest and execution. In spring 1455 the court faction arranged alleged 'arbitration' of the York/Somerset dispute, which was expected to come down heavily in Somerset's favour and legalize punitive measures to ruin York's power. This was to be dealt with by a 'Great Council' (dominated by the Beaufort faction) at Leicester – well away from turbulent London, which could riot in York's favour – on 21 May.[24] The royal entourage of Household and armed court nobles set out with its army for the meeting, and York decided to intercept it en route and prevent himself being punished. As shown by the outcome, if he could not secure 'justice' from the King (which would entail removal of his enemies from court) he intended to fight to regain physical control of the sovereign. Not since 1387 had a group of alienated major subjects decided on this course, and not since Simon de Montfort's revolt in 1264 had a king been attacked in person. The lesser and slower military preparations than in 1452[25] may reflect Henry's personal confidence that York would keep to his 1452 oath not to attack him in arms again, and it is possible that the court's decision to leave London and advance on the Midlands implies fear of anti-court rioting in London as in 1450. The court was again to concentrate on the Midlands, not London, in the 'royalist' faction's period of predominance after 1456. Staying in London would have been unlikely to alter the course of events to York's detriment, as holding out in the Tower against an arriving insurgent army had not been an option for similarly embattled Richard II in 1387. The King's worst miscalculation was probably to pardon both Somerset and Exeter, which renewed the impression that he was an unjust tool of a faction and so boosted York's support. Notably, official letters to York, Salisbury and the latter's son Warwick ordering them to disband almost all their followers or be treated as traitors – the likely precursor to a 'showdown' – were not prepared until 19 May, two days before the King's departure from London.[26] This would suggest that he or his 'minders' were not expecting an imminent attack; instead York and his allies were already at Royston and their reply to the orders could be sent back on the 20th and received by the King at Kilburn on the morning of the 21st as he marched north.[27] They demanded that the Chancellor, Archbishop Bourchier (another royal cousin), excommunicate Somerset and Exeter and summon a more representative, i.e. pro-York, assembly than the one that was due to meet at Leicester. But the royal army moved on, and early next morning received supposed assurances of their opponents' goodwill and desire to 'protect' Henry from his 'evil counsellors' from York's confessor and envoy, William Willeflete.[28] The option of returning to London once they knew York's proximity on the 21st was not followed; nor was the option of halting at Watford when Willeflete arrived daring York to attack.

The armed attack on the royal army as it advanced north against the defiant York and his allies on 22 May 1455 turned political confrontation into bloodshed. The King himself seems to have hoped to negotiate a truce with the defiant rebels as in 1452, not least as his army outnumbered theirs, and replaced the confrontational royal commander/ 'Constable' Somerset with the more conciliatory Duke of Buckingham. It seems to have been Buckingham's advice to move on into St Albans as originally intended – and a herald was then sent to York to order him to withdraw or face forfeiture for treason, which he ignored. The only cleric with the King and so available to launch a mediation-effort was the Bishop of Carlisle, a Percy and 'court' ally – would Bourchier have been able to calm York down, or was it a hopeless cause with Somerset clearly still in the King's confidence? The talks that followed this failed bluff collapsed, with one source claiming that York demanded the handover of his enemies. The Duke's messages may have been intercepted before they reached Henry, and the subsequent pro-York Parliament blamed Somerset and his ally Thorpe for the battle. But in any case, Henry referred York's envoy (the Duke of Norfolk's official herald) to Buckingham for a reply, rather than mediating himself, and he took up his position in warlike mode by his standard in the town centre.[29]

York and his brother-in-law the Earl of Salisbury now launched an attack on the King's camp in the centre of St Albans. It was not so much a traditional battle as a series of assaults by York's troops on the barricaded streets around the royal camp, and a succession of skirmishes ended with the principal court lords in flight and Henry, hustled from house to house, being captured. Somerset was deliberately cut down as he tried to hold out at an inn, and the Earl of Northumberland – as the head of the house of Percy, principal northern rival of the Earl of Salisbury's Nevilles – and Lord

Clifford were killed in more dubious circumstances. The Duke of Buckingham, who had taken sanctuary in the abbey, was arrested in violation of its right of sanctuary but spared and the Earl of Wiltshire (the new royal appointee as Treasurer) escaped; most of the forty or so royal troops killed were from the King's household and so would have been defending him and his standard. Other royal troops were despoiled by the victors, an example of blatant illegality and disrespect to men who had been defending their sovereign.[30] The overall impression given is one of York's arrogance and disregard for politic moderation – a problem for his 'image', which was to recur in 1460. Henry was now escorted to London, with official honour but effectively as a prisoner, and York resumed his Protectorate as the King had another bout of his illness.[31] Bourchier continued as Chancellor, and Wiltshire was replaced as Treasurer by the Chancellor's brother Lord Bourchier (who was to continue off and on in this role under Yorkist regimes to his death in 1483 so was clearly capable and trustable). It was the first time that a king had been made prisoner of a political faction since Richard II had had to surrender the Tower to the 'Lords Appellant' in 1387; before that Edward II had been captured (not in battle) in 1326 and Henry III had been captured in battle at Lewes in 1264. The personal 'targeting' of the victors' foes was worse than on either of these occasions; the 'Appellants' had at least used (rigged) legal procedures. This time the physical incapacity of the sovereign made a formal regency by his captor legally defendable. But how long would this last, and what of the situation if or when Henry recovered? Was his mental condition likelier to save him from deposition (as a useful puppet and guarantor of legality for whoever held real power) or lead to his removal?

### (ii) After St Albans – 1455 to 1460

Henry's reputation as a saintly innocent uninterested in politics and above the sordid magnate struggles only followed his mental illness, appearing in the mid-1450s. He was regarded as being seriously complicit in his senior ministers' abuses of authority by at least some of those involved in the popular uprisings of 1449–50, from the evidence of threats to depose him – particularly for endeavouring to save Suffolk from justice by letting him escape abroad. But after his illness the King's reputation improved, and his decline in health and mental capacity was only sporadic. It appears that he was genuinely ill when the York-organized Parliament that followed his capture at St Albans resumed the 'Protectorate', rather than being deprived unwillingly of power. The terms of the regency were as they had been during his first illness, and significantly made provision for it continuing until his son was of age; though he was probably not catatonic as reference was made to consulting him about matters touching his person.[32] He may have suffered delayed shock after his first exposure to battle in the streets of St Albans, in which he received a minor wound. But he was well enough in February 1456 to be brought into Parliament by various lords who opposed a controversial act of 'resumption' (cancellation of royal land- grants) put forward by York. This meeting could be seen as being as politically biased as the assembly that the royalists had summoned for May 1455, but in the opposite, 'Yorkist' cause, as only twenty-seven out of fifty-three peers summoned turned up to the first session of Parliament in July 1455 and forty-five out of a hundred summoned turned up to the second in December. On the second occasion the absentees were sent threats of what would happened if they did not attend the third session in January.[33] A substantial part of the political 'nation' must have seen the meeting as illegal – or regarded their participation as too risky as a restored royalist government could condemn them later for attending. This was a threat to the stability of the new government, though its vigour in setting up committees to take control of various aspects of governance, assert Duke Humphrey's innocence of all charges in 1447, and 'resume' royal grants of lands to 'Somerset faction' favourites need not be written off as merely opportunistic.[34] The King's absence from Parliament in November was probably due to illness rather than York preventing him from attending, though York secured the useful Parliamentary ordinance that his new, second Protectorate should be terminable by the King and lords in Parliament not by the King alone so he was secure from arbitrary royal displeasure.[35] The restriction of financial grants to the Queen and absence of any to the King's half-brothers Edmund and Jasper Tudor (all future arch-foes) were, however, provocative. So was the drastic demand in the second planned Act of 'resumption' of past royal grants that anyone who accepted a new grant in defiance of it should be indicted for breaching the Statute of Provisors and fined1000 marks.[36]

Henry was able to use his authority to veto the controversial Act of Resumption and cancel the grant of the Protectorate in a personal appearance in Parliament in February 1456. Apparently, the majority of lords opposed to the Act brought him in to overrule York – a sign of the latter's overweening over-confidence.[37] Without this, would the Protectorate have lasted much longer or would York's enemies have been able to undermine it anyway as the King recovered his wits? Although Henry was probably prompted he was clearly seen by all to be capable of a formal role in governance. His physical capacities were probably limited thereafter, however, and he spent long periods of the next few years away from the dangers of unruly London with his Queen taking the lead in building up her clientele in the north Midlands. He spent much of his time visiting monasteries, and significantly it was the Queen (whose castle at Kenilworth was his main secular residence) who took part in a ceremonial 'entry' to Coventry.[38] The withdrawal of the court from the London area was prolonged (three-and- a-half years) and unprecedented for a mediaeval English sovereign resident in England. But was it prompted by a French queen used to Valois practices of long periods of residence at large chateaux away from the capital? Special arrangements were made to provide Westminster 'central' funds for the court, and more were raised by use (or abuse?) of the Crown's hereditary revenues – as was to be done again in 1629–40 with similar results. There was no Parliament, perhaps due to the use York had made of the one in 1455 and the death of the court's effective 'Parliamentary manager' Somerset. While the French mounted raids on the Kent coast, as in 1377, the government made no effective response – despite the levying of archers for war in 1453. There were apparently paid troops in existence in 1457, as after 1459 the Yorkists were to allege they had been raised to terrorize the King's subjects.[39] But no more was heard of endeavouring to regain the King's French dominions, even in Bordeaux. Possibly, the main royalist military preoccupation was fear of another rising by York as in 1452 and 1455 – particularly after the blatant dispossession of Carmarthen Castle and imprisonment of the King's local lieutenant, Edmund Tudor (the new Earl of Richmond), by York's allies Sir Walter Devereux and Sir William Herbert in August 1456.[40] This incident led to Edmund's death – the removal of one major future 'prop' of the House of Lancaster and the resulting fatherless upbringing of his son Henry (VII), with possible long-term psychological effects on the ultra-'insecure' founder of the House of Tudor. The semi-mutinous Yorkist allies in the southern Welsh Marches could easily form the nucleus of a new rebel army. However, at first York was still recognized as the King's principal councillor and military 'stand-in', in which capacity he was able to take a royal expedition north to Yorkshire in summer 1456 to force the invading James II of Scotland to withdraw from Northumberland. Also, his wife's nephew Warwick was now finally admitted to his governorship at Calais by the mutinous garrison, by royal command.[41]

The eventual dismissal of Lord Chancellor Archbishop Bourchier, half-brother of the relatively conciliatory court magnate Buckingham, and other York-appointed ministers was apparently the work of the Queen.[42] She was also accused of wanting to deal with York at the Council meeting of October 1456 and being stopped by Buckingham. The meeting of a 'great council' at Coventry in 1457 may have seen another requirement of York to swear an oath of loyalty and an appeal from Buckingham to make this the last time York would be pardoned for his part in unnamed disturbances, though this is uncertain.[43] Parliament did not have to meet for over three years due to the customs and subsidies having been given to Henry for life. Possibly this abeyance was used by the Queen's faction as a means to avoid having to summon York's allies to any potentially problematic mass-meeting, and hence the French naval raid on Sandwich in August 1457 did not lead to a response. Only court-allied magnates were allowed onto a Commission of 'oyer and terminer' into the Devereux-Herbert activities in South Wales during Henry's progress to Hereford in summer 1457.[44]

In this atmosphere, is it any wonder that York chose to defy the court's moves to arraign him in 1459? The King's only personal intervention in the rising ill-trust was the well-intentioned but politically naïve 'Love-Day' he organized at St Paul's Cathedral in March 1458. This followed a potentially dangerous meeting of the great lords in London, which saw York's faction assembled at Blackfriars, near his residence at Baynard's Castle, and Somerset's son and successor Earl Henry and the heirs of the similarly murdered Northumberland and Clifford encamped at the White Friars in Fleet Street while mediators shuttled between them.[45] There was an evident danger of a brawl between their followers turning to something worse, with the Somerset faction seeking revenge for the killings at St Albans. Persuading the principal political rivals to attend the church service together and hold hands in public was, as might have been expected, a polite gesture of goodwill to the King by his reluctant senior subjects, which solved nothing. In practical terms, local land-disputes (such as that between the Earl of Warwick, York's nephew, and the Beauforts over the lordship of Glamorgan and the Courtenay vs Bonville feud in the West Country) continued unabated.[46] Disarming the rival magnates in the counties required a bolder king than Henry – who had no personal army anyway except the garrison at Calais.

Nor did Henry manage to secure an even nominally stable government involving men from both factions, with a division of patronage that might have temporarily bought off the great lords. Given his mental weakness, he would have needed a determined and non-partisan queen to effect this – if it was possible at all. If a 'centre party' existed its logical leader was the Church under the new Lord Chancellor installed by York in 1455, the new Archbishop of Canterbury, Thomas Bourchier – closely related to both York and the Beauforts. The distribution of senior offices to pro-York figures in 1455 was not immediately reversed after Henry resumed his powers in February 1456; nor was York's faction removed from the Council. This opened an opportunity for mediation, not to settlement – the blood-grudges from St Albans were probably too deeply felt for that. Even if the Queen was cautious for a year or so, the well-armed northern heirs of York's principal

1455 victims (the Earl of Northumberland and Lord Clifford) would seek revenge. Crucially, the combination of personal revenge and defending their estates from local pro-York rivals provided them as a ready-made nucleus for a royalist 'ultra' faction. But Henry did nothing to prevent the subsequent deposition of the pro-York Chancellor Bourchier, and other ministers in favour of more 'reliable' figures, and his only possible political initiatives were connected to the abortive Anglo-French peace-embassies. He was still supposed to be furious with the 'treacherous' Duke Philip of Burgundy for violating his oath to him in defecting to Charles VII in 1435; thus a French defector, the Duke of Alençon, received no royal support when he arrived at court in 1456 to ask for aid against Charles VII. Instead, Henry complained that both kings' vassals were too treacherous.[47] Had any expedition been planned against either Charles or Duke Philip, York was the obvious leader – Somerset was too young – but the (French) Queen would not exactly support this boost for his position. However, the story that Margaret encouraged the French attack on Sandwich, by her 1460–1 ally Admiral Pierre de Brezé, to embarrass York is probably incorrect.[48]

The lack of governmental direction and tangled motivations of the English participants (e.g. York and his court defector ally Sir John Wenlock, Speaker of the 1455 Parliament) make it impossible to work out whether the English were sincere about the alleged treaty and marriage-alliances or, as the Count of Foix told Louis XI in 1461, York was really seeking aid to overthrow Henry.[49] By the summer of 1459 the court-connected chronicler Abbot Wheathampstead of St Albans was reckoning that royal justice had collapsed, i.e. that the court was unashamedly partisan in seeking to ruin York's party.[50] On a military level, attempts were made to remove Warwick as commander of the large and well-trained garrison at Calais, and when he refused to resign he was supposed to have suffered a murderous attack in Westminster.[51] Possibly the emergence now of a story that the Prince of Wales was not Henry's son was deliberately sponsored by York as a way to remove the danger of Margaret as regent for the boy if the King died or was deposed – and caused her obsessive hatred of him? Accordingly, as the subsequent indictment of York makes clear, he and his closest allies refused repeated summonses to court in mid-1459. Apparently, a repeat of the armed defiance of 1452 and 1455 was planned, with a summons for loyal subjects to meet the King at Leicester on 10 May armed for two months' campaigning and a reinforcement of the royal supplies of arrows for a large body of archers.[52] A great council then met at Coventry towards the end of June, which York, Salisbury, and others did not attend in defiance of their summonses.[53] This time the Queen's faction struck first – probably with more success as they were already in the Midlands with a large escort, not in

London, when the summons to the dissident peers was issued. (Had they turned up, a repeat of Duke Humphrey's arrest in 1447 was probable – and possibly murder by the vengeful Lord Clifford, whose later activities in 1460–1 imply that he was thirsting for retaliation for 1455.)

As the Earl of Salisbury started to advance south from Yorkshire, the royal army moved quickly forwards to Nottingham to deny him the castle and he was forced to march south-west to join York at Ludlow. The Queen's army (many of them Cheshire levies, as last used as a royalist 'private army' by Richard II) intercepted Salisbury at Blore Heath on 23 September, but was routed; the royal army then pursued him to Ludlow.[54] Henry was again paraded at the head of the royal army in the advance on York's Marcher base – and proved a major psychological weapon as the court propagandists played up the treason of fighting against the King and his standard. York's men had had no such scruples in 1455, but this time Andrew Trollope, commander of the Calais troops, declared that he had not known he was being brought along by Warwick to fight the King in person and deserted after the 'showdown' at Ludford (across the River Teme bridge from Ludlow). Apparently outnumbered, York and his older sons, Edward and Edmund, Salisbury, and Warwick (all of whom could face execution for treason) fled Ludlow overnight across the Teme bridge – with the royal commanders too incompetent to guard all the bridges and trap them. The crucial role in the confrontation, for the final time, was played by Henry in person.[55] He was clearly unable or unwilling to assert himself as mediator again after the 'Love-Day' – and thus became more of a partisan figure to the danger of his throne.

Henry's role in 1459 was that of a talisman of his Queen and her allies, used to show that resistance to their army was treason. But was his incapacity sufficient to justify removing him as king? The first rumour of this eventuality after the 1450 crisis surprisingly emanated from the court camp pre-1459, with the Queen the alleged instigator – no doubt aiming to make herself regent for Prince Edward.[56] It may have been a 'security measure' to counter-act any York-led seizure of her husband. The growing anarchy and private wars of powerful nobles showed up the King's ineffectiveness, but this did not lead to widespread desertion. For the moment the Queen was able to assert her faction's power after her military victory, and at the quickly summoned Parliament at Coventry, York, his elder two sons, Salisbury and his son Warwick, Salisbury's wife (as heiress of the Earldom of Warwick), and their principal adherents were attainted and all their lands seized.[57] Pardon was possible if the accused submitted, but the sweeping and legally dubious nature of the conviction aroused support for them and was as counter-productive as York's killing of the court leadership at St Albans had been. Worse, the means used implied that Parliament could be used for legal pillaging of any court critic in future, an implicit threat to the entire social elite's safe possession of their property. Such a sweeping 'purge' of 'traitor' nobles had only been seen before by the restored regime of Henry III in 1265 (later wisely modified) and by Richard II in 1397–9.

This politically unwise triumphalism therefore can be seen as a factor in the failure of the majority of the peerage or landed gentry to rally to the King and Queen as York's heir, Edward, Earl of March, and Warwick led an expedition back from their refuge at Calais to Sandwich on 26 June 1460. A papal legate joined them, and so did Archbishop Bourchier – and Sandwich, pillaged by the Queen's countrymen the previous year, was hardly likely to hold out on her behalf.[58] The expedition entered London unopposed on 2 July, with only the Tower holding out, and marched on to encounter the King's army near Northampton on 10 July. Crucially, the warlike Queen was not with her husband and heavy rain accompanied Warwick's assault on the royal army, which crumpled in half an hour.[59] From now on the King was a prisoner in the hands of York's faction, and his removal from the throne with his supposed consent became one way to counter the control his wife and her party had over him. But support for his right to remain king was strong enough to make his threatened deposition in autumn 1460 by York's clique unpopular with a majority of the lords – and the well-informed French observer Jean de Wauvrin believed that non-partisan peers had been reassured by Warwick's group swearing not to depose him as they invaded.[60] Had this oath tipped the balance against any serious rallying to the royal army in July 1460? The resistance to Henry's deposition cannot be blamed on opportunist aristocrats fearful of the rule of a strong king who would halt abuses of power, as the 'Yorkists' could argue. In any case, to the fifteenth-century 'mind-set' the importance of keeping sacred oaths of allegiance outweighed such practical considerations as the King's competence. At the time, the Queen and her army in the north were still a major factor, with their advance on London expected. The infant Prince of Wales was with them, so deposing Henry would not neutralize the Lancastrian dynasty. Ludlow had been sacked for assisting a 'rebel' after its fall to the royal army in autumn 1459 – would it be London's turn next if the King was deposed and his wife returned? Fear of the possible revenge to be expected on Lancastrian deserters by Queen Margaret meant that self-preservation should induce those nobles supporting her dynasty's displacement to grant York, their champion, what he wanted and prevent their enemies securing a compliant King again. The scale of 'courtier' reprisals against the York faction in 1459 seems to have altered the balance of support by uncommitted nobles, though not to the extent of enthusiasm for Henry's immediate deposition. York's bold legal claim to depose Henry, made to the House of Lords on 16 October 1460, was promptly passed on to Henry himself as a weighty matter that only the King could decide; and as Henry refused to abdicate the question was passed to the senior judges who also equivocated and preferred to leave it to the decision of the 'blood royal'. It was also pointed out that York claimed the throne now as direct heir of Edward III's second son, Lionel, Duke of Clarence (senior to Henry VI's ancestor John 'of Gaunt') but until this he had displayed the arms of, i.e. relied on the claim of, Edward's fourth son Edmund, Duke of York.[61] He was thus changing the rules of the game to suit his current position.

Eventually, the King agreed to a compromise put by Warwick's brother Bishop George Neville – he would remain king until his voluntary abdication or death, but his son would be disinherited. This gave York the role of heir apparent and its estates (the Principality of Wales, Duchy of Cornwall, and Earldom of Chester) plus legal immunity from prosecution, as stripped from Prince Edward. Quite apart from the excuse of apparent rumours of the late Duke of Somerset being the boy's real father, nobody had taken any oaths of allegiance to the Prince yet and disinheriting him removed the threat of Margaret seizing power if Henry died leaving an under-age successor. The initiative may have come from the papal legate Copponi, as Pope Pius later claimed credit for the idea – and the support of the Pope for its legality would persuade the cornered King to give in.[62] If abdicating a position given him by God was a sin, the Pope could absolve him.

Despite his failure to gain the throne, York had secured the succession, legal immunity, and vast estates to reward his family and friends – always a major inducement for a medieval semi-royal magnate. He had also secured the support of many peers– although with the Queen's party so vengeful they had little alternative to agreeing. The bloodthirsty Warwick had killed the Duke of Buckingham, Lord Beaumont, and other leading court peers in the clash at Northampton,[63] clearly aiming to wipe out the opposition leadership as York had done in 1455 and thus inviting later reprisals. As of 1455–9 the perceived 'aggressor' in the inter-royal feuds had been seen as York, who had attacked the court's army at St Albans in 1455, killed senior nobles of the rival faction in cold blood, and taken the King captive. In 1459 the Queen had been the moving spirit in the 'coup' that ended the uneasy political truce, leading the royal army on York's headquarters at Ludlow and demanding his surrender. The Yorkist reply to their forced exile, as to the threat of arrest in 1455, had been unnecessarily violent and personal.

Who was responsible for the escalation of the crisis in 1459–60? It must be remembered that we can see events with hindsight and thus know that years of instability were to follow, but as of 1459 political actors' attention was focused on York's recent armed insurrections. The Queen's army's attack on Ludlow in 1459 was partly pre-emptive, to prevent York and Salisbury from another attack on the court as in 1452 and 1455. Technically, by levying war on the King they had committed treason and their lands could be forfeited as was done at the Coventry Parliament after their flight. Any action of armed defiance of the King and the royal army was taken as treason rather than self-defence, and so the Coventry Parliament had a legal excuse to deprive York and Salisbury of their vast landed estates so as to cripple their political-military power. But this was politically counter-productive, quite apart from the inevitable reaction to the planned enrichment of the victorious pro-court nobles (led by the Percies). As with the confiscation of Roger Mortimer's lands in 1325 and Henry of Bolingbroke's lands in 1399, this only led to invasion by the aggrieved party at the first opportunity. Luckily, York was able to defy the government and secure his ancestral lands and troops in Ireland, where he had been a popular governor in the late 1440s. The Dublin Parliament ignored all orders to remove him, and he could invade England (belatedly) in 1460. He also secured the major military force at Calais, from which his son Edward and cousin Warwick (captain of Calais) invaded the south-east in July 1460. The new court nominee to govern Calais, the late Duke of Somerset's son and successor Duke Henry, was kept at bay and captured by Warwick, and the latter's navy gained control of the Channel and a link to Ireland to co-ordinate the invasion. In June 1460 Warwick and York's son Edward, Earl of March, landed at Sandwich to be joined by Archbishop Bourchier.

### (iii) Deposition – 1460–1

As seen by the new government and its allies in autumn 1460, it was essential to avoid the Queen's party regaining the legitimacy automatically awarded by physical control of the King. From 1451–2 onwards she had become seen as an irreconcilable foe, starting with her building up armed support in the north Midlands in 1456 and then the dismissals of pro-York ministers. Margaret had driven York and his family into exile in 1459 in revenge for the 'usurpation' of power in 1455 and the killings of her allies at the battle of St Albans; what would she do if she regained power this time? Making York king (not just regent) as he requested was the only way to keep the vengeful Queen out of power permanently, but a significant number of nobles resisted this. By the time of the 'Yorkist' faction's seizure of power that summer, Henry's illness and an apparent unworldliness may have saved him from the fate of the equally politically 'incompetent' and resisted Edward II and Richard II. Luckily for him, his son was still at liberty to serve as a figurehead if York had murdered him. (As soon as the boy was killed, in May 1471, York's son announced Henry's allegedly fortuitous demise.) Apart from a sense of honour for a sick man apparently 'touched by God', on this occasion – unlike in 1327 and 1399 – there was a powerful, unscrupulous, and masculine queen to blame for the King's misdemeanours and grievances against the late regime could be deflected onto her. The legend of the 'Tigress of Anjou' was born, and was to be much enhanced by her party's bloody revenge on York and his family in December 1460 and her pillaging northern army's march on London thereafter. As with Richard II and III and Henry V, the popular conception of her was to be 'fixed' by Shakespeare – who had used somewhat 'sensationalized' sixteenth-century chronicles such as Hall's history of York and Lancaster.[64]

The drama of York's killing in December 1460 added to the notion of the political conflict over patronage and the succession as a 'blood-feud', with elements of treachery that the Yorkists could play up. Fighting during the Church's Christmas festivities was unusual, and implicitly not chivalrous. York had gone to his south Yorkshire residence, Sandal Castle, to raise troops against the gathering court/Percy army based at nearby Pontefract, but had not taken the offensive; instead, the enemy advanced by surprise to blockade him and cut off his supplies. A sortie into Wakefield to gather supplies was then ambushed in dubious circumstances and the Yorkist leadership 'targeted' for killing. In fact, contrary to Shakespeare's story, Margaret was not present at the battle or the executions, though she exulted in them afterwards; the surprise attack on York's force – possibly at a time of truce – was led by the Dukes of Exeter (who had a distant claim to the throne himself) and Somerset, the Earl of Northumberland, and Lord Clifford. The last three, sons of the principal lords killed at St Albans in 1455, had old scores to settle. Nor was York's 17-year-old son Edmund of Rutland a youthful non-combatant, whose killing was seen as unprecedentedly shocking;[65] he was old enough to fight and be killed by contemporary reckoning. (Henry V had played a leading role at the battle of Shrewsbury in 1403 aged 16.) But the killings left York's heir Edward at large in the Welsh Marches, where he had been raising troops, and the local court force under the Earl of Wiltshire and Jasper Tudor (Henry VI's half-brother) was unable to complete the Queen's victory by killing Edward. Instead, the latter took the offensive and destroyed the 'Lancastrians' at Mortimer's Cross on 2 or 3 February before marching on London to link up with the Earl of Warwick.[66] After the battle he executed the King's stepfather, Owen Tudor, whose grandson Henry VII was to kill his brother Richard in 1485; the blood-feud escalated.

Henry's eventual deposition by Edward (3 March 1461) was not carried out with the confirmation of most of the political 'nation' as had been the agreement of October 1460. There was no formal meeting of the Lords, though the unsettled state of the war-torn country and the need for speedy action after Edward's arrival in London on 26 February made that impossible anyway. The only major magnates involved in the 'Great Council' at Baynard's Castle, the York residence in the city, that backed Edward were Warwick and the (Mowbray) Duke of Norfolk; the churchmen were led by the Archbishop of Canterbury and the Bishop of Exeter. The latter, Warwick's brother George Neville, was also Lord Chancellor, in which capacity he had set out Edward's genealogical claim and the misrule by Henry to a public meeting at St George's Fields on 1 March.[67] The seizure of power was unrecognized in the northern counties occupied by the Queen's forces.

The accession of Edward IV was at least partly due to recent actions by Queen Margaret. Following Wakefield, the Queen advanced into the Midlands with her feared northerners, as recorded by the panicking Croyland chronicler, and took the usually competent Warwick by surprise at St Albans on 17 February. This time Trollope's Calais troops won the day for the Queen's party; Abbot Wheathampstead reckoned that the soft southerners in Warwick's army were terrified of the Percy/Scottish levies' élan and bloodthirstiness.[68] Henry himself, rescued from the Yorkists by the Queen's faction at St Albans, passed from being a prisoner of Warwick to being a virtually powerless talisman of his wife's army. As York's son Edward destroyed the court army in the Marches at Mortimer's Cross and advanced to join up with Warwick the Queen retreated, possibly nervous of the damage to her reputation if London was sacked. Negotiations at Barnet to admit a token force of court lords and troops were unsuccessful. A deputation of leading figures pleading for her to leave the city unoccupied may have played a part, but in any case London was less important than defeating Edward's army.[69] (In similar circumstances a decade later in March 1471, Edward took care to secure London even with his enemies rapidly closing in.) The responsibility for her failure to press on to London is unclear, but the decision lost her the south as she retreated to her strongholds in Yorkshire. Warwick, who had retreated to the Cotswolds, was left unmolested to join up with the advancing Edward's Marcher army somewhere around Burford in mid-February and then regain London.

The removal of Henry VI – and his son – to the north in March 1461 left a legal vacuum in government in London. Edward could not carry out the government in Henry's name (as his father had been forced to do after the Lords' rejection of his own claim to immediate usurpation in October 1460) as he did not have physical possession of him. The decision of Edward and his backers, led by Warwick, to depose Henry in his absence in March 1461 was partly a reply to the recent killing of York, his second son the Earl of Rutland, and his brother- in-law Salisbury (Warwick's father) at or after the battle of Wakefield. Placing the victims' heads on Micklegate Bar in York afterwards further embittered matters between the York-Neville faction and their enemies, though technically traitors' heads were legally liable to public display (as seen at London Bridge for centuries.) If the killings and posthumous humiliations of December 1460 were the act of a psychopath, it was Clifford not Margaret, contrary to later legend. York had already started the practice of killing captured foes in cold blood at St Albans in 1455; this was merely the expected retaliation. Had he been captured at Ludlow in October 1459, judicial murder would have been probable. But the blood-feud between the York dynasty and the Beauforts intensified with these killings, and served to justify Edward deposing Henry once he had destroyed the Lancastrian army in the Welsh Marches at Mortimer's Cross (February 1461) and raced to London ahead of the Queen's forces. Technically, the court party's breach of the truce at Wakefield could be presented as a reason for Edward to abandon his allegiance to his 'faithless' King and Queen; the settlement of October 1460 had involved York paying allegiance to Henry but Edward had not done so.

Henry's rescue from Warwick's Yorkist army at St Albans ahead of Edward's arrival thus made his deposition by the Yorkist leadership in London easier, a contrast to the situation the previous October when York's similar claim had been blocked by his peers. Until the point when York claimed the throne all forced seizures of government had been subject to the fiction that they were in the King's name to save him from 'evil advisers', as when York and his allies in the 1455 'revolt' had claimed that they were only seeking access to Henry's presence which their court foes were denying.[70]

The Queen, whose expected personal role as a fifteenth-century female did not encompass deputizing for a weak or preoccupied husband, could still have induced Henry to go at the head of an army – as he had done earlier to confront York and did in 1459 – but was now regarded as partisan rather than in the traditional role of a queen as peacemaking conciliator. This was inevitable by 1456–8 given the rumoured threat of York to her husband's throne, however much rumours of her son's real parentage may have been current to add to her resentment. (The extent of this factor before 1460 is unclear.[71]) But she was not the first queen to be regarded as a dangerous political partisan – Henry III' s Provencal Queen, Eleanor, whose relations had been monopolizing patronage along with his half-brothers in the 1240s and 1250s, was pelted with refuse by angry Londoners as she tried to sail under London Bridge in 1262 and the initially popular Queen Isabella, leader of the 1326 rebellion, was attacked for giving power to her lover Roger Mortimer and was supposed to have murdered her husband, Edward II. In both cases their political role was ended after the resolution of the conflicts in which they were leading figures, Eleanor by reason of age and eclipse by her son Edward I after 1265 and Isabella by forcible marginalization by her son Edward III in 1330. Both were French, like Margaret, so her origin was not to blame despite the recent humiliation of a complete French victory in Normandy. Margaret remained the leader of her cause in exile in 1461–70, and so continued to be vilified by the new regime.

As of autumn 1459 the Queen's and her factions' full intentions are unclear, with exile and confiscation for any captured Yorkist leaders as likely as a bloodbath in retaliation for St Albans. But the fleeing York's wife, Cecily Neville, prudently sent her youngest sons abroad. Even if York, his two elder sons, his brother-in-law Salisbury, and the latter's son Warwick had all been captured and judicially murdered by their foes Somerset, Buckingham, and Clifford in retaliation for the 1455 killings the younger sons of York and Salisbury would have survived to claim their fathers' lands in due course. The ascendancy of the Queen's faction could not have lasted indefinitely, and any mass-confiscation of Neville lands to benefit her Percy allies would have left embittered exiles at large ready to attack England at the first opportunity with the backing of the House of Burgundy, 1460s rivals of the Queen's French allies.

Had Henry not been in a state of mental incapacity after the shock of St Albans (his first exposure to combat) in 1455 York would not have had the same excuse to resume his Protectorship, though he could have kept Henry away from Westminster so that potential doubters did not know the royal condition and exaggerated the latter. A king normally lived in public, but after Henry slipped into some form of catatonic state he had been kept in seclusion at Clarendon near Salisbury from July to December 1453 without much controversy, with limited access by official delegations once he was thereafter installed closer to London at Windsor. If necessary, access to Henry could have been restricted again under pretence of renewed illness, though details of the truth would have duly leaked out. The fact that York was deprived of his Protectorship, probably with clear evidence of Henry's full recovery used in Parliament by his opponents and possibly at Henry's own insistence, within nine months of his victory in 1455 shows his limited grip on power. Even with the King incapacitated and York's principal enemies dead or powerless his faction could not maintain full power for him, and his continuation on the Council from February 1456 (apparently at the King's request and against the Queen's wishes) only led to his gradual eclipse by the 'court party', led by Margaret and the Beauforts, over the next year or so. Clearly a 'middle party' of peers (and the bishops?) were unwilling to see either of the two rival factions predominant in 1456–8 and neither could stage a coup to deprive the other of all offices and lands, while lack of clear direction in policy or judicial 'police action' against local feuds increased private conflicts in the counties. But this stalemate could not last long term.

## The struggles of 1450–61: some further points for consideration

### *(i) A third royal deposition in 133 years, autumn 1460/ March 1461 – how legal was it?*

In 1459–60 the struggle for control of the government led to naked military conflict, with York eventually victorious. As in spring 1455, the anti-York party at court (now led by Margaret) resorted to military confrontation; but this time they sought to move in on York's estates to pre-empt an attack on London. The first clash duly took place as royal troops intercepted Neville forces en route to aid York at Blore Heath, and the most was made of the King's presence with the army to make all who resisted seem to be traitors. Having escaped from the advancing royal army converging on his base, Ludlow Castle (centre of his Welsh Marches lands inherited from the Mortimers), York was able to take refuge in loyal Ireland – an ironic result of his court enemies sending him there out of their way in 1447. His eldest sons, Edward and Edmund, and his wife's nephew Warwick were able to secure control of Calais, with its largest and most coherent body of disciplined troops in the country, and returned to England to defeat the court party at Northampton. The important role of the Calais garrison in England's military conflicts in 1455–71 has been underestimated; and from 1455–70 they were under Warwick's control. Crucially, when Edward IV sacked and drove out Warwick in spring 1470 the Earl's deputy at Calais, Lord Wenlock, stayed loyal and refused Warwick entry so he had no choice but to seek aid from Louis XI and the exiled Queen Margaret (though Wenlock himself later defected to Margaret and died fighting for her at Tewkesbury in 1471).

For the moment the Yorkist dominance of 1455 was restored. But even then their victory in summer 1460 preserved enough support for the King among the peerage for York's claim to the throne in October to be blocked. His military triumph was achieved by Warwick, Salisbury, and his own heir Edward of March in invasion from Calais while he remained in Ireland; would he have risked an attack with 'inferior' Irish troops on the court had Warwick not been able to secure the well-armed and disciplined troops at

Calais? When he belatedly arrived in London flaunting the royal arms and physically laid his hands on the throne in Westminster Hall, a sign of confidence, he met unexpected resistance. Even Warwick, to whose victory he owed his return, argued fiercely with him in private,[72] while the principal peers and bishops objected to York now claiming to be the rightful king via descent from Edward III's second son Lionel on the grounds that he had always previously borne the arms of (i.e. claimed descent via) the fourth son Edmund, Duke of York. By that legal argument, York had always acknowledged that he was the representative of a line junior to Henry's, not of the genealogically senior line of Lionel. The use by York of the 'heir of Edward III's second son' argument as his justification implied that Henry had never been rightful king, and neither had Henry IV or V; it was more legally dangerous than the argument for deposing a – rightful – king for misrule that had disposed of Edward II in 1327 and Richard II in 1399. The arguments used against Edward and Richard could have been used against the equally incompetent and partisan Henry VI,but his mental illness was a potential argument for sparing him the harsh political fate of these rulers.

Both these men had voluntarily abdicated in public in front of assemblies of leading (hand-picked) nobles, Edward at Kenilworth and Richard in the Tower, and this semi-public renunciation had been followed up by confirmation of the act by an incumbent Parliament.[73] York lacked the presence of either a large body of acquiescent peers or the Commons, and thus could be accused of a coup – which could be reversed by armed force later if Margaret's army defeated him. He thus sought to allege that he had been rightful king all along; had he based his claim on the descent from Edward III's fourth son, Duke Edmund of York, the legal grounds would have been shakier as Richard II had never explicitly and publicly named Edmund as his heir. Edmund had been named regent – the normal role for the next adult male kin of the king – when Richard left for Ireland in 1399, but the then heir of Lionel's line, Edmund Mortimer, had been unavailable as he was underage.

The legal controversy was then put to Henry as king and supreme legal arbiter, and he stood by his own right to the throne. This meant that there would be no voluntary abdication, as in 1327 and 1399, and Henry would have to be deposed involuntarily. This had never been done since the rebel barons of 1216 had withdrawn their allegiance from King John for misrule, and transferred it not to his son but to his niece's French husband. Finally, on 31 October a compromise, proposed by the new Chancellor George Neville (Warwick's brother), left Henry the Crown for his lifetime under the political control and direction of affairs by York – a sort of permanent regency without the excuse of mental illness. There were potential legal precedents for this, in the direction of political affairs by committees of rebel lords who could not trust their adult sovereign to govern responsibly in 1264, 1310, and 1388. But none of these committees had ever been seen as permanent. The possibility arises that some people who joined the invading Henry of Bolingbroke in 1399 anticipated this solution to the problem of a vengeful and unstable Richard II, short of deposing him – if the later allegations of Henry promising not to depose Richard were accurate.

The grounds for deposing Henry by the 'Great Council' on 3 March 1461 were set out in a petition to Parliament that autumn,[74] which presumably followed the same lines as Bishop Neville's arguments to the public rally at St George's Fields on 1 March and the case made to the Council on the 3rd. Henry and his father and grandfather had been usurpers, as the correct claim to the Crown had lain with the line of Lionel, Duke of Clarence, not his younger brother John 'of Gaunt'. York had been the rightful heir as senior descendant of Lionel, and Edward had inherited that claim. Moreover, Henry's reign had seen endless disorder, misrule, injustice, violence, rapine, and vicious living – which could be taken as a sign of God's disfavour as well as his unfitness to rule. He had violated the truce-agreement of October 1460 and was thus a perjurer[75] – though he could hardly be blamed for the uncontrolled actions of his partisans at Wakefield; he had joined and headed their army in February 1461. This left unanswered the argument that if Henry and his ancestors had been usurpers, their royal actions could be illegal – which invalidated all royal laws and grants of lands and titles since 1399.

### (ii) The existence of Edward, Prince of Wales: the crucial reason for armed conflict, or only an excuse?

The disinheritance of Edward, Prince of Wales, was necessary for York's claim and his long-term consolidation of power. Had the Prince not been born the removal of Henry would have given York the Crown – though the Duke of Exeter claimed an alternative right as the nearest descendant of Henry's great-grandfather John 'of Gaunt', in the female line (and unlike the Beauforts fully legitimate). The enmity of the Queen meant that York could not rely on exerting power as a principal councillor during a minority for the Prince as Henry's successor, which would have been a problem had Henry continued in his catatonic state after 1454; hence York's securing a Parliamentary act in 1455 that only the King in Parliament (could remove him. (Of course, another Parliament, 'fixed' by the Queen and the Beauforts, could cancel this.) The blatant disinheritance of the Prince of Wales for political reasons in October 1460 was unprecedented for England, apart possibly from the disinheritance of John's son Henry by those rebel barons who had invited Prince Louis of France to reign instead in 1216; and that could be excused by the argument that an adult king was necessary, plus the doubts about his parents' marriage. (John had divorced Isabella of Gloucester to marry Henry's mother, Isabella of Angouleme, in dubious circumstances.)

The Dauphin (Charles VII) had been disinherited in France in the Treaty of Troyes in 1420 on similar grounds of not being his father's son. The long time between Henry's marriage (1445) and the child's conception (early 1453), and the chances that the unworldly King was incapable of siring a child, made the idea that a desperate queen had resorted to a 'stud' to produce an heir – and thus thwart York's claim to the throne – plausible. It was politically convenient but possible, although it is only speculation that it was news of the Queen's pregnancy had helped Henry's first mental collapse in 1453.[76] Rumours of a move by York or his supporters to secure his long-term domination of politics after his return to power in 1453 by this means could have caused the irrevocable alienation of him and the Queen – as the King's closest companion, vital to control of influence and appointments – after the Prince's birth. But tension between the two was already apparent in 1452.

Logically, then, it is possible that if the King's increasing mental incapacity had been less apparent, rumours as to the Prince's parentage would not have arisen, or gained enough currency for them to alienate Margaret from their perceived Yorkist sources. Her first English court 'patron' as a new arrival, Suffolk, had been killed in 1450 and it was vital to the development of private magnate feuds into bloodletting during the 1450s that she backed the Somerset/Exeter faction against York. This was apparent before the Prince's birth, with York's role as heir to the throne being linked to the rumours of 1450 that the Cade revolt had been carried out with his connivance to depose Henry. But the birth of a son added to her reasons to turn implacably against the Duke – particularly as the King's illness meant that York was able to exert full political control of the government for the first time in 1454–5 as the sick monarch's closest adult heir.

The right to an English regency (or headship of the governing Council) crucially lay with the monarch's male kinsfolk – Edward III's cousin Lancaster, not Queen Isabella, in 1327, Gaunt not Princess Joan in 1377 and Henry V's brothers in 1422. Had either Duke Humphrey or his elder brother Bedford produced a son they, not York, would have been the legal claimant to Royal guardianship, regency, and the succession and thus York would have seemed less of a threat. He could still have been leader of the anti-Suffolk faction and a potential military challenger to the King's power and favourites, as was the royal cousin and senior magnate Thomas of Lancaster to Edward II in 1310–22. Nor would the closest royal male relative automatically win control of political affairs on the removal of the King's 'bad advisers' by magnate revolt – Henry of Lancaster had been prevented from assuming this role despite personal guardianship of Edward III in 1327. Roger Mortimer had won out over Henry of Lancaster in gaining political power then; York could still have been more powerful in political terms than a surviving son of Humphrey or Bedford on the defeat of the Suffolk/Beaufort faction.

The position of the Queen as 'head' of the court faction, in opposition to the 'reversionary' claimant, was more marked after 1455 when Edmund, Duke of Somerset and the senior magnate of the Suffolk/Beaufort faction, was killed; (as was the veteran head of the Percies, 'Hotspur's heir); Somerset's heir Duke Henry was younger and even more inexperienced than the French Queen. The senior magnate of this faction was now the Duke of Exeter (Holland), who as a royal descendant and self-proclaimed potential heir to the throne could threaten Margaret's position and so was not trusted by her. His claim lay via male descent from Earl Edmund of Kent, son of Edward I's second marriage, and was thus more remote than that of the Dukes of Buckingham (who were descended from Edward III's youngest son Duke Thomas of Gloucester) but was not complicated by female descent.

By the confrontation between the royal army and York at Ludlow in 1459 Margaret was seen as the head of the 'court' party, trailing the King along behind her as she led the army on York's headquarters, and in winter 1460–1 she was raising an army of northerners to attack the Yorkist leadership in London. Her role as the symbol and spokesperson of royal authority on behalf of her weak husband made her a crucial political player beyond the normal role of a Queen (usually a mediating figure, though not in the cases of Henry III's Eleanor of Provence and Edward II's Isabella). Instead of being a force for stability, Margaret was seen as fiercely partisan – with the threat to her son's succession at York's hands an obvious reason for her to be his implacable opponent. It should be said in her defence that the 'Tigress of Anjou' as she was later nicknamed, the implacable foe of the York dynasty, did not become a partisan political player until the mid-1450s and was not necessarily only inactive as she was finding her feet in English politics earlier. Despite her links to Suffolk and the Beauforts it was only after the deaths of the senior male court leadership at St Albans in 1455 – 'targeted' for elimination by their foes in front of her and Henry, in the manner of a blood-feud – that she rose to prominence as an implacable defender of their faction.

## Was the escalation of the struggle in 1451–9 inevitable? And how and why did this confrontation differ from earlier power-struggles?

The first resort to military intimidation had been by York (1451–2), though he had been excluded from political influence and been virtually banished to

Ireland and he had the fate of Duke Humphrey hanging over him; he was also the first to start killing his senior foes in battle (1455). His resort to violence in the face of his foes blocking his power and controlling the King was in line with the actions of Thomas of Lancaster in 1322, Mortimer and the Queen in 1326, the 'Appellants' in 1387–8, and Henry of Bolingbroke in 1399 – it was the continuation of the normal court struggles for power by other means when politics failed. What was new was the length of the dispute; the previous confrontations had quickly seen the excluded faction either defeated or victorious, and even in the more evenly-balanced political confrontation between Simon de Montfort and the 'royalists' around Henry III the long-term control of power was resolved within a year (1264–5). York was mostly to blame for the escalation of the dispute into bloodshed, given that violence had been avoided in 1451–2 by both sides drawing back from military confrontation in contrast with what happened at St Albans in 1455. But York's forbearance in challenging the magnates around the King to battle in 1451–2 had not met a reciprocal restraint; arguably in 1455 he must have reckoned that he had no alternative but the permanent physical elimination of his foes (as resorted to by the victors in 1322, 1326, 1388, and 1399). De Montfort showed restraint in 1264, and ended up hacked to pieces on a battlefield.

The nature of magnate and court politics also argued for a resort to drastic measures by an 'excluded' senior political figure. Given the nature of the political structure in the localities, most regions saw the evolution of 'spheres of influence' over land-grants and local office by rival magnate families – in some cases, expressed in physical confrontations between them at times of weak central control such as the 1450s and 1460s. (The *Paston Letters* give a good example of this in Norfolk, where the Dukes of Norfolk, the Mowbray dynasty, opposed the 'upstart' Pastons as heirs to Caister Castle.[77]) The outbreaks in the Welsh Marches in the mid-1450s were more normal, given the militarization of the area and the fierce loyalties of the inhabitants to long-term dynastic lords rather than to the Crown – the English king was historically and culturally an 'alien' foreign overlord to the Welsh tenantry anyway and most local Anglo-Norman barons had a hereditary claim on their loyalties.

Similar outbreaks of lawlessness and open armed feuds had occurred at times of other weak royal government, in the 1220s (when the original 'Robin Hood' may have flourished?), the aftermath of the 1264–5 civil war, and the early and late 1320s. Ominously, it had commenced again in Henry VI's reign well before 1450. The political 'point' here was that a strong king usually intervened to reverse this, as the new ruler Henry II did to illegal castles in 1155–7 – or an heir did it for him, as Prince Edward did for Henry

III in 1266–70. There was no such reassertion of non-partisan power by a vigorous king in the 1450s, although Henry VI and his court did visit Hereford in 1457 (with a suspiciously partisan commission of courtiers) after the Devereux/Herbert vs Tudor clashes.[78] In an intensively competitive political world, loss of access to patronage and influence at court led to loss of confidence in a patron by his followers – he could not 'deliver' security and grants of land and office. If this continued, he could easily face desertion by his supporters; self-assertion was thus vital for his own interests. Thus York had to back up his local supporters in conflict with rival magnates such as Exeter, and each act of challenge to a 'pro-court' magnate backed by the King (or Queen) was easily interpreted as defiance and implicit rebellion. Many localities had their own feuding noble dynasts who each had a court patron and alignment in the 1450s, most notably the pro- Beaufort Percies and the pro-York Nevilles in the north. This conflict extended to their friends and relatives as proxies, like a mid–late twentieth century clash between two 'Third World' powers threatening to drag in the latter's patrons, the USA and USSR. 'Flare-ups' causing escalation were thus a risk, as seen by the proxy disputes involving Percy and Neville allies in the north. Any settlement of grudges between the rival provincial dynasties by a 'truce', as endeavoured in 1456–8, would have required a mixture of compromise and goodwill by all sides to last; both would have had to refrain from provocation or from backing up their rival local allies too firmly. This goodwill and restraint was notably absent, and the Nevilles and Percies were already fighting as of August 1453 (before news of Henry's incapacity would have arrived in Yorkshire and reassured them that the paralyzed government would not react). If goodwill was absent, order would have to be enforced by the King or his nominee, a reaction notably absent in government in the turbulent 1440s and 1450s. This failure to punish local armed conflict duly encouraged others to take their grudges into their own hands, arm their tenants, and attack their enemies. The bloodshed at St Albans in 1455 was a cause for retaliatory acts at the first opportunity by the heirs of the aggrieved Beaufort, Percy, and Clifford families. Warwick then made matters worse by more killings at Northampton in July 1460 – though had the Queen and Lord Clifford secured their foes at Ludlow in 1459 a 'Lancastrian' massacre of the Yorkist leadership was possible before Warwick provided the Queen's faction with such an excuse. All this made another outbreak of struggles for power very likely, with the absence of a strong executive figure in London to adjudicate and force a conclusion to disputes an added reason for pessimism.

In 1267–70 Prince Edward (acting on behalf of the enfeebled Henry III) had enforced the terms of victory by one struggling faction, with some diplomatic concessions to de Montfort allies required by the strength of resistance after the battle of Evesham; in 1322–6 Edward II and the Despensers had temporarily won out but later been overthrown, as had the 'Appellants' after 1388. Mortimer and Isabella had lost personal control to Edward III in 1330 and some enemies had been rehabilitated, but the destruction of Edward II's faction was not reversed; Henry IV had permanently won out in 1399 despite severe challenges. Stability and a firm sense of purpose at the centre of power was apparent on each of these occasions; there was no such stability backing compromise in 1456–8 or the permanent victory of one faction in 1455 or 1459. The absence on these occasions of a strong, legitimate, and unchallengeable executive authority was vital; ironically, if Henry VI had been permanently mentally incapable from 1453 the chances of a permanent settlement being enforced by a 'royal substitute' regent (York) would have been greater.

Also, unlike in 1265–70 and 1326, the defeated faction of 1455 (the Beauforts) still possessed some residual power with the slaughtered court magnates' heirs being in possession of lands and private retinues with a capacity to take revenge; the de Montforts had been destroyed in 1265–6 and the Despensers had been destroyed in 1326. The necessities of compromise had left Richard II's 'duketti' and some allies with a degree of power in 1399, despite the destruction of Richard II's 'new men' Bushy, Bagot, and Greene – and in 1400 and 1403–5 the defeated Ricardians had duly challenged Henry IV. By 1459 the Queen and her allies were duly seeking a similar political (and personal?) elimination of the Yorkist leadership.

The Queen's perceived enmity made the succession of her son Edward as Henry's successor unacceptable to York and his supporters, making the danger of implacable factional feuds at court seem long term. In return, the rumours about his parentage (perceived to come from the Yorkists) and the violence York had shown in enforcing control of politics in 1455 would not make the Queen willing to see York as regent or as 'guardian' of her son as king. If Henry died, who would control political life until 'Edward IV's majority, c. 1469? (Henry VI, born December 1421, came of age in 1437.) Given recent precedents, the new King's nearest male kin – i.e. York – had the prior claim to being his personal governor or Protector, as had Henry of Lancaster for Edward III in 1327, John 'of Gaunt' for Richard II in 1377, and Duke Humphrey for Henry VI in 1422 – but not to full power as regent. Margaret had every reason to fear York in either role, and he had reason to fear for his safety from his vengeful rivals if excluded from power. There was thus every prospect of a long-term vacancy of strong kingship under an enfeebled king and a young heir, and by 1459–60 a solution was being sought by York's party in terms of the Prince's exclusion from the throne – and later in 1460 by removing the King too. This drastic measure duly alienated assorted nobles who were prepared to back York against the court faction, as seen in the shocked reaction to his claim to the throne in 1460. It was the mixture of this prospect of long-term instability and the physical/political survival of part of the defeated factions in the confrontations of 1455 and 1459–60 that made the struggles for power after 1450 far less easy to resolve than those of earlier centuries.

The deaths of York's chief court foes at St Albans in May 1455 only transferred the enmity to their heirs who became close to the Queen. Equally, the weak control of the government – King or substitute – over defiant armed magnates meant a plethora of local clashes and the danger that if York seemed to be backing his local partisans against a court ally this could be interpreted as treason (as over his attitude to the Courtenay/Bonville clash of 1456).[79] Nor could Margaret and her allies trust York's headship of a regency Council if Henry died or became permanently incapacitated. Once the succession of Prince Edward could not be trusted to guarantee York's position, the drastic step of removing him and his mother was inevitable. This, in turn, brought the danger of this controversial step adding to the number of magnates who would rally to the Queen and the Beauforts against a Yorkist 'usurpation'. The resulting conflict would be resolved by force, and the physical survival of the rival contenders (even in exile) would lengthen the conflict – as York and his sons were able to restore their position after the 1459 debacle at Ludlow in 1460, and as Margaret and the Beauforts were able to challenge York in December 1460 and his son Edward IV in 1462-4 and 1470.

### (i) Ludlow 1459 and the deposition of Henry VI. A missed opportunity for the Queen to prevent further revolts?

This emphasizes the importance of what did not happen at Ludlow in 1459, and the crucial fact that York was able to escape from encirclement. Unlike in 1455, the challenged court party had a large army – centred on the men the Queen had been raising in Cheshire – at its disposal, to add to the presence of the King to lead the army as a sign that resistance was treason (which had not worked in 1455). York had blocked the royal advance at Ludford, across the River Teme south of Ludlow, but then Andrew Trollope's Calais troops had defected to the King. Only the narrow Teme bridge now protected Ludlow from assault on 13 October. In physical terms, the royal army could easily have sent troops round the mile or so of woodlands on the south-west bank of the River Teme from Ludford Bridge (the south entrance to the town) to the western bridge, by which York escaped, to block the latter. Were they unfamiliar with the layout of the town, did they fear ambush by York's men in the thick woods, or did some 'moderate' leaders of the royal forces seek to avoid a bloodbath and thus let York escape?

Certainly, when the town fell there was some killing by the royal troops, although Duchess Cecily and her younger children were spared and were not placed in permanent secure custody as hostages.[80] Had York, his two elder sons, and their Neville ally Salisbury and his son Warwick been killed by Margaret's men in a Wakefield-style slaughter at Ludlow in 1459 there would have been a chance of a long era of court supremacy as there would have been no major adult royal challenger at large in exile (as in 1326 and 1399). But, as seen in France over the killings of Louis of Orleans in 1407 and John of Burgundy in 1419, a blood-feud by the murdered dynast's heirs was liable to make such drastic solutions temporary. The Percies had survived two shattering defeats and the deaths of their male leadership ('Hotspur' and Thomas, earl of Worcester, in 1403 and the Earl of Northumberland in 1405-8); the Nevilles would have survived the loss of Salisbury and Warwick, both of whom had a multitude of younger brothers and married sisters to plan revenge.

It is one of the forgotten facts of the mid-fifteenth century dynastic conflicts that the large number of males in successive generations of the Neville and Percy families – each in need of lands, titles, and an heiress wife – made the chances of major conflict in the north far more likely. York's brother-in-law Salisbury was the son of the second marriage of Earl Ralph (Neville) of Westmorland, and so in need of a landed base of his own with most of the ancestral Neville lands going to his elder half-brother. He had three younger brothers who acquired secular lordships (Bergavenny/ Abergavenny, Latimer, and Fauconberg) plus one who became Bishop of Salisbury. His son Richard Neville, Earl of Warwick by marriage, acquired a crucial claim on his wife's ancestors' Despenser lands in South Wales – also claimed by the Beauforts, which led to armed conflict in the mid-1450s. Richard Neville would not have been in this position to quarrel with the King's Beaufort favourites had his wife's brother Henry Beauchamp, Earl of Warwick, not died childless in 1446, leaving her sole Beauchamp heiress. It is also notable that it was a younger son of the (Percy) Earl of Northumberland, Lord Egremont – also keen on carving out his own lands – who was the principal aggressor in the Percy vs Neville clashes of the mid-late 1450s, with Warwick's younger brother Thomas as his principal foe. These local feuds were 'side-shows' to the tension at court, but the existence of rival claims to lands and of restless and acquisitive younger brothers of major peers added to the escalation of violence.

*(ii) York's genealogical luck*

It was important that the position that York was in as heir to a childless King – and then rival to his son – was exacerbated by the near-extinction of the Lancastrian male line. Henry V's next brother, Thomas, had married (Margaret Holland) but been killed in 1421 before he could have children. John, Duke of Bedford, had had none by either Anne of Burgundy or Jacquetta of St Pol – and the latter was to produce over a dozen children by her next husband, Sir Richard Woodville. Nor did Duke Humphrey have children by his wives, Duchess Jacqueline of Holland (a brief 'political' marriage to enable him to claim her lands) and the socially 'inferior' ex-lady-in-waiting Eleanor Cobham. Any male children of these marriages would have had precedence over York in the 1440s and 1450s, and a daughter would have posed a problem to his claims as he could not disavow her rights to the throne without putting at risk his own claims to inherit by female descent (from Edward III's second surviving son Lionel, senior to the Lancastrian progenitor John 'of Gaunt').

Had such a rival Lancastrian male heir existed, possibly born as early as c. 1420 (Thomas' son), he would have had prior claim to the Protectorship during Henry's illness in 1453. York would still have been in a strong political/military position as the spokesman of the 'war party' in France in the 1440s and arch-rival of the popularly loathed Suffolk, but not have been next heir male to Henry. He would have had to base any claim to the throne solely on the prior rights of the heir of Lionel of Clarence over the House of Lancaster, not on the bastardy of Prince Edward from 1453. This would have lost him even more support among the peers, adding to those who in real life objected to his claim in October 1460. A son of a brother of Henry V could still have been 'bought off' or excluded by a militarily more powerful rival, as Henry IV had enforced his right to the throne on the country in September 1399 despite Richard II naming the Mortimer claimant as his heir. But the superseded Lancastrian dynast, probably born between 1420 (Thomas' son) and c. 1435–40 (Humphrey's son by Eleanor), would have been as much of a threat to York as Edmund Mortimer was to Henry IV.

*(iii) The battle of Wakefield, 30 December 1460; if there had been no catastrophe how would it have affected the 1460s and 1470s?*

It should be remarked that York's unexpected death on 30 December 1460 was entirely avoidable. Controlling most of the south of England, he was being defied in arms in Yorkshire by Somerset, Exeter, and other magnates who had marched unopposed from their base in the south-west to link up with the Percies while the Queen collected a new army in Scotland. Somerset's father and the late (Percy) Earl of Northumberland had died at

York's hands, as had the father of the energetic young northern magnate Lord Clifford – thus the principal 'Lancastrian' leaders could not be expected to accept or trust York as controller of the government. Clifford, as memorably portrayed by Shakespeare (based on Tudor chronicles with memories of contemporary accounts), was particularly implacable and ready for vengeance. Owen Tudor, Queen Catherine's widower, and his second son, Jasper, were also resisting York in Wales – and Owen's eldest son Edmund (father of Henry VII) had died in captivity in 1456 after capture by York's allies in a struggle to control south-west Wales. Another round of warfare could be expected within months, and York's attempt to make his ascendancy in London permanent by claiming the throne had met large-scale resistance from the peerage.

Marching north early in December to defend his pillaged Yorkshire estates from the Lancastrians, York was based at his residence of Sandal Castle over Christmas 1460 while Somerset with a larger army was based nearby at Pontefract Castle awaiting the Queen. Some sort of a truce was negotiated, but Somerset returned to the offensive and harassed the Yorkists, possibly infiltrating his men into Sandal Castle to spread reassuring stories that his army was smaller than in reality. Lured out to respond to the provocations, York was ambushed outside Wakefield as two hidden Lancastrian 'wings' emerged from nearby woods to assist the relatively small force he was facing openly. He fell fighting; his second son, Edmund, and Salisbury's younger son, Thomas, also fell (Edmund reputedly killed by Lord Clifford in cold blood) and Salisbury was captured and later beheaded.[81] The Yorkist claim to the throne thus passed to York's eldest son, Edward, currently raising their levies in the Welsh Marches, who first had to defeat the Tudors' army and occupy London ahead of the Queen. On 3 March a group of Yorkist peers and prelates in London chose Edward as king, and he assumed the Crown by occupying the throne in Westminster Hall on the 4th.

York had shown one serious miscalculation in claiming the throne as opposed to merely another Protectorship in October. He had been implacable towards Somerset's father in having him thrown in the Tower of London while he was 'Protector' in 1453–4, thereby showing his attitude to compromise. His death at Wakefield was due to another miscalculation, and although his cause in the north needed urgent reinforcement in December he could easily have sent the veteran Salisbury (a local Neville) and his son Thomas on their own. Alternatively, as holding out at Sandal would expose him to a siege when the Queen's army arrived, he had the option of withdrawing south and evading battle. He could then have linked up with Warwick in time to meet the Queen and Somerset at a more evenly-matched battle as they marched south in February. Edward would still have been preoccupied with the Tudor army (which he defeated on 2/3 February at Mortimer's Cross).

Despite the fear aroused by the plundering carried out across the East Midlands by the undisciplined Scots, York would have had the advantage of Warwick's force of Burgundian cannoneers and crossbowmen to pit against the ferocious but probably ill-armed Scots and the professional soldiers from Calais that Lord Trollope had brought over to the Queen. He would also have had the extra legal 'boost' for Yorkist claims to the throne that his heir was to use in March to justify usurping the throne – Henry had sworn oaths of protection to the Yorkist leadership in October but the treacherous attack at Sandal had broken these so he could be deposed. Unlike in autumn 1460, there was now direct evidence of Henry's 'treachery' to his kin to cite as an excuse for deposing him – and it echoed the similar untrustworthiness of Richard II in promising to pardon the 'Lords Appellant' for their actions in 1387–8 and then systematically murdering or exiling them in 1397–9.

Henry was not physically in arms against York until he was recaptured from Warwick by the Queen's men at the second battle of St Albans; if York and Warwick had won at that battle they would not have had that excuse for withdrawing allegiance. Ironically, Henry's rescue from custody may have politically doomed him. Warwick may have miscalculated that parading the King with his army added to his chances of winning as it had done for Margaret at Ludford Bridge in 1459, by showing that the sovereign was on his side and encouraging the 'moderates' in the enemy leadership to defect to avoid arrest for treason. He would have done better to keep Henry away from the battlefield, ready to be evacuated to a Yorkist stronghold if Warwick lost the battle. But if Salisbury and his son alone had been killed at Sandal/Wakefield, York's and his son Edward's anger could easily have led them to depose Henry once the Queen had been defeated; it was not solely Henry's recapture that lost him the Crown. The arrival of Edward in London with his Marcher troops (26 February 1461 in real life) would have given York's army the necessary reinforcement to match the Queen's Lancastrians had the latter won or been able to withdraw in good order from their first clash with York.

Outnumbered in Yorkshire, either York or Salisbury could not have held on there in January 1461 as the Scots army arrived even had a lucky or skilful encounter with Somerset's larger force checkmated the latter. York had campaigned in France in the early 1440s; Somerset was younger and inexperienced. The decisive battle would have come as the Queen marched south, or possibly back in Yorkshire had she had to withdraw in the face of Edward's joining up with his father's army after victory in the Welsh

Marches. The Yorkists might well have still held possession of King Henry, not losing him to the Queen at St Albans in February, and as the retention of Henry on the throne would have entailed keeping him separate from his belligerent and irreconcilable wife it would be easier to depose him. 'Richard III' would have assumed the throne in spring 1461, without his rival being at large in Scotland and the north of England as a focus for resistance until 1465. Queen Margaret would have used the Prince as her rallying-point instead of her increasingly feeble and bewildered husband, until forced to flee to France as in real life.

### No bloodbath at Wakefield: York as king, followed by his son Edward IV?

It is possible that York, born in 1411, would have lived into his early sixties like his grandfather Edmund and great-grandfather Edward III, i.e. into the 1470s. His mother's Mortimer ancestors were shorter-lived, but most of the Plantagenet males in Edward III's immediate family who were not killed lived into their fifties apart from the mysteriously afflicted 'Black Prince' and Henry IV (dead at 46 and at 45/6). His eldest son, Edward, would then have succeeded, with the probability that with his father still alive and able to command his adherence he would not have dared to take the controversial step of his secret marriage to Elizabeth Woodville in 1464. He would have been in a weaker position to defy the Council's expectations of his marital choice as heir rather than king; his father is likely to have been as keen as Warwick was in real life to marry Edward off to a French royal bride to achieve reconciliation with Louis XI.

The kingship of York as 'Richard III' would also have meant a less powerful role for his nephew Warwick, fourteen years older and much more experienced than the real-life King Edward IV but in no such relationship to the older York. Had Salisbury still been killed in the northern campaign of winter 1460–1, Warwick would have had his father's estates to add to his marital (Beauchamp Earls of Warwick) lands and still been the wealthiest landed magnate at court, adding to his prestige as the victor of Northampton who had restored Yorkist fortunes in 1460. Once Richard died he could be expected to take a leading role at the court of Edward IV as its leading 'power-broker', and given his ambition still have tried to marry off his daughters to the King's brothers.

If there had been no bloodbath at Wakefield in December 1460 Edward IV's next brother Edmund, earl of Rutland (born in 1443) would have been next in line if the King had no son or had a 'dubious' secret marriage. This would have materially altered the nature of any subsequent struggle for power involving Edward IV's wife's family and his brothers, and Duke

Richard of Gloucester would have been at a substantial disadvantage. The survival of Rutland would have provided him with the landed estates, probably well-dowered bride, and dynastic claim to stand in the way of both George of Clarence and Richard of Gloucester in their manoeuvrings for power after 1469. Nothing is known of Rutland's capacity as a leader, but it is unlikely that he would have been as treacherous to Edward IV as Clarence was to be in 1469–71 and 1477–8. He would probably have been married off before Warwick's elder daughter Isabel (born 1451, so eight years his junior) was available – would this have stymied Warwick's ambition to marry his daughters off to Edward IV's heirs at the time when the King had no son, i.e. pre-November 1470? It is likeliest that Rutland would have been married to a foreign princess, possibly in the negotiations with France that were ruined in real life by Edward IV's secret marriage; but the need for Clarence to secure an heiress and a landed affinity would have still made him keen to secure Warwick's daughter in the late 1460s. If Rutland had been at Edward's side loyally in 1469, Warwick would not have had the temptation of deposing the King to place Clarence on the throne as his puppet – so would this have given him second thoughts about seizing the King then? Logically, too, a 27-year-old Rutland in possession of a strong landed base and clientele would have been a major block to Warwick revolting successfully in 1470; without Rutland, Edward was more vulnerable. His main supporter in real-life 1470, his youngest brother Richard, was only 18, new to governance (though titular Lord Admiral since his pre-teen years), and untried as a commander.

## Chapter Three

# The Yorkist Regime, 1461–83:
# Insecurity and Alternatives

**What if Warwick's men had managed to catch and kill Edward IV in autumn 1470 as he fled the country – and Henry VI had been restored as nominal ruler without a serious military challenger?**

E dward, the charismatic victor of Mortimer's Cross and Towton Moor over far more experienced Lancastrian commanders at the age of eighteen in 1461, had unexpectedly saved the 'Yorkist' dynasty's position after his father and uncle's killing by Margaret of Anjou at Wakefield at the end of 1460. He had rallied the Yorkist supporters in the Welsh Marches – where he had inherited the Mortimer lands and their descent from the royal house of Gwynedd, of which his propagandists made use[1] – to destroy the local royal forces of the Earl of Wiltshire and Jasper Tudor, then had secured London. Finally, he had destroyed the Queen's superior forces in a lucky blizzard at Towton on Palm Sunday 1461, in a bloodbath where the Pastons had reckoned that around 28,000 men were killed. (The battle may have served as a model for witness Sir Thomas Malory's depiction of the bloody final battle between King Arthur and the rebel Modred in his 'Morte d'Arthur'.[2]) The excessive loss of local life in the Queen's army at Towton Moor may well have encouraged anti-Yorkist risings later in the 1460s but was effective in defeating the Queen, who had to flee to Scotland.

**Towton and after: Edward IV's skills and luck. The Scottish factor**
The 'official' Yorkist version of the events of 1461 may have exaggerated in portraying the Yorkists as having the majority support of the south and east of the country and the ex-King as having the support of the north and west, but the latter provided the backbone of the Lancastrian army that was crushed at Towton. The latter had had the larger army, with the adherence of much of the militarily active nobility (two dukes, four earls, a viscount,

and eight barons) and over sixty knights, twenty-five of the latter MPs. Their chances of winning must have seemed high, and the loss of the capital to Edward in March was not decisive and could have been reversed. The northerners were on familiar home ground outside York; the Lancastrian army included many of the northern nobility and gentry who were more used to war (against the Scots) than the southerners and had a more militarily coherent and battle-hardened tenantry. These posed a substantial danger of unrest to the new King, but were destroyed at Towton; the bloodthirsty victor of Wakefield, Lord Clifford, and other senior nobles like the young Earl of Northumberland – head of the most powerful family in the north-east – Lords Dacre and Welles, and the ex-Calais commander Andrew Trollope were killed (Clifford in a pre-battle clash). The effects of the bloodbath were devastating nonetheless, with the King following his father's and Warwick's practical ruthlessness in executing the captured Earls of Devon and Wiltshire afterwards.[3] (With them eliminated rather than pardoned, their lands in the south-west and Wales could be distributed to Yorkist lords to add to regional security.) The victory was gained by boldness, with the smaller Yorkist force pressing forward aided by a hail of arrows and persevering until the enemy broke, a tactic repeated at Barnet and Tewkesbury in 1471 and clearly ordered by the new King not the more cautious Warwick.[4] For all his subsequent reputation as the warlord 'par excellence' of the 1450s and 1460s, the so-called 'Kingmaker' had a limited record for winning battles. His skills seem to have been political and as a publicity-monger rather than as a warrior; he lost control of Henry VI at St Albans in early 1461, although he nearly won at Barnet in March 1471.

Edward had gained and secured the throne by his own boldness rather than by relying on Warwick, in contrast to the latter's leading role in the 1460 attack on the south-east. His victory forced the Queen and her surviving noble adherents to retreat to Scotland, where Edward had the bonus that the warlike young pro-Lancastrian King James II had been killed in a cannon-explosion while besieging Roxburgh Castle in July 1460 leaving an eight-year-old son. James II, a ferocious warrior and ruthless political operator known for his harrying of the southern uplands in the 1450s to drive out the rebel Douglas clan, could have been expected to aid the Queen, who had handed over Berwick to him earlier, and thus to require another major English campaign against Scotland. His mother, Joan, had been the sister of the Duke of Somerset killed by York's men at St Albans in 1455. With his leadership removed the Scottish regents, Queen-Mother Mary of Guelders and Bishop Kennedy, gave their Lancastrian allies little effective help; the latter were only able to hold onto parts of Northumberland, studded with semi-impregnable castles loyal to the late Earl's Percy family and each requiring a costly siege to reduce. The geography and local partisanship by the tenants of the defeated Lancastrian nobility enabled the area to hold out for Henry VI into 1462, as did north and south-west Wales under Owen Tudor's son Jasper (Earl of Pembroke to 1461 and from an Anglesey dynasty). Edward had killed Jasper's father at Hereford after the battle of Mortimer's Cross, and now confiscated the Earldom of Pembroke and Jasper's estates. Warwick's murder of the Duke of Buckingham, lord of Brecon and the other principal magnate besides himself in south-east Wales, after the battle of Northampton in 1460, had left the Buckingham title and estates to a minor, Duke Henry. Warwick was duly granted their wardship, but was soon eclipsed as the King's main lieutenant in South Wales by a 'new man', Sir William Herbert (who later replaced Jasper Tudor as Earl of Pembroke). Herbert had been the lowly Sheriff of Glamorgan under Warwick's command in the 1450s, and the acquisitive Earl seems to have fiercely resented his rise; at the first opportunity he was to arrest and murder Herbert too (1469).[5] Edward, in contrast to Warwick, was able to show a degree of reconciliation; of the fourteen peers attainted by the 1461 Parliament seven were already dead and six others still defying him in arms.[6] His future wife Elizabeth Woodville's father, Lord Rivers, and brother Anthony Woodville, Lord Scales, had both fought for Henry VI at Towton but were pardoned, as were the new Earl of Shrewsbury, Lord Grey of Codnor, and others.

Neither 1461 'rebellion' against Edward IV was a major danger, although it took until September for Edward's local lieutenant Sir William Herbert to reduce Pembroke Castle and for Warwick, now lieutenant of the east and west Scottish Marches, to reduce Alnwick and Dunstanburgh Castles. The latter was riskily left to its ex-Lancastrian commander, Sir Ralph Percy, whose father and brother had both been killed by the Yorkists; his adherence was thus dubious but his family needed to be won over so the risk was taken. Herbert defeated Jasper Tudor outside and reduced Caernarfon in October, leaving the Tudor forces in possession of strongly fortified and isolated Carreg Cennen (reduced 1462) and Harlech (reduced 1468); Herbert now took over the pro-Lancastrian Tudors' role as the King's lieutenant in Wales. Warwick commanded the north of England, based on his inheritance of part of the Neville dynasty's lands and the support of the senior branch of the family, the Earls of Westmorland – though the necessary reliance on the Nevilles, Edward's maternal kin, risked the further enmity of the Percies. (The confiscated Percy title of Earl of Northumberland was not given to a Yorkist, Warwick's brother John, until 1469 – a sign of hope for the Percies' submission?) The removal of Queen Margaret to France to seek aid and Yorkist-aided revolt against the Scots regency brought the latter to terms in summer 1462, although Margaret's return with a small French force under the veteran mercenary commander Pierre de Brezé in the autumn led to the garrisons of Bamburgh, Alnwick, and Dunstanburgh all deserting to them. The fact that the French-born Margaret relied on help from her homeland was useful in alienating people from her – and in 1461 she had offered the Channel Islands to France, leading to de Brezé invading Jersey.

This rebellion led to another northern campaign by the King, who was held up by measles at York while Warwick took over the sieges. Once Margaret and Henry VI fled to Scotland the rebel castles could be invested without fear of relief. The Yorkist triumph seemed decisive enough for the young Duke Henry of Somerset, son of the late Duke of York's foe and victim Duke Edmund, to surrender to Edward.

### Signs of Edward IV's weakness? The mid-late 1460s

Edward was clearly willing to pardon all but the most senior Lancastrian partisans in order to secure his kingdom with a maximized degree of unity. He had kept on the locally influential Sir Ralph Percy at Dunstanburgh Castle after his surrender, only to see him revolt again, and the defeat of the autumn 1462 revolt left Percy submissive – and pardoned – for a second time. He was not even removed from or forced to share Dunstanburgh's command, which would have been wise. Predictably, he abused Edward's trust and/or need of his support and revolted a third time as soon as Queen Margaret and a Scottish army reappeared in Northumberland in spring 1463. The Scots besieged Norham Castle, only to retreat after a large-scale raid into their country by Warwick and his brother John, Lord Montague; Edward promised to come to the Nevilles' aid and raised a large sum from Parliament to fund an army but for some reason his attack on Scotland never materialized. The immediate danger over, he remained in the Midlands amidst considerable criticism in contemporary chronicles of his laziness.[7] A truce was secured with France in October 1463, ending aid from Louis XI to Margaret who finally gave up her efforts and sailed from Scotland to exile in France; Henry remained in the ever more precarious area holding out for him in northern Northumberland until the imminent fall of its castles led to him going into hiding. From his subsequent adventures and capture it appears that he was protected by the gentry of the Lake District in 1463–5. Their steadfast loyalty to their king was a tragic reminder of the wasted opportunities the Lancastrians had had in the 1450s to retain the goodwill that their dynasty had built up since 1399 – even in October 1460 a majority of peers had baulked at allowing York to depose the already mentally feeble Henry.

Sir Ralph Percy had already abused Edward's pardon, and now in winter 1463–4 it was Somerset's turn to betray him. Already the object of hostility as undeserving of Edward's notable favour in London in 1463,[8] he had been sent to North Wales out of the way. But he used his isolated location – and lack of supervision – to send letters to Henry promising support and plotted to raise a Welsh revolt on his behalf; when this was betrayed to the King he fled to northern England to join his real sovereign. Intending to raise some of his ex-soldiers who were part of the Newcastle garrison to declare for Henry, he was spotted and nearly captured at Durham and fled to Bamburgh to join Henry instead; the rebellion was thus restricted in location to the remote north beyond the Tyne. Hemmed in by the advancing Yorkists, Somerset and Sir Ralph Percy ambushed Edward's commander Montague on Hedgely Moor in April but were routed; Percy was killed and Somerset was taken prisoner at a second encounter at Hexham in May and was belatedly executed. He and Percy were not the only ex-rebels pardoned by Edward in the ranks of the 1464 revolt, Sir Humphrey Neville of Brancepeth also taking part. Notably, it was Warwick not Edward who organized the series of executions of captured rebels after the defeat of the revolt, which literally decapitated dissent in the north for a few years – a sign of greater Neville realism and ruthlessness? The King had to build a consensus and thus take the risk of pardoning rebel leaders, particularly those with local support in the hostile north, but overall Edward gave an impression of weakness in 1461–4, which encouraged further revolt.

The question remains of why Edward had trusted Somerset in the first place, or at least – given his importance as the lynch-pin of a possible reconciliation with the Beauforts – why he had been allowed to go to North Wales in 1463, not kept under surveillance in southern England. Edward's failure to go north on campaign in 1463 was probably partly due to lack of ready money for an advance into Scotland, but he could easily have shown his face in the far north without moving on to invade Scotland. Instead, all the action of the sieges was left to Warwick and Montague. Coupled with his excessive trust in a major Lancastrian partisan, these actions indicated a lack of energy or ruthlessness by the young king and can be seen as early signs of his well-recorded laziness in later years. It would have been more politic to show his eagerness for a Scots war in 1463, given that a major criticism of Henry VI had been the latter's failure to fight the national enemy (then France).

Denied long-term support from Scotland or France and with his senior local partisans now executed or killed in battle, Henry's 'mini-state' on the Borders now collapsed. He lost his final castles in northern Northumberland in 1464, went into hiding with loyal local gentry, and was captured wandering around Lancashire in 1465. He was placed securely in the Tower of London. The ex-Prince of Wales and his mother remained at large in France, with Louis XI willing to use them for an invasion when needed, but by 1465 the charismatic young 'Sun of York' had seemed to have secured the crown permanently for his family. The local disturbances that marred the 1460s, as reflected in the *Paston Letters*,[9] were more a case of the unruliness and defiance of authority endemic to a time of weak central control with disbanded fighting-men on the loose (c.f. the 1260s, 1320s, and 1450s) than of a serious threat. Edward had done his best to suppress such local violence in the early 1460s,[10] though the East Midlands risings of 1468–9 assumed a wider and more worrying dimension – probably due to encouragement by disaffected senior lords, principally Warwick.

Edward's reign suffered major problems in 1468–70, which were clearly unanticipated in the hopeful mood of 1461. There was a young and vigorous king who already had a military reputation as of his accession, like Henry V, a sharp contrast to Henry VI. So how did he come to face two major revolts – both successful – after a mere eight years of rule? The blame cannot be placed solely on Warwick, despite the latter's leadership of both revolts; Jean de Wauvrin's well-informed chronicle and other sources make it clear that there was not exactly a popular rush to volunteer for Edward's army during the revolt of 1469. He was reliant on an army of Welshmen and West Countrymen raised by his local supporters (Sir William Herbert, now Earl of Pembroke, and Humphrey Stafford, Earl of Devon) to save him from Warwick on that occasion, and was helpless when they were defeated.[11] Nor did he have popular support as the banished Warwick returned in arms in 1470; if anything, men flocked to the rebel's standard.[12] This cannot be written off as fear or a prudent desire to back the winner. And were all the apparently large rebel Yorkshire host of 'captain of the commons' 'Robin of Redesdale' in 1469 bribed Neville tenants gathered by Warwick's men?[13] It appears that Warwick was able to use a sense of disillusionment with Edward in 1469 and 1470, even if fear of being caught on the losing side inhibited men from backing the King against his militarily experienced, immensely powerful, and skilful challenger. He was also known for his lavish generosity – useful in gaining recruits.

Edward's unexpected and initially secret marriage to Elizabeth Woodville (see next section) in May 1464 had been symptomatic of or had actively caused his rift with his most powerful vassal, his cousin Warwick. The latter, boundlessly acquisitive, was probably bound to be frustrated at Edward limiting his acquisitions of land and office at some point in any case, particularly as Edward built up Herbert's power in Wales at Warwick's expense, removed his brother George Neville from the Chancellorship

(1467), and failed to follow his desire for alliance with France. The latter was connected to the occasion for the first open conflict of interest between King and Earl, when Edward failed to inform Warwick that he could not marry the French princess who Warwick was negotiating for as he had already married in secret (summer – autumn 1464). The loss of 'face' for Warwick, shown up to the French negotiators as he did not know his king's plans about matrimony, no doubt exacerbated his grudges – though it is questionable how much this affected his attitude to Edward as well as to the new Queen, whose family Warwick already despised.[14] But what was Edward doing by not announcing his betrothal, let alone his marriage? We do not even know the date or location for certain, though circumstantial evidence backs the traditional legend that the date was 1 May 1464 and the location a chapel near Elizabeth Woodville's manor-house at Grafton Regis. The witnesses were apparently limited to a few members of her family, led by her mother the Dowager Duchess of Bedford (later accused of masterminding the event, and of using witchcraft to ensnare Edward); no courtiers appear to have been present, and possibly Elizabeth's father was not.[15] The hurried nature of the event and the lack of witnesses was connected to Edward's current journey north with a small entourage to commence a campaign against the latest rebellion in Northumberland – according to Robert Fabyan, writing decades later, he pretended to be going hunting for a few hours and slipped away from his companions.[16] The marriage was not revealed until a 'Great Council' was held at Reading in September to plan the forthcoming Anglo-French 'summit' at St Omer, where Warwick intended to finalize the marriage of Edward to Louis XI's sister-in-law Bona of Savoy.[17]

The very fact of a secret marriage was unprecedented for the post-Conquest kings, and its existence could be queried as there were so few witnesses; it was not revealed for four or five months and then by the King. The fact of the ceremony could not be certified by reliable witnesses – and it may not have been only fear of the Nevilles' reaction that caused Edward to keep it secret. Did he always intend to honour it, or did he think of denying it if necessary? The legend that Edward, recorded around 1510 by Sir Thomas More (who had access to Edwardian court veterans such as Bishop John Morton) as a notorious rake in his youth, tried to force himself on Elizabeth at dagger-point but that she held out for marriage may reflect the 'truth' that she was more interested in marriage than he was.[18] The stock 'Woodville legend' (fostered by Warwick and by Richard III) accuses her entire family of being greedy social climbers, intent on leeching off the King, but it is possible that Edward's secrecy was not only due to fear of what Warwick would make of the 'mis-match'. There is the unresolved issue of his other mistreatment of vulnerable young women – his alleged devious avoidance of carrying out (legally valid) 'pre-contracts' to marry Eleanor Butler, a young widow from the aristocratic Butler dynasty (daughter of the late Earl of Shrewsbury), and Elizabeth Lucy. More is the only person to name Elizabeth Lucy, who is known to have been the mother of Edward's bastard son Arthur Plantagenet, Lord Lisle.[19] But did he mix Elizabeth and Eleanor up, intentionally or accidentally? The dates for these incidents – two separate occasions, which have been confused as one, or only one with the female participant confused? – seem to be 1462–4, so did the more worldly Elizabeth Woodville insist on a marriage instead of a betrothal-ceremony? (Both were seen as equally legal in the fifteenth century; a century previously the Church had ruled that Richard II's mother Joan had been 'married' to a man she had been betrothed to and could not marry again in his lifetime.[20])The Butler/Lucy case was only revealed in 1483 so some historians claim Richard III invented it.[21] Elizabeth Woodville, 'unsuitable' or not from her gentry background, was six years or so older then Edward and was of a lower social status than most royal brides, although her mother was the royal Duke of Bedford's high-born Continental widow Jacquetta of St Pol. Her father, Sir Richard Woodville, Bedford's ex-steward, had already been publicly abused by Warwick and his kin for his insolence in marrying above himself;[22] this was more important than Woodville, his son Anthony, and Elizabeth's late husband, Lord Grey, having fought for Lancaster. (Grey had been killed at Towton.)

Warwick, his plans for a Continental marriage-alliance with the still hostile France undermined behind his back by his sovereign and at odds with the new Queen's acquisitive family, exploited tension at court, rising faction, and civil unrest to suddenly revolt and capture Edward in 1469. As with the treachery of Henry Beaufort in 1464, it appears that Edward was slow to listen to rumours of his intentions and did nothing to pre-empt his rebellion by raising troops – indeed, he did not even hurry north as the 'Robin of Redesdale' rebels advanced on Nottingham. Warwick was able to slip away to Calais to marry his elder daughter, Isabel, to Edward's next brother (and current male heir) George of Clarence, a match that Edward was refusing to allow, and then to march on London proclaiming his intention to 'rescue' Edward from his 'low-born' councillors (Herbert, the Woodvilles, and others named). The peers of royal blood had been excluded from their 'rightful' places around the King by these 'arrivistes', and now sought to reassert their 'rights' by force. The terminology used in Warwick's proclamation was that used by the – successful – rebels against the then King's unpopular councillors in 1326, 1387, and 1399, a fact that would have been apparent to all parties and a warning of what fate Edward could face.[23] The fact that Clarence was with Warwick, and married to his daughter, implied that Warwick had a replacement king ready to hand if he wanted to depose Edward, though in the event he did not carry out his implied threats.[24]

Ironically, the Duke of Bedford's early death in 1435 contributed to the breakdown of trust within the Yorkist regime in the mid-late 1460s, as his widow, Jacquetta, was able to re-marry and produce Edward IV's future wife and her brood of acquisitive siblings. This was an example of unexpected long-term political consequences from a seemingly remote event – and arguably it even affected the stability of the young Edward V's regime and contributed to the Tudor success in seizing the throne in 1485. If Bedford had lived longer, his widow would not have been free to marry Sir Richard Woodville – though Edward could still have married a 'low-born' bride instead of Bona of Savoy. Whether or not the 'Kingmaker' ever intended to depose the King, he made the most of his opportunity to kill the Queen's father and one of her brothers and Edward's powerful supporter, William Herbert, Earl of Pembroke, brutally restoring his pre-eminence at court. But Warwick's military abilities may have been exaggerated as the cause of his success in July 1469, although his advancing rebel army was able to secure London and reach the Midlands unopposed. Edward still had a large army of Welshmen and West Countrymen advancing to assist him at this point, though peculiarly he made no move to join them. Warwick's successful attack on Herbert's army at Edgecote Field in July 1469 was due to the Welsh and West Countrymen quarrelling over billeting and having to be quartered separately, miles apart, thus enabling Warwick to attack the Welsh on 25 July while most of the archers were with Herbert miles away. But for this he could well have faced a dangerous royal army, and been defeated; Herbert, an ex-official of his, would have known how best to fight him. Instead, he was able to destroy the royal forces, capture and execute Herbert, and then advance to capture the powerless King.[25] As in 1461, Edward showed what speed and decisiveness in action he was capable of in a crisis after a sluggish response to the 1469 revolt. Having been caught out by Warwick whose secret encouragement to the 1469 Midlands rebels clearly surprised him, he made no attempt to evade the Earl's forces and relied on his supporters to put pressure on Warwick to free him. It is possible that the Parliament that Warwick initially announced was intended to replace Edward with Clarence, but if so the Earl lost his nerve.[26] There was no purge of Edward's Council or senior office-holders beyond Herbert and the Woodvilles – indeed, a wider move would only have raised the probability of revolt by well-armed magnates. Warwick could not raise troops to face another Lancastrian revolt in the north (by two minor Nevilles, ironically) without the King's legal authority, and he did not have the option of getting supportive Councillors to declare him governor or 'Protector' of the realm with the King adult and in full command of his senses. In September he gave in and allowed Edward to leave custody at Middleham Castle for York to raise peers and soldiers for the northern campaign, and the King then summoned the Councillors (plus their armed entourages) from London to join him as he advanced on his capital. For the moment, Warwick escaped with the loss of some of the offices he had seized from his victims – most of his Welsh acquisitions went to Edward's youngest brother Richard, Duke of Gloucester, who Edward now built up as a counter-weight to the unreliable Clarence. Officially, Edward proclaimed reconciliation with Warwick, though according to the *Paston Letters* his supporters were more hostile.[27] But the effective truce was unlikely to last, although there is controversy over Warwick's responsibility for the next 'popular' revolt in spring 1470, which escalated into the decisive King vs Warwick confrontation. This rising broke out in a pro-Lancastrian area, Lincolnshire, and was led by the Lancastrian sympathizer Lord Welles. Having indulged in a relatively commonplace 'private war' against Edward's local stalwart Sir Thomas Burgh and sacking his manor-house, he reacted to the rumour that Edward was about to launch a personal judicial 'purge' of local rebels by proclaiming himself as 'captain of the commons' and summoning local support to resist the King. This escalated the disturbances into a direct challenge to Edward, as the 1469 revolt of 'Robin', though without implicit threats to depose Edward. His confession after capture that Warwick had put him up to it has been excused by pro-Warwick historians as forced by Edward IV in order to incriminate the Earl and excuse his banishment.[28] The official version of the royal attack on the rebels at 'Lose-Coat Field' – where the lack of rebel preparedness and their easy rout argues for their spontaneity – put it out that the rebels had worn Warwick and Clarence's livery and shouted their names. Contemporaries with no apparent ulterior motives asserted that Warwick and Clarence were involved in the revolt, and there were other risings in areas of the north and the West Country where they were the leading magnates.[29] The fact that ex-Lancastrians joined in may be opportunism or part of that unlikely Warwick-Lancastrian alliance that was to emerge that autumn. At the least, the two leaders failed to obey Edward's orders to join him in repressing the revolts, even after the Lincolnshire rising had failed when it was clear that refusal would mean a royal attack on them next. The majority of peers backed Edward, although Warwick seems to have had a solid base of support among minor gentry, and as the King's army advanced Warwick and Clarence failed to secure support from close allies such as Lord Stanley in Lancashire (or even Warwick's younger brother, Lord Montague).Facing defeat and arrest for treason, they fled abroad to France and in May 1470 a bizarre and no doubt reluctant reconciliation between Warwick and Queen Margaret was staged at Amboise by their mutual ally, Louis XI. Warwick's younger daughter Anne Neville, aged fourteen, was now married off to Margaret's son Prince Edward, who Warwick had been instrumental in disinheriting as a bastard.[30] In reply to the threat of Warwick linking up with the Lancastrians, Edward now reinstated the Percy heir, son and grandson of the two Earls of Northumberland killed by the Yorkists in 1455 and 1461, as Earl after five years in the Tower of London. He was now meant to bring the Percy lands and tenantry into the Yorkist 'fold', though the reconciliation meant stripping the earldom from Warwick's brother John Neville who was compensated with the Marquisate of Montague but was reported by the chronicler John Warkworth to be furious with the King.

### Edward's flight and return, 1470–1. Some elements of the 1399 invasion repeated?

Edward had to flee for his life from the East Midlands in October 1470 as Warwick, invading from exile, received the support of the Yorkist commander in the north, his younger brother John Neville, Marquis of Montague. The King had gone north in July to deal with a local rising by Warwick's brother-in-law Lord Fitzhugh, despite the possibility that Warwick's French-backed fleet would land in the south (e.g. notoriously turbulent Kent where he had landed in 1460 and 1469). His personal presence there was logical, given that Montague – soon to defect – was of dubious loyalty and the new Earl of Northumberland was young and inexperienced. But the Pastons reckoned it unwise for him to go north at all, given the invasion-threat, and he had not returned weeks after the rebels had been dispersed. According to Edward's own correspondence, as of 7 September he expected Warwick to land in Kent, where the royal fleet was patrolling the Channel waiting for him.[31] However, when a storm dispersed the King's ships on 9 September and Warwick was able to sail from France the Earl headed for Devon instead. Possibly, Warwick incited his relative Sir Humphrey Neville of Brancepeth to revolt to lure Edward up to the Borders and intended to mislead him about landing in Kent, and if so it worked. As in July 1469, Edward's inactivity is puzzling; it gave Warwick his chance. In mid-September the Earl and Clarence landed in Devon and moved north-east into the Midlands, being joined by Lord Stanley (his brother-in-law) en route.

Returning south, Edward was caught unawares at Doncaster as news arrived that Montague, raising an army for him at Pontefract to his rear, had declared for Warwick – a repeat of his being caught out by Somerset in 1464 and Warwick in 1469. Edward and a few close associates, including Lord Hastings (a local magnate so able to guide him) and Lord Rivers, headed swiftly to the nearest port at King's Lynn and found a ship; within days they were in Holland, part of the Burgundian domains of the King's brother-in-law Duke Charles. This left the south of England to the invaders and enabled Warwick's brother Archbishop George Neville of York to head for London unopposed, with Warwick following; on 5 October the Archbishop secured the abandoned capital and the person of Henry VI, who was still in the Tower and was now moved into the abandoned royal apartments. Their most recent occupant, heavily-pregnant Queen Elizabeth Woodville, took refuge in the sanctuary at Westminster Abbey. Edward's decision not to fight was probably wise, given the speed with which Montague could intercept any attempt by him to raise troops and the possibility of further defections, and it is possible that the Marquis deliberately let him escape to save the embarrassment of what to do if he was captured. (If Edward could be executed as a traitor to Henry VI, what of the rest of the Yorkist leadership who Warwick now needed to woo as a counter-weight to the Beauforts and Henry's Queen?) Notably, the official records of Coventry reckoned that up to 30,000 men flocked to Warwick and Clarence as they arrived in the Midlands to confront Edward, suggesting lack of enthusiasm for the King as much as eagerness to back the winners.[32]

Once Edward had fled Warwick's faction was confident enough to summon all but seven peers to the next Parliament despite the potential problems this would cause in requiring many loyalists of Edward IV to perjure themselves by abandoning the man they had sworn allegiance to and recognize the man they had deposed in 1461. Four of the seven were in exile with Edward already, the exceptions being the Earl of Wiltshire and Lords Dudley and Dinham.[33] Warwick certainly did not rely on fear or the use of a narrow faction of his own supporters to impose recognition of Henry VI, though the majority of peers had stood aside from his challenge to Edward and now, as he reckoned correctly, preferred the safe course of recognizing a *fait accompli* to arguing about legality. Arguably, the swift course of events in September to October 1470 had taken them by surprise; but they did not rally to Edward's side when he returned in March 1471 either. As far as we can tell from the absence of records for this Parliament (destroyed by Edward IV), nobody dared to suggest on Clarence's behalf that attainting Edward IV – thus debarring him from his York estates as well as the 'illegally seized' Crown – would make Clarence his legal heir to all the York inheritance. (The matter of Edward's supposed illegitimacy could also count.) The number of Parliamentary attainders was minimal (headed by the ex-King and Richard of Gloucester);[34] despite the need for acquiring lands and titles to buy support, Warwick dared not stir up extra opposition. Typically, he secured not only the militarily necessary leadership of the new government (as 'Lieutenant of the Realm'), and his old Captaincy of Calais but extra offices seized from the ex-King's close supporters, e.g. the Admiralship and Chamberlainship, and the control of the Duchy of Buckingham's Welsh estates, which Edward had taken from him.[35] Only one Yorkist loyalist, the much-reviled ex-Treasurer and alleged sadist Lord Tiptoft who was accused of assorted unjust executions as Constable of England, was executed and others who were arrested were soon released.[36] The ambiguity and embarrassment of the political leadership recognizing their past actions of 1461–70 as illegal were avoided as far as possible, with no investigation of Archbishop Bourchier for crowning a 'usurper' and no re-coronation of Henry VI as had been necessary for the 'deposed' and re-acclaimed Stephen in 1141 (a Saxon-style 'crown-wearing' ceremony in St Paul's Cathedral on 13 October sufficed).[37]

'Realpolitik' evidently impelled most of the political nation to recognize reality and abandon Edward's cause for Henry's in October 1470, though there was no enthusiasm for the new order. The new King was not even placed in a royal palace, but lived under supervision at the Bishop of London's residence pending his Queen's return. Fortunately, the uncomfortable political result of Warwick's alliance with ex-Queen Margaret and Louis XI – the return as his allies of his arch-enemies in the Lancastrian faction – was not immediately tested. Margaret and her son, the Duke of Exeter, and the Duke of Somerset (Edmund, brother of the Duke executed in 1464 and son of the man killed by Warwick's father and uncle in 1455) were all still abroad; the latter two did not return until February 1471 and Margaret was still in France as Edward IV invaded. The inevitable quarrel over patronage and renewal of old mistrust was thus put off, though there was already a major problem over the status and estates of the Duke of Clarence, Warwick's son-in-law. Edward IV's male heir until the birth of the ex-King's son in sanctuary at Westminster on 2 November 1470, he had been lured by his father-in-law to support his brother's arrest and probable overthrow in 1469 and had joined Warwick in rebellion and flight in 1470. His allegiance to the Lancastrian cause brought in more ex-Yorkists than the 'hard core' Neville partisans in autumn 1470. He owned massive estates across the country, especially in the West Country, whose tenants would follow his standard – though many of these lands had been confiscated from prominent Lancastrians by Edward IV and in March 1471 Clarence had to hand some of them over to endow Queen Margaret and her son. This transfer of lands was accepted in the documentation as a breach of the promises Warwick and the Queen had made that Clarence was to keep all his lands until properly recompensed – and it is probable that his resentment at this was one reason why he listened to messages sent from Edward IV promising a pardon if he defected.[38] There was also the unresolved question of Clarence's acquisition of the lands of the Earldom of Richmond, which had been taken from the Tudors by Edward IV; the late Earl Edmund's posthumous son Henry (the future Henry VII) now appeared at Henry VI's court as the protégé of his uncle Jasper, the new regime's 'strong man' in South Wales. Would he be endowed at Clarence's expense next? Clarence's accepting Henry VI as legitimate king – and by implication his son Prince Edward as heir – was not the end of his ambitions for the throne, and it seems that he was promised the succession next in line after the Prince. He may well have initially hoped to be named as Henry's direct heir as he prepared in invade in 1470, and been reluctant to accept that the terms of Warwick's alliance with Queen Margaret ruled that possibility out.[39] Naming him as next heir would also dash the hopes of the Beauforts, who were technically illegitimate but could be legitimized by Act of Parliament. The lack of any public declaration of the new line of succession in the early months of 1471 may show that Warwick had to balance the competing claims of Clarence (who brought with him ex-Yorkists) and the 'hard-line' Lancastrian Beaufort partisans to be Henry VI and Prince Edward 's next heirs. Legally, Clarence had the better claim. If the 1461 claim of Edward IV as rightful king as heir of Lionel of Clarence was disallowed, that still left the York line as rightful heirs after the Lancastrians, as descendants of the younger brother of John 'of Gaunt', Edmund of York – and if Edward IV was debarred and his son illegitimate, Clarence was next male heir to this line. The priority of other matters may be a reason why there is no hint of any attempt to investigate the legality of Edward IV's marriage – or his mother's alleged affair with his 'real father' Blaybourne – during the five months of his exile. Declaring either would have been to Clarence's legal benefit and added to Warwick's ability to justify his revolt, but nothing is recorded as happening.

Warwick was able to gamble successfully on the grudging neutrality of almost all the senior figures in English politics during winter 1470–1. The ambiguity over who exactly was now legitimate king – with two rival crowned kings to choose from – and the sheer attractiveness of not running risks worked to his advantage. There was no great exodus of peers or Household loyalists to join the ex-King in exile, as loyal Lancastrians from the ex-King's Household had gone into exile in 1461 – and the relatively bloodless nature of the invasion meant that the new regime did not have to consider naming many who had fought against it recently as traitors. Nor did Edward's host in exile, his brother-in-law Duke Charles of Burgundy, hasten to raise an army on his behalf. He treated Edward coolly, did not let him come to his court to be feted as rightful king, and did not loan him troops or ships until Margaret and Warwick's ally Louis XI of France attacked him in December 1470. Only when Louis attacked Picardy did he condescend to meet Edward and given him a few ships, after a two-month delay.[40] Warwick had had to agree at the Angers 'summit' in 1470 to commit English troops to Louis' planned war with Charles, thus placing himself at imminent risk of Burgundian attack if Edward or his heirs escaped to Burgundy, but this did not work out to his immediate disadvantage. Arguably, the notoriously calculating 'spider-king' Louis miscalculated on this occasion. If Louis had not bound Warwick to assist him, Duke Charles – who at first recognized Henry VI that autumn – would not have reacted and the chances of Edward IV receiving adequate aid to invade England would have been minimal. He could have invaded without official support and then secured adequate backing within England, as Henry of Bolingbroke was able to do from France (an official ally of his 'target', as Duke Charles was of Henry VI until December 1470). But Charles' support secured Edward a fleet of thirty-six ships and around 1200 men, many of them local Flemings, with whom he sailed from Flushing on 17 February 1471 – giving him a better chance than he would have had with no official backing.[41]

The uneasy alliance of Warwick's and Clarence's ex-Yorkists and the 'die-hard' Lancastrians was always problematic, and Warwick's fear of betrayal is shown by the limited number of magnates who he gave commissions to raise troops as he faced invasion in early 1471.[42] In Yorkshire, where Edward was to land, the Earl could not even entrust a commission to the young Earl of Northumberland, allegedly a reliable Lancastrian and the son and grandson of two Earls killed by the Yorkists (who had then included Warwick). Nor was it clear where Edward would land, and he made an initial descent on Cromer in Norfolk to be warned by his 'contacts' that the local pro-Yorkist Duke of Norfolk (the Pastons' enemy) had been arrested and there was no opportunity to rally support there with the Earl of Oxford advancing. Instead, he landed at Ravenspur in Yorkshire, where Henry of Bolingbroke had landed in 1399, and like him cleverly dissuaded immediate attack from local magnates by claiming that he recognized the current King and was only coming to regain his confiscated dukedom.[43] This gave waverers who had sworn allegiance to Henry VI and/or were Percy foes of the Nevilles an excuse not to have to attack him, as he had legal justice in claiming that he had been illegally despoiled of his inherited estates (as Henry had been in 1399). He was duly admitted to the city of York as a publicly professed subject of Henry VI, and both the armed magnates who had troops in the locality – the Earl of Northumberland and Warwick's brother Montague –

avoided attacking him. Either could have crushed his small army, but instead Edward was left alone to march on south and slowly bring in adherents as he closed in on Warwick at Coventry. The only detailed source for the campaign, the so-called 'Arrivall' of King Edward (first compiled within weeks of the events), was undoubtedly crafted as propaganda to show the 'miraculous' nature of Edward's success and so present his cause as divinely blessed, but there is no reason to doubt its accuracy concerning the small numbers of Edward's army and the luck that he had in evading disaster in Yorkshire. It also states that memories of the slaughter at Towton Moor in 1461 were so strong locally that sympathies were generally Lancastrian and pro-Percy, meaning that Montague (a Yorkist until 1470, and a Neville) could not have guaranteed that his troops would follow if he defected to Edward; the crucial reason for Edward's success was thus the Earl of Northumberland standing aside. Edward IV's restoration of the earldom to its rightful owner in 1470 thus now paid off, and he was able to march on south unmolested.[44]

Montague and Northumberland enabled Edward and his small army to move on southwards and gain more recruits than they had done in York, building up their force until they could challenge Warwick. No major pro-government peers came in to support Edward, although his East Midlands ally Lord Hastings' supporters brought recruits; the Duke of Somerset had gone to Dorset to meet Queen Margaret and the pro-Lancastrian Dukes of Exeter and Oxford fled south to join Warwick. The latter, evidently fearing desertions, refused to fight and stayed immobile in Coventry, probably to await Clarence's arrival with his tenants to make his army larger. But when Clarence arrived from the south-west on 3 April he joined Edward and Richard of Gloucester near Burford. This crucial defection boosted Edward's army enough for him to risk leaving Warwick undefeated behind him and head for London, where he arrived without resistance on 11 April. Archbishop Bourchier of Canterbury (who had crowned Edward) and most of the other civilian government figures stayed to welcome Edward; the only pro-Henry VI figure of importance left in the capital, Warwick's brother Archbishop George Neville of York, tried parading Henry VI through the streets to win support but was treated with indifference. Apparently, according to Warkworth's chronicle, the time-serving Neville then entered into secret communication with Edward and agreed to keep Henry secure and out of sanctuary until the Yorkist army arrived to recapture him.[45]

Had Neville had the loyalty to take Henry out of danger to join Warwick in the Midlands or to wait for Queen Margaret in Dorset, the King would have had a reasonable hope of escaping abroad as his cause collapsed. He would have been a poor figurehead for a declining and militarily lost cause with Prince Edward dead, but would have been able to live out his final years in peace (perhaps in France). But Neville, more of a politician than a cleric, took care of his own interests instead, and duly survived the ruin of his brothers' cause to keep his archbishopric for the rest of his life. Deprived of his chancellorship again so probably not trusted, he was arrested on suspicion of renewed contacts with his exiled brother-in-law Oxford in April 1472, deprived of his revenues, and locked up in Hammes Castle near Calais (safely out of England) until Oxford was in custody and it was safe to release him in 1474.[46] He died in obscurity in 1476.

When the other Neville brothers, Warwick and Montague, finally joined armies and confronted Edward at the battle of Barnet (Easter Sunday, 14 April), they were without a significant part of the Lancastrian forces as Somerset (and Warwick's veteran captain Sir John Wenlock) had gone south-west to meet Queen Margaret at Cerne Abbas. Ironically, she landed on the same day as the battle. Had she and her French mercenaries had time to reach London and join Warwick things would have seemed much more hopeless for Edward, who had around 9,000 men but probably the smaller army. Indeed, her failure to return to England sooner, as expected (Warwick had gone to Dover to meet her in February), was a disaster for her cause. It may have doomed her husband, who was left in the treacherous Archbishop Neville's hands in London, and it left the Lancastrian armies short of leaders and troops; Somerset, for example, was not able to fight at Barnet. It also kept her warlike and possibly inspiring teenage son, a useful rallying-point for his family's cause, away from the main Lancastrian-Neville grouping at the Court in London in the crucial early months of 1471. (On the bonus side, her absence helped to avert a clash between her, Warwick, and Clarence over patronage.) Her party, in fact, boarded their ships at Honfleur on 24 March, to be held up by northerly winds until 13 April; the factor of an adverse wind thus arguably seriously weakened the Lancastrian cause in 1471 as it undermined King Harold's chances of defeating the Norman invaders in 1066.

At the battle of Barnet, the two ex-Yorkist Neville peers were finally defeated by their royal cousin Edward IV. Montague was killed along with Warwick after a hard-fought hand-to-hand combat in early morning fog – and as his body was discovered to be wearing Edward's heraldic device under his armour he may have been considering changing sides again. Thanks to a muddle in the thick fog, Warwick's possession of a large, coherent army did not secure him victory despite his men pressing the Yorkists back alarmingly at one point. His right wing under the Earl of Oxford drove their opponents off the battlefield, leading to panicking fugitives fleeing back to London crying that all was lost, but as Oxford returned to the battlefield Warwick's men mistook their 'Silver Star' banner for Edward's 'Sun in Splendour' and fired at it. Oxford's men attacked them or fled, securing Edward the vital chance for an assault and victory.[47] The Duke of Exeter was wounded and captured, and some surviving Lancastrians were able to escape to Dorset to inform Queen Margaret of the disaster.

Edward was then able to catch Queen Margaret's army at Tewkesbury as it headed for the Severn valley to link up with Jasper Tudor's army in Wales, having left Windsor on 24 April after the St George's Day ceremonies to head for Malmesbury. Initially, a clash east of Bristol at Chipping Sodbury on 1 May seemed probable and Edward drew his army up there. But the Queen chose to avoid a clash, withdrew her men from Bristol without Edward's scouts finding out quickly, and raced north to secure Jasper's assistance; she was at Berkeley that evening while Edward was still waiting for battle.[48] Edward headed the Queen's army off the Severn crossings in time in a desperate race across the western Cotswolds, luckily managing to send a force ahead to secure Gloucester where she arrived early on the 3rd. The Queen had been able to raise local troops from the Beaufort and Courtenay estates in the south-west, and had received support in Bristol; more time would have made her even more formidable. Instead, the arrival of the victorious royal army meant she had to retreat from a direct confrontation and try to link up with the Welsh levies. Luckily Edward was only a few hours behind the Queen's army, giving them no time either to rest or to secure a Severn bridge once they failed to secure Gloucester. Instead, the Lancastrians arrived at the next town and bridge upstream (Tewkesbury) later on 3 May with the enemy so close behind that they had to stand and fight. The resultant battle in the water-meadows saw both sides exhausted from the pursuit but Edward's with the advantage of a recent victory to boost their confidence, and the Lancastrians made more mistakes as Somerset (possibly goaded by Edward's artillery) abandoned his strong defensive position in front of the town to attack southwards across open fields. This advance brought his right wing within reach of a Yorkist force hiding in a spinney adjacent to the battlefield, who then emerged to take him in the flank. The Lancastrians were pushed back, and in the resultant chaos one of their generals axed Lord Wenlock, claiming that his failure to back up the attack meant that he had been bribed. The Queen's army was destroyed, and Somerset and other leaders captured hiding in Tewkesbury Abbey were dragged out and hastily tried by a 'kangaroo court' before execution (4–5 May). Prince Edward was killed either in the battle or in the 'round-up' afterwards (according to Warkworth calling out for help to Clarence),[49] Queen Margaret and Anne Neville were taken into custody at a nearby priory, and with them dealt with the captive Henry VI's death was announced within hours of Edward's return to London on 21 May. The blatant nature of Henry's convenient demise was obvious, though it was arguably politically 'necessary', and it was later claimed to be the first of the future Richard III's murders. In 1483 the French historian Philip de Commignes heard that Richard (as Constable of the Tower) had either done the killing or watched it; Robert Fabyan, a London chronicler, heard that Richard had stabbed Henry and the 'Croyland Continuator' recorded that Henry was found dead and Richard was blamed for it. Edward almost certainly ordered it, though Sir Thomas More (a generation later) claimed Richard had acted alone.[50] A final descent on London by yet another army of Kentish rebels, led by the Nevilles' naval commander the 'Bastard of Fauconberg' (son of Warwick's late uncle), was driven off in time as Edward arrived back in his capital.[51] This left only Jasper Tudor and his young nephew Henry (who fled to Brittany and were interned) and the fugitive Earl of Oxford at large to rally the Lancastrian cause, and Oxford was to be captured on landing in Cornwall in 1474.

Edward was thus able to pick off the various Lancastrian armies one by one and kill off almost all their leadership from March to May 1471, securing the Yorkist cause for another fourteen years. But he could easily have been trapped and defeated or killed during the first weeks of his invasion, failed to win over Clarence, lost at Barnet, or faced a more dangerous combination of Warwick and the Beauforts or Queen Margaret and Jasper Tudor. Not all invasions of an area safely remote from London succeeded in the mid-fifteenth century civil wars; Henry Tudor (later Henry VII), not a crowned king like Edward IV but facing a controversial usurper and allied to the partisans of the deposed Edward V in autumn 1483, was forced to abandon his landing in the south-west. Edward IV owed his success to the fatal 'fault-line' in the unwieldy alliance of Nevilles and Lancastrians, as personally exemplified by Clarence, and the unwillingness of two men who he had helped generously in the past – Montague and the fourth Earl of Northumberland – to confront him in arms in early-mid March 1471. But the number of peers who refrained from either boycotting the 'Readeption' of Henry VI or from aiding Edward as he landed showed that politics were now so unstable that many senior figures preferred to stand back and wait for a clear victor to emerge before committing themselves. That phenomenon was to reappear in 1485 and 1487, as the number of magnates fighting for or against their king during an invasion was notably small – and the confused state of rightful possession of the Crown after three reversals of occupation hardly gave confidence in any particular possessor of power.

**The roles of Edward's brothers had he been killed in 1470–1**

Edward's still-loyal brother Richard (later Richard III) was only eighteen in October 1470. If he had escaped alone, was he willing to take the risk of returning to claim the Duchy of York as his hereditary right in 1471 without nominally threatening the Crown at first, as Edward did? The technical heir to the Duchy of York had Edward been dead would have been his infant son, hidden in sanctuary at Westminster and no doubt barred from the claim, and after him Clarence – but giving the York lands to Clarence would have made him nearly as powerful a magnate as Warwick so Queen Margaret is likely to have blocked it. (Her men killed Clarence's father and brother Edmund in 1460; she had no reason to trust this rival to her son as Henry VI's heir.) The York lands were likely to have been a bone of contention between the rival factions at a Lancastrian court in 1471,and perhaps to have been divided up among several leading magnates. But would Richard have won enough adherents in invading, especially Clarence, and have won at Barnet without the military experience that Edward had? Edward nearly lost to Warwick at Barnet, until the latter's troops got muddled in the fog and fired on each other. If Edward had been killed in flight or in prison in 1470, Clarence would have been the Yorkist heir and may well have been trying to secure the Duchy of York for himself from Henry VI's ministers as Richard was landing. If the Lancastrian leadership had refused to grant Clarence what he wanted, he would have been likely to join Richard – but the question of the York lands may well not have been settled by the time Richard invaded, with Margaret not yet landed. Thus Clarence would not yet have been finally alienated from Lancaster. Would Richard have risked an invasion in order to muster troops before Margaret returned as Edward did? It is more likely that Richard, an untried youth of eighteen, would have waited until a breach between Clarence and Henry VI over the succession to the throne (and/or the Duchy of York) and then aided his brother in revolt. Thus even if Edward had been killed in autumn 1470, a split among the Lancastrian ranks could have led to Richard invading in 1472 or 1473.

If Richard had been killed too in 1470, would the unlikely alliance of the triumphant Warwick as Henry's restorer and Queen Margaret of Anjou – who had murdered Warwick's father in 1460 – have been likely to last? Margaret's son Edward was rumoured by the Yorkists not to be Henry's as he was incapable of siring a son, so his succession to the mentally feeble Henry would have been controversial. Margaret had every reason to fear Warwick as much as she had done York in the1450s – not least as he had married his elder daughter to Clarence, her son's rival. Besides that, Clarence may have been endeavouring to secure a promise of the heirship to Henry in return for his allegiance to the rebels and was apparently accepted as the heir after Prince Edward. Margaret's Beaufort allies would not have allowed that to continue once the Lancastrians did not need Warwick's immediate support against a Yorkist invasion.

Edward IV, if still alive and in exile after 1470, could be written off by Lancastrian propaganda as a claimant with the story that his mother had committed adultery with the archer Blaybourne so he was not the son of the Duke of York and thus Clarence was the legitimate heir. This story first surfaced in 1483, or possibly in 1478 when Edward's mother, Duchess Cecily, was furious at Edward killing Clarence, but may have been current earlier as gossip. Margaret would have defended the rights of her son as Henry's heir and sought to oust Clarence, and a clash between her and Warwick would have followed with a vicious court struggle between their partisans over control of the supine Henry. The Beauforts and Jasper Tudor would have been likelier to back Margaret than Warwick on account of the 'blood-feuds' between Warwick and their families (Warwick had been involved in the death of the Duke of Somerset's father at St Albans in 1455, and the Yorkists had executed Jasper's father, Owen, at Hereford in 1461).

### Clarence or Prince Edward of Lancaster as the next king after Henry?

Clarence would presumably have insisted on receiving all the York family estates as his right and would have been a formidable foe if refused. In due course, at the latest at Henry's death (in the mid- or later 1470s if he had lived to something like his Valois grandfather's age of fifty-four), Margaret – or Prince Edward and Somerset on her behalf – and Warwick/ Clarence would probably have come to blows on the battlefield or engineered a sudden arrest or murder. As a senior peer resident in England who had spent the 1460s building up a vast northern lordship and an experienced commander, Warwick – aided by Clarence – would have had massive resources of men and arms and been more likely to win than Margaret and her Beaufort/ Tudor allies. The final coup of the 'Kingmaker' could have been to secure his elder daughter, Isabel's, husband Clarence's succession to Henry VI – though as he had married his younger daughter, Anne, to Prince Edward she would have been the latter's queen. The marriage of Edward and Anne had, however, been the idea of Warwick and Margaret's mutual patron in exile in 1470, Louis XI of France, and Warwick is more likely to have backed his elder son-in-law Clarence. Prince Edward, apparently a vindictive young man from the little evidence we have of him, would have been less likely than Clarence to accept his father-in-law's direction due to Warwick's past role as arch-enemy of Lancaster. At the least, his determined character would not make him an easily controlled or trustable son-in-law as king; his accession would pose dangers to Warwick that Clarence's accession did not.

Whichever of the contenders won, Warwick would have been the King's father-in-law and potential grandfather to a king. His rivalry with Margaret leaves it open to doubt if he could trust the latter and her son 'Edward V' not to turn on him once Henry was dead. The death of Henry VI, probably by 1480, might thus have seen Warwick install 'King George' and 'Queen Isabel' (if the latter had still been alive), and the Yorkist line returning to the throne. If the possibly tubercular Isabel had died in 1476 as in real life, Clarence would have been available for the prestigious foreign marriage that he then sought – though not to Mary, heiress of Burgundy, as the union of England with the latter would have been commercially problematic. (Clarence could seek her hand in real life as he was not sovereign or heir to the throne, though Edward IV still vetoed the idea.) But if Warwick had managed to remove Prince Edward and his mother to secure Clarence's accession, this would have left Anne Neville – divorced or widowed – free to remarry. On or before Warwick's death there would have been a major struggle for the hand of Anne Neville and her half of the Warwick inheritance. Indeed, it is not impossible that if Richard of Gloucester – brought up as Warwick's protégé at Middleham Castle in the 1460s – was alive in exile Warwick might even have called him back to England once he had disposed of Prince/King Edward and Queen Margaret.

Richard would make a capable new husband for Anne and co-heir to the Neville inheritance, provided that Clarence – now king – could be persuaded to accept his brother's return. Richard could also be a valuable ally for the diminished Yorkist dynasty in their relations with the Beaufort and Tudor families, who would have received an access of lands and power under Henry VI's regime from 1471 and would have been probable backers of Prince Edward in a power-struggle. The amount of confiscations and exiles among the pro-Yorkist peers in autumn 1470 had been very small so there would still have been a substantial number of landowners loyal to Edward in the 1460s available to back Clarence in a 'showdown' with the Queen and Prince, to add to Warwick's own clientele. But a regime with a narrow base of support was at risk of serious revolt, as Richard was to find in 1483–5, so Clarence would have needed as wide a range of support among the peers as possible to survive. The recall of his brother Richard would add to his trustable supporters and diminish the need for gaining the backing of Lancastrian peers.

Thus Clarence, as king after Henry following the elimination of Prince Edward and Queen Margaret by himself or Warwick, could have recalled Richard. It is possible that Clarence's son Edward, born in 1475, was feeble-minded and so a dubious heir – though his apparent limitations in real life in 1499 may have been due to his years isolated in the Tower of London. If he had succeeded to the English throne as an under-age ruler or as one with limited political capability, there was potential for new strife or even a coup by Richard. Clarence's death in this case would have seen a brief reign by 'Edward V' – Clarence's young son, the Earl of Warwick – and a coup by Richard, ruling as in real life as 'Richard III'. It would be crucial whether at this point, possibly the 1490s, the 'Kingmaker' (born in 1428) was still alive and who he backed – and if he were dead whether Clarence had secured all his vast estates and military affinity for the Crown or had allowed part of them to go to Richard. Richard was a natural choice as the next husband for the younger daughter, Anne, of the 'Kingmaker' after Prince Edward had been eliminated, and the claims of Edward IV's disinherited son Edward would have been unlikely to meet much support. The 'usurpation' of Richard III over a genealogically senior candidate, in this scenario not occurring until Clarence had died naturally, would have been likelier in the 1490s or even 1500s than in the 1480s.

Given that the main Lancastrian line would now be extinct, the chief dynastic rivals to Richard would have been the Beauforts (assuming that Edmund, Duke of Somerset, had not been killed as Warwick defeated Margaret and Prince Edward).The senior Beaufort line, though of female descent, was represented not by the Dukes of Somerset but by Henry Tudor, son of Duke Edmund's cousin Margaret Beaufort. (Edmund had inherited the Somerset title from his brother Henry, killed in 1464 for revolting against Edward IV, and his father Duke Edmund, killed in 1455 at St Albans; the latter's elder brother John, d. 1444, had been Margaret Beaufort's father.) As a stalwart of the Lancastrian cause since 1461, Henry's uncle Jasper Tudor would have been loaded with lands and titles by Margaret after 1471 and presumably been the regime's leading supporter in Wales; Henry himself would probably have regained his father's Earldom of Richmond. As long as the Tudors had avoided being brought down with Margaret and Prince Edward in a confrontation between the latter and Warwick, Henry Tudor would have been in a good position to become a major player at court. If Clarence (born in 1449) had been succeeded in the 1490s or 1500s by his son who then proved an inadequate ruler, the House of Tudor would have stood a chance of aiming for the throne in competition with that of York.

**Another possibility – what if the Yorkist leadership had not fractured in 1468–70? Was the quarrel of Edward IV and Warwick inevitable?**
Given the senior political and military position and personal dominance of Warwick in 1461, Edward's maternal cousin (fourteen years his senior) was clearly going to play a powerful role under the new King. His role in 1459–61 as commander of Calais, an important source of trained professional soldiers

at a time of armies made up of noblemen's personal retinues (usually part-time soldiers, their tenants), made him a vital captain. This was added to by his role as head of the junior branch of the Nevilles when his father, Salisbury, was killed at Wakefield, which added Salisbury's landed and military affinity to his own marital Warwick one. These earldoms had been occupied by Henry V's top commanders, who died in 1428 and 1439, before coming into Neville hands – their tenantry thus had a usefully long military tradition. His prestige had suffered from his losing the second battle of St Albans to Margaret – with possession of Henry VI – but his political 'weight' and his seniority to the nineteen-year-old Edward quickly restored his position and he became the new King's chief adviser and military commander, with his brother George Neville (Archbishop of York) as Chancellor. His landed base and control of leading castles in the Yorkshire region (based on Middleham, later his son-in-law Richard III's home, and Sheriff Hutton) made him as dominant in the north as Richard was later to be. This was inevitable, given the debt that Edward owed to him and his father – the closest landed allies of York in 1455–61 – and the Lancastrian allegiance of the only rival power in the north, the Percies (whose current head fell fighting for Queen Margaret at Towton in March 1461). One junior Percy, Sir Ralph, who was allowed to keep his castle (Dunstanburgh), on surrendering, promptly defected to the Queen in 1462. The Percies' hostility was a major factor in enabling Lancaster to hold onto the north-east of Northumberland in 1461–4, with local castles that had surrendered to the new King promptly revolting whenever Queen Margaret and/or a French force were in the vicinity. To do him credit, Edward risked trusting Sir Ralph – several times – and in 1470 was to endeavour to return the confiscated Percy Earldom of Northumberland from its new holder, his cousin John Neville, to the rightful heir.

The Percy Earldom of Northumberland was granted in 1461 to Warwick's younger brother, John Neville, a capable commander who defeated the rebel risings in Northumberland in 1463 and 1464, and with their brother George as archbishop the Neville brothers dominated the north. In military terms, their firm control was needed to combat the Queen and her adherents who were at large in Scotland and in control of the northernmost castles in Northumberland in 1461–2. Some royal reaction from this position was inevitable when Edward became older and more confident, and the apparent arrogance, intense family pride, and prickly nature of Warwick made it probable that he would take it badly. But could he have been credibly expected to go to the lengths of arresting and threatening to depose Edward? Edward did not rely entirely on the Nevilles – the Lancastrian Henry Beaufort, Duke of Somerset, a major court magnate of

1455–60 following his father's death at York's hands at St Albans, was rehabilitated and trusted on his surrender. He betrayed the King's trust and in 1464 treacherously joined the Lancastrian rebels in the north-east; on their defeat John Neville executed him. Edward was necessarily generous to those Lancastrian magnates who surrendered, having had a relatively small number of peers in his camp when he took the throne in March 1461 and needing to acquire solid support from the nobility. Indeed, his future wife, Elizabeth Woodville, had a Lancastrian husband, Sir John Grey, killed at Towton, with the confiscation of his estates allegedly the reason for her first seeking out the King;[52] her father, Sir Richard Woodville, had fought for Henry VI, as befitted his former role as the ex-King's uncle Bedford's retainer. Luckily, the chances of foreign meddling to aid the Queen's party was reduced by the deaths of the Lancastrian allies James II of Scotland (in a cannon-explosion while besieging Roxburgh Castle) in 1460 and Charles VII of France in 1461.

Their heirs aided the Queen to invade Northumberland in 1461–2, but the substitution of a regency under Bishop Kennedy for the vigorous young warlord James II in Scotland made the kingdom's disengagement from Henry VI's cause more likely. The ruthless James II had not scrupled to kill his principal magnate foe (the Earl of Douglas) in a fit of rage in Edinburgh Castle in 1452, had driven the Douglas clan out of their effectively autonomous domains in the Southern Uplands in 1455, and had been endeavouring to restore full Scots control of the Border strongholds when he was killed. Henry VI's failing government had returned Berwick to him as a vital ally; he would have been likely to continue the struggle against the national foe with more vigour than the regency did in 1461–3 and to have led major armies to aid the Lancastrian strongholds of Bamburgh, Dunstanburgh, and Alnwick. The most serious Anglo-Scots military clash since Henry IV's wars would then have been inevitable, with an English march on Edinburgh likely following the precedents of 1385 and 1400 – and the weight of numbers of men and artillery makes it probable that England would have prevailed. Noticeably, in real life Edward IV promised war on the Scots and raised large sums of money from Parliament for it in 1463 but did not go through with it, only going north belatedly and then not fighting. His fleet was not used, the expected army was not raised, and there was much domestic criticism of his inactivity.[53] Lack of money has been claimed as one cause for his inactivity. But the war lacked political urgency, as it would not have done had it been an aggressive and experienced James II invading the north – if that had been the case, the King's presence with a large army would have been essential.

In retrospect, indeed, Edward's failure to march north looks more like an early example of that laziness and over-reliance on his lieutenants that was to mark his northern policy in the last decade of his reign. Arguably, he failed to act quickly enough to counter the Neville threat in 1468–9 either; and he was taken by surprise by the successive treachery of Somerset in 1464, Warwick in 1469, and John Neville in 1470. The later criticism of his indulgence of his personal appetites (in both women and food) should be remembered in assessing his apparent sloth; and this criticism was not restricted to Richard III's partisans, though the latter made most use of it. Philip de Commignes, Louis XI's adviser, was commenting on it – and on Edward's weight- problem – as early as 1475.[54] The lack of a need for a major Scots war in the early 1460s may well have been a major contribution to his lack of swift activity compared to his role in 1460–1 and his masterly campaign of spring 1471. Edward could act decisively and show military skill when necessary, but did not go out of his way to do so. It had its uses, not least in avoiding unnecessary loss of life and treasure in warfare; a more aggressive king might have been expected to retaliate for Louis XI's aid to the Lancastrians in 1461–3 by sending English aid to the French rebels, the 'League of Common Weal', in 1465.

Edward avoided all temptations to use the Franco-Burgundian confrontation to rally national unity with a French war, as Edward III had done after 1337 and Henry V had done in 1414–15. (It seems likely that Henry IV would have pursued this policy to a more limited degree had his health not collapsed, as there were indications of it.[55]) Edward, like Henry IV and V, had a recent civil war to consider and restless nobles whose loyalty had been lukewarm to distracted, plus armed entourages to either occupy or 'demobilize'. The danger of neglecting to deal with their 'low-level' lawlessness had been shown up in the 1450s, and such unchecked violence added to grumbles in Parliament about an ineffective king.[56] Indeed, according to one modern theory (by Colin Richmond) all the successful medieval English kings distracted their nobility and united the nation in foreign war; peace caused disorder and conspiracy.[57] Arguably, inaction diminished Edward's reputation among his expectant subjects and built up that of his commander-in-chief, Warwick, who a vigorous young king in his twenties could have been expected to outshine in military affairs. He was not the first new young king to be overshadowed by a powerful landed magnate with a vast bloc of landed possessions, a military reputation, and a close relationship to the royal family – Gilbert de Clare, the 'Red Earl' of Gloucester, had had this relationship with Edward I in the 1270s. De Clare had not sought to intervene in foreign policy as Warwick did in the 1460s, but his local power in Wales had made him a potential threat to his king and their relationship before Edward's accession had been marked by mistrust. However, they avoided a disastrous confrontation, evidently by mutual caution; and Edward made up for his contentious and partisan role in the civil wars of 1264–5 by leading his nobility in war against Llywelyn 'the Last' of Gwynedd in 1277 and David of Gwynedd in 1282–3. Edward I, like Edward IV, built up a 'bloc' of royal power in Wales, which was arguably aimed at his over-resourced Marcher barons as much as against rebel Welshmen; he took over the lands of Gwynedd and western Deheubarth as direct royal patrimony. But in Edward IV's case his chosen instrument in the 1460s, Sir William Herbert, was overthrown and executed by Warwick – an act of defiance that nobody dared show to Edward I – and he had to fall back on Richard, Duke of Gloucester and later on the Council acting for the Prince of Wales, Edward, after 1473.

### The state of the nation and the failure to fight Scotland: a disappointing or a wise king?

Edward had been built up as the national saviour from decades of Lancastrian misrule by a careful propaganda campaign in 1460–1, aided in the Marches by his useful Welsh descent via the Mortimers from Llywelyn 'Fawr' of Gwynedd. He, not Henry VII, was the lineal heir of the royal line of Gwynedd back to the time of Cunedda in the fifth century, the 'Son of Prophecy', and his first victory at Mortimer's Cross had been attended by celestial portents (a perihelion, the original 'Sun of York').[58] Yet serious disappointment was apparent in public attitudes as early as 1463, over the failure to fight the Scots, and Edward was not to receive any enthusiastic public backing in the crises of 1469 and 1470. His army melted away at the news of his allies' defeat at Edgecote and as Warwick's treachery became apparent in late July 1469, with the authorities in London admitting the advancing rebel – which they did not do to attackers when the City was similarly at risk and no royal army at hand to aid them in May 1471. The inevitable disillusionment following high expectations in 1461 does not entirely explain this decline in support, and it appears that there was a lack of cohesion and direction in the government's policies, renewal of faction, and a sense by 1468–9 that there had been little improvement from the factional feuds of the 1450s.[59] The local disorders of the 1450s had returned by 1467–8, and according to subsequent charges – by Edward's enemies, but believable – the King was accused of partisanship and injustice. He had fed the troubles by allowing great lords' large armies of retainers to get away with intimidation – the same charge made against Henry VI's regime, but now implicating a fully sane and active young adult king. Among the worst cases of perceived favouritism were the execution of Henry Courtenay, brother of the executed and forfeited Lancastrian Earl of Devon, as arranged by his rival Humphrey Stafford (soon to be made Earl), and the intimidation of the jury trying and seizure of the household goods of the ex-Lord Mayor of London, Sir Thomas Cook, in 1468.[60] Both were accused and possibly guilty of Lancastrian plots, but irrespective of this it was felt that they had not had fair trials. The Queen and her kin were blamed for 'framing' Cook in order to loot his possessions, although the main chronicler to record this was Cook's employee so not an unbiased witness.[61] There was also the case of the blatant attack on disputed Caister Castle by the Duke of Norfolk to evict his rivals the Pastons, with Edward doing nothing to give the latter justice. (To complicate matters, the Duke's wife, Elizabeth Talbot, was the sister of the King's discarded mistress or 'wife', Eleanor Butler.[62])

As in 1381 and 1450, outbreaks of apparently spontaneous armed disturbances by the provincial lower classes followed; and rebel leaders assumed the populist pseudonym of 'Robin' (i.e. Hood). The implication of this name, as used in the popular ballads, was that the authorities were corrupt and partisan and the oppressed people should rely on 'vigilantes' to dole out justice. The rebel leadership, sometimes gentry as with 'Robin of Redesdale' (aka Sir John Conyers) in 1469 and Lord Welles in spring 1470, had their own political agendas as Neville agents spurred on by Warwick to defy the King; the Earl used 'Robin' to lure Edward north and then to ambush his army at Edgecote Field. But all their local followers cannot be written off as bribed hirelings or Neville tenants following their lords; there was apparently a large army of ordinary Yorkshiremen and Lincolnshiremen in arms in 1470.[63] There was an underlying discontent at the lack of royal leadership, which ironically would not have been apparent had Edward led England into war against the Scottish regency or Louis XI (though then complaints about high taxes could have been expected).[64] There were complaints at high taxes anyway in 1469, but without the other, more beneficial, effects of a war in distracting the lords' armed local retainers. Both Edward III and Henry V used foreign warfare to send potentially disruptive bands of warriors abroad to plague France not England, most notably in the case of the 'Free Companies' in the 1360s; Edward IV did not, although he was wise to distrust any promises of long-term alliance from either Louis XI (who abandoned him in 1482) or Duke Charles of Burgundy (who ignored him as an exile in 1471). Edward ignored the attempts of Louis XI to lure him into alliance in 1465–7, despite the proposed handover of Holland and Zealand (plus Louis' daughter Jeanne) to his brother Richard in an Anglo-French attack on Burgundy – a revival of the English interest in a Low Countries domain pursued by the previous Duke of Gloucester, Humphrey, in the 1420s.[65] Warwick's 'showy' embassy to France and close involvement with French embassies to England achieved nothing, which probably added to his proud disgruntlement at being 'sidelined' from policy-making – and a major proponent of the preferred Burgundian alliance was a Woodville, Anthony, Lord Scales. An anti-French alliance was arranged with the new Duke Charles of Burgundy in 1467, despite the unpopular financial demands connected to Edward's dowry for his sister Margaret, Charles' bride.[66] (The long-term results of Edward's choice of ally were to include a 'Yorkist' haven at Margaret's court in Burgundy for anti-Tudor pretenders after 1485.) No specific Anglo-Burgundian expedition to dismember France was laid down in the alliance, but this was a probable outcome given Charles' recent involvement in the abortive 'League of Common Weal' French magnate revolt against Louis and the history of Anglo-Burgundian attacks on the French Crown. Edward did not attack France in alliance with Charles in 1469 or 1470, but the French reaction to his alliance with Charles was as dangerous as if there had been open war – Louis' sponsorship of Warwick's reconciliation with ex-Queen Margaret in 1470.[67] But it should not be assumed that it was only Edward's snubbing of Louis' embassies in the mid-1460s that caused the resulting French-backed Lancastrian-Neville coup of September-October 1470. Louis was reported to be considering backing Margaret as early as 1467, and the French King's fear of encirclement by an Anglo-Burgundian-Breton alliance meant that he was likely to act against England once his offers had been turned down. The fact that his reaction was sufficient to overthrow Edward was due to the alienation of Warwick, which gave 'teeth' to his plots; the extent of French backing to other Lancastrian invasions of England (Oxford in 1474, and Henry Tudor in 1485) was more limited. What is unclear is if Warwick could have lived with an English alliance with Burgundy, given his combination of arrogance, a sense of grievance, and apparent intense dislike of Duke Charles.[68]

Had James II been alive and active or Edward responded to Louis' armed aid to rebels in the north in 1461–3 with military retaliation, the probability is that the 1460s would not have seen this sense of 'drift' and disillusionment. Given the hopes expressed of Edward in 1461, a sense of national goodwill and unity could have been expected of his commencing a major war as in 1415 and 1337 – though eventual grumbling at the cost of war would have followed. Luckily, Louis XI could not have used Henry VI as a political weapon to recall English subjects to their old allegiance if Edward invaded; the ex-King failed to follow his wife into exile in France and after years of being hidden away by partisans in the north-west was captured and placed in the Tower of London in 1465.

The cost and disruption from prolonged civil strife in the 1450s made Edward's caution a wise choice financially. But politics among the high nobility in the medieval period was a constant study in 'man-management' and personal leadership for the sovereign. Other vigorous young kings who had assumed the throne in controversial circumstances, such as Edward III (and Henry V as his father's heir), chose to unite their fractious nobility round them by invading France. Cost was no less a problem to Edward III's regime than it was to Edward IV's; the former had to rely on lavish promises to and huge loans from the Italian and Low Countries bankers, and defaulted on the former. Indeed, in his early years of French campaigning one reason for basing himself in the Low Countries was to serve as a personal pledge for his loans; at the time his third surviving son, John, was born in Ghent (hence 'Gaunt') he could not leave the city as he owed huge sums to local merchants. Edward IV's avoidance of this military route to successful leadership saved money and lives, and Louis XI offered him large sums for his alliance unsuccessfully in 1463–5 and successfully when he did invade France in 1475. (The latter treaty was notably unpopular in England as a disappointment to belligerent expectations.[69])

Arguably, the King aided English economic recovery by his choice, as he did by his eventual decision to accept alliance with Burgundy not France, which aided the traditional economic partnership with the destination of England's cloth-exports (though Louis offered rival trade-opportunities, successfully in 1475). But his decisions – and the absence of a need to invade Scotland – meant that large numbers of landed magnates' retainers who were used to a permanent state of warfare, first in France to 1453 and then in a divided England, were not rounded up and sent out of the country to fight elsewhere. This meant a risk that their lords would use them in local conflicts against their rivals, as their enemies notoriously did in evicting the Pastons from Caister Castle. If the King did not act firmly to halt this and make an example of offenders it would add to the sense of disappointment and 'drift'.

The combination of the Woodville marriage and the alliance with Burgundy illustrated and contributed to Warwick's estrangement from the King, and thus to his armed assertion of his power over the latter in 1469. The loyalty that he had shown the Yorkist cause so far made his revolt surprising, and he was needed as a commander and the master of huge tenant levies if Margaret of Anjou and/or Louis XI invaded. The King cannot be blamed for trusting him in the way that he can be blamed over excessive trust of the ex-Lancastrian Somerset, who he seems to have treated as a Court intimate to no avail.[70] But he had already received warnings about the Earl, who had refused to attend court to explain himself, and by standing in the way of Clarence's marriage to Isabel Neville in 1468–9 Edward showed that at the least he feared to let Warwick have a tempting candidate as the next king in the form of his ambitious brother as son-in-law. Warwick was already over-willing to respond to insults or seeming challenges by 1460–1, as seen by his alleged abuse of the captive Sir Richard Woodville (not yet his rival as father of his new Queen) for his upstart marriage to Bedford's widow, Jacquetta.

If Edward IV had accepted his terms for alliance with Louis in 1466 and been available to marry Bona this would not necessarily have avoided a clash in the future. (The proposed alliance would have married Edward's brother Richard off to Louis' daughter and given him part of the Low Countries if conquered; it would thus have removed the future Richard III from English politics and a Neville marriage.) Warwick could still have turned to alliance with his elder daughter Isabel's new husband, George of Clarence, in c. 1469–72 to intimidate or replace Edward IV; and if Edward had blocked the marriage it would have aroused his anger. (The Burgundian alliance of 1468 raised the possibility of Clarence marrying Duke Charles' heiress Mary, which would have meant he could not marry Isabel as Warwick wanted.) The King's surprise marriage to Elizabeth was by no means the main factor in his breach with Warwick, and even if the double 'snubs' of the marriage and the Burgundian alliance had gone ahead Edward had the option of setting spies to watch his cousin and arresting him at the first rumour of a plot. He had suspected him and (vainly) ordered him to come to court to explain himself in 1468 after earlier allegations, but in summer 1469 he failed to keep an eye on Warwick's movements.

It is hardly coincidence that Edward was taken by surprise four times by treachery – Somerset in 1464, Warwick in 1469 and 1470, and Montague in 1470 – and arguably ignored the potential threat of an 'over-mighty' Richard of Gloucester to his heir in the early 1480s. He was clearly too willing to trust his leading supporters, and would have been slow to react to signs of a threat from Warwick at whatever date this occurred. His over-confidence in 1469 was such that he stayed inactive at Nottingham during the height of the 'Robin of Redesdale' crisis in July, waiting for his allies Herbert (in Wales) and the new Earl of Devon (in the south-west) to arrive with their troops, and did not send scouts to find out what Warwick was doing. He had already summoned Warwick to his presence and been ignored, and had presumably heard by the time he left Nottingham that the Earl had slipped over to Calais to marry his daughter Isabel to Clarence and returned in arms to take over London. The Earl's manifesto made it clear that he intended to remove the King's alleged 'evil counsellors', led by Herbert, Devon, and the male Woodvilles,[71] and Edward sent the latter away to safety. He was unaware of his allies' defeat by 'Robin' when he set out south, and when news of the battle of Edgecote reached him many of his attendant lords abandoned him. He did not realize the hostile intent of Warwick's brother Archbishop Neville (sacked as Chancellor in 1467) who intercepted and arrested him.

### The Woodville marriage: why the secrecy? Could it have been denied later?

It is quite feasible that Edward would not have married Elizabeth Woodville despite their physical relationship; the secrecy in the nature of the ceremony and delay in announcing it are suspicious. The urgency of the northern campaign in May 1464 could have caused an immediate delay in announcing it, though the Nevilles would hardly have risked allying to the rebel Somerset – a hereditary foe and associate of their Percy rivals – if they were furious at the marriage. Conceivably, Edward was keen to consummate the relationship at once and Elizabeth would not agree without a ceremony so the impatient King did not wait for a more propitious time and a more public ceremony. (One story had it that he tried to ravish Elizabeth and put a dagger to her throat.) Elizabeth wisely refused to accept any sexual relationship without a marriage ceremony; was the delay due to Edward considering denying its occurrence? Elizabeth or her family may have forced his hand by publicizing it. Indeed, in spring 1464 King Henry of Castile was offering Edward the hand of his sister (and eventual successor) Isabella, which Edward turned down. If this offer had been accepted Elizabeth Woodville would have stood no chance – and Isabella would not have been in Spain to succeed Henry and unite Castile with Aragon by marrying Ferdinand of Aragon. Would Spain have stayed disunited?

The nature and reasons for the allegations made of Edward's other 'legal' contract to marry Eleanor Butler, revealed by Richard III in 1483, make it impossible to say that the King had succeeded in having his way with Eleanor (who possibly had a child) without a full marriage ceremony but Elizabeth was not so naïve and made sure that the marriage was legal and publicized. It is not proven that the 'contract' existed and was not drawn up by Richard in June 1483 to justify his coup – and whoever informed Sir Thomas More of the accusations made by Friar Shaa at St Paul's on 23 June seems to have had an idea that the supposed contract was with Elizabeth Lucy, not Eleanor.[72] Was this just confused memories, seeing as Elizabeth had definitely had a son by Edward (Arthur, Lord Lisle)? Or was it a deliberate attempt to confuse More's contemporaries? The chances of Edward having some legal arrangement with Eleanor are probable, not least as the supposed witness to the contract – Bishop Stillington – was arrested for words prejudicial to the King in 1478 at the time that Clarence was claiming that Edward's children were illegitimate so he was heir to the throne. At the time of the marriage Stillington was a junior court cleric and Lord Privy Seal, i.e. in charge of the King's private administrative arrangements; and he received the first available bishopric after the Woodville marriage was announced (plus the Lord Chancellorship in 1467). Edward was capable of shameless illegality when convenient, as when he declared the Countess of Warwick (the widow of the 'Kingmaker') legally dead in order to pass on her lands to her sons-in-law, his brothers. In 1481 he did not return the estates and titles of his second son Richard's defunct child-bride Anne Mowbray, heiress of the Dukes of Norfolk (and niece to Eleanor Butler), to her cousins as was legally required.[73] Ironically, the king who righted this illegality was the 'tyrant' Richard III in 1483.If Edward had intended to deny marrying Elizabeth Woodville if convenient and then done so, Elizabeth and her family lacked the political power to force his hand; it remains possible that he would have gone on to commit a French or Castilian marital alliance. In that case, his ambitious brothers Clarence and Gloucester could then have used the marriage ceremony with Elizabeth Woodville as evidence to disinherit Edward IV's children instead of the Butler 'pre-contract'.

**Different results for the 1469 crisis. What if Edward had won at Edgecote, and what if he had had to flee England?**
Even if the Woodville marriage had gone ahead, Edward need not have faced disaster in 1469 or 1470. As mentioned above, he was dangerously slow to react in July 1469 and stayed inactive at Nottingham for weeks as the Redesdale rebels advanced and Warwick and Clarence evaded a summons to court and fled to Calais to carry out the marriage that the King had banned. Arguably, Edward was waiting for the arrival of Herbert's Welshmen and Devon's south-westerners, under commanders more loyal and aggressive than the lords in his own retinue who duly abandoned him at news of the defeat at Edgecote. Edward may have been correct not to trust his backers at Nottingham, or risk their loyalty in an attack on 'Robin of Redesdale', but he made no effort to hasten south-west to link up with Herbert or Devon and put himself in the hands of men he could trust. As events turned out, the two nobles quarrelled over lodgings when they met up and lodged their men separately so 'Robin' and his pro-Neville force were able to take Herbert's men alone by surprise on 2 July and rout them. Devon's men were, at best, late to the battle, and the arrival of a small force of Warwick's men (rumoured by the royalists to be the Earl himself in force) completed the rout.[74]

Had Edward been there to enforce harmony on his commanders, or the two men co-operated better, the royal forces should have outnumbered the rebels (who lacked an experienced and aristocratic general) and won. With the rebels defeated and royal forces more confident, Edward, Herbert, and Devon could have taken on Warwick and Clarence with a better hope of victory. Warwick had the Calais garrison troops but he was not that successful or innovative a general and had lost to the ex-Queen at St Albans in 1461; Edward had won against superior numbers at Mortimer's Cross and was to do so again at Barnet, and Herbert had defeated Jasper Tudor in Wales in 1468. The chances are that Edward would have won against Warwick in August 1469 as he was to do against him in April 1471, not least as on the latter occasion he lacked the Herbert and Devon armies and Warwick had his brother Montague at his side. The open treason Warwick had committed would have been adequate grounds for forfeiture of his estates, though Edward would probably have forgiven Clarence as he was to do after worse desertion in 1470–1; as Isabel Neville was related to Clarence (via the latter's mother, Cecily Neville, Warwick's aunt) their marriage could be legally annulled if Edward wished it.

Edward would have faced the dilemma of keeping Clarence loyal (he still lacked a son) by allowing him to keep Isabel as his wife and to receive her father's forfeited estates as a bribe, or to break up the Neville 'power-bloc' by giving the Earl's lands to loyalists. As Warwick's brother Montague had not yet entered the field against Edward, there would be no reason to strip this so-far-loyal Neville of his power (which currently included the confiscated Percy estates and Northumberland title); it was Edward's enforced return of the Percy grant to its rightful owner in 1470 that caused Montague to join the next revolt. Warwick would have had to flee into exile, as he did in 1470 when his next revolt failed, and would thus have been likely to link up with Queen Margaret in France under Louis XI's patronage as in 1470; they could be expected to invade in due course. With the Woodvilles still dominant at court and Elizabeth's father alive as Lord Treasurer, this could be used as a stimulus to encourage affronted magnates to desert the King at the first opportunity – but if Clarence had been bought off with (part of?) Warwick's estates he would have been unlikely to desert Edward as he did in 1470.

Even after Edgecote, with his demoralized men slipping away, Edward could have shown more speed and purpose in his retreat and evaded Archbishop Neville's pursuers – although his lack of a ready army to fight another battle would have probably meant exile. Warwick would thus have had the choice of making his new son-in-law Clarence king, as he had apparently considered as early as 1467, or of deciding for Henry VI. He had some ex-Lancastrian backing in his 1469 rebellion, but in 1470 – when he did restore Henry – he was in a weaker position as an exile who had been forced to ask Louis XI for aid and accept his invitation to link up with Margaret, his family's arch-enemy. His manifesto in 1469 spoke of coercing not deposing the King, though this may have been subterfuge to maximize his support and reassure Yorkist lords that he aimed at removing the greedy Woodvilles not restoring Henry VI. If he had been successful in overthrowing and exiling Edward in 1469 – possibly not his original intention – he would have been in a different position from that of real-life August 1469, with Edward safe out of his reach. He was more likely to have backed Clarence as king than Henry, not needing French and Lancastrian aid as desperately as he did in real-life 1470. England would thus have been in the position of having two ex-kings, one at large and one in the Tower, the latter's wife and heir in exile in France, and a weak 'King George' as a Neville puppet. The resulting potential for chaos and counter-coup would have been even greater than that of real-life spring 1471.

## Chapter Four

# The Fatal Blow to an Otherwise Stable Yorkist Government: The Early Death of Edward IV?

**What if he had not died aged forty and there had been no division of the dynasty's adherents in a vicious and controversial fight over the succession?**

The Yorkist regime seemed firmly established from May 1471, with Henry VI and his heir both incontrovertibly dead and the nearest Lancastrian claimant now the exiled Henry Tudor, son of Margaret Beaufort and Edmund Tudor. The 14-year-old suffered both from a lack of connections with the higher nobility (at most he had been to court once, during Henry VI's 're-adeption'[1]) and from the fact that the Beaufort line had been barred from the throne by Act of Parliament in 1396 as illegitimate. This could be reversed, but all his landed male Beaufort kin (the line of his grandfather John Beaufort's next brother) had been wiped out between 1455 and 1471 and his mother was safely re-married to the Yorkist stalwart Thomas Stanley. Henry's only military backer from 1471 was the exiled Earl of Oxford, Warwick's commander at Barnet in March 1471, who vainly seized St Michael's Mount on his behalf but was blockaded, captured, and deported to the isolated castle prison of Hammes near Calais. Margaret of Anjou's cousin and patron Louis XI recognized Edward IV's restoration, no other English enemy had an interest in overturning the Yorkist order, and the young and vigorous Edward seemed set for a long and successful reign free from the overbearing presence of his cousin Warwick. Had he learnt from his mistakes in 1464–70, or would he repeat them?

The break-up of Warwick's concentration of land and power left the only figure able to challenge the King as the latter's next surviving brother, Clarence, who had inherited half the Warwick estates via his wife Isabel and endeavoured to seize them all. Edward prevented that by acquiescing in the marriage of Isabel's younger sister and co-heir, Anne, to his other brother Richard, which Clarence vainly resisted (supposedly by having Anne hidden in disguise in a London cook-shop).[2] When it came to a confrontation between the King and Clarence after Isabel's death in 1476, the King had his brother imprisoned in the Tower and tried for treason. Clarence's recent behaviour had been provocative and foolish in the extreme, given his luck to be pardoned for his past desertion of Edward in 1470, and he had apparently consulted astrologers about the succession and openly challenged Council decisions. The fact that he had one of Isabel's maids arrested, tried before a private 'court' composed of his adherents, and executed for 'poisoning' her suggests that he was crazed with grief and/or paranoid. But he had also had hopes of securing Duke Charles' young heiress Mary of Burgundy as his next wife, which would give him the resources to invade England on Edward's death if he wanted the throne, and Edward refused to accept this.[3] The unstable Clarence might well revolt in retaliation, so securing him in the Tower avoided a repeat of his treachery in 1469 and 1470.

Clarence was a major threat, given his vast landed estates and 'affinity', and Edward's firm reaction was wiser than his extreme caution in 1469. The trial and condemnation for treason meant that he could seize Clarence's estates and militarily neutralize him. But executing rather than imprisoning his brother would have been a major embarrassment for the King and some observers do not seem to have thought he would do it. In the end the death-sentence was carried out in February 1478, though Clarence was privately killed (supposedly being drowned in a butt of Malmsey wine) not beheaded.[4] It is possible that we can see another instance of Edward's already twice near-fatal lassitude in his initial lack of reaction to Clarence's excesses in 1477; the Duke had been making wild allegations and his partisans had been breaking the law openly for months before Edward acted to arrest him. As in Henry VI's years in power from c. 1440, great men close to the King seemed to be immune from punishment. The fact that the usually indulgent King was prepared to commit fratricide has led to modern speculation that he had to silence Clarence in order to prevent him revealing that the marriage to Elizabeth Woodville was illegal – or that Elizabeth and her family drove him to do it.[5] This thorny issue is entangled with the question of whether the 'Eleanor Butler betrothal' actually occurred or was invented by Richard III in 1483.

The years after the crisis of 1477–8 saw a return to domestic calm, though some historians have criticized Edward for his continued over-reliance on a small group of trusted lieutenants who had local power over a wide area concentrated in their hands. He had built up Warwick before 1469 (not that he had much choice, given his military/political debt to his cousin) and faced revolt; he had allowed similar licence to the less reliable and proven traitor Clarence after 1471 and faced open defiance. Now he granted extensive local power to Richard of Gloucester, making him his lieutenant in the north in Warwick's old role (as was logical due to his marriage to Anne and ownership of Warwick's principal castles of Middleham and Sheriff Hutton) but also creating a judicially autonomous principality for him on the Borders. The latter was a potential problem to the Crown, though it may have been mainly aimed at equipping and financing the Duke for future expansion into southern Scotland; it was unwise to alienate royal judicial and financial rights to any subject, however loyal.

This might not have mattered to English politics had Edward continued to lead the government, Richard being as unswervingly loyal as William Herbert, Earl of Pembroke (Edward's other grantee of extensive local power) had been in Wales in the 1460s. But Edward died suddenly on 9 April 1483, just short of his 41st birthday, leaving a boy of 12 as his heir. Another round of domestic strife followed, this time with Richard and Edward's wife's family as the main protagonists, and the nature of Richard's resulting usurpation of the throne was to give Henry Tudor an unexpected reversal of fortune. But what would have happened had Edward IV lived longer?

**The unfortunate timing of Edward IV's death – and the potential role of Clarence. How the fall of Clarence fundamentally altered events in 1483**

As a result, Edward V would have been able to succeed as an adult or near-adult. Even at the age of 12 he did not need a formal 'regent', hence the confusion over what exactly was entailed by his uncle Richard being 'Protector' and for how long. By tradition, the closest male relative of the under-age King would serve as head of the regency council, with the most recent precedent having seen the Council refuse the right of Protectorship (in England) to the infant Henry VI's uncle Duke Humphrey of Gloucester in 1422. (Humphrey was not the closest male relative, but his older brother the Duke of Bedford had been given the governorship of France by the late King's will.) Ironically, if Edward IV had not killed Clarence in 1478 he would have been head of the Council in April 1483, and the record that the latter had for treason to his brother from 1469 was not reassuring. Given the difficulties of 'back-dating' the story of Edward's alleged 'pre-contract' to Eleanor Butler beyond the sudden claims made by Richard in 1483, it is not certain that Clarence did regard himself as having a superior right to the throne to Edward V's. Why was the supposed 'witness' (or backer of any witnesses) Bishop Stillington arrested at the time of Clarence's fall in 1478 – to shut him up? However, irrespective of the 'pre-contract' claim Clarence had defied Edward IV to marry Warwick's elder daughter and joined the Earl's revolt in 1470, only returning to his brother's side after Edward had landed in March 1471 and marched on his base at Coventry. He was politically unreliable and a potential threat to Edward V anyway, and we can see from his public resistance to Richard marrying his wife's sister Anne Neville in 1471–2 that his ambitions had not been curbed by his near-escape from treason-charges in 1471. Technically Anne, widowed aged only 15 when her first husband Prince Edward of Lancaster was killed at Tewkesbury, was his 'ward' and he thus had the right to veto her choice of husband; and keeping her unwed kept her lands in his, not her husband's, hands. But he would have been wise to submit the decision to the King, not insist on his rights and quarrel openly with her suitor, Richard, as testified to by the *Paston Letters*.[6]

Clarence was an unstable and politically rash character, who Edward did not trust as a potential husband for the heiress of Burgundy in 1477 after his wife Isabel died in childbirth. Sending him to Burgundy with his armed retainers would keep its leaderless lands out of French hands, and keep him out of England for years to come, but the King presumably feared that he would use Burgundian resources to attack him or his heir later. Technically, English intervention by Clarence might also spark a war with the acquisitive Louis XI of France, long kept at bay from annexing Burgundian territories by the militarily superior Duke Charles – and Edward had shied away from fighting Louis during his invasion of France in 1475, signing an unpopular peace treaty. Protecting Burgundy from Louis would lead to the French King cancelling his subsidy to Edward, although the unreliable 'Spider King' had already violated his 1462 truce with Edward by backing Warwick and Queen Margaret in 1470 and was clearly capable of betraying Edward whenever convenient. Was Edward prepared to gamble – correctly – in 1477 that Louis' other rival Maximilian of Habsburg, son of Emperor Frederick III, would save Burgundy from Louis and avoid him having to intervene?

The surprise death of Edward IV's unreliable brother-in-law Duke Charles (aged only 43) in a snowstorm while attacking a well-armed Swiss infantry force at Nancy in January 1477 thus precipitated major crisis in England and altered the balance of power at court. Clarence was refused the right to woo Charles' daughter, the young Duchess Mary, and stayed in England where his conduct became ever more unstable. Seemingly driven by a grudge against the King, he claimed that Isabel had been poisoned (by whom? the Woodvilles?) and peremptorily arrested (i.e. kidnapped), tried and executed her ex-lady-in-waiting for murder; he then started putting about prophecies that 'G' would be the next King. Quite apart from the illegal nature of dabbling with black magic, referring to the King's demise and seeking to find the name of his successor was treason rather than bad taste in mediaeval England, and Clarence turned up uninvited at a Council meeting to make noisy allegations against his enemies. After a surprisingly long period of indulgence, Edward arrested him and arranged for a Parliamentary trial and death-sentence, delaying carrying the latter out until he was officially 'reminded' and then killing the Duke privately.

There was no indication of Edward IV being in poor health in 1477–8, so the danger posed by Clarence to the succession was probably not an urgent reason for the King removing him. The fact that Clarence had participated in politics in 1469–71 as an ally of his father-in-law Warwick, who had killed Queen Elizabeth, Woodville's father and brother and may have been behind charges that her mother was a witch, may indicate that the Queen was a lead actor in Clarence's downfall as she feared his open boasts that he was Edward's real heir. It remains unproven that Richard 's claim of June 1483 that Elizabeth and Edward's marriage was irregular was correct and that Clarence's boasts meant that he had found this out – logically, from the story's 1483 'witness' Bishop Robert Stillington. But it would make Clarence's near-treasonous behaviour logical, as a grudge-driven assertion of his 'rights', rather than totally surprising.

Edward had contemplated the Clarence-Mary match as part of the Burgundy alliance in 1468, but circumstances had been different – Mary's father had been alive (meaning that Burgundian lands and power would not go immediately to the unstable Clarence) and Clarence had not yet betrayed Edward as he did in 1470–1. Similarly, a Low Countries domain for a brother of King Edward (Richard not Clarence) had been contemplated in the abortive Warwick-Louis XI talks of 1466. The scheme could be traced right back to Henry V's brother Duke Humphrey's efforts to take over Holland as the husband of Duchess Jacqueline in 1424–6 so it was not unprecedented. It had a degree of logic, in removing a restless and ambitious royal prince from English politics, as Humphrey's plan had done in the 1420s – but then his brother Bedford had vetoed it due to its infuriating Jacqueline's previous husband's brother, Duke Philip of Burgundy. Now Edward apparently feared what use Clarence could make of the Low Countries' resources in invading England. It was unfortunate that Isabel died when she did, reviving confrontation between Edward and Clarence, but it had a major impact on events in 1483. It is possible that Isabel (died aged c. 25) and her sister Anne (died aged c. 29) were both tubercular; the latter's condition was also to be a major factor in English politics, in 1483–5.

Had Isabel been alive the confrontation between Edward and Clarence would not have come about over the Burgundy marriage, if at all, and the Duke would still have been alive and in possession of half the Warwick inheritance in April 1483. He was as much of a danger to Edward V as Richard was, and from his past activities would have seemed a more apparent threat. It has been plausibly suggested that it was the realistic Elizabeth who persuaded her husband to destroy Clarence in 1477–8, with Edward as hesitant about responding to his provocations as he had been to Warwick in 1469. Edward had been accused of conniving at legal intimidation and fraud by his magnate allies' retainers in the 1460s, as the Pastons could bear witness given what had happened at Caister Castle.

### The Stony Stratford incident: was Richard not Rivers the plotter in April–May 1483?

Edward V's maternal uncle and guardian, Anthony Woodville, Earl Rivers, had been chosen by the late King to superintend the boy's upbringing at Ludlow Castle – headquarters of the York family's hereditary Mortimer lands – in the mid-1470s. This also involved supervising the new 'Council for the Marches of Wales', of which the Prince was titular head. He was the equivalent of the usual respected and experienced knight chosen to supervise well-born fifteenth century boys' upbringing, and train them as his squires, instead of them being kept at their parents' residence. Warwick had brought up Clarence and Richard in his household at Middleham Castle; usually this knightly 'fostering' had not applied to royal male children, though even the young Henry VI had been entrusted to a veteran noble warrior (Warwick's father-in-law, Richard Beauchamp, also Earl of Warwick) as personal 'governor'. Prince Edward's presence at Ludlow served to keep an eye on the Marcher lords and build up their loyalty to the royal heir, and was to be repeated by Henry VII with Prince Arthur and by Henry VIII with Princess Mary. A noted jouster and devout pilgrim who had visited Santiago de Compostella, Rivers was suitable to train the next king as a knight as well as politically reliable. He was duly in control of Edward V at his accession, and set about escorting him to London for his coronation; but as a Woodville he was supposed by the 'official' later Ricardian account to have been in league with a plot by his kin to keep Richard from becoming 'Protector'. By precedent, the under-age King could have both a personal guardian – Rivers' role – and a political 'Protector' who held royal rank; in the 1420s Warwick and (in France) Bedford had held these roles for Henry VI and Duke Humphrey had sought the 'Protectoral' rank within England. In 1327 Edward III's personal 'guardian' had been his kinsman Earl Henry of Lancaster; political power had lain with Queen Isabella and Roger Mortimer. There was thus no reason for Rivers and Duke Richard to quarrel over the late King's arrangements, apart from personal ambition and mistrust.

Rivers and the new King's escort were not in a hurry to ride to London, but according to Richard's version of events Rivers did not inform him of his intentions. Worse, Rivers had been plotting with his sister the Queen to 'hurry' Edward V to London for an early coronation so that Richard's authority as Protector would lapse, giving full political power to the Woodville-led Council not Richard. Only the late King's Chamberlain and personal friend William, Lord Hastings, prevented this; alarmed at the Woodville 'plot', he wrote to inform Richard (then in Yorkshire) and advise him to hasten to London to take up his Protectorship before he was outmanoeuvred and the late King's will sidestepped. Richard decided to intercept the royal party en route from Ludlow, and was offered help by his distant cousin, Henry Stafford, Duke of Buckingham (married to the Queen's sister but kept from influence at court for years and out for revenge). Richard and Buckingham met up and closed in on the royal party, and Rivers blithely rode into a trap at Stony Stratford when they intercepted him and the new King en route to London at the beginning of May 1483. Evidently not expecting treachery, he rode over from his nephew's lodgings to dine with Richard, retired to bed in the inn rather than insisting on returning to the King, and woke up next morning to find Richard's men surrounding his lodging.[7] He would not have been so careless had the aggrieved royal brother out to intercept him been Clarence, a man with a long record of deceit and desertion of his allies, not to mention violence. If Edward had died leaving Clarence as his next adult male heir, the unstable Duke would have had every legal right to demand the 'governorship' of the new King and senior place on the regency Council, as had gone to the next adult male heir in 1327 and the next adult male heir in England in 1422.

We have only Richard's subsequent word for it that Rivers and his escort intended to bring Edward V quickly to London before Richard arrived so that they could crown the boy and declare a Protectorship unnecessary. It is far from clear that a coronation ended the requirement for an under-age king to have a 'Protector'; the legal tutelage of Edward III had continued beyond his coronation (1 February 1327) and that of Henry VI beyond his English coronation (6 February 1429). Edward had been crowned soon after accession, without any change to his status; Henry had been too young at accession and had had to wait for seven years. At the most, crowning Edward V would have been the occasion to legally 'fix' arrangements for the governance of England until his adulthood. Given that Edward IV had died on 9 April 1483 and news must have reached Ludlow within a few days (probably on the 14th),[8] Rivers does not seem to have acted with much haste to be as far from London as Northamptonshire on 29 April. The likelihood is that he had no intention of denying Richard his rights, whatever Queen Elizabeth intended to do, and that he was 'framed' by Richard to justify removing him; he was kept away from London so he could not defend himself before his peers and was quietly executed in Yorkshire in June. At best he faced a short trial, before a tribunal hand-picked by Richard within the precincts of his place of captivity.[9] The nature of his disposal was unprecedented for peacetime since the 1390s, though similar politically dangerous peers had been executed without a public trial (if any) in the recent political disturbances since 1455. Even Richard II had held full royal power when he disposed peremptorily of his enemies the 'Appellants' in 1397–9; Richard was not yet king and thus showed his contempt for traditional legal practice. His equally sudden and ruthless arrest and beheading of Hastings on 13 June 1483 was to be even more blatant, and both events led to panic in London. One recent suggestion is that Richard had found (circumstantial and unprovable?) evidence by mid-June that Rivers and the Queen's son Dorset had poisoned Edward IV so they could run a regency for Edward V – but this can only be a guess.[10]

Had Clarence been the potential threat to the alleged 'Woodville plot' to seize control of the regency, or the Queen and Rivers quite reasonably feared his potential given his past record, Edward V would have been likely to be brought to London far more quickly. The new King's escort would not have trusted Clarence as they evidently did Richard, and if Richard was seeking enhanced power (or the throne) this early he was not certain to have backed his long-term rival Clarence against the Woodvilles. We cannot be certain if Richard backed, opposed, or cold-bloodedly stood aside from Clarence's disgrace in 1477–8, or if he blamed the Woodvilles for it. Much has been made of contemporary Mancini stating this – but was it only gossip?[11] But had both brothers been alive and in charge of large armed affinities in April–May 1483, as would have seemed probable until 1477, the struggle for control of Edward V's person would have taken a different course from real events – and Richard could have linked up with Rivers to deny Clarence control of the new King's person and government. Clarence, like Duke Humphrey of Gloucester in 1422, would have faced implacable hostility from elements of the Council.

### Was Edward V doomed in 1483? The disputed evidence of the More account and the bodies

The older Edward V was at succession the less likely he was to be overthrown, and it is apparent that even in May 1483 he was able to express disquiet at Richard's allegations about his Woodville relatives' motives.[12] He was supposed to be healthy in May/June 1483, but the incipient illness (and/or morbidity) that affected him after his deposition, when he had need of the royal physician, Dr Argentine, and according to Dominic Mancini said he feared for his life,[13] was linked to the signs of osteomyelitis found in 1933 in the jawbone of the elder body found in 1674. The latter evidence, however, has since been interpreted by other medical experts to point out that the osteomyelitis in this case was advanced enough to indicate long-term serious ill-health, which was not the case with what is known of Edward V – so was the body his after all?[14] In 1933, it was not proveable that the body in queston was male – unlike an autopsy today. The probable source of Mancini's story was Dr Argentine, given that the latter was one of the few visitors that the deposed King was allowed to receive in the Tower.

If the bones discovered then were those of the Princes – they were certainly approximately the right age – Edward could easily have died before his accession or as a young adult king. Due to the lack of a DNA test, however, it cannot be said that the bones were genuine; the age of victim was approximately correct but some post-1485 sources denied the bodies had been hidden in the White Tower. More to the point, was the site – a staircase leading from the original structure of the White Tower to a later, lower annex built alongside its south wall – correct? If Sir Thomas More's story of c. 1510 was correct a priest had dug the remains up after the initial burial and put them somewhere more fitting, in consecrated ground – though possibly the site of the 1674 discovery was close enough to St John's Chapel in the Tower to count as 'consecrated'. There had been other children's bones discovered earlier in the seventeenth century somewhere hidden in the White Tower. Or was More's account really feasible? How could the murderers dig under a stone staircase at night in an inhabited part of the royal palace in the Tower without someone hearing them and coming to investigate, or at least telling Henry VII where to look after Richard's overthrow?[15] Are the 1674 bodies evidence of anything?

If Edward V had died his next brother Richard, Duke of York, aged ten in 1483, would thus have succeeded as 'King Richard III' with another struggle over the next regency a possibility. He had been married off by Edward IV as a small child to the equally young Anne Mowbray, heiress of the Dukes of Norfolk, and when the girl died in 1481 the King shamelessly defied the law by keeping the vast inheritance for himself in Richard's name rather than passing it on to Anne's relatives. The claims of the latter were ignored until Richard of Gloucester seized power, when he gave the Norfolk title and most of the lands to one claimant – conveniently his own henchman, John Howard. A loyal Yorkist veteran in his early sixties, this minor Norfolk nobleman of semi-royal descent was one of the few men not of a northern background who Richard could trust and was to lead his vanguard at Bosworth in 1485. If Richard of York had succeeded to the throne on Edward V's death as still the nominal possessor of the Dukedom of Norfolk, it is uncertain if he or his regents would have merged the latter with the Crown (which already held the dukedoms of Lancaster and York) or handed it to a claimant like Howard in return for political support.

**1483: An unexpectedly early succession**

The succession of either of Edward IV's sons to the throne could have been as late as the 1500s if Edward IV had lived into his 60s – among his ancestors Henry III had lived to 65, Edward I to 68, Edward III to 64, John 'of Gaunt' to 59, and his great-grandfather Edmund of Langley, Duke of York, to 60. His mother, Cecily Neville, lived to around 80. Edward IV's death on 9 April 1483, a few weeks short of his 41st birthday, was unexpected despite his apparent sluggishness in recent years. The contemporary writer of the continuation of the 'Croyland (Abbey) Chronicle' – possibly Bishop John Russell – and the slightly later Polydore Vergil, neither with a patron to please with biased writing about Edward, reported that Edward's court in its later years was notable for gluttony, licentiousness, and exhaustive high living, which logically would have undermined the King's health. Edward's close friend and Chamberlain William, Lord Hastings, and his stepson Thomas Grey (Marquis of Dorset) were named as the King's principal encouragers in dissipation.[16] Mancini stated that the King's death followed a chill caught on the Thames at Windsor in the aftermath of one session of gluttony. Vergil said the cause was unknown and hinted at poison; by 1548 Hall believed it was fever (malaria?) caught in France in 1475, exacerbated by gluttony. The caustic evidence of the French chronicler Philip de Commignes states that when he saw the King at his 'summit meeting' with Louis XI on the fortified bridge at Picquigny in 1475 he had developed a serious weight-problem since their last encounter a few years before,[17] and Edward's willingness to be bought off during that campaign has been attributed to laziness as much as prudence.

Richard III's propaganda, such as the petition calling on him to assume the throne on 25/6 June 1483, undoubtedly made much of the excessive gluttony and debauchery at Edward's court,[18] and exaggerated that as in its lurid claims about witchcraft by Elizabeth Woodville and her mother to ensnare Edward into marriage in 1464. The written accounts of Edward's court bear similarities to stock writings about such behaviour, traceable back to the biographies of the more unrestrained Roman emperors such as Nero and Elagabalus. This is not to deny their essential truth, only that their recorders resorted to stock phraseology in describing them and some details may have been invented. Logically it is arguable that a sustained programme of over-indulgence could have undermined Edward's health so that a chill could carry him off at the age of 40, and Richard's subsequent attacks on Edward's boon companions – Lord Hastings and the Marquis of Dorset in particular – for leading the King astray have exaggerated rather than invented their role. The Italian observer Dominic Mancini, written off by his detractors for not understanding English adequately so not a trustable witness, was, however, a uniquely valuable 'outsider' with no patron to please in his account of what he saw and heard in London in May–July 1483. He also states that Edward IV was well known for making free with his subjects' wives, including middle-class Londoners – in which category 'Jane Shore' can be placed. (The Shore 'legend' unfortunately owes much to later plays, not traceable fifteenth century facts; her real name was 'Elizabeth'.[19])

Compared to his vigour in the 1460s, Edward had not shown much of an interest in campaigning or in visiting the north since the mid-1470s. Even in the earlier period, he had allowed himself to be taken by surprise by the 1469 rising and had no agents spying on the Earl of Warwick whose discontent could have been anticipated by a shrewder king. As noted earlier, he had unexpectedly refrained from using his Parliamentary grant and fleet or raised an army for a Scottish campaign in 1463. Nor did he hasten to link up with Herbert and Devon to confront the rebels in 1469. The grip of his government on the country in 1482–3, as analysed by Charles Ross, showed no sign of weakness or a loss of control despite his reduced itinerary and his careful and determined build-up of royal wealth to outmatch his magnates was noted by the Croyland Chronicler.[20] His delegation of authority over a large part of his realm to his brother Richard then was not new – he had given similar power to the equally trusted Duke of Somerset in the north in 1462–4, Warwick in the north in 1462–8, Montague in the north-east in 1464–70, and Herbert (created Earl of Pembroke) in Wales in 1461–8. Three of the four had played him false, but he did not learn his lesson and use more men with less power given to each. Henry VII, by contrast, was a master of 'divide and rule' and did not trust the northern frontier to its traditional magnates (after 1489) or lavish grants on his nobles.

Edward showed no interest in personal involvement with the Scots crisis of 1480–2 compared to the northern revolts of 1464 and 1468, not responding to the major raids on Northumberland in person, staying in southern England, and leaving the planned invasion of Scotland to Richard. The serious magnate discontent in Scotland as a result of James III's reliance on 'low-born' favourites, coupled with the apparent mixture of fear and greed for power shown by James' surviving brother Duke Alexander of Albany, was a major opportunity for the English King to intervene. It would have provided Edward with a bonus for his military reputation after the anticlimax of the French campaign of 1475, even if he marched all the way to Edinburgh and back without much to show for it or – as happened to Richard – Albany and his faction linked up with the English to coerce James but turned against them once they had gone home. He did not avoid war on account of the cost or the futility as he arguably did in 1463, when Scotland was no major threat once Henry VI's northern English allies had been driven out, or Richard would not have been sent to invade Scotland. Edward had been more careful of his reputation as an active hero in the 1460s, sponsoring the propagandist claims that he was the 'Son of Prophecy' of Welsh legend (as a descendant of the Princes of Gwynedd via the Mortimers) and having been linked to a revival of the 'Arthurian' chivalric cult. (The extent of his active involvement via his brother-in-law Anthony Woodville with Sir Thomas Malory's commission to write the *Morte d'Arthur* is more uncertain.) Even in the 1470s his miraculous return to power had been quickly 'written up' and cast in a heroic light in the *Historie of the Arrivall of Edward the Fourth*, apparently composed by one of his followers and distributed abroad.[21] The 'spin' placed on his achievement conveniently avoided asking why he had been overthrown in the first place if he was such a great leader. So why was he not quick to head north in 1482, even if he left the fighting to Richard?

The King's lack of personal intervention in this crisis – he did not even go as far as York – may reflect no more than a desire to give Richard a chance to 'earn his spurs' as his principal northern commander, and cannot be linked definitively to Commignes' criticism of his laziness. As seen in 1463, he had little personal concern with his northern frontier. (The one time he did march to Newcastle, in 1464, he fell ill with measles.) But his lack of action may indicate a decline in health or undue lethargy. Nor did he show signs of reacting with a new Continental war to the French abandonment of their treaty-obligation from 1475 to marry the Dauphin to his eldest daughter, Elizabeth, by allying with his other principal neighbour, Archduke Maximilian in 1482 – a serious insult. It is possible that this foreign reverse, uniting his two principal neighbours who until now he had striven to keep apart, caused the onset of depression in winter 1482–3, but if so it did not lead to plans for retaliation. The obvious target of such an action would be Louis, now aged 59/60 and usefully in declining health and living like a hermit at the Loire chateau of Plessis. Louis' fear of Edward was such that there was one story that he had poisoned him to head off an English invasion in 1483,[22] and if Edward had been contemplating retaliation to the insult shown to him there should have been some sign of it at the early spring 1483 Parliament or in an embassy to Maximilian.

His death apparently followed a chill caught on a fishing-expedition on the Thames at Windsor at the beginning of April, with the King unaware of its seriousness until he was dying. Given its suddenness, poison was inevitable rumoured, with Louis XI of France the prime suspect. One modern theory has even suggested his wife, Elizabeth Woodville – though it would have been a 'high-risk' strategy to remove her husband in favour of a regency headed by herself without being sure of dealing with Richard or

Lord Hastings first. Arsenic has been suggested as a means of poison, and Edward's failure to recover from his 'chill' may be suspicious but may only mean that he had some underlying problem (perhaps due to alcohol). Even when his condition started to deteriorate, he did not take it seriously enough to make efforts to resolve the factional disputes among his intimates, principally the quarrel between his stepson Dorset and his chamberlain Lord Hastings until a late stage or to make it publicly known who was to be in charge of the effective regency for his 12-year-old elder son. The latter was not summoned from Ludlow Castle, his residence as titular head of the 'Council of the Marches', whereas if the Prince had been en route to London well before the news of Edward's death reached Yorkshire Richard of Gloucester would not have had the time to arrange to intercept the party. (If the Queen was poisoning her husband, logically she would have had an idea how long he would last and thus would have summoned her son in time.) Even though Edward's illness may have been relatively short (perhaps around ten days at most), he had time before he died on 9 April to give orders to have the Prince brought quickly to London, which should have stimulated Anthony Woodville into speedier action had they existed. Instead, Woodville lingered at Ludlow for several more weeks.

**Results of Edward IV's survival. Even less excuse for a Protectorship if Edward V had been older?**
What if Edward, even if overweight and in poorer health than as a young man, had lived for another few years – or a decade or two? A physically inactive king restricted to touring the parts of the south nearer London was not a major problem if there was a vigorous and loyal deputy to act for him in outlying regions, as Prince Edward (later Edward I) had done for his ageing father in 1265–9 and as John 'of Gaunt' had done for the young Richard II. A trusted close male relative could act (militarily and administratively) for an incapable king in France, as Bedford had done for Henry V; Edward IV had not trusted Clarence with a Burgundian 'power-base' in 1477 but he gave Richard such military powers in the north in 1480–3. As the most vocal opponent of the 1475 French treaty Richard was the logical leader of an expedition to France, and was very unlikely to be bribable by Louis XI. His hostility to the 1475 treaty was notorious.

Had Edward IV been in poor health throughout his last years (his forties?),there was the precedent of Henry IV who had been struck down by a mysterious illness at the age of, at most, 39 in June 1405. On that occasion it had seen the King's eldest son and Archbishop of Canterbury at odds over the control of the Council and the Prince's temporary triumph in 1410 had been reversed when the King reasserted himself. When Edward III was in his dotage, restricted to his Thames valley estates, and the 'Black Prince' was chronically sick at Berkhamsted in 1372–6 John 'of Gaunt' had been their effective deputy in government, with accusations of a greedy court clique (headed by the King's mistress, not his wife as with the Woodvilles) benefiting from the over-indulgent King. The fact that Edward V would have acceded at an older age would have meant no need of or excuse for a Protectorship even for the few weeks until the coronation, thus giving Richard of Gloucester no excuse for arresting his alleged would-be deprivers of that role. As explored below, that did not rule out a military challenge from Richard at a later date, with the fate of the previous royal uncle Duke of Gloucester (Humphrey) in 1447 hanging over him.

Legally, the last official 'regency' had been that of William Marshal for the 9-year-old Henry III in 1216 so Edward V had not needed a regency even in 1483 – as his mother's faction apparently endeavoured to effect. This is assuming that Edward' IV's grant of a 'Protectorship' to Richard amounted to real legal power, as opposed to a personal 'governorship' of the under-age King. We do not have any unbiased record of what role Edward IV intended for his brother as of April 1483, only Richard's 'post facto' claims – and it is improbable that Edward IV would have feared his wife's relatives' acquisitiveness enough to give supreme power to Richard.

We can only use precedents of what was usual in working out what Edward IV intended, not Richard's subsequent justifications of his coup – though Lord Chamberlain Hastings was apparently alarmed enough at the Queen's activities to summon Richard to London in late April 1483. The 10-year-old Richard II had succeeded without any 'Protector' or 'Governor' in June 1377, though as a legal minor he had not exercised royal authority and the Council had collectively done so under the leadership of his eldest surviving uncle, John 'of Gaunt'. The 14-year-old Edward III had succeeded without one in January 1327, merely with his eldest male relative Henry of Lancaster as titular head of the Council and the King's guardian. In reality, Edward's mother, Isabella, and her lover, Roger Mortimer, had controlled the government until they were overthrown in October 1330 and had been able to brush Lancaster aside. The Council had ruled in the name of the infant Henry VI from September 1422, rejecting the claims of his uncle Humphrey, Duke of Gloucester, to become Protector under Henry V's will; Henry VI had been declared adult and the governance of the kingdom by his Council ended in November 1437, just before his sixteenth birthday.

Even in 1483, the assumption was that the Protectorship that Edward IV's will gave to Duke Richard was only to last until the coronation. The 'Woodville faction' led by the Queen-Mother were thus presumed to be hastening Edward V to the capital in early May for a quick coronation to obviate the need for Richard to hold power even for a few weeks, and

Richard's propagandists declared this thwarting of the late King's will to be their aim.[23] Incidentally, the coronations of Edward III and Henry VI had not ended their supervisors' governorships, so a crowned king was not automatically 'adult'. Nor was declaring Edward V free of legal tutelage at his coronation following the legal 'norms'; though its end to a legal 'Protectorate' could have been feared by Richard as meaning that the Queen would persuade her son to have him arrested. Timing was crucial in any case, with the excuse for any legal tutelage for the new King lessening as he grew older. If Edward V had succeeded at the age of 14 or 15 in 1485–6 there would have been less likelihood of a royal will by his father creating any 'Protectorship' (personal or political), and if he had succeeded at the age of 16 in 1487–8 virtually none. Thus even if Edward IV had still died early, in his mid-forties, the new King would have been in the charge of a Council, which could still have exercised the use of the royal signet and determined policy (Queen-Mother Isabella had held the signet for Edward III in 1327–30) but would not have needed any legally-appointed head. As Humphrey's claims had been seen off in 1422 with a much younger king, so a majority of the Council under men such as Hastings and Dorset could have constrained Duke Richard's authority to that of one among many equals. He could have been personal guardian of the young King, as Earl Henry of Lancaster, the nearest male relative, had been for Edward II and Earl Richard Beauchamp of Warwick had been for Henry VI – both of them without political control of the government. Indeed, it remains possible that Edward IV intended him as only a personal guardian, and that Richard deliberately inflated the extent of his Protectoral powers in his claims of what Edward IV's will had meant. This may not have been a sign of his designs on the throne as of May 1483, merely a legal manoeuvre to protect himself from any indictment by his foes on the Council and/or a Woodville-prompted Edward V. It must be remembered that he had arrested Earl Rivers and Sir Richard Grey, uncle and half-brother of the new King, at Stony Stratford and had a tense interview with the latter who clearly did not trust him.[24] The last 'regent' to arrest a young king's relatives and ignore his protests was Roger Mortimer in 1330, who had ended up arrested by the affronted young Edward III and dragged off to Tyburn as a traitor. Thomas, Duke of Gloucester, executed his nephew Richard II's tutor Burley despite his protests in 1388, and was killed (probably on his orders) a decade later.

### The issue of political alliances at Edward V's accession: which mattered more, Edward V's young age or Hastings abandoning the Woodvilles?

But Edward V's age in 1483 might not have been decisive in leading to his maternal relatives' neutralization by Richard and his later deposition. Other under-age kings had not been at their paternal uncles' mercy, so why was 1483 an exception? Notably, the new government for a king aged under one year had been able to hold off an ambitious royal uncle's demands in 1422–3. Then the royal Council had been united, and Duke Humphrey had been unable to secure his alleged right as Protector of the new King in England although the Council had conceded such a right to Bedford as governor of France. They had also been able to use Bedford, their ally and possessing more troops than Humphrey, as an agent to block Humphrey's demands. Bedford had been granted legal precedence over Humphrey when in England, and he and his Council allies had been able to block Humphrey's ambitions; indeed, the frustrated Duke had become violently antagonistic to Bedford's main ecclesiastical supporter on the Council, their uncle Bishop Henry Beaufort, for frustrating him.

This unity of 1422–3 was lacking in 1483, which may well have been more crucial than the thorny question of whether Edward IV's will – never published – had appointed Richard as 'Protector' (and if so with what powers). It is also important to note that in 1422–3 the leading clerics on the Council, Chancellor (Bishop) Thomas Langley and Bishop Henry Beaufort, were both willing to stand up to Duke Humphrey's demands to be Protector. Humphrey could not remove Beaufort, despite threats of violence to him; in 1426 Bedford seems to have persuaded Beaufort to go to Bohemia on 'crusade' to get him out of Humphrey's way. In 1483 the Archbishop of Canterbury, the aged royal relative Thomas Bourchier, was not active in politics and the equally aged Chancellor, Archbishop Thomas Rotherham of York, lost his nerve over what to do when he heard of Rivers' arrest and illegally handed the Great Seal to the Queen.[25] Richard duly sacked him. Could younger and more determined clerical councillors in 1483 have stood up to Richard, as Langley and Beaufort had stood up to Humphrey? Or if the crisis had come a few years later, would Edward IV have appointed a younger and more capable Chancellor by then? The Yorkist dynasty favoured trustable clerical protégés for this office, and the logical next appointees were either Bishop John Russell of Lincoln (the real-life Chancellor under Richard in 1483–5) or Bishop John Alcock of Worcester, one of the Prince of Wales' Council at Ludlow. Alcock is likelier, having held the office briefly in 1475 while Rotherham was abroad, and was likely to be loyal to Edward V; in 1486 Henry VII made him Chancellor after Rotherham's final retirement. Stronger clerical leadership on the Council could have shifted the balance of its members against Richard, with or without Hastings joining them.

Even in the circumstances of 1483, it would have been possible for Hastings to choose to back the Woodvilles not Richard and to seek to contain the latter via a 'normal' Council of State not by backing their overthrow. It was apparently his warning that brought Richard to the Midlands in time to intercept the new King, and he who rallied the Council to limit Edward V's armed escort. As seen in 1422, precedent favoured government by a collective Council not one 'regent'. The possibility thus arises that it was his personal dislike of the Queen's eldest son, the Marquis of Dorset, his recent rival for Edward IV's patronage, that led Hastings to seek alliance with Richard and invite him to come quickly to London. Or was it fear that Dorset and the Queen would use their planned 'army' to arrest him? This was to be fatal to him and probably fatal to Edward V – though Richard could still have arrived uninvited to confront the Council after Edward V's arrival and to demand his rights as Protector. As he showed in June 1483, he had substantial numbers of armed tenants from his northern lands who he could use to overawe the Londoners – a politico-military weapon entrusted to him by Edward IV who had granted him a large autonomous 'palatinate'. It would make little difference if he arrived before or after the coronation; as seen by the poor attendance of peers at Edward IV's coronation in 1461, a coronation was no less legal for being enacted in the absence of major figures. But a royal uncle parading his troops near London making noises about his exclusion from power might not win such a confrontation; the mutinous Earl Henry of Lancaster had been faced down by the Queen-Mother's regency in 1329.

A united Council holding Richard at bay in May 1483, or a later accession of an older Edward V, would not have prevented potential discord. There could still have been quarrels over the exercise of authority, the destination of patronage, and the implementation of policy – e.g. towards France and Scotland – with the grant of significant military forces to Richard for a campaign feared by his enemies. The physical possession of the King would have been important, as was more nakedly the case in regencies in Scotland where James III, in particular, had ended up kidnapped by rival magnate factions. In England in 1329 Henry of Lancaster had tried to march on the court to seize possession of Edward III from Isabella and Mortimer. But Richard would have been at a disadvantage compared to his London-based rivals, with his estates concentrated in the north so the court would have adequate warning if he was marching south to attack them. He would have been better-placed if the alleged greed or monopoly of patronage by the Queen's clique had given him an opportunity to exact political capital out of it and propose redress by armed force as the saviour of the nation (see below).

### Results of Edward IV remaining an active king
If Edward IV's regime had continued into the later 1480s, or even the 1490s, the pattern of power and patronage of the period 1471–83 are likely to have

continued. The exercise of power would have seen continuing Woodville influence at court and an enhanced role for Anthony, Lord Rivers, and the Queen's other brothers. Bishop Lionel was too young to be made Archbishop of Canterbury when Archbishop Bourchier died in 1486, even by the brazenly nepotistic Edward IV, so the reliable Bishops Alcock or Russell were the likeliest candidates. The real-life choice to be Archbishop, Bishop John Morton of Ely, was chosen as a leading plotter for Henry Tudor in 1483 by his grateful protégé. Indeed, it was the 'Richard vs Hastings' showdown on 13 June 1483 that caused Morton to throw in his lot with the Tudor cause – Richard had him arrested and put in the custody of the 'loyal' Duke of Buckingham, whose rebellion later in 1483 was supposed to be partly due to Morton.[26] When the revolt failed, Morton fled to France to join Tudor. In the case of Edward remaining king, Morton would not have been disgraced by the Yorkist regime in 1483 but would have been less close to King Edward IV than others. His main court ally as of 1483 appears to have been Henry Tudor's mother, Margaret Beaufort, Countess Stanley, a potential threat to the Yorkists as the Lancastrian Beaufort heiress but entrusted to her 'loyal' husband by Richard after her arrest in June.[27] Had Bourchier died under a Yorkist king around 1486, Morton was far less likely to have secured the Archbishopric than John Alcock, Edward V's former tutor.

Archbishop Rotherham of York, trusted as Chancellor by Edward but only appointed to his see in 1480, was unlikely to be moved from that post to Canterbury by Edward V c. 1486. There was, however, a precedent of moving a politically useful Archbishop of York on to Canterbury when a vacancy arose – Bourchier's predecessor John Kemp in the early 1450s. Kemp, like Rotherham, was a long-serving civil servant (twice Chancellor). Edward's other senior advisers of 1483, especially Lord Hastings, would have dominated affairs through the 1480s and into the 1490s under both Edward IV and Edward V. Hastings (born c. 1420) was probably the former's closest intimate, and had been a companion on his return to retake the throne in 1471; he was supposed to 'share' Mistress Shore's charms with the King.[28] He would have remained the Crown's chief magnate in the East Midlands, while the lack of an opportunity to gamble for high political stakes would have saved Henry Stafford, Duke of Buckingham (executed for rebellion against Richard in October 1483) from ruin and his Gloucestershire/South Wales estates from confiscation. Elizabeth Woodville's elder son by her first marriage, Thomas Grey, Marquis of Dorset – who had already secured an important heiress by 1483 and was Hastings' rival as the King's boon companion – would have been an important figure, especially in his half-brother Edward V's reign. His younger brother Richard, executed in real life in June 1483, had been in the Prince's entourage in 1483 and was likely to have received a title and heiress. The same could be expected for the Queen's youngest brothers, Sir Edward and Richard Woodville.

### Husbands for Edward IV's daughters: different from the men Henry VII chose in real life?

Allied noble families would have been angling to marry their sons off to Edward IV's daughters, who would have made better matches than they did under the suspicious Henry VII whose principal female adviser was his mother, Margaret Beaufort, rather than his Yorkist Queen. Henry (and probably Margaret) were to marry off two of Edward's daughters, Cecily (born 1469) and Catherine (born 1479), to Lancastrian loyalists, William Courtenay and Lord Welles, and a third – Anne, born 1475 – to the son of a senior pardoned Yorkist, Thomas Howard. By this date, Elizabeth Woodville, mother of Henry's Queen, was in (forced?) retirement at Bermondsey Abbey after alleged support for Lambert Simnel's revolt. Her removal was probably a personal effort by her rival as senior female adviser at Court, Henry's formidable mother, Margaret Beaufort.[29] By contrast, Edward IV and Elizabeth could have been expected to select more prestigious marital partners – possibly from the extensive Neville connection, though Anne could still have been married to Howard whose grandfather John Howard was a senior Yorkist. (Edward IV had cheated him out of his share of the Duchy of Norfolk estates and titles in 1481.) They would have been more likely than Henry VII to consider foreign bridegrooms too, as Henry notably avoided using his sisters-in-law to build up foreign alliances in c. 1486–1500 despite having no daughters old enough. (He may have feared being overthrown by an ambitious and 'unsafe' brother-in-law.)

Luckily for Edward, he had six surviving daughters in 1483, aged from 3 to 18, so he could have used them as political bait for Continental allies for well over a decade. Elizabeth, the eldest daughter, had been deprived of her French fiancé the Dauphin Charles (Charles VIII) by Louis' double-dealing in 1482 but Edward would have been looking for another crowned bridegroom for her. Given her age, she was too old for Maximilian's son Philip (born 1478), thirteen years her junior, and the Habsburg would have regarded Ferdinand and Isabella of Spain as more valuable allies than England – as in real life – although England would have seemed more stable than it did in the real-life late 1480s. Ferdinand and Isabella's son Juan, heir to Spain, was also born in 1478. There was a current shortage of eligible heirs to thrones of the right age, with the Kings of Denmark (Hans/John) and Portugal (John II) married, Hans' elder son Christian married, the Burgundian family virtually extinct, and Maximilian and Charles VIII without brothers. A domestic magnate was possible as husband for Princess Elizabeth if Edward could not find a suitable European partner, and it is possible that the girl had inherited her mother's ambition as in real life she was plausibly believed to be angling for political rehabilitation by marrying her own uncle early in 1485.

The contemporary 'Song of the Lady Bessy' and a letter she sent to John Howard suggested that she was as ambitious then as her mother had been in 1464. Incidentally, her apparent willingness to throw herself at her uncle Richard III implies that she did not believe that he had killed her full brothers Edward V and Richard of York – her half-brother Sir Richard Grey and her uncle Rivers were evidently more expendable. An alternative theory has it that the account of Elizabeth's marital plans in early 1485 refers to a foreign marriage, probably to the Portuguese prince Manuel, not to the King. If this is correct, a successful negotiation (talks were underway in summer 1485) would have removed her from English politics and she would have become Queen of Portugal in 1495.[30] Edward IV had married (secretly) for personal rather than political reasons and evaded his advisers' attempts to arrange a foreign match; Elizabeth may have been capable of seeking – or being used by – an aristocratic 'catch' at court if she was still unwed in the late 1480s. Edward IV, like Richard, might have found a Portuguese match useful to prevent her from having a husband who could challenge his male heirs. Given that Princess Cecily had already been earmarked for Prince James of Scotland, closer to her age than was Elizabeth, and there were no sovereign duchies in the Low Countries available, the eldest Princess might have had to make do with Hans of Denmark's second son, Frederick, or an English noble. One obvious family to tie to the House of York was the powerful northern dynasty of Percy, originally staunchly Lancastrian, to whom Edward had had to return the Earldom of Northumberland in 1471. If a noble of semi-royal blood was essential the Bourchier, Fitzwarin, and Stafford descendants of Edward III's youngest son, Thomas, were closer to the throne than the Percies. The ambitious Duke of Buckingham, in real life Richard III's lieutenant then betrayer, might have used his talents at intrigue to link Elizabeth to his son, Edward Stafford (born 1478), provided that the latter's being Elizabeth's cousin did not stop this (perhaps dependant on a papal licence). But the lack of use Edward made of Buckingham may indicate mutual mistrust between them.

In a continuing Yorkist regime, some of the clerical ministers would have been the same as for Henry VII in the 1480s and 1490s. Edward's own most trusted clerical advisers, given the Chancellorship since 1471, were Robert Stillington, Bishop of Bath and Wells and allegedly privy to the secret of his 'pre-contract' first marriage; and the ageing Thomas Rotherham,

Archbishop of York. Stillington, briefly arrested in 1478, may have been suspected of passing on the secret of the 'pre-contract' to Clarence and thus been unlikely to be re-employed; Rotherham was to be briefly reappointed by Henry VII in 1485–6 but soon superseded by John Alcock. Most bishops continued to serve whoever was King, even in the swift changes of fortune from 1483 to 1485, though personal contacts at court were vital for promotion so Edward V's tutor John Alcock would have been a likely candidate for promotion under the Yorkist government. Promotions could have been expected for senior royal clerks such as Edward's secretary Oliver King and Richard's choice of Chancellor, John Russell.

## Political alliances

It is unlikely that the acquisitive Edward would have taken the illegally-seized Dukedom of Norfolk from his younger son Richard – its late heiress' widower, not a relative – for John Howard, which Richard III was to do later in 1483 (though Edward V might have done so to secure support as an adolescent King if he could compensate his brother Richard of York elsewhere.) Shuffling peerages around for political reasons was normal policy for Edward, who had handed the untrustworthy Percies' Northumberland title and lands over to John Neville in 1461 but returned it to win their allegiance in 1470. Edward also had the lands and titles forfeited by Clarence to use as sweeteners to potential allies. It is uncertain if Edward would have rehabilitated Edward, Earl of Warwick (born 1475), the disinherited young son of the executed Clarence, who was in the wardship of the Queen's sister Catherine and her husband, the Duke of Buckingham, in 1483. Warwick was taken into the household of Richard III in real life and was treated as a possible heir once the latter's son died. Warwick was Edward IV's nephew and technically closer to the line of succession than Richard of Gloucester and the royal family was short of adult males so he could have been a useful new peer once he was old enough – assuming that his alleged 'simpleness' in real-life 1499 was due to prolonged incarceration in the Tower not mental feebleness. Reversing his father's attainder and giving him land could have roused Richard's jealousy. From the mid-1480s Edward IV's nephew John de la Pole, Earl of Lincoln, son of his sister Elizabeth, could have been a rising military commander in campaigns in Scotland or Brittany as James III faced revolt and conflict resumed with Charles VIII's regency. Lincoln, born around 1464, was the real-life military leader of the Yorkist revolt in 1486-7.

If Edward IV had lived the special jurisdiction created in the north of England – a 'palatinate' like the Bishopric of Durham – for Richard would have continued as a northern equivalent to the Marcher lordships, but with

Richard's son dying in 1484 he would have had nobody to pass it to unless he had married again after 1485 and had a son.[31] It could have been given to Edward's and Richard's nephew John de la Pole, an adequate military leader in real life so capable of handling Scottish border raids, if he had outlived Richard. The younger sons of Edward IV's sister Elizabeth de la Pole, John's brothers, were also potential grantees of peerages and a role at court and in administration, and Clarence's daughter Margaret (born 1473) was likely to have received a more advantageous marriage from her uncle than she did in real life from Henry VII.

**Foreign policy**

Would the newly ineffective Edward have bothered to intervene in France to save Brittany from being swallowed up by the kingdom when Duke Francis II died in 1488 – sending a large expedition under a Woodville general like Rivers for a civil war like that of the 1350s? Keeping Brittany out of the hands of the French central government had been a major aim of the English regime at times of Anglo-French hostility, and Brittany was also a matter of concern in 1471–83 for its harbouring Henry Tudor. Edward IV had endeavoured to lure Henry home with a promise of a royal bride before 1483; and after the pretender invaded England in autumn 1483 Richard III was to bribe Duke Francis' minister Landois to have Henry seized and extradited. (He was forewarned of the plan and escaped to Paris.[32]) Had the crises of 1483 not unfolded as they did, Henry would presumably still have been in Brittany when Francis died in 1488 and Brittany faced annexation by France; and his role as a Lancastrian pretender would have made him an embarrassment to an Anglo-Breton alliance. Would he have prudently fled to Paris to seek aid from the regency for Charles VIII, and the latter used him against England as Louis XI had used Margaret of Anjou?

In real life Henry VII, a French ally in 1485, now lent troops for Breton resistance, with traditional English efforts to keep Brittany independent continuing. He sent Sir Edward Woodville to aid the Duchy against Charles VIII's regency;[33] however, the French secured Francis' heiress Anne and the Duchy. Edward IV, betrayed by Louis XI who had abandoned their political/ marital alliance in 1482, would have been equally if not more hostile to France in 1488. It is possible that the belligerent Richard of Gloucester would have successfully urged intervention to save Brittany from the French regency regime, leading an armed force there if not himself preoccupied with the succession-crisis in Scotland.

The overthrow of James III in June 1488 by a coalition of his principal nobles, led by the Border magnates under Archibald ('Bell-the-Cat') Douglas, would have occurred irrespective of events in England and been of concern to their neighbour Richard. He had attempted to manipulate a Scots revolt to coerce or remove James in 1481–2. The heiress of Duke Francis II of Brittany, Anne, born in 1476, was of a reasonable age to be married off to Edward IV's eldest son Edward (born November 1470) in a potential union of crowns, as revenge on France for its 'desertion' of the English alliance in 1482. Alternatively, if the hand of the future Edward V had been bestowed elsewhere (perhaps one of Ferdinand and Isabella's daughters) she could have been married to his next brother Richard, Duke of York. Either would have been fiercely resisted by the French regency, and entailed a long war in which taking sides in a Breton succession-dispute served as a means of drawing England and France back into open war as in the early 1350s. Edward IV being unfit for major foreign campaigning, the obvious person to lead an expedition to Artois to link up with the Yorkists' Habsburg allies was Richard of Gloucester. Maximilian of Habsburg would have been no more reliable for the English than his father-in-law Charles of Burgundy had been for Edward IV in 1470–1 or 1475, and ultimately an Anglo- French treaty would have been possible securing Brittany for England (or at least its junior line as represented by the Duke of York). If Edward IV wished to keep his sons for a more senior princess, Anne of Brittany could have been bestowed on his eldest Pole nephew – the older and militarily active John, Earl of Lincoln.

Would Richard of Gloucester have intervened in Scotland again as rebels rose against James III in 1488 – or done so earlier to impose James' brother Alexander as king? The treacherous Alexander had deserted him in 1482 but was still ambitious enough to link up with England again. Richard had the men to invade, and the Scots leadership was seriously divided with James III's low-born 'favourites' a source of aristocratic anger. Presumably the English would have been unable to forcibly keep a nominee like Alexander on the throne indefinitely against the resistance of most of the Scots nobility, as Edward III had found with Edward Balliol in the 1330s. A small English army had installed Edward Balliol in Perth in 1332 and after his eviction Edward III had intervened in greater force in 1333–4, ultimately to no effect; the English could at best dominate the Eastern lowlands and hold onto key castles with local help. (Edward had also had local aristocratic backing from the 'disinherited', partisans of the deposed John Balliol expelled by Robert Bruce in 1307–14; Richard did not have such a 'bloc' of support.) Richard would have had no better luck than Edward III if the nobility turned against Alexander, and the French were liable to assist any anti-English contender as they had backed David Bruce in the 1330s. Like Edward Balliol facing the young David Bruce after his seizure of the Scots Crown in 1333, the English-appointed usurper would have been at the risk of a long civil war and then deposition (in favour of James' son) as soon as his sponsor became preoccupied elsewhere.

If Richard had had the troops to force Alexander onto the throne as an English vassal in 1488 and the unpopular James III been unable to stage a comeback (as he was captured and murdered?) James' son James IV would have been the beneficiary of a 'backlash' in Scotland against an English-imposed king. Richard, possibly adding parts of Galloway or Lothian to his northern principality with the ruthless brutality he showed in dealing with opponents in real-life 1483, would have had to campaign hard year after year to keep his lands and his candidate as King of Scots. He could have ended up being forced to abandon his efforts due to the cost causing complaints in London (Parliament) and Edward IV refusing him more aid, and then blamed the withdrawal of his brother's support on the Woodvilles. If Edward IV was physically failing, the Queen and her brothers would have been wary of allowing Richard a large army lest he turned it on them in a succession-dispute. As an over-powerful 'Lord of the North', Richard would have seemed as threatening to his rivals in London in the mid-late 1480s as Warwick was in the 1460s or the Percies were to Henry IV in 1403. Conceivably, the brave but rash Richard, campaigning in person in Scotland, would have ended up killed in battle and the Scots venture abandoned as Edward IV had to come to terms with the new regime of James IV – presumably by the marriage of one of the King's daughters to James as an ally. Princess Cecily had been considered already by 1483.

### Richard of Gloucester and a more adult Edward V: a king at odds with his uncle like Richard II's and Henry VI's uncles?

If Edward IV, apparently in poor health and not campaigning in person by 1482, had died when his elder son was aged over fifteen or so (c. 1486) there would have been no need of a 'Protector'. A semi-adult Edward V would have succeeded with the Woodvilles as the main power at court. Richard would then have been isolated and unable to secure influence with the King, but with his military power in the north would have been too powerful to be dealt with decisively except by a trick. The messy expense and defeat of his attempts to take over Scotland for a client king could have provided his enemies with an opportunity to undermine him. Like the previous Dukes of Gloucester, Thomas and Humphrey, he would have been vulnerable to a sudden arrest and execution by a distrustful nephew encouraged by his rivals. He would have been very much aware of their fates, and of the fact that they had both been seized by surprise by a 'treacherous' King – Thomas arrested in person by a royal-led 'posse' at his Essex residence of Pleshy Castle, and Humphrey arrested at Parliament at Bury St Edmunds.

Richard's alternative course was to put himself at the head of a coalition of disaffected lords complaining at a monopoly of patronage by the Queen's kin, in the manner of Simon de Montfort against the Poitevins in the 1250s or Thomas of Lancaster against Gaveston and other royal allies in 1308–22. The chances are that Richard would not have challenged them in his brother's lifetime, unless Edward IV was seriously ill or 'senile' and perceived to be the helpless puppet of a greedy clique as Edward III had been in 1376. Both ambitious nobles such as the Duke of Buckingham (Richard III's real-life chief assistant and then betrayer in 1483) and a 'reforming' Parliament impatient at the abuse of power, as in 1376, could have aided Richard's ambitions to overturn the power of the King's current favourites as Edward IV aged and lost control of politics and patronage through the 1490s.

The dynamics of inter-state relations would have been the same, with England balanced against France and the Empire. Would Edward V or Richard, Duke of York been married off to Catherine of Aragon or a sister of hers – not the oldest, Juana, as heiress to Castile – as part of an alliance with Ferdinand and Isabella against the old enemy, France? (There were no French princesses near their age available.) The sister of Philip I of Burgundy and daughter of Emperor Maximilian, Margaret (born 1480), was an alternative and would have been useful in an anti-French alliance; Edward IV's sister Margaret (real-life Yorkist pretender-sponsor from 1486 to 1499) was available to negotiate with her stepson-in-law Maximilian. It is possible that the French regency-government would have retaliated for Edward IV's support for Breton independence from 1488 by smuggling Henry Tudor into France and using him as a Lancastrian pretender – if Edward had not had him extradited from Brittany first. Richard III attempted to get his hands on Tudor in real-life 1483–4, bribing Duke Francis' chief minister Landois, only for Tudor to flee to Paris; Edward IV could have done this too.

Until the major rift in the Yorkist regime caused by Edward V's real-life deposition and disappearance Henry had negligible support in England, as shown by the failure of the Earl of Oxford to win support in his Cornish venture in 1474. If Edward IV had died while the Anglo-French dispute was still underway Henry was no real threat to a (semi?-) adult Edward V. The Woodville alliance with Henry Tudor of Christmas 1483 only followed the disappearance of the deposed Edward V and his brother, and the scale of ex-royal Household men's involvement in the autumn 1483 revolt showed that many Yorkist stalwarts did not accept Richard. It is unlikely that Richard could have had the backing of many major nobles to depose an adult Edward V. Edward II, Richard II, and Henry VI had all been perceived as inadequate, faction-dominated kings for many years (22, 22, and 38) before they were deposed; Edward IV's deposition in 1470 was a 'special case' as his legitimacy as king was more in question and he had a deposed, 'legitimate' predecessor to hand for rebels to use. The rebels were led by Edward's cousin and ex-chief adviser Warwick, who had many clients from the vast Neville estates ready to back him, and included Edward's next adult male heir Clarence. Richard could only have removed Edward V on the grounds of legality, using the supposed 'pre-contract' of Edward IV to marry Eleanor Butler to argue that Edward V was illegitimate; and the story relied on at most one live witness (Stillington?) as of 1483. The question of its believability is obscured by the frantic efforts Henry VII made to 'airbrush' the incident out of history after 1485[34] – which themselves argue that Henry feared it was believable. But could Richard have won the Council to his side if he did not have Stillington (who died in 1495) to hand, as the latter was the key figure in the 'revelations' made in mid-June 1483?

If Richard had secured a client on the throne of Scotland (Alexander of Albany or Prince James?) in alliance with rebel Scots nobles around 1488 and/or led a successful expedition to Brittany or Artois, he would have boosted his military reputation. If he also had the manpower of his 'palatinate' to call upon against Edward V's unpopular Woodville relatives' domination of patronage and had allied nobles such as Buckingham, an attempt to coerce an ageing Edward IV or more likely a young Edward V was possible. But even if the rebels had been as effective against an untried new king as those of 1387–8, yet another royal deposition was an unlikely result. The previous depositions of adult kings – Edward II, Richard II, Henry VI, and Edward IV – had all been spearheaded by an ambitious rival, or in Edward II's case the mother of his heir and her lover, after either a period of weak government or the domination of government and patronage by one contentious person or faction. There was a chance that the Queen-Mother and her Woodville relatives could dominate politics and amass lands and titles for themselves in a similar manner under a young Edward V, perhaps from c. 1488 for five to ten years, and that Richard could act as a focus for resentment. Alternatively, the Woodvilles – or the King – could have seen him as a military threat and confiscated his 'palatinate', driving him into exile as Roger Mortimer had been imprisoned by Edward II or Henry IV had been exiled by Richard II, and thus caused an invasion. In that case Charles VIII's regency or Richard's favourite sister, Margaret, Dowager Duchess of Burgundy, were possible allies for him; in real life Margaret was to back Richard's heir Lincoln against Edward IV's daughter and son-in-law in 1486–7.

The deposition of an untried young king was unlikely to win support from the great nobility; the removal of his 'evil ministers', as the Lords Appellant had done to Richard II in 1387–8, was a more likely precedent. Richard of Gloucester would have found it more difficult to claim the throne from an adult king (and his younger brother Richard of York) by inventing or publicizing the conveniently-discovered story about the illegality of Edward IV's marriage. But if he had been responsible for having Edward V's chief ministers and maternal relatives rounded up and killed he would have been in the same position as Thomas, Duke of Gloucester, in the 1390s – facing the hostility of a chastened King determined on revenge at a later date and so with a reason to secure his position by usurpation. A confrontation between Richard of Gloucester and the Woodvilles over control of the young Edward V's government could have seen a repeat of the 1390s in the 1490s, and much would have depended on the personal capacity and leadership of the King. If Richard did not defend himself he could have shared the fate of Thomas of Gloucester in 1397, arrested and quietly murdered by his vengeful nephew. His extensive lands would have been a powerful inducement for his nephew to remove him and auction them off to royal supporters.

The Franco-Spanish showdown over Navarre in 1512 would have been a good opportunity for Edward V – or if he was dead, his brother Richard – as king to invade France. The English king, aged 41/2 (Edward V) or 39 (Richard of York), would have been unlikely to have had much military experience unless there had been an Anglo-French clash in the 1490s following the Breton succession-war. Burgundy, and thus their Habsburg allies, would have been the Yorkist government's principal Continental ally in 1485–1503, in contrast to real life where Maximilian as well as Duchess Margaret backed the pretender 'Perkin Warbeck' against Henry VII (in return for the pretender naming Maximilian as his heir). France would, however, have still had Italy as its priority under Charles VIII and Louis XII, with an invasion of England to back a Lancastrian claimant – Henry Tudor? – a much more risky affair than it was in real-life 1485 when Richard III lacked legitimacy or support.

James IV, as a French ally even if married to Edward IV's daughter, would have been likely to invade England if England attacked France. Assuming a war between the two in 1512, he would have been in the same position of aiding Louis XII against the English King as in real life; he could have been killed at Flodden in 1513. His mother, one of Edward IV's daughters (Cecily?), would then have had a claim to the regency for their son James V if enough nobles backed her. Either Edward V or his brother Richard would have been able to marry and produce heirs to England, with one of the brothers possibly still on the throne into the late 1530s. Born in 1470 and 1473, they would have been a generation older and more experienced than either Charles V or Francis I in the diplomatic conflicts of the 1520s.

Henry Tudor, left isolated in Brittany or France with no major split in the Yorkist 'power-base', would have been an unlikely choice for Edward IV as his eldest daughter's husband and would have lacked the support to challenge the adult Edward V or his brother. If the Plantagenet male line had continued, would there have been no 'Break with Rome' as there was no Henry VIII? There would still have been rising interest in Continental religious affairs and Lutheranism, but without the impetus of Henry's marital disputes the English state's attitude would depend on the personal piety and tolerance of the King. A fairly relaxed approach to dissident theology, like that initially in France, could have seen 'reformers' active in the major port of London in the 1530s and new ideas seeping into the universities, aided by imported books. There would still have been calls for Erasmian-style reform of clerical 'abuses' – the crucial choice facing the King would have been whether or not to suppress them.

## Chapter Five

# The Fall of the House of York, 1483–5

**What if Richard III had won at Bosworth and stayed in power?**

*The coups of May–June 1483*

As analysed in Charles Ross' biography, Richard III relied on a far narrower power-base than Edward IV due to the shocking nature of his usurpation in June 1483.[1] The surprise announcement of Edward V's bastardy (on account of his parents' marriage) on 22 June, initially in Ralph Shaa's officially-approved sermon on the text 'Bastard slips shall not take root', was probably based on the 'pre-contract' of Edward IV and Eleanor Butler as stated by the author of the *Croyland Chronicle*. There is some confusion over the identity of the betrothed woman cited, but not over the legal reason – which would have been more difficult to use if Edward IV had married in public with unbiased witnesses. Did the Woodvilles' unpopularity with some nobles enable Richard to risk this highly unusual action? The original texts of the sermon and of the Parliamentary Act sanctioning the change in succession, *Titulus Regius*, have not survived. After August 1485 Henry VII was keen to have them expunged from people's memories, as he partly based his appeal on his wife's being Edward IV's eldest daughter and thus bastardized with her siblings by Richard. Sir Thomas More was confused as to who the 'pre-contract' had been with, citing Edward's known mistress Elizabeth Lucy not Eleanor.[2] Was this just a slip, or a genuine sign that the announcement made on 22 June 1483 was not specific as to the name of the late King's betrothed?

Eleanor Butler has been traced, and the first biography of her written.[3] The original identity given to her in post-1483 literature was accurate, and she was indeed a daughter of the Earl of Shrewsbury, Henry VI's great general killed in 1453, and was buried in the nunnery church of the Carmelite Order in Norwich. Dying in 1468, this young widow was both 'available' for Edward to marry in 1462–4 and dead by the time that Edward was arrested and threatened with deposition by Warwick in 1469. Technically, even if Edward had legally 'married' her he could have re-married Elizabeth Woodville in time to legitimize his eldest son, born in October 1470 – but his daughter Elizabeth of York, Henry VII's wife, would still have been illegitimate as she was born in 1466. Ironically, canon law provided for Edward and Elizabeth's 1464 marriage to have been legal not 'bigamy' if it had been public and Eleanor had failed to speak up for her rights at the ceremony – but the Woodville marriage was private and poorly-attended. The arguments against the legality of the Woodville marriage in *Titulus Regius* apparently included that it was not in church and had not been approved of by the peers.[4] Under contemporary canon law, the private circumstances invalidated the marriage – whether or not there was a 'pre-contract' to anyone else. Thus, the question of who Edward IV's 'other wife' was (and if Richard invented her role) is in a sense irrelevant. The Butler genealogy reveals two interesting facts – Eleanor's sister Elizabeth, with whom she probably lived at Kenninghall in Norfolk after 1461, was married to the Duke of Norfolk and they were closely related to Warwick. (A rumour c. 1462 did say that Edward was sexually involved with Warwick's niece.[5]) This poses two questions about the 'marriage that might have been' between Edward and Eleanor and its effects on post-1464 politics. Did Elizabeth, Duchess of Norfolk, and/ or her husband know of the betrothal-ceremony and Edward have to avoid alienating the Duke, e.g. by backing his blatantly illegal attack on the Pastons at Caister Castle? And what if Warwick had found out about the betrothal – could he have administered the *coup de grâce* to the Woodvilles in 1469 by forcing the Church to examine the evidence and declare Edward a bigamist? His execution of Elizabeth Woodville's father and husband would then have been followed by annulling Edward's marriage to Elizabeth, whether or not Edward was deposed too. Either Edward would have had to marry a bride of Warwick's choosing, or Clarence would have been restored as Edward's sole legal heir in place of Edward's illegitimized daughters.

The promiscuous young Edward IV of the early 1460s was certainly capable of making a promise of marriage in order to seduce a woman and going back on it later. His actual marriage in May 1464, was secret and gave rise to confusion over its legality when he eventually admitted it. The bishop who had seemingly performed the betrothal-ceremony to Eleanor – or else received the confession of the priest who had done so – Robert Stillington, was arrested for unknown reasons by Edward IV when the King's brother the Duke of Clarence, was laying claim to be Edward's heir in 1478. This suggests that he may have told Clarence the story and thus inspired the latter's endeavours to cut Edward's children out of the succession.[6] It makes more sense to suppose that Clarence's threatening hints about 'G' being the rightful heir in 1477 arose from a sense of (justified?) grievance at his brother's underhand behaviour rather than simple lust for power. The relative paucity of knowledge of or interest in Eleanor in Tudor times may reflect writers' recognition that it was a dangerous topic to pursue – if Edward IV had been legally contracted to her, Henry VII's wife had had no claim to the English throne. Thus Henry VIII was not the rightful king, and logically Clarence's daughter Margaret Pole should have been queen or else have handed over her rights to her son Henry, Lord Montague. Henry VII claimed the throne in his declaration to Parliament in autumn 1485 by his, not his wife's, descent– though this was presumably partly to avoid making himself legally dependant on her rights and partly out of loyalty to his mother, Margaret Beaufort, whose claim he had inherited.[7] Raking up the Eleanor Butler story could be interpreted by the paranoid Henry VIII or Elizabeth I as backing their Plantagenet challengers, so was it suppressed deliberately? There is evidence that the Butler claim was still 'live' as a political issue in the 1530s.[8]

It also appears that mention was made (probably by Richard's chief supporter, Henry Stafford, Duke of Buckingham) in a speech on 24 or 25 June 1483 of the rumour that Edward IV was illegitimate too due to his mother's affair with the archer Blaybourne in 1441/2. Polydore Vergil claimed he had heard witnesses confirm Duchess Cecily's anger at this – though there is no evidence of her quarrelling with Richard, who was living at her residence at the time. The story, which Louis XI of France used against Edward in the latter's lifetime,[9] may have been current earlier than 1483 and inspired the clumsy claims to the throne (or the reversion to it) made by Clarence in 1470–1 and 1477–8. Did Warwick think of using it to depose Edward in 1469? It is an alternative explanation for Clarence's behaviour to his being told about Eleanor Butler. Indeed, recent discovery of evidence about Edward's father's itinerary as commander in Normandy in 1441 may indicate that he was not with Edward's mother, Cecily Neville, at Rouen at the likely time of Edward's conception and that there may be truth in the claim about Blaybourne.[10] At the time, much was made of the fact that the six-foot-four Edward did not resemble his undersized father but Richard did; at the public declaration of Richard's rights as lawful king in the City on 22 June 1483 he made an appearance before the crowds to remind everyone of this fact.[11] No doubt it was carefully arranged so that his partisans in the crowd could 'spontaneously' acclaim him as king.

It is far from certain that Richard did not have a legal claim in 1483, provided that the exclusion of Clarence's seven-year-old son Edward (possibly mentally sub-normal) by reason of Clarence's attainder was accepted. The exclusion of an under-age if genealogically closer heir in favour of a more distant, adult claimant had a precedent – in 1399, when Edmund Mortimer had been Richard II's expected heir but was only eight and was ignored by the usurping Henry IV. The political power at the time had lain with Henry, as it did with Richard in June 1483, and nobody dared oppose the new ruler.

Whether or not Richard had any legal claim on the throne, the surprise discovery of his nephews' bastardy was very convenient for his own ambitions and was cynically seen as such by contemporaries. Edward IV had nominated Richard as Protector for the twelve-year-old Edward V, at least until the latter's coronation when a king supposedly attained his majority, and Richard was the senior adult male of the House of York and the greatest magnate in the country (recently awarded a new 'palatinate' over parts of the north). He was the most experienced war-leader and was more able to lead the Council than the two most senior political magnates resident at court, Edward's friend and Chamberlain William, Lord Hastings, and stepson the Marquis of Dorset, who were at odds at the time of Edward's sudden death on 9 April. But the powerful family of his queen, Elizabeth Woodville, were critical of the measure and possibly tried to keep the contents of the will secret to reduce Richard's authority over the Council. The apparent efforts to hurry Edward V from his residence as Prince of Wales, Ludlow Castle, to London for an early coronation without waiting for Richard's arrival from Yorkshire would indicate a means of preventing the Protectorship – if Richard can be believed. (See previous section.)

The extent of and reasons for Elizabeth Woodville's enmity towards Richard are unclear, though it has been speculated that she bore a grudge against the Neville clan for the 'Kingmaker' Earl of Warwick's execution of her father and brother in 1469 and had transferred this to Richard as Warwick's son-in-law and principal heir to estates in the north. But she did a land-deal with Richard in 1472 – as current rival to her foe Clarence? Her brother Anthony Woodville, Earl Rivers, showed that *he* was not at odds with Richard (or expecting Richard to interfere in arrangements for the government) in the way that he took no precautions after meeting Richard and Buckingham on the road to London at Stony Stratford on 29 April. He rode back from Edward V's quarters to dine with the Dukes and was arrested in his inn the next morning. It was clearly Richard that was the plotter on that occasion, not Rivers, though he later displayed barrels of weapons that he claimed Rivers had been taking to London to be used in a Woodville coup. Richard certainly claimed to fear the Woodvilles' intentions, sending to York for a large body of his tenants and allies to come armed to London in June to protect him. The semi-hysterical and abusive references to treachery seems to be an obsession of his, implying self-righteous insecurity.[12] When news of his seizure of Rivers and others reached London the Queen chose to take sanctuary with her other children and her son Dorset and brother Edward Woodville to flee the country with what men, treasure, and ships they could lay their hands on. Was this due to genuine fear, or to win sympathy? An uneasy impasse followed Richard's arrival in London with his and Buckingham's armed retainers escorting the new King, until sometime in early June the question of the legality of Edward IV's marriage surfaced and Richard began to consider deposing his nephew. The dates of this, the question of who was plotting against whom, and the truth of assorted claims about the 'pre-contract' are still disputed. But the evidence would seem to indicate that at some date Hastings, formerly an ally of Richard's against his foe Dorset's mother Elizabeth Woodville, became reconciled to the Woodvilles – possibly with Edward IV's mistress 'Jane' Shore acting as an intermediary – and Richard came to see him as a threat.[13] Given that Hastings had been responsible for summoning Richard to London and was an enemy of Dorset, this reversal of alliances was somewhat bizarre and would indicate that Hastings was seriously worried for Edward V's welfare.

On 13 June the Protector, in an act of blatant violence unusual even for fifteenth-century politics, had a Council meeting at the Tower stormed by his retainers and Hastings was dragged outside and beheaded on Tower Green without any attempt at a trial. The nearest parallel was what Richard's father-in-law (and mentor at Middleham Castle in the mid-1460s), Warwick, had done to those male Woodvilles he could lay his hands on in 1469. Warwick had also killed the late Duke of Buckingham, father of Richard's ally, in this manner after the battle of Northampton in 1460 and Edward IV had killed the Duke of Somerset and other captured Lancastrian peers after the battle of Tewkesbury in 1471. All these victims had been in arms against their captors, and been arrested and killed after battles; Rivers and Hastings in 1483 were not. Richard also arrested Lord Stanley, Archbishop Rotherham of York, and Bishop Morton, though the first two were soon released and the latter was placed in the custody of Richard's close ally Buckingham at his residence at Brecon (and may have encouraged his later revolt). Hastings' estates were not confiscated, indicating that Richard accepted that he had no legal reason for doing so and needed to make a gesture of reconciliation, but Mistress Shore was required to do penance as a prostitute in a clear act of personal spite and ostentatious criticism of the debauchery at Edward IV's court. Richard's propagandists notably kept returning to this theme of the late King's moral faults, implying Richard's superior qualities; it may well reflect a personal obsession of Richard's.[14] Richard also executed Rivers and his associates Sir Richard Grey (the

Queen's second son by her first marriage) and Haute in custody in Yorkshire in mid-June, possibly after a brief trial. The Queen was required to hand over her youngest son Richard, Duke of York, to join his brother in the Tower, and the deposition of Edward V followed. On 25 June Richard was proclaimed king following a hasty 'election' by an assembly of magnates, and on 6 July he was crowned in place of Edward V.

### How ruthless was Richard? The case of the disappearance of the Princes

The question of the murder of Edward V and his brother has long exercised historians, novelists, and others and remains one of the most written-about historical mysteries. It is, of course, the central problem in the question of whether Richard was a potential success as king had he not been overthrown in 1485 – and the charge by his defenders that his reputation has been maligned. What did contemporaries think of him before all their writers had a vested interest in denouncing him, to please his overthrower after 1485? And need proof of his ruthlessness mean that he was going to be an unpopular ruler, easily attracting plotters to replace him – or was it potentially to his advantage? As Shakespeare (his most influential 'blackener') reminds us, treason is a matter of dates – 'if treason prosper, none dare call it treason'. Would Richard have gone down in history as no more ruthless than Edward I or John had he fought off his challengers successfully? John murdered Welsh hostages and starved baronial captives to death, and Edward conducted mass-executions in Scotland and paraded his female Bruce and Buchan captives in cages for 'treason' to him as its king. Both men reportedly committed crimes in rages, John killing his nephew Arthur and Edward assaulting his son and tearing out his hair. Henry II memorably made wild calls for Archbishop Becket's destruction for breaking an agreement about their terms of political truce on the latter's return in 1170, which was acted upon by his servants.[15] Were any of them worse than Richard? Would his alleged murders of his nephews been brushed aside had he had a long and successful reign thereafter – or was the story (true or not) a symptom of why he failed to secure his throne in the first place?

The 'Richard III Society', a unique society of supporters devoted to the memory of a divisive English king over 500 years after his death, have long argued that he had no reason to kill the Princes after they had been bastardized by Parliament – although such Acts could be and were frequently reversed in the fifteenth century after a change of regime. Supposedly Richard, the loyal ally of his brother in the struggle to regain the Crown in 1471 and the trusted viceroy of the north in succession to Warwick, would never have abrogated his personal motto of *Loyauté me lie* or, as a deeply religious man whose reign was marked by acts of public piety – including towards the cult of Henry VI, the king who had been murdered at his brother Edward IV's orders – would never commit the serious sin of murdering his nephews. (But what then of his interest in early 1485 towards marrying his niece Elizabeth, also regarded as a sin by the Church and apparently unpopular among lay opinion too when it was rumoured?) All his other victims were adults who were a political threat, and the 'Tudor myth' of his wickedness (of which More's biography was the main vehicle) that Shakespeare took up was full of falsehoods and relied on rumour. The playwright was, of course, writing literature not history, but his account of Richard follows the 'historical' (though polemical) Hall chronicle of 1547 closely – and both 'covered up' such circumstances as the fact that if Richard did personally kill Henry VI in May 1471 it would have been on Edward IV's orders. The killing of Henry's son Prince Edward after the battle of Tewkesbury a few days earlier was also a 'collective' act by the Yorkist leaders, if he was captured alive at all rather than being killed in the rout as the Lancastrians were fleeing the battlefield.[16] Certainly, Richard did not have a withered arm, which casts doubt on the accuracy of at least one of the scenes in More's biography where he supposedly exposed his arm at the Council meeting on 13 June 1483 and accused his enemies of causing it. (Was Bishop Morton More's source?) He could not have fought so successfully at Barnet, Tewkesbury, and Bosworth had he been so hampered, and no contemporary mentions it. The circumstantial minor details in More's account – e.g. Richard asking Morton to send him some strawberries from his garden a few minutes before suddenly turning violent – suggests that More relied on an eye-witness account. One recent suggestion has been that Richard really meant that his 'arms' – his heraldic escutcheon – had been 'withered' by Woodville treachery, probably by the Queen covering up her illegal marriage to deny Richard the throne.[17] What is apparent is that Richard chose to portray the 'plot' against himself as 'treason', which was the war-cry of his retainers as they burst into the Council chamber to seize Hastings, Stanley, Rotherham, and Morton.[18] It was also his cry as he was surrounded by the defector Lord Stanley's men and hacked down at Bosworth; it seems to have become an obsession with him. The most famous portrait with the 'withered arm' attribute, one in the royal collection at Windsor dated by the dendrochronological evidence to c. 1520, was 'doctored' at a later date to add the deformity, and it was also shown in the original version of the Royal Society of Antiquaries' portrait of c. 1540.[19] Apart from one mention of Richard as having a 'crook back' in recorded abuse of the late King in York c. 1489, there is no evidence of it from contemporaries who met him – including foreign visitors with no interest in praising or abusing him, such as the 1484 Court visitor Nicolas von Poppelau from Silesia.[20] The Italian source of much information on events in London in 1483, Dominic Mancini, makes no mention of it, and when the former Yorkist propagandist John Rous re-wrote his 'Rous Roll' under Henry VII to condemn Richard (and altered his flattering portraits of the royal family) he did not put in any deformity.[21] The discovery in 2012 of the bones matching Richard's description at the site of the Greyfriars church in Leicester, where he is recorded as being buried, adds confirmation to the 'crook back' story. DNA confirms that the body is Richard's and he did have curvature of the spine – so that story is not 'Tudor propaganda'. Did his disability add to Richard's religious fervour, or to his sense of alienation from his brother's court? Hall and Shakespeare are also wrong about his involvement in the removal of Clarence, as far as the evidence stands – though he and the Duke had quarrelled bitterly over Clarence seeking to prevent him marrying Anne Neville in 1471–2.[22] If Richard was a major foe of the 'Woodville faction' in 1478–83 as 'back-dated' from the way the Queen plotted against his Protectorship in April 1483, it made no sense for him to remove his brother Clarence to the Woodvilles' benefit.

Some claims of the 'Ricardians' are, however, equally unlikely. Importantly, they were made in an era of less brutal politics than the fifteenth century and seem to have forgotten the 'norms' of behaviour by Richard and his contemporaries. The *Historical Doubts on the Reign of Richard III*, Horace Walpole's reasoned reassessment of Richard's reign and crimes, started the ball rolling in 1768, and by 1906 the extreme Ricardian Sir Clements Markham was claiming that Henry VII had murdered the Princes in 1486.[23] (This is very unlikely, given that someone among their captors in the Tower over this long period would surely have managed to reveal the story.) Paul Murray Kendall's biography of 1955 is the main mid-twentieth century 'defence' of Richard. His sympathetic portrayal of Richard's energetic actions to improve justice for ordinary citizens – e.g. by having legal business done in English not Latin – and his public proclamations of his desire for just government argue for the King's good qualities as a ruler, if ignoring the value of this stand to an insecure regime.[24] But Kendall's view of Richard's marriage to Anne Neville as a love-match has no contemporary evidence; Richard had sound practical reasons to seek her as his wife in 1471–2 to add her half of the Warwick inheritance to his lands. If they were so much in love, why did rumours spread that he had poisoned her even before the battle of Bosworth made this allegation congenial to the current authorities? The attention that he paid to his niece at Christmas 1484, while his wife was dying, Richard's seeking of Church advice on the possibility of divorcing Anne early in 1485, and the warning that his henchmen Ratcliffe and Catesby gave him about a revolt if he dared to marry Elizabeth of York cannot be dismissed as post-Bosworth calumny.[25] Nor was it necessary for him to execute Rivers, Haute, and Vaughan in June 1483 once they had been placed in secure custody and were no threat. It is clear that he deployed terror as an instrument of intimidation in 1483.

Any consideration of Richard's character and chances of long-term survival must centre on the most notorious allegation against him, that of killing the deposed king and his brother. Admittedly, the 'Princes in the Tower' were not placed there as part of a move to have them isolated and then quietly killed off; the Tower was the normal place of residence for a monarch before his coronation. It was prudent for Richard to keep Edward V there and have his brother join him – under the guard of Richard's own attendants rather than those selected pre-1483 by their parents – in case the boys were carried off by the Woodvilles as figureheads of the rebellion that did, in fact, break out late that summer. Thus the boys' 'sinister' withdrawal into the inner apartments of the Tower and increasingly infrequent sightings, attested to in July by the Italian observer Dominic Mancini, were only a security-measure. Indeed, recent new evidence shows that there was a plot in London to rescue them in late July or early August 1483, with secret legal investigations held at Crosby Hall.[26] Removing their attendants implied that Richard feared the latter would spirit them out of the Tower to serve as figureheads for a revolt, not a move to surround them with his own 'trusties' ready for murder. It was undeniable that they had then disappeared, sometime between late June and early September 1483, and Richard was not able to produce them for a public parade to show that they were alive in the way that in 1487 Henry VII paraded Clarence's son Edward in London (to show that he was not leading the 'Lambert Simnel' revolt and that Simnel was an impersonator). The deaths of the boys were rumoured at the time of the rebellions that autumn, which had started out in the name of Edward V but shifted focus to the cause of the obscure Lancastrian claimant Henry Tudor.[27] Mancini provides evidence that a rumour to the effect that the boys were dead arose in the late summer, though not who was spreading it (perhaps Elizabeth Woodville's agents), and the revised version of Rous' originally pro-Yorkist account dates the murder to three months after Richard seized the elder Prince in early May. At best, recent evidence found in the Colchester records shows that the rumour of their killing had not reached there by September.[28] Murder by Richard was openly claimed by the French government in January 1484. The *Croyland Chronicle* – written at a Fenland monastery some way from London – dated the rumours of their disappearance to Easter 1484, and stated that Richard was believed to have 'suppressed' his nephews (the original Latin may or may not encompass the notion of 'smothered', as in More's story).[29] The author of this part of the text may have had connections to the regime, but was critical on occasion and is now thought less likely to be Bishop Russell (Richard's Chancellor). Louis XI of France had apparently heard the rumour before his death on 30 August 1483.[30]

When the Duke of Buckingham shockingly betrayed Richard and joined in the widespread revolt in October he did so in Tudor's name, though it has been speculated that that was merely to gain more support from the Tudor and Woodville alliance and he ultimately wanted the throne himself (he was the senior male descendant of Edward III's youngest son). Presumably his captive at Brecon, Bishop Morton who Richard had seized at the Council table in the coup of 13 June and put in his custody, had persuaded him to link up with the Tudor/Lancastrian cause that Morton had been supporting as late as 1471.[31] Logically, if the ex-King was believed to be still alive Buckingham would have been more likely to rise in his name than that of an unknown Welsh-French fugitive with no popular English support. Buckingham was married to the ex-King's aunt, Catherine Woodville, and thus would have had a claim to be his guardian or chief minister as his 'uncle' on the maternal side. Buckingham, if anyone, would have been able to know if the boys were alive in secure custody in the Tower as of September 1483 – though his apparent failure to rise in rebellion in their name has been interpreted as implying that he had a motive for killing them.[32] It would have taken a very Machiavellian character to kill the boys and spread rumours that Richard was to blame for it, thus improving his chances of a successful revolt, and to only pretend to back Tudor when he wanted the throne for himself all along. It is not impossible, but it can only be speculation. The claim that the boys were murdered by the 'advice' of Buckingham can be interpreted in different ways depending on the meaning of the word in the late fifteenth century.[33] It may indicate that he advised Richard to do it, in the modern sense, or that he was the 'means' i.e. he carried out the King's orders. But his urgent request to see Richard as he was awaiting execution at Salisbury after his failed revolt may mean that he wanted to bargain for his life and had some important news to use – the location of the disappeared Princes? This may be linked to the claim made by the pretended 'Prince Richard', Perkin Warbeck, in 1499 that an unnamed lord rescued him from the Tower but sent him abroad and warned him to keep his identity secret or else.[34] Logically, Buckingham could have wanted his wife Catherine Woodville 's nephew(s) safe from potential killers but not able to interfere with his own bid for the throne, being planned at the time of his 'rescue' (July or August 1483?).

By Christmas 1483 Henry could make a public promise at Rennes Cathedral to marry the Princes' sister Elizabeth as if she was now the 'legitimist' heiress, apparently by co-ordination (perhaps via his mother Margaret Beaufort, Stanley's wife, and her physician Dr Lewis) with Elizabeth Woodville in sanctuary in London. Queen Elizabeth thus had reason to suspect that the boys were dead and seek Tudor's alliance rather than come to terms quickly with Richard. In the New Year the French Chancellor made a public accusation against Richard of infanticide in the Estates-General, though as early as August Louis XI may have heard a rumour of it as he then turned against Richard according to Commignes. In March 1484 the Queen finally reached terms with Richard on her leaving sanctuary. Her insistence that he take public oaths to protect her and her daughters suggests that she did not trust him,[35] though her daughter Elizabeth may have been of a different opinion as she was rumoured to have favoured the bizarre plan made on (or before) the death of Richard's wife Anne in spring 1485 that she should marry her uncle. The contemporary ballad, the 'Song of the Lady Bessy', indicates her favourable attitude to her uncle at this time. Elizabeth Woodville's eldest son, the Marquis of Dorset, attempted to abandon Henry's cause and return to England in spring 1485, which suggests that he had strong hopes of a pardon (perhaps via his mother or half-sister).Dorset did not think that Richard was the losing cause at the time.

Even the Princes' disappearance in Richard's custody has not stopped claims being made that he was not a killer. One theory is that he allowed them to leave the Tower to join his illegitimate children in obscurity at Sheriff Hutton Castle in Yorkshire, based on a claim that Edward V, not Richard's son John, was the 'Lord Bastard' referred to in the household accounts. Alternatively, a family tradition connected to Sir James Tyrrell (the murderer according to More's version) has them being smuggled out to live quietly with the Queen and her daughters at Tyrrell's home, Gipping Hall in Essex, and then leaving the country. This was first discovered by Audrey Williamson (*The Mystery of the Princes*, Alan Sutton, 1981).[36] Supposedly, Richard baulked at murder, but required them to reside abroad away from plotters who could restore them (or 'Tudor agents' intent on murdering them to make their sister's would-be fiancé the only legitimate claimant to the throne). Was Tyrrell's apparent mission to Flanders in 1484 to arrange a refuge for the boys there, or even to escort them? And what of the large sum of money that Tyrrell was granted by Richard in 1484[37] – a fund to set up a safe hiding-place for the boys? Or just money to bribe spies in the Low Countries for normal intelligence information?

The fact that Tyrrell was pardoned twice early in Henry VII's reign could be interpreted as meaning that he had either done some illegal deed for Henry between the two occasions (royal murder according to Markham), or that Henry had found out about something he had done for Richard. He was required to reside abroad in command of Guisnes Castle near Calais, and when he was arrested for apparent Yorkist plotting in 1502 and brought back to London for execution his supposed 'confession' to killing the Princes was not public or widely circulated.[38] Either he was being used as a scapegoat, or Henry was unwilling to make a detailed public statement of the 'truth' about the killings until he had located the Princes' bodies, which he never did. The confusion over Henry's reasons for arresting Tyrrell is increased by the escape of Richard's nephew Edmund de la Pole to the Continent shortly before Tyrrell's 'plot' and arrest. This Yorkist pretender was a major threat to Henry, whose eldest son, Arthur, had just died leaving him with only one underage son, so Henry may have feared Tyrell was working for the Pole cause rather than wanting him disposed of to provide 'proof' that the Princes were Richard III's victims. Edmund, incidentally, was not a 'die-hard' Yorkist motivated by a violent grudge against Henry for 'cheating' the de la Poles of the Crown, though his elder brother, the Earl of Lincoln, may have been recognized by Richard III as his heir. When Edmund had the chance to desert Henry and put himself at the head of a large army of rebellious Cornish tax-protesters in their march on London in 1497, he obeyed Henry's summons to assist him instead. Indeed, he ignored his Neville relation Lord Bergavenny's specific suggestion to join the rebels, and stole the latter's breeches and saddle so he could not ride off and join them either.[39]

The mysterious 'Perkin Warbeck' from Flanders, the pretender with Yorkist family looks who surfaced in 1490 as a protégé of Richard's sister Margaret of Burgundy and asserted that he was the younger Prince, claimed that he had been smuggled abroad by an unknown magnate in 1483 and warned to stay hidden because of an unidentified threat to murder him.[40] He did not name the man or provide one coherent story of what had happened to him or to the missing Edward V, but the unnamed 'rescuer' could have been Buckingham. He was the boys' uncle, and had his own reasons for not wanting them on the throne if he aimed for it himself. The Portuguese-born adventurer Sir Edward Brampton (Duarte Brandao), who had long connections to Edward IV and other links to 'Warbeck's home town of Tournai and 1490 employer Pregent Meno, could have taken him abroad on behalf of Richard or of Richard's enemies. Brampton was also responsible for bringing 'Warbeck' to Portugal at the start of his adventures c. 1489, as a page to his wife – though he alleged that 'Warbeck' was a Flemish boy in search of adventure who could not even speak English. (He made this claim in 1496, before it was clear 'Warbeck' would fail to overthrow Henry, so it probably was not forced to secure the victors' favour.[41]) If Brampton was not merely seeking Henry's favour, it would appear that 'Warbeck' was not an English boy who had left England at the age of ten in 1483 – as a rescued 'Richard of York' would have done. A ten-year-old would not have forgotten his native language so easily. Nor would 'Richard of York' have had reasons to hide the fact that he could speak English well from Brampton around 1489–90; the latter was a trusted ex-follower of Edward IV, not someone who if he knew 'Richard' was really English could hand him over to Henry VII.

Tyrrell was another candidate for the 'lord' who had smuggled the boys abroad. He was close to Richard, and was sent by him from his touring court at York in late August or early September 1483 to London on a private mission – according to More, to take over the Tower of London for a night and murder the Princes for Richard. In any case it was possible that 'Warbeck' could not explain what had happened to Edward V because he did not know; the boys had been separated for security. There was a garbled story that Edward had drowned, possibly while being smuggled to a ship on the Thames to sail abroad, or had been thrown into the sea. (One version had it that the boys had both been drowned – to excuse the lack of bodies?) It may also be significant that in his confused 'confession' after capture by Henry, the pretender made much of an irrelevant detail that he had been 'ill' for a long time around 1483.[42] Was this a hint that he had replaced the 'real' Perkin Warbeck in the family household in Tournai at this time, with the boy kept out of view? The inconsistencies in the confession of 'Warbeck' to Henry in 1497, as published and sent abroad to his patrons, may suggest that he made deliberate mistakes to show the latter he was not speaking freely. Why did the captured pretender not correct Henry's men about the mother of 'Warbeck' being called Catherine, not Nicaise de Faro?[43]

Did Henry's interrogators present him with a prepared statement to sign, based on their (inaccurate) research in Flanders, and did he let their mistakes go uncorrected? And why did Henry claim that the most dangerous plotter was the fairly (socially) insignificant John Taylor, a former member of the Duke of Clarence's household? This man's arrest in France was greeted with delight,[44] and we know that he had been mixed-up in the pretender's first appearance in Cork in 1490. Taylor's importance was surely not just his early role in the plot and thus knowledge of where the 'feigned lad' had sprung from; it was Sir Edward Brampton (a former employee of Edward IV) who had provided that information to Henry. Taylor, if anyone, knew the truth as well as many names of 'high-level' plotters. But when 'Warbeck' had first appeared in his company at Cork, he had not been identified definitively by him as Richard of York. And was it just ambition that made senior court figures such as Sir William Stanley, Lord Chamberlain and brother of Henry's stepfather Lord Stanley (now Earl of Derby), promise aid to

'Warbeck' in 1493–4? Did they think him genuine, as Stanley claimed? The extent of the Yorkist conspiracy at the time was large enough to suggest that the pretender was seen as potentially genuine, with statements being made that if 'Richard of York' was really who he claimed his father's ex-loyalists would back him against the Tudors. There was also a network of Church supporters,[45] as previously seen for the 'legitimate' would-be 'Richard IIs' and Edmund Mortimer against Henry IV in the 1400s. The extent and identity of the plotters suggest a genuine belief that a legitimate claimant was at large and that the current King was a usurper, as seen under Henry – and neither Henry IV nor Henry VII could be accused of misrule.

But even if 'Warbeck' was really a Plantagenet he need not have been Edward IV's son; there is also the mysterious case of a plot in 1477 to smuggle Clarence's son abroad as a potential threat to Edward. The man who had masterminded this, the later 'Warbeck' plotter John Taylor, could have taken an apparent illegitimate son of Clarence abroad in 1477 and then used him as 'Warbeck' to challenge the Tudors in 1490. It was Taylor who first prompted pro-Yorkist Irishmen to recognize 'Warbeck' as a Plantagenet when he sailed to Cork on Pregent Meno's ship in 1490.[46] Could 'Warbeck' not speak English as he had left England as a baby?

The boy may have been the unknown lad who Margaret of Burgundy appeared to be fostering in the early 1480s, subsequently claimed by Tudor propaganda to be her illegitimate son. But Margaret of Burgundy need not have been convinced of Warbeck's truthfulness about being 'Prince Richard of York' in order to use him to overthrow Henry, and the same applies to his other patrons Maximilian of Habsburg and James III of Scotland. Maximilian shamelessly forced Warbeck to nominate him as his heir, so if he was killed invading England Maximilian had a claim on the throne. (Henry's supporters spread a story that Warbeck was the illegitimate son of Margaret and the Bishop of Cambrai.[47]) The sceptical Spanish sovereigns Ferdinand and Isabella notably referred to Warbeck in the special diplomatic code that they used for legitimate sovereigns.[48]

It has been claimed that even if the boys were killed in August or September 1483 Richard may not have been responsible or have approved of it. There were contemporary claims that they were put to death by the 'vise' – means, or advice? – of Buckingham, as recorded in the anonymous 'Historical Notes' of the period 1483–8 by one or more Londoners (published in the *English Historical Review*, vol. 96).[49] By extension it could be argued that the Duke killed them to do Richard a service, or in order to remove them ahead of his own bid for the throne. Could he have carried out the murder as part of a plan to have Richard blamed for it and ease his own way to power? In practical terms, it is difficult to see how Buckingham's agents could have gained access to the royal apartments in the Tower without being stopped by Richard's own men, particularly Constable Sir Robert Brackenbury. It is not impossible, however, that if the Duke had arranged the killing without informing Richard, the King would have baulked at announcing it; public opinion would conclude that he himself was behind the convenient murders and was using Buckingham as a scapegoat.

### The 1483 rebellion: a sign of Richard's precarious position?

Whether or not Richard was the guilty party, his usurpation proved a fatal split in the Yorkist power-structure. A number of Edward IV's household officials and other loyalists took part in the abortive risings across southern England in the late summer of 1483, suggesting a deep-seated disgust that overcame their loyalty to the regime, with revolts as far scattered as Kent, Surrey, Berkshire, Wiltshire, and Devon. The geographical extent of the revolts and their 'low-status' leadership were unusual for a revolt aimed at 'regime change' in that period. The 'Peasants' Revolt of 1381 and the Cade revolt in 1450 had had wider social and economic aims, as well as protesting against governmental corruption and injustice, and had been aimed at the entire governmental leadership; the rebels of 1381 had protested loyalty to their King, although in 1450 there had been rumours that 'Cade' or his backers were Mortimer agents aiming to remove Henry VI. Other revolts had had more in common with 1483, being led by 'higher-status' personnel with narrow political aims. The endemic revolts since York defied Henry VI in 1451, as with the 1387–8 and abortive 1400 and 1415 plots, had been aimed at removing the sovereign or his close advisers, and usually had been led by great magnates; the involvement of members of the northern gentry in the disturbances against Edward IV in 1469–70 had camouflaged secret backing by Warwick. Usually figures excluded from influence at court, or fearing for their power there, had been the ringleaders – as with York in 1451–5, the exiled Yorkist leadership in 1460, and Warwick in 1469–70. (In 1459 York was forced into defiance of a 'counter-coup' against his influence at court by the Queen's party.) Sometimes a prominent exile invaded to reclaim his rights, and was joined by sympathizers within the country – Henry of Bolingbroke in 1399, Warwick and Edward (IV) in 1460, Warwick in 1470, and Edward IV in 1471. The exiled Henry Tudor did sail to England to join in the 1483 revolt, but he was hardly in the same league as these men – he had never had influence at court to regain, or held a senior peerage (as opposed to claiming one, i.e. his father's Earldom of Richmond).

This time few senior alienated nobles were directly involved, apart from Queen Elizabeth Woodville's refugee son Thomas Grey, Marquis of Dorset (in hiding since Richard's coup of early May) and his Woodville uncles – and at a late stage the 'semi-detached' involvement of Buckingham (based in South Wales far from the main centres of revolt). The only senior figure in the immediate royal family implicated was Richard III's brother-in-law St Leger. It was former officials of Edward IV's Household and their friends and relations who led the revolt, some with Woodville associations such as Sir George Browne of Betchworth, the stepson of Rivers' fellow-victim Sir Thomas Vaughan, and assorted Hautes. Analysis of those involved shows a mixture of local family connections, a lack of strong pro-government magnates in the areas affected (e.g. the perennially restless Kent), some men with former service to Clarence as well as Edward IV, and little signs of involvement from anti-Yorkists except possibly a few Courtenays in Devon.[50] According to the contemporary Croyland Chronicler it was anger at Richard's coup and executions, added to by fears that the Princes had been murdered, that caused the revolt.[51]

The dates of Richard's replacement in office of those court office-holders who joined in are not clear enough to say that they acted in revenge after their dismissal or if they feared replacement. Apparently the involvement of Henry Tudor, in Brittany with no obvious links to the rebels, was the suggestion of his mother Lady Margaret Beaufort, who had been implicated in the 'Hastings conspiracy' against Richard in mid-June along with her current husband Sir Thomas Stanley (briefly arrested). Their ally Bishop Morton, Henry VII's future Archbishop of Canterbury and Lord Chancellor (and formerly a Lancastrian in 1470–1), had been arrested at the Council meeting of 13 June and placed in Buckingham's custody at Brecon; he presumably brought Buckingham into the plot. Given the physical and political distance between Buckingham and the other rebels, he was hardly a prime mover in the plot – quite apart from his close involvement with Richard in Edward V's deposition, which would have alienated him from the main body of rebels who would not have trusted him. His participation was clearly a late bonus to a plan hatched after Edward V's deposition and timed to be carried out while Richard was away from London on his post-coronation tour; probably Morton worked on his alienation from Richard while in custody. (Would Buckingham have revolted at all had Richard not entrusted Morton to him?) It remains a moot point whether it was remorse, calculation that Richard's unstable regime would not last long, or greed for the throne that was Buckingham's main motive, and as early as c. 1500 Polydore Vergil was writing to deny the probability of rumours that Buckingham's alleged conversion to Henry Tudor's cause had been a screen for his own bid for the throne.[52] More called a halt to his 'Life' of Richard III at the Buckingham rebellion and did not complete it; this was problematic as he could have portrayed the Duke as another victim of Richard's power-crazed duplicity who had nobly deserted the infanticide to back Henry Tudor. Did he discover that Buckingham's role was less creditable and decide to call off the biography sooner than damage his reputation and thus infuriate his son, the then-current Duke and a senior courtier?

The southern rebels were unlikely to succeed without backing from major magnates, even if they had temporarily secured control of London in Richard's absence – which seizure had not brought success to the non-aristocratic rebels of 1381 or 1450. In a parallel case, the senior noble anti-Henry VI rebels led by Warwick had taken London in an attack from Calais via Kent in 1460 but Queen Margaret had held out in northern England; Richard also had a northern power-base. Warwick had taken London as he revolted against Edward IV in 1469, but had not been sure of success until Edward's Welsh/south-western army had been defeated at Edgecote. Richard's reaction, however, stored up trouble for the future. His appointments to county offices across the south depended strongly on loyal 'outsiders' he had brought in from his extensive northern lands. Having brought an army south to intimidate London at the time of his coup and been keen to revisit the north as soon as possible on his summer progress of 1483, he never achieved as wide a degree of support and service among southern magnates as Edward IV had done.[53]

The number of actual exiles in Brittany and later France as a result of the southern English revolt was small, but Buckingham's revolt was a serious threat due to his Marcher tenantry and it was lucky for Richard that heavy rain flooded the Severn crossings, discomfited the rebel's men, and held him up long enough for Richard to gain the initiative. The rebel plan to co-ordinate the risings for 18 October– with Richard out of the way in the north and only John Howard, the new Duke of Norfolk, in charge in London – also failed and Norfolk was able to have enough warning to block the rebels' advance on the capital from Kent. Had better weather enabled Buckingham to cross the Severn and link up with the rebels in Devon and Wiltshire before Richard arrived from the north the outcome would have depended more on the new King's military capacity. Richard was an experienced commander and Buckingham was not, while the rebels in the south of England also lacked a 'professional' commander to make up for their inexperience – in 1485 the Tudor forces had John de Vere, Earl of Oxford, Warwick's lieutenant at Barnet in 1471.But Buckingham and the southern rebels combined would have posed as much of a threat to the northern forces loyal to Richard as the combined armies of Welsh and south-western troops (loyal to Edward IV) had done to the rebel Nevilles in the 1469 campaign – though the Nevilles had won the encounter, at Edgecote Field.

**Richard III in power: a dangerously isolated regime, or par for the late fifteenth century?**

When it is not seen in isolation, was Richard's position as of summer 1483 really that desperate? Are we too dependent on hindsight to assume that his overthrow in 1485 was inevitable? Buckingham, Richard's senior ally, like Warwick under Edward IV before 1469 or both Clarence and Richard under Edward after 1471, had been loaded with titles and office by a dependant sovereign. He was virtually unchallenged in Wales, controlling the vital Marcher lordships with their manpower; but Edward had given a similar role to Warwick (which had included the wardship of the underage Buckingham's lands). When Edward tried to build up William Herbert as a rival to the Earl, Warwick had him killed at the first opportunity. Edward also gave a dangerous local concentration of power in the north to Richard after 1471, amounting to a legally autonomous 'palatinate' on the Cumbrian frontier – though Richard was less likely to betray his brother Edward than Buckingham was to betray his cousin Richard. Buckingham's power indicated a danger to the Crown should he revolt.

Admittedly, the sovereign needed reliable allies with large resources to come to his assistance in an emergency, and relying on a major local magnate to 'bring in' his tenants from a large area was normal Late Medieval practice. In Northumberland (and to a lesser extent Durham and Yorkshire), Henry IV and later Henry VI had relied on the locally dominant Percies. A 'build-up' of lordships in a district in one family was a genealogical hazard, given the nature of early mortality of male heirs, which could unexpectedly bring extra lands to their sisters' or daughters' husbands. This was how Warwick had acquired his eponymous earldom, by the extinction of the Beauchamps in 1446; and his father the Earl of Salisbury had also inherited his earldom by female descent. A powerful family with large numbers of acquisitive sons – like the fifteenth century Nevilles – could amass heiresses to marry the boys and add to the family estates and titles. In addition, political 'in-fighting' at court meant a concentration of grants of lands and titles on a few 'reliable' candidates – a fault to which Henry VI was particularly prone (see above). The nature of the inter-nobility feuding of 1455–61 meant that Edward IV had a reduced 'pool' of trustable allies led by his close blood relatives and needed to bring in a few prestigious ex-supporters of Henry VI like the Beauforts if possible. Edward, an inexperienced youth, had had little option but to trust the available Henry Beaufort, Duke of Somerset, to govern Northumberland in the early 1460s (the local Percies were pro-Lancastrian) and to give similar authority in the Midlands and Yorkshire to his cousin Warwick, the senior figure in his mother's Neville family and a loyal ally in 1459–61, but it was unfortunate that both then revolted. His attempts to build up William Herbert, Earl of Pembroke, and his own

Woodville father-in-law as rival figures of importance only led to Warwick having the two of them executed during his first revolt. He did not learn his lesson about giving too much power to one man with Warwick, and gave Clarence and Richard similarly huge estates and powers after 1471.

Buckingham, one of the excluded senior nobles of part-royal blood in the 1470s, had to make do with a Woodville wife but no local posts, and may well have felt aggrieved and so taken his chance to show his support for Richard in spring 1483 in return for an understanding that he could control his local area (the Welsh Marches). His accumulation of offices in the Marches was a gamble that did not pay off for Richard, for whatever reason – a devious long-term plan to seize the Crown in which Richard was his pawn according to his modern detractors. Once Buckingham proved disloyal Richard fell back on a small group of supporters, among whom only Lord Lovell was a peer – hence the famous satirical rhyme by the Tudor agent William Collingbourne that:

> The Rat (Ratcliffe), the Cat (Catesby), and Lovell our dog Rule all England under the Hog (the Ricardian boar emblem).[54]

Technically Lovell, resident at Minster Lovell in Oxfordshire, was a peer; but he had few resources compared to the usual aristocratic families who the Crown relied on. Ratcliffe was from the Yorkshire gentry, and Catesby from the East Midlands. A similar group of much-criticized 'low-born' ministers had served Richard II in his final years, and Richard III elevated a new leading aristocratic supporter by granting the Dukedom of Norfolk with its estates to his ally Sir John Howard. His coronation was relatively well-attended, even if many peers from remote provinces must have set off for London expecting to be attending that of Edward V. But the only other two senior nobles to be entrusted with great office after autumn 1483 were Lord Stanley, who had already been arrested once as a Hastings partisan in June and was married to Margaret Beaufort but was the senior magnate in Lancashire, and Henry Percy, Earl of Northumberland, senior magnate in the north-east. At least one, if not both, of them betrayed him at Bosworth. But the fact is that Stanley had a long record of unreliability, not only to Richard; he had abandoned his brother-in-law Warwick's cause in 1471. Northumberland, who failed to bring his troops at the Bosworth battlefield into action, had already stood aside from Warwick's cause to let Edward IV march through Yorkshire unhindered in 1471.

The poor attendance of loyal peers at the royal camp at Bosworth in 1485 indicates a lack of willingness by potential supporters, which the controversial nature of the usurpation must have exacerbated. But this was not unusual or especially dangerous for Richard among mid-fifteenth century sovereigns. The way in which power and the Crown had changed hands frequently since 1455 was a warning to cautious magnates not to risk their lives and property by eagerness to support one particular candidate in battle, and Henry VI (really Warwick and Queen Margaret as his proxies) and Edward IV in 1471 had had a similar lack of support. On a lower social level, the Paston letters are full of indications of the anxieties of members of the 'middling' gentry over which royal candidate or senior noble to support in the case of a revolt and the risks of making a wrong choice and having your estates confiscated.[55] In 1487, there was not exactly a major 'turn-out' of peers to support Henry VII against the invasion of the Earl of Lincoln and his protégé 'Lambert Simnel', and Henry may have preferred to rely on a few trusted peers than on many unreliable ones. The level of violent inter-gentry feuding from c. 1450 to the early 1470s independent of high politics indicates a contempt for the supremacy of the law and the 'King's peace' inconceivable under a strong ruler who could concentrate on enforcing the law.

The use of private retinues as bodyguards and 'enforcers' in violent incidents is apparent from the time of the rash of incidents that preceded Henry VI's first period of incapacity in 1453, and has been linked to the return of large bodies of disgruntled demobilized soldiers from France after 1450. The actions of the Bonville family in the 1450s are among the most notorious of the era, and the like had not been seen since the turbulent early years of Edward II (another time of weak central power and a discredited monarchy). The Pastons were involved in a notorious feud with the more powerful Mowbray Dukes of Norfolk over the inheritance of Caister Castle, in which the armed might of the stronger party prevailed, well into the first reign of Edward IV when a vigorous young king should have been putting down such behaviour. In these circumstances, the fact that many local magnates able to raise troops did not bother to come to the King's camp in 1485 was a symptom of the general lack of central control by the monarchy rather than a personal reaction against Richard's alleged villainy, however much the rumours about his nephews were widely believed from early 1484. Neither Warwick/Henry VI nor Edward IV had attracted spontaneous mobilizations of eager adherents in 1470–1, as shown by the small size of the armies involved in their final confrontation.

**1485 and 1487: was Henry VII as short of support as Richard?**
At the time, no contemporary observer would have had a sense of Bosworth as a 'new beginning' and an end to the dynastic strife of the mid-fifteenth century, despite subsequent Tudor propaganda. It would have seemed another remarkable, but reversible, turn of events in an unstable country in the same pattern as Henry VI's 're-adeption' of autumn 1470. The difference was that the new government was more politically secure as its ousted

predecessor, Richard III, was dead unlike Edward IV had been in 1470; however, Henry Tudor lacked the political experience and local 'power-base' of Warwick and his brothers. He had been in exile for fourteen years, never held rank or acquired close political allies in England, and had as uneasy a relationship with 'defecting' Yorkists as Henry VI's regime had had with the defector Clarence in 1470. His predecessor's pardoned heir, the Earl of Lincoln, was to flee to the Continent in 1486 to join the next Yorkist rebellion as Clarence had deserted Edward IV in 1469 and Warwick in 1471. His new mother-in-law, Elizabeth Woodville, was shortly to be disgraced – possibly for plotting, possibly out of royal desire to seize her estates. He lacked Warwick's military reputation and skill, and was reliant on the veteran Lancastrian commander John de Vere, Earl of Oxford, who had been Warwick's lieutenant at the battle of Barnet in 1471, his stepfather Thomas Stanley, and the latter's brother Sir William Stanley. Indeed, within two years England was to be invaded again and Henry had to confront a Yorkist army in the Midlands, acting on behalf of an impostor impersonating the 'legitimate' heir (Clarence's son Edward).

Nor did Henry VII have a large-scale 'turn-out' to assist him in defending the new dynasty against the Simnel/Lincoln invasion in 1487. The latter army, based on a body of foreign mercenaries (German) like Henry's (French) in 1485, was able to march right across England from its isolated landing in the west (Simnel landed at Barrow-in-Furness, Henry at Milford Haven) to take on the King waiting for them in the East Midlands. If Richard's failure to tackle Henry – or send loyal troops to hold him up en route – before the pretender reached the East Midlands is an indication of weak support among the magnates, the same can be said of Henry in 1487. No pragmatic noblemen would have realized in 1487 that the Tudor regime would last for another 116 years; the precedents available to them would have suggested the possibility of another sudden reversal of fortune as in 1459–61 or 1470–1. As Richard depended on one senior supporter with military experience – Norfolk – as his main general in 1485, so in 1487 Henry depended on the Earl of Oxford (who had fought for Warwick at Barnet in 1471). Lincoln, Richard's nephew and senior commander of the rebels at Newark in 1487, was an untried young man in his mid-twenties like Henry had been in 1485 but had the advantage of having been named as Richard's heir when the King's son died in 1484. It was Simnel and Lincoln's defeat at Newark, not Bosworth, that established a period of comparative peace and security for the English Crown – and Henry still had to face the lesser threat of Warbeck in 1497. He was lucky in that Warbeck did not land in Cornwall until the most serious local threat of that year, the popular revolt against excessive taxes for the faraway Scots war, had already been put down. That large body of rebels, led by a blacksmith from

St Keverne and a minor lawyer in the populist tradition of Cade's Kentish revolt of 1450, reached Blackheath in their march on London.[56] As we have seen, some ex-Yorkists contemplated joining the rebels. Had Warbeck arrived from Scotland in time to promise redress and persuade them to accept him as their leader he would have had far more supporters than he could muster in reality. Nor should it be forgotten that the absence of revolt after 1497 was not necessarily a sign of 'inevitable' triumph by a wise and widely-accepted king. Henry may have been paranoid, but his intense fear of foreign-backed plots continued after 'Warbeck's execution and was centred on the escaped Edmund de la Pole, Lincoln's brother. The latter fled to the Continent in 1499, and Henry did all that he could to deny him the military aid that had been given to 'Simnel' and 'Warbeck. Finally, in 1506 Duke Philip of the Netherlands, the son of 'Warbeck's ex-host Emperor Maximilian, was driven ashore in Weymouth Bay by a storm and Henry 'invited' him to London for talks. Before Philip and his wife, Juana, left England they had agreed to have Edmund handed over, and the pretender languished in the Tower until the new King Henry VIII executed him a few years later. Fear of another Yorkist plot was not limited to the King either, as it was reliably reported that when his elder son, Arthur, died in 1502 senior nobles were discussing if the throne was secure for his second son Henry. The latter was only eleven, younger than Edward V had been in 1483, and his succession was not seen as secure. The witness was treasurer Sir Hugh Conway – speaking in the relative safety of Calais, but terrified of Henry VII's reaction if he was accused of discussing the succession seditiously.[57] One plausible adult alternative was said to be Duke Edward of Buckingham, the son of the 1483 rebel and direct descendant of Edward III's youngest son Thomas – and his boasts of his 'rights' apparently continued into Henry VIII's reign.[58] It is possible that some senior ministers rumoured to be in touch with Edmund de la Pole after his flight (e.g. Sir Richard Guildford, recently 'marginalized') were doing this as an 'insurance policy' just in case the regime crumbled – as senior figures at William III's court were to keep in touch with James II in the 1690s. Hindsight should not make us believe that the Tudor throne was seen as secure after 1499, especially once Henry VII's health declined after 1503. Certain of his extortionate ministers, e.g. Empson and Dudley, were as resented by nobles as Richard III had been.

### Bosworth: could Richard have won?

Richard, an experienced commander at Bosworth though dependent on his magnate allies, had the advantages of reputation, high ground, and possibly of numbers on 22 August 1485. (The actual battle-site is still not beyond doubt; the latest 2009 discoveries suggest a different site from the usual one.[59]) His wait in central England for his enemy to advance to meet him has been interpreted as a sign of weakness, and certainly none of his supposed allies moved to intercept Henry Tudor's small army when it emerged from the isolated Welsh hills into the Cheshire plain. But Richard's defensive strategy was only a repeat of that of Warwick's government when facing Edward IV's invasion (from Yorkshire) in 1471, and of Edward IV's when facing Warwick (from Devon) in September 1470. It gave him time to muster a larger army rather than hurry forward to take on the invader. Henry, like Richard II when facing Henry of Bolingbroke in 1399, was initially out of reach in western Wales, and could not be tackled safely until he reached the English lowlands. If Richard had moved forward to block Henry's exit from Wales at Shrewsbury, could he be sure that the Earl of Northumberland (son and grandson of Lancastrians killed by Richard's kin in 1455 and 1460) would not attack his rear?

Henry was a cautious man who had refused to land in Devon when he arrived to join the 1483 revolt, rightly fearing that the assurances of support he had had from on shore were insincere and he would be arrested. His August 1485 landing in his home country of Wales (in Jasper's Earldom of Pembroke) avoided that risk but meant that he had a long march into England. Marching to attack him as soon as he landed was not an option for Richard, given the distance to Milford Haven and the hostility of the landscape (and potentially the locals). Luckily for Henry the local magnate, Rhys ap Thomas, had politely refused to send his young son to Richard's court and could delay his reaction to the invasion, allow Henry to march into mid-Wales without resistance (or many recruits), and belatedly join him a week or so later. (The link between the two men was supposed to have been Rhys' ex-tutor Dr Lewis, now an agent of Henry's mother Margaret Beaufort, Lord Stanley.[60]) The failure to block Henry's advance into Shropshire and the Midlands lay with the principal magnate of Lancashire, who had enough armed tenants to do it – luckily for Henry, his stepfather Thomas Stanley. Stanley avoided joining either side ahead of Bosworth, although Richard was driven to make threats to execute his hostage son if he did not obey his sovereign. His brother Sir William apparently gave Henry enough private assurances of due – not immediate – support to persuade Henry to move on to attack Richard, which kept momentum with him and arguably gave him his only real hope of winning a battle.[61]

Richard may have commanded a wing at the battle of Barnet in 1471, aged eighteen, and he led armies against the Scots in the early 1480s, whereas Henry had never been on a battlefield and had spent the years 1471–84 as a minor diplomatic pawn of Duke Francis of Brittany, lodged under watch in his castles and at risk of being extradited to England. Henry's uncle Jasper

Tudor had military experience from the 1460s, as a long-standing Lancastrian commander in Wales who had held out at Harlech Castle for years after defeat by Sir William Herbert in 1461. The senior Lancastrian commander at Bosworth, Oxford, had commanded Warwick's left wing at Barnet in 1471 before years in exile; having failed to stir up revolt in Cornwall from his base on St Michael's Mount in the mid-1470s, he had been arrested by Edward IV and spent years more in prison near Calais before escaping. Richard faced a potential for treachery by Lord Stanley, the commander of the Lancashire and Cheshire area levies, as Henry Tudor's stepfather and a pardoned participant in the nebulous 'Hastings plot' of June 1483 – he had refused to take his troops to join Richard' s forces on the field. His brother Sir William Stanley was also strategically positioned with his levies near the battlefield (at what site is unclear), and joined his brother in attacking Richard when the King got into difficulties – and in 1495 was to be executed by Henry Tudor for apparent links with the Yorkist pretender Warbeck.

There was allegedly a warning to Norfolk beforehand that Richard was to be betrayed, presumably by the Stanleys. It is also uncertain if the Earl of Northumberland, commanding his north-eastern levies as part of the royal infantry, held back from following Richard down Ambien Hill into the melee out of cowardice or treachery. It should, however, be pointed out that the risk of commanders of the sections of a mid-fifteenth century army defecting to the opposition in the middle of a battle was not a special problem unique to Richard. At Barnet the Marquis of Montague, Warwick's brother, was found to be wearing the enemy colours under his armour when he was killed, possibly indicating an intention to defect when opportune; a few weeks later chaos among the Lancastrians at the battle of Tewkesbury allegedly led to one commander having his brains dashed out by another who feared he had been suborned by Edward IV.[62]

The battle of 'Bosworth', in fact of Sutton Cheney or Stoke Golding, is still contentious as it is not clear what positions the rival armies held and where. The battle took place adjacent to a 'marsh', which has since dried out, and scholarly argument has raged over which way the armies were facing. Richard was apparently to the north-east or north of Henry, who had marched out from Atherstone on Watling Street. But enough is agreed by the sources to make it clear that Richard had to attack Henry by moving west or south-west down from a hill – traditionally seen as Ambien Hill, though the latest finds of cannon-shot and royal badges are enough to cast this in doubt. It started poorly for the royal forces when Howard was killed leading the royal vanguard. The Stanleys did not yet join in on Henry's side and merely continued to disobey orders to move to the King's support It is unclear why Northumberland did not move his troops forward to aid Norfolk's men in breaking Henry's line, and it may have been due to geography rather than intended treason. Was the ground too marshy or the hill too steep for an advance on the royal army's right to reinforce the vanguard – or did Northumberland fear a Stanley attack on his flanks?

The two vanguards were left engaged on approximately equal terms in the centre, without Richard's forces being brought fully into action. Richard's were the more experienced and thus likelier to prevail in a long combat. But the King attempted to put the issue beyond doubt by a personally-led cavalry charge downhill against the pretender, presumably to pre-empt a Stanley advance to rescue the rebels. His frontal attack with his Household knights could have won the day – he got close enough to Henry to cut down his standard-bearer, Sir William Brandon, and several others who would have been near the invaders' leader. But, as would have been feared, both Stanleys then attacked Richard in the rear and he was surrounded and hacked down. Allegedly, he refused to escape in the few minutes available. But if the Stanleys had delayed for a few more minutes, Northumberland had moved into the fight with Richard to give him the advantage of numbers and thus dissuaded the Stanleys from intervening, and Richard had had the luck to reach Henry in time, the outcome of a personal combat between them would have been in little doubt. Those magnates who had hung back from the battle to see which way it went would have had no option but to hasten to the King's assistance with assurances of their support. Lacking a broad base of support and with his main general Norfolk dead, Richard would not have been able to risk punishing them for fear of causing more rebellions – Stanley controlled much of Lancashire and the Isle of Man, and Northumberland was head of the powerful Percy clan and crucial to the safety of the Border now Richard himself had moved south to London. Richard, like Henry VII in 1485 and 1487, would have had to make the most of what support he had among the peers and seek to establish a secure regime with the passive quiescence of men he knew he could not trust.

Richard had sought to project an image of himself as a man concerned with his subjects' welfare since 1483, acting swiftly to carry out justice, dealing with concerns raised in Parliament, and pointing out his moral standards and piety in contrast with the 'luxury' and immorality of his brother's reign. His use of moral issues in his propaganda was noted, with foes who had been known for their wild living at Edward IV's luxurious court (e.g. the Marquis of Dorset) being placarded as immoral and Edward IV's ex-mistress Elizabeth/Jane Shore having to do penance as a whore. Richard's sympathetic biographers, Paul Murray Kendall (1955) in particular, have paid extensive tribute to his abilities, public-spiritedness, and hard work as king. His critics have, however, noted his obsessiveness with sin and his extensive founding of chantries, and analysis of his personal 'Book of Hours' has pointed out the hints at a sense of guilt – and a personal devotion to St Julian who had killed his relatives. His loss was particularly lamented in York, the centre of his power, where the Council records paid him a generous tribute.[63]

### Richard III's policies after Bosworth: would he have been more insecure than Henry VII?

As unchallenged king from 1485 Richard would have continued these policies, sincerely or not, and with Henry Tudor dead or in flight to France he would have faced no major challenges for at least several years. The unusual and disquieting circumstances of his removal of a legitimate sovereign meant that, like the similarly-placed Henry IV, he would not have been secure from a series of potential challenges even after one crushing victory. The continuing acquiescence of Elizabeth Woodville and powerlessness of her 1483 southern English allies could not be taken for granted, and it is indicative of Richard's sense of this dynastic threat that even before his ailing wife died in winter 1484–5 the idea was floated that he should marry the Princes' sister Elizabeth. It is unclear if he was ever serious or just raising the issue to see if this drastic solution to his dynastic illegitimacy was possible, but the fact that it was considered despite the 'sin' of incest involved indicates his (or his supporters') sense of weakness and need to neutralize Edward IV's children as a threat. The marriage would have been rare for medieval Europe and particularly since the introduction of Church canon law, the main known examples of a similar uncle-niece dynastic alliance having been in Rome (Claudius and Agrippina) and Byzantium (Heraclius and Martina). Unfortunately, neither had ended well – Agrippina had murdered Claudius and some of Martina's children by her uncle had been born disabled. The next outbreak of uncle-niece marriages was to occur among the Habsburgs, as a measure to keep their vast inheritance within the family – Philip II married his niece, Anne, in the 1570s. (The Church did not seek to prevent this 'incest', but its champion Philip was in a stronger position than Richard III was in 1485.) Marriage among first cousins was more normal, and was common practice among the Spanish and Portuguese royalty. Richard and his brother George of Clarence both married their first cousin's (Warwick) daughters, Anne and Isabel Neville. Reaction at court and among the 'political nation' to any idea of his marrying Elizabeth of York was so hostile that Richard was forced to deny that it had ever been seriously considered. Some modern writers also think that the apparent enthusiasm of Princess Elizabeth for a marriage – and her appeal to Howard for support – refers to a planned Portuguese marriage, not to her marrying her uncle.[64] His return to the idea after a victory at Bosworth was possible, given his ruthlessness and the fact that the possible rebellion that Catesby and Ratcliffe had warned could follow the marriage was now impractical.

After Bosworth he would have been unwise to have dared to carry out the marriage even to consolidate his links with the 'legitimist' cause represented by his nieces and to prevent more Edwardian Household loyalists plotting to raise a pretender against him as Elizabeth of York's next fiancé. Any foreign prince who was married to Elizabeth could now be a target for plotters seeking to use him to depose Richard. All of Edward IV's daughters could not be removed as political threats by putting them in nunneries; logically, the best solution was to marry Elizabeth to Richard's own chosen heir John, Earl of Lincoln (about two years her senior). Richard, like Henry after 1485, would have been marrying off Edward IV's daughters to his own loyal supporters as they became old enough – probably mostly northern magnates. The Duke of Norfolk's grandson Thomas Howard (born c. 1478), married to Elizabeth of York's sister Anne in real life, would have been one obvious candidate. The girls would have made better matches than they did under Henry VII, though foreign marital agreements would have been more difficult than under Edward IV as the issue of their 'bastardy' had now come into the open, which would have made foreign suitors conscious of rank wary of marrying them.

The English Crown, unlike the Scottish, had not passed by female descent since the twelfth century (1135, aborted by a challenger, and 1154), although Edward IV could claim descent from Edward III in female as well as male lines. When Richard II had named his heir as Edmund Mortimer in 1398–9 that had legitimized female descent, as Edmund was the grandson of the daughter of Edward III's second surviving son Lionel; but Henry IV's accession had overturned this. Edward IV's father Richard of York had returned to the Mortimer claim as his excuse for usurpation in 1460 – and been opposed in the House of Lords by most of the nobility. Once Richard III's son Edward died in 1484 he was left with the choice for heir of his attainted brother Clarence's young son Edward, born in 1475 – who may or may not have been weak-minded – or his sister Elizabeth de la Pole's eldest son John, born around 1464, and chose the latter. Indeed, it has been argued recently that Richard's marriage in (?) 1472 to Anne Neville, within the proscribed degrees of dynastic affinity, did not have an adequate legal permit so his son's succession could have been challenged if the latter had lived. Is it possible that if Prince Edward had not died in 1484 and Richard III had died in the 1490s or 1500s, the new King would have been open to challenges about his legitimacy? Richard III's actions in dragging up obscure legal claims to justify a naked 'power-grab' in 1483 would then have come to haunt his dynasty as his son faced a challenge on similar grounds – perhaps by John, Earl of Lincoln.

Richard III would need to re-marry as soon as possible to produce his own heirs, and would be advised to choose a foreign princess, which would mean a long delay during diplomatic arrangements. In the meantime John, Earl of Lincoln, would succeed if he died suddenly. The succession of John as King John II would have been unusual though as 'legitimate' as the Yorkists claiming the throne in 1460–1 by female descent from Edward III's second son Lionel or as Richard II naming Lionel's great-grandson as his heir in 1398. It was possibly capable of touching off a revolt by a rival who could also claim royal descent, such as a member of the Stafford and Bourchier families (descendants of Edward III's younger sons) or a supporter of Clarence's son.

### Rival heirs: Clarence's son and Edward IV's daughters

Edward Earl of Warwick, born in 1475, was the focus of the initial Yorkist plots against Henry VIII and was to be kept in the Tower for twenty-four years and finally executed on a trumped-up charge of plotting to escape with Perkin Warbeck in 1499. The execution may have troubled Henry and was widely seen as unjust; in terms of 'realpolitik' it halted Yorkist threats on Warwick's behalf and may have been secretly insisted on by the sovereigns of Aragon and Castile, Ferdinand and Isabella, as part of their marital alliance with Henry. It is unclear if Warwick was really feeble-minded in 1499 or only naïve from long incarceration in the Tower, but as an inexperienced youth lacking military experience he could not have been a serious threat to the veteran Richard in the 1490s – or even to Lincoln as the new king – except as the puppet of disgruntled nobles. It is unclear if Richard had ever seriously considered Warwick as an heir in 1484, the sources being contradictory, and in practical terms Lincoln was older and thus more able to succeed securely if Richard died before any new royal offspring of a second marriage reached maturity. Lincoln had already had some administrative experience as head of the Council in the north, and would have continued to acquire titles and offices into the 1490s – possibly in the role of chief supporter in the north that Richard had held under Edward IV. In due course similar powers could be given to his younger brothers Edmund and Richard, born around 1466–70, and other royal stalwarts should have included Norfolk's son Thomas, Earl of Surrey (born c. 1445).

There is the possibility that the question of Edward IV's marriage would have continued to hang over the English Crown, with Elizabeth of York's husband a potential threat to Richard or his heir unless she had been sent abroad to an allied prince. The Yorkist ally Maximilian of Habsburg, stepson of Richard's sister Margaret of Burgundy, had a son (Philip, born 1478), but he was twelve years younger than Elizabeth and is unlikely to have been a candidate given his father's prior concern with a Spanish alliance. Her original engagement to Charles VIII of France had already been broken by his father, and a cordial Franco-English rapprochement is unlikely given their probable clashes over Brittany around 1488. Elizabeth Woodville could have continued to intrigue against Richard unless she had been found to have encouraged Henry Tudor in 1485 and been pensioned off minus her income to Bermondsey Abbey as in real-life 1487. Even if her eldest daughter had been married to Lincoln or some accommodating foreign prince, Elizabeth Woodville could have encouraged another daughter's husband to depose Richard and take the Crown – or overcome her probable enmity to Clarence's family to attempt to marry one of her daughters to Warwick. Any forced reconciliation between a politic Richard and a chastened Elizabeth Woodville after 1485, with her son the Marquis of Dorset recalled (if not killed fighting for Henry Tudor) and an attempt to win back Edward IV's disgruntled ex-Household men, might have led to attempts to press for the legitimization of Edward IV's daughters – who foreign princes would be reluctant to accept as wives if they were illegitimate. The King could then have legitimated them as personal concessions rather than by having to cancel his contentious law *Titulus Regius* that had bastardized them, while making it clear that they had no legal claim on the Crown – as the Beauforts were legitimated in 1396 but barred from the succession. The death of Lincoln preceding Richard's cannot be ruled out, possibly in battle on Richard's behalf against the Scots or French, and in that case Richard would have had to make a choice between Lincoln's next brother Edmund de la Pole and the younger Warwick, Clarence's son, as his heir. Reinstating Warwick would have necessitated reversing his father's attainder of 1478.

### Would Richard marry again after 1485?

Richard was only thirty-two in August 1485, and had plenty of time to marry again and father heirs who could be adult before he died. Assuming that he did not dare to solve the conundrum of Edward IV's delegitimized daughters by marrying Elizabeth of York himself, he would have been looking for a foreign princess to cement an alliance after the diplomatic isolation that had afflicted England since the rapprochement between Louis XI and Maximilian of Burgundy (Habsburg). There were no Scots princesses available, quite apart from James III's hostility towards Richard for the 1482 invasion, and the young Charles VIII of France's sisters were married. The daughters of Ferdinand and Isabella were too young (the eldest, born in 1470, was ear-marked for the more important King of Portugal), as was Margaret, the daughter of Maximilian and Mary of Burgundy, born in 1480. As of summer 1485, a marriage between Richard and the Portuguese princess Juana (b. 1452) was being explored as part of the 'deal' that would have married off Elizabeth of York to Prince Manuel – with the ubiquitous Sir Edward Brampton as the 'go-between'. The devout Juana, later to be known as 'the 'Holy Princess', would have shared Richard's strong and ostentatious morality.[65]

One possible solution was the heiress of Brittany, Francis II's daughter Anne (born in 1476), the Duke's chief minister Landois having obligingly tried to aid Richard in 1484 by handing over Henry Tudor who had to flee to France. (The Breton ducal house was descended from Edward I.) This would entail a long wait for children, but England had been a long-term ally of Breton independence from France (involving a civil war in the 1350s) and Brittany was strategically vital. Unlike in the fourteenth and early fifteenth centuries, there was no multitude of sovereign ducal houses in the Low Countries that England could use for a marital alliance – the territories had been united under the House of Burgundy and had then passed via Richard's sister Margaret's stepdaughter (Mary) to the Habsburgs.

Marrying Anne would end the current French attempts to secure Anne for King Charles and unite Brittany with France, though it would have entailed a war with France over control of the Duchy. The real-life Breton succession-crisis erupted in 1488, long enough after Bosworth for Richard to be looking around for a foreign war to bolster his regime and soon enough for him to have still been unmarried. In addition, Richard had been a rare critic of Edward IV for allowing Louis XI to buy him off during the invasion of France in 1475, and had refused a generous 'present' from Louis for his acquiescence; he had been noted for past hostility to French power and to a peaceful settlement with the country. In 1488/9 France was a credible target for a Continental expedition, quite apart from having sheltered and funded Henry Tudor. Richard was capable of leading an expedition to France himself, either to Brittany to secure the borders from French invasion or to Picardy to link up with Maximilian for a more successful version of the 1475 invasion. Ultimately, an expedition to Picardy was most likely to end up bogged down in sieges with the Habsburg prince losing his enthusiasm for the war, though Richard was likelier than the less martial Henry VII in 1492 to have fought a long war and have taken one or two towns (Boulogne or Tournai?). The logical course of a war in Artois was to extend the English 'Pale', as Henry VIII was to attempt in 1513–14 and 1544.

It would need a long English commitment, as in the early 1350s, to secure Brittany against a determined French attack backed by some local nobles and force the French King, an inexperienced teenager at this time, to accept any 'union of crowns' between Ricardian England and Brittany. In real life Henry VII sent a small force to assist Brittany in 1488, commanded by the rehabilitated Sir Edward Woodville, and had to abandon the project; but the vigorous and determined Richard could have fought a war with France lasting several years and with luck have secured Anne's person and hand (had the pro-French faction not kidnapped her and carried her off to be married to Charles VIII). English troops could then have remained in Brittany to ensure that the French did not invade, and Richard had the prestige of success against the national enemy without the expense of a long war. The Bretons being noted for their independent spirit, it would have had to be agreed by Richard and the Breton Estates that the two countries would be governed separately. Presumably if Richard and Anne had had two or more children, one would succeed to England and one to Brittany.

## Other aspects of foreign policy and the succession

The deposition of James III of Scotland by a magnate revolt on his son's behalf would have been likely to take England by surprise under Richard as it did under Henry. Richard had had long personal experience of fighting in southern Scotland, though also of Scots nobles and princes going back on their promises. Concentrating on France and Brittany in 1488–9, he would have been unable to take advantage of the situation but could subsequently have threatened invasion and induced the new King to marry an English princess (possibly one of Edward IV's daughters as the late King had planned, possibly Clarence's daughter Margaret). Richard had a valuable resource for international diplomacy in his nieces, provided that their illegitimacy (or not) was not an insuperable bar for status-conscious foreign princes. Given that the Princes were still missing and any reversal of *Titulus Regius* on the girls' behalf would imply that Richard had been wrong to declare them all bastards and might have had the Princes killed as well, it would be easier for a special Parliamentary Act to declare the Princesses legitimated without rights on the succession. If Richard was still childless and his heir Warwick or Lincoln was intended to marry Elizabeth of York, this sort of resolution would aid their union as a reconciliation with partisans of Edward IV's children. Whether Richard would have felt confident enough to grant more southern sheriffdoms, keeperships of royal estates, and other positions of local power to the local gentry instead of key northerners is uncertain and would probably have depended on the risks of new revolts. Without such conciliatory gestures the chances of revolt would have been higher, particularly if Henry Tudor had still been at large and had been backed by France in retaliation for Richard's 'interference' in Brittany. Richard would have needed to build up loyal magnates to control the south of England from the threat of revolt or invasion (East Anglia would have been under the control of John Howard's son Thomas, second Duke of Norfolk, disgraced in real life by Henry VII.) But granting extensive lands and titles to newcomers not of ancient – or local – birth would have run the same risks of abuse for the 'parvenus' as Richard II faced for his 'duketti' in 1397–9.

The usurpations of Henry IV and Edward IV had been controversial, but armed force and the acquiescence of most of the magnates had kept them on their thrones for their lifetimes (though Edward had had to regain his once). Provided that his health survived better than Henry IV's, Richard would have had the advantage of having seen off his main challengers in 1483 and 1485 and his success would have disconcerted potential opponents. If he had married a princess nearer his age than Anne of Brittany, or even an English relative from among the senior aristocratic families, he could have had several adult sons by the mid-1500s. The husband or sons of Elizabeth of York would have posed a threat to Richard's children, with the question of Edward IV's marriage unresolved whatever the legal fictions that Richard had enacted about it, and some ambitious noble or a foreign power could have sponsored a pretender claiming to be Edward V or his brother in the 1490s. The likeliest offender was France, as the real-life backers of the pretender 'Warbeck' were Richard's sister Margaret and probable ally Maximilian – who would have been Richard's supporters. If Richard was to be killed in battle or die naturally leaving young children, there was a strong chance of another civil war with Warwick, Lincoln or his brother(s), and a husband of one of Edward IV's daughters involved. But with luck Richard III could have lived into his sixties and died as late as 1515 or 1520, after a long and successful reign that had started no more rockily than Edward III's did in 1327–30, Henry IV's in 1399–1405, or Henry VII's in 1485–7. The convenient death of the King's predecessor had thrown shadows over the reigns of the first two, though at least they had been able to produce the deposed sovereign's bodies (there is a question over the case of Edward II[66]) and pretend that they had died naturally.

The question of his nephews' murder would have continued to hang over his dynasty, but there is less likelihood under Richard III's own rule (or that of his son) of any writers in England daring to mention it openly. If the story of Tyrrell being commissioned by Richard to organize the murder during the post-coronation 'progress' was true, Tyrrell would not have been talking about it as he would have remained a loyal, probably well-bribed supporter of Richard and not been arrested for treason in 1502. He would have hidden his secret and at the most told his family who might have been willing to talk about it after Richard was dead. Richard could hardly have replied to any invasion by a French-backed 'Edward V' by producing the body of the real ex-King and claiming that he had been killed by Tudor agents, even assuming that Richard knew where the bodies had been buried. As with Henry VII, the problems outweighed the benefits of reminding people about the disappearances. If, on the other hand, Buckingham or Tyrell had smuggled the princes abroad, one of them could have asked for the French aid as an adult – but been unable to prove their authenticity? Even if Richard's death, around 1500 or 1510, led to another civil war no husband of one of the sisters of 'Princes' (or Warwick) would have wanted to publicize the idea that they might still be alive and available as a rival contender. Nobody (except the French or a surviving Henry Tudor in exile?) would have had a motive to publish stories about the murder as long as Richard was alive and king.

The Ricardian regime might well have outlived those few senior courtiers who knew the truth, and nobody have been left alive with knowledge of events by the time that the matter was considered by some historian – conceivably More himself – once Richard was dead. The King would have had an unsavoury reputation, but the scandal have been as conveniently ignored in English politics as were the mysterious and convenient 'natural' deaths of Edward II, Richard II, and Henry VI. Unlike that trio or the 'martyred' Thomas of Lancaster, there would have been no shrine to serve as a potentially embarrassing centre for criticism of the current dynasty. Even his successor might well have found the episode too embarrassing to refer to it, unless that ruler – a husband of one of Edward IV's daughters? – had his own reasons to blacken Richard's name. The chances of any bodies being recovered in 1674 would have been minimal, and the mystery would have been even more insoluble than in reality.

## Chapter Six

# The Afterglow of the 'Sun of York', 1485–1525: A Possible Yorkist Restoration?

**August 1485 – early 1486: a weaker royal position than 1461 or 1471?**

Contrary to later simplification, the battle of Bosworth was not the 'end of the Wars of the Roses'. This was the image presented by Shakespeare, as mooted by the 1548 Tudor chronicler John Hall, with the battle as the end of a cycle of vicious dynastic feuding and Henry VII restoring harmony by marrying Edward IV's eldest daughter, Elizabeth of York. It was a neat and logical ending to the thirty years of political instability, but – as mentioned in the previous section – the truth is rather more messy. Bosworth solved nothing, as like Mortimer's Cross and Towton (1461) or Barnet and Tewkesbury (1471) it left one regime deposed by military force but potential rivals for the throne still alive. After 22 August 1485 Henry swiftly had his lieutenant Sir Reginald Bray collect Princess Elizabeth, his promised bride, and Clarence's son the Earl of Warwick from Sheriff Hutton Castle and escort them to London so neither could be used by refugee Yorkists as a pretender; he also had the adherence of Richard III's nephew and presumed heir, John de la Pole, Earl of Lincoln.[1] Richard's closest ally, Lord Lovell, had disappeared and was clearly intent on escaping to do further mischief, but ended up in sanctuary at Colchester Abbey[2] rather than raising a rebel army to hold out in a remote location as Queen Margaret did in Northumberland after Towton and Jasper Tudor did in North Wales after Mortimer's Cross. Of Richard's two senior commanders at Bosworth, the Duke of Norfolk was dead (and his son Thomas, Earl of Surrey, in custody) and the Earl of Northumberland had possibly failed to support Richard in battle and duly swore allegiance to Henry but was given no immediate trust.[3] The other two members of Lovell's alleged triumvirate, Ratcliffe and Catesby, were dead – the first killed in the battle and the second executed afterwards. But was this 'clean sweep' of opponents any more impressive than Edward IV's in 1471? The battles of Barnet and Tewkesbury had also left the defeated faction in disarray minus its existing leadership – Prince Edward, Warwick 'the Kingmaker', Lord Montague, and Lord Wenlock were killed in or after the battles, Queen Margaret was in custody, the Duke of Somerset was executed, and Henry VI was disposed of and then claimed to have died naturally. The Lancastrian cause had been crushed for twelve years and in 1483 had only been revived when new pretender Henry Tudor (not even of fully legitimate royal blood) allied himself to the revolt of Edward IV's 'loyalists' against the usurper Richard III. The autumn 1483 revolt had at least started out in the deposed Edward V's name and once he was presumed dead Henry still had to promise to marry his sister and heiress (Elizabeth) to hitch the Lancastrian cause to that of Richard's enemies. Arguably, the Yorkist cause was no worse off in 1485 than their enemies' cause had been in 1471; and it had the bonus of at least one adult male Yorkist claimant, the Earl of Lincoln, pardoned and active at court ready to defect from the (temporary?) winners. He duly did so despite all the rewards Henry had given him and fled to Burgundy early in 1487 as a new Yorkist claimant emerged there.[4] The young Earl of Warwick, Clarence's ten-year-old son, was in the Tower but if not executed could be used as a figurehead; on past precedent he could be released by defecting court politicians during an uprising as Archbishop Neville had released Henry VI in the 1470 revolt. Notably Lincoln defected just after Henry had paraded Warwick in public – thus he knew that new pretender Simnel, aka 'Warwick', was a fake.

Moreover, Henry VII had a far weaker claim to the throne than Edward IV had had in 1461 and 1471 – he claimed the throne by right of his Beaufort descent, his mother, Margaret, being the daughter of John, Earl/ Marquis of Somerset (d. 1444), eldest son of the eldest son of the third marriage of John 'of Gaunt'. As mentioned earlier, the problem with this was that all John's Beaufort children were born illegitimate, in the lifetime of his second wife Catherine of Castile, and were legitimated but excluded from claiming the throne by Act of Parliament in 1396.[5] In fact, Margaret should have been proclaimed queen herself by this argument, and her resignation of her claim in her son's favour was never legally confirmed;[6] it was presumed that only a man could rule and/ or an adult male war-leader was needed for turbulent times. The only female ruler of England to date had been the disastrously contentious and allegedly arrogant Empress Matilda, Henry I's legal heir who was recognized as such by his vassals at his request but superseded by her cousin Stephen on her father's death in 1135 and only ruled 'de facto' briefly in 1141 before a successful revolt drove her out of London. Henry could also claim the throne by unofficial 'right of conquest', i.e. proof of Divine support, as Henry IV had done in 1399 when he superseded the arguably superior legal claim of the under-age Edmund Mortimer.[7]

Ingeniously, Henry VII dated his reign from 21 August, the day before the battle of Bosworth,[8] so he could claim that everyone who had fought for Richard III had committed treason and would therefore forfeit their lands if they did not surrender and swear allegiance to him – his subtle use of legal blackmail was well-established from his accession.

His claim on the loyalties of the remaining Yorkist adherents was centred on his Christmas Day 1483 oath at Rennes Cathedral to marry Elizabeth of York, as heiress of Edward IV, if her brothers were presumed dead. He duly did this as promised, but there were two legal problems – which explain the delay in the marriage from his arrival in London (3 September) to 18 January 1486.[9] This was not due to the insecure new King preferring to have himself crowned first (30 October)[10] so as to assert the primacy of his personal right to the throne and head off any Yorkist attempt to make him merely a 'king consort'; for one thing he and his leading adherents had to have their past attainders reversed by Parliament (which met on 7 November) and for another Parliament and the judges had to invalidate Richard III's Act *Titulus Regius*, which had bastardized Elizabeth and her sisters. As seen above, this contentious legal centrepiece of the Ricardian usurpation had exhibited (or invented?) the story of Edward IV's 'pre-contract' to marry Eleanor Butler, making his marriage to Elizabeth Woodville illegal, and it had to be reversed to make Elizabeth of York legally the heiress of her father and the transmitter of his claims to the throne. But reversing it also restored the rights of Edward V and his brother Richard if they were still alive – and the indications are that Henry had no idea if this was true or not. As a result, the indictment of Richard III as a usurping tyrant referred to him as someone who had committed 'infanticide' without giving names or dates,[11] and if the story that Sir Thomas More was to record c. 1510 about Sir James Tyrrell doing the murders was already current he was not treated as a scapegoat and forced to confess. Instead, he was pardoned – twice in quick succession – for unspecified crimes committed under Richard and removed from the country to serve as commander at Guisnes Castle, near Calais. Indeed, when *Titulus Regius'* was struck from the legal records as invalid its contents were not listed, as would have been normal practice; the judges recommended to Parliament that when they cancelled it by a new Act its scandalous contents were not mentioned. Similarly, everyone possessing a copy of it was required to hand it in by April 1486 or else – a clear attempt at a 'cover-up'.[12] (It is significant that Henry ordered Bishop Stillington, allegedly the witness to Edward and Eleanor's pre-contract and certainly the man cited as such by Richard III, to be arrested as soon as he took the throne.[13]) This indicates that Henry feared that the question of the alleged Butler betrothal was unable to be conclusively settled and so suppressed it. The two linked questions of Elizabeth's illegitimacy and the potential survival of her missing brothers made Henry's position far more unstable than Edward IV's had been in 1461 or 1471 – the question of whether Edward was illegitimate does not seem to have been raised until later. The matter of Henry and Elizabeth being fourth cousins and so needing a Church court decree of absolution before they could marry – or even a papal ruling, which would take longer to obtain – was also a cause for delay. In fact, the decree was granted just before they married so the King clearly intended to marry as soon as it was legally 'safe' to do so. There is thus no question of Henry seriously considering abandoning his oath to marry Elizabeth once he was on the throne; if he had done so the chances were that her mother, Elizabeth Woodville, and half-brother the Marquis of Dorset would have quickly been plotting to place another Yorkist claimant on the throne as Elizabeth's husband. Lincoln was the obvious choice, Warwick being nine years Elizabeth's junior.

As far as the political situation appeared in early 1486, the battle of Bosworth was merely another reversal of fortunes in the perennially unstable English kingdom – which was almost unique in Europe at this period for coups among its elite and appeared to be in modern parlance a potential 'failed state'. There was stable dynastic descent from one ruler to another, usually father to son, in France, Burgundy, and the states of the Iberian peninsula; the major and minor sub-states of the Holy Roman Empire were usually inherited by the legal heir, although they could be partitioned among brothers or cousins; and in the British Isles itself the new Stewart dynasty of Scotland from 1371 saw direct succession of father by son, even in a minority (though James III's brother Alexander attempted to subvert this in 1482). A dynasty that ended in female succession could have problems as potential husbands for the heiress or her male relatives tried to seize power, as faced by Hungary and Poland after 1382 and by Naples after 1343 and 1414; and in these circumstances an 'excluded' royal cousin such as Henry VII could seize the throne. There were also coups against 'tyrants' or underage rulers in Italy, most notably in Milan in the late fifteenth century – though the Duchy there was a relatively new polity and not as secure as the kingdom of England. 'Separatism' was also a problem in some multiple dynastic states, particularly in Sweden (where resistance to the 1397 'Union of Kalmar' meant that the merger of Denmark, Norway and Sweden was repeatedly challenged) and Poland-Lithuania where the nobles of the latter preferred to be ruled by their own Duke not by the absentee King of Poland. But the repeated dynastic coups in England since 1455 were only matched by the instability of the Grand Duchy of Moscow, where the weak Vassily II (ruled 1425–62) was repeatedly removed by his uncle and then his cousins in the 1430s and 1440s.

## The first plots and 'Lambert Simnel', 1486–7

As of 1486, there was no guarantee that the endemic instability in England was over; and indeed even that spring there were abortive plots to raise a Yorkist rebellion in the Midlands, as arranged by the veteran Edwardian loyalist Sir Humphrey Stafford of Grafton, Warwickshire, and aided by Lord Lovell from sanctuary.[14] There was some sort of plot to raise a rebellion in Yorkshire, heartland of Richard III's estates and home of much of his 'affinity', where his death had been recorded with defiant written declared sorrow in the official records of the city of York.[15] Henry's local 'strongman', the Earl of Northumberland, seems to have been unable to secure the loyalty of his subordinates, possibly out of anger that he had betrayed his King at Bosworth. As a result the new King had to make an unexpected progress north to York, and there was a plan to assassinate him when he arrived in the city – apparently involving Lovell, who had escaped from sanctuary in Colchester without detection and headed north (possibly to Richard III's old home, Middleham Castle). En route Henry was warned by Bray that Lovell was planning to flee sanctuary, but when he received Bray's informant Sir Hugh Conway he discounted the story.[16] It is surprising that he had not stationed men around Colchester Abbey to keep Lovell safe, as he was to do to Stafford and his brother Thomas when they fled to sanctuary a few weeks later and to 'Perkin Warbeck' at Beaulieu Abbey in 1497. Presumably he thought Lovell likelier to flee abroad than to launch a coup.

The murder plot, possibly involving Lovell in person, was prevented at the last minute by the detection of the would-be assassin, either at High Mass in the Minster or later at a banquet in the Archbishop's palace.[17] Had the plot succeeded, the plotters apparently intended to proclaim Warwick as king, presumably hoping he would not be killed by the Tudor adherents as soon as the news reached the Tower of London, and the Stafford brothers would raise the tenantry of Warwick's West Midlands estates. (Their home at Grafton was near Warwick Castle so some would have been known to them personally.) If the plan had succeeded there would have been chaos in London as Henry had no son and heir yet and his only male kinsman, his uncle Jasper Tudor (now Duke of Bedford), had no claim to the throne; presumably Margaret Beaufort would have had to defer to Elizabeth of York as the new queen sooner than split the regime's adherents by claiming the throne. The West Midlands rising by Stafford and his brother Thomas went ahead, but was put down; they fled to sanctuary at Abingdon Abbey's 'cell' at Culham near Oxford but were dragged out and tried for treason. The Abbot, John Sante, dared to speak up for them and claim that the breach of sanctuary was illegal; he was to be involved in a further Yorkist plot so he was clearly not merely defending Church rights. Humphrey was executed on 8

July and his quarters displayed in the Midlands but Thomas was pardoned on the scaffold in the first of the Tudor 'set-pieces' of State executions.[18] The revolt in Yorkshire opened as planned, but soon disintegrated as Henry issued promises of pardon; according to his 1620s biographer Sir Francis Bacon (using the contemporary Polydore Vergil's account) Henry had believed that the rebels were 'left-overs' from Bosworth and had been surprised to find them a serious threat. A riot, planned to co-ordinate with the date of the murder plot and the Stafford revolt, occurred at the same time in London as a mob displaying the heraldic badges of the Earl of Warwick assembled at Highbury but it was dispersed.[19] Lovell now fled north-west to join Sir Thomas Broughton, a Yorkist stalwart, at his isolated house at Broughton-in-Furness. The latter's participation in the Simnel plotters' invasion (which landed nearby) a few months later implies that he and Lovell would have been planning together and that when Lovell soon fled abroad to Burgundy Broughton promised to aid an invasion.[20] Lovell now joined Richard III's sister Margaret, Dowager Duchess of Burgundy, who held her court at Malines in the Low Countries. One modern theory has linked Lovell and his 'hideout' at Colchester Abbey to a presumed 'son' of Richard III, the later Kent labourer 'Richard Plantagenet' who was recorded in the 1720s as having claimed to have been brought to see the King at Bosworth by an unnamed 'lord' (Lovell?), told that Richard was his father and would acknowledge him if he won the battle, and then to have fled into hiding and hidden his identity, training as a bricklayer. This man, who died at Eastwell (ironically, a Victorian royal residence) in 1550, may have been connected to the Abbey and have worked later at its sub-priory, Creake in Norfolk, as 'Richard Grey' – though he is unlikely to have been Edward IV's son Richard, as David Baldwin suggests.[21] But if he was known or available to Lovell as a potential pretender in 1486 – he was then about fifteen – he was not used, and the new King was to arrest Richard III's openly acknowledged bastard John of Pontefract and to execute him in 1490.[22]

The potential for 'Richard Plantagenet' as a focus for revolt in 1486 was thus unlikely, and in any case the adult Earl of Lincoln or the teenage captive Warwick were the acknowledged Yorkist heirs. Instead, the next conspiracy focussed on an obscure youth known to posterity as 'Lambert Simnel', apparently aged around ten in 1486/7[23] – whose unusual name has led to suggestions that it was a pseudonym. The very fact of his emergence suggests the weakness of Henry's regime and/or the determination of its opponents; Edward IV had been on the throne for eight years before he faced a serious revolt in his 'heartland', in 1469, though the Lancastrian remnants in Northumberland had held onto isolated strongholds in 1461–2 and had risen in revolt again several times until 1464 aided by the Scots and

French. As of 1486 Henry had had no opportunity to make serious mistakes and alienate senior supporters, as Edward IV had done in 1464–5 by announcing his secret marriage to Elizabeth Woodville and then in 1465–9 by building up the power of his Queen's relatives. 'Simnel', an organ-maker's son, appears to have been trained in courtly manners and set up as a pretender by an obscure Oxford priest called Richard Symons/Symonds, whether or not with local backing, and was presented as the Earl of Warwick.[24] The latter was really in the Tower, but his survival there may have been dubious to contemporary rumour considering what had happened recently to his cousins Edward V and Prince Richard. Was Symonds relying on the real Earl being dead, or was 'Simnel' an 'insurance-policy' for use in a planned rising – there was no point in Henry killing the real Warwick before rescue as then the pretender would assume his identity.

The boy was now smuggled abroad to Dublin, where the weakly-supported new regime had had to keep on the loyal Yorkist partisan Gerald, Earl of Kildare – greatest feudal Anglo-Irish magnate of the 'Pale' – as its Lord Lieutenant in 1485 despite his probable disloyalty. The attention and justice that Richard III's father had displayed in Dublin as Lord Lieutenant in the late 1440s had paid dividends for the Yorkists ever since; York and his adherents had fled there after Queen Margaret's attack on Ludlow in 1459 and Edward IV and Richard III had had no trouble from the island. Dublin was clearly teeming with Yorkist adherents, and Symons and his 'Earl of Warwick' received a warm welcome from assorted senior local lords. The news was taken to London in February 1487, just as writs had been sent to Cornwall and Devon for the arrest of several prominent local gentry headed by Sir Hugh Bodrugan. (The latter was said by local legend to have escaped capture by jumping his horse over a cliff at 'Bodrugan's Leap'.[25]) Henry had the real Warwick taken out of the Tower and paraded through London to a meeting of the Church Convocation, where assorted senior clerics (led by the Chancellor, Archbishop Morton) could vouch for his being genuine. He then spent the night with Morton at Lambeth Palace and was taken on to the royal country residence at Sheen (i.e. the later Richmond) up the Thames to be shown to the court.[26] But this precaution did not stop the treachery of the Earl of Lincoln – the alternative Yorkist claimant to Warwick. Lincoln had been present at a Council meeting to discuss what to do about Simnel and had spoken to the genuine Warwick at the Convocation, so he knew that the boy was a fake; nevertheless at the end of the Council discussions on 9 March he headed home to Suffolk and immediately took ship for Duchess Margaret's court.[27] On 19 March, according to Lincoln's attainder, he was meeting unknown persons – probably Lovell and/ or Duchess Margaret – in Flanders. Meanwhile, his servants were tracked by royal agents on an apparent mission to Hull and Yorkshire with saddlebags full of gold, no doubt recruiting more rebels.[28]

The defection of Lincoln was a major blow to Henry and gave the planned rising a credible military leader as well as an alternative candidate to the throne to Warwick, should the latter be murdered or set aside as too young or barred by reason of Clarence's 1478 attainder. Indeed, it was subsequently claimed that Lovell had come to see Lincoln during the royal visit to York, shortly before the planned attack on the King, and asked him to join in the plot but had been turned down as the attack was too risky.[29] The prospect of a successful revolt would have been increased then had Lovell succeeded in attracting Lincoln's support. It was perhaps a little odd that Lincoln should set aside his own claims to the throne in favour of an untried boy of eleven or twelve – but, like the Duke of Buckingham in 1483, he may have hoped to supersede his allies' pretender later in the rebellion. He also knew Simnel to be a fake; but he and Lovell may have intended to supersede the Oxford youth by the real Warwick once they had rescued the latter, a twist of plan worthy of Anthony Hope's *Prisoner of Zenda*. The most surprising potential ally for the plot was, however, ex-Queen Elizabeth Woodville, who suddenly had all her lands and property seized at the time of the plot's discovery in February 1487 and was required to retire to the apartments of the Queen Dowager at Bermondsey Abbey near London for the rest of her life. The reason given was that she had betrayed the Christmas 1483 agreement with Henry by proposing to arrange marriages for her daughters (including Elizabeth of York) with Richard III;[30] but Henry had known that when he took the throne and had then restored all the lands that Richard had taken from her. She had been welcomed back to court, and had been in attendance at Henry's son Prince Arthur's baptism at Winchester Cathedral in September 1486 as the baby's godmother.

Why did Henry wait until February 1487 to strip her of her lands? Some historians have argued that she was in ill-health (she was aged around fifty and died five years later) and genuinely wanted to retire from court; and she was to receive some future signs of royal goodwill such as a Christmas present of fifty marks in 1490. In November 1487 he was to propose her as a potential wife for the widowed King James III of Scotland (fifteen years her junior), which admittedly would get her out of the country for good; and in November 1489 she was summoned to court to meet a visiting French relative.[31] But all these acts may have been signs of necessary political goodwill and 'normality' in the royal family to impress observers; the previous Queen-Mother 'exiled' to Bermondsey Abbey, Henry's grandmother Catherine of Valois, had recently had her secret second marriage and children exposed and died a few months after her 'retirement'.[32] There is a strong possibility that Henry's mother and principal adviser, Margaret Beaufort, did not get on with the ex-Queen, her successful rival for court power in the 1470s, and their rapprochement over the Henry–Elizabeth betrothal of December 1483 had been out of political necessity and mutual dislike of Richard III. There was not room for two formidable matriarchs at the Tudor court by this argument, and Margaret made sure that Henry removed his meddling mother-in-law – who may have been angry at the long delay before Henry had his wife crowned.[33] It would seem illogical for Elizabeth Woodville to retaliate by planning to dethrone her son-in-law, particularly in favour of the son of the Duke of Clarence who had threatened her, her royal sons, and her husband's position in 1477–8. (According to one theory discussed earlier, she had even been responsible for having Clarence killed.) She would hardly have believed Simnel to be the genuine Warwick, nor was she likely to have been on good terms with Richard III's chosen heir, Lincoln – supplanter of both her royal sons (assuming they were alive) and her daughter. It has been suggested that she could have intended to have Henry murdered or forced into exile so her daughter, the Queen, could re-marry – Lincoln or the genuine Warwick? – and retain her title, with Elizabeth Woodville not Margaret Beaufort as the new 'power behind the throne'.[34] One theory even has it that Simnel was a 'stalking-horse' for the real Edward V, alive and hidden in exile as Elizabeth Woodville knew, and that the boy who was to land in England and lead the rebel army at Stoke Field in 1487 was not the Oxford Simnel but the older ex-King, installed in his place. The boy captured at Stoke was said to be around fifteen – older than Simnel – and some Irish rebels had said that they were fighting to 'restore' the King, i.e. to restore Edward V.[35] But this is unlikely in the extreme; it is more probable that the ex-Queen was targeted by the suspicious Margaret Beaufort as a potential 'kingmaker' for Warwick (on good grounds or not) and that Henry wanted to secure her property for himself.

Whether or not Elizabeth Woodville was hedging her bets in case Lincoln and the fake Warwick won the forthcoming conflict, the Yorkist plan now proceeded to invasion thanks to military support from Duchess Margaret. Given that Henry was an ally of France and had hired mercenaries from there in 1485, France's rival Maximilian (sole ruler of Burgundy since his wife's death in 1482) had no reason to interfere in Henry's favour. On 5 May Lincoln and Lovell landed from the Low Countries in Ireland, with 2,000 Swabian and Swiss mercenaries loaned by Duchess Margaret under a professional commander, Martin Schwartz. This was equivalent to the aid that Charles VIII's French regency had given to Henry in 1485 – and unlike Henry in Wales in 1485 the invaders had a substantial body of local Anglo-

'Celtic' nobles waiting to join them. Kildare and his allies welcomed them to Dublin, as did a body of English Yorkist refugees, including Bodrugan and the ex-commander of the Calais garrison, Thomas David. The Church under the Archbishop of Dublin recognized Simnel as the Earl of Warwick, and on 26 May (Whit Sunday) he was proclaimed as rightful king by the Bishop of Meath at Christchurch Cathedral and then crowned as 'Edward VI' by him with a circlet taken from a statue of the Virgin Mary at a nearby church.[36] (The theory that Simnel was really Edward V does not explain why in that case he was not crowned under his real identity, avoiding muddle later.) The Archbishop of Armagh stayed away, but to all intents and purposes Simnel and his controllers were as firmly in charge of Ireland as the refugee Duke of York had been in 1459–60; as in 1460, invasion of England was the next move. The last claimant to be King of England who had been crowned outside London due to a 'usurper' occupying the city had been the child Henry III (crowned at Gloucester) in 1216, when Prince Louis of France held London – and that had not stopped him from going on to regain the lost areas of his kingdom later. He had been re-crowned in Westminster Abbey in 1220 after winning the civil war – and possibly Simnel would have been re-crowned later in a similar manner. But the *Chronicle of Calais* and Polydore Vergil heard that Lincoln intended to supersede him in case of victory.[37]

The Yorkist army landed in Furness in Lancashire, safely cut off from loyalist territory by the Fells and by Morecambe Bay, on 4 June. They first landed on Foulney Island off shore to occupy undefended Peel Castle, indicating caution in case of loyalists in the vicinity, and then were welcomed to the mainland by local Sir Thomas Broughton – Lincoln's host and fellow-plotter in 1486.[38] As of 8 May Henry was at Kenilworth Castle awaiting invasion, well-placed in central England as Richard III had been in 1485 but also facing a rebel force that landed in an isolated region and was able to advance across mountains to central England unopposed. The situation appeared to be one of *déjà vu* from 1485, or even from Warwick's invasion of south-west England in 1470, and there was no guarantee that all the great lords would be more loyal to Henry than they had been to Edward IV and Richard III. In these circumstances, it is perhaps surprising that Henry had not summoned most of the garrison of Calais to aid him, as this compact and fully-trained body of 6–700 troops could make all the difference. Or did he fear treachery from them? Lincoln's small army marched unopposed across the Pennines into Yorkshire, joined by the two Lord Scropes (of Bolton and Masham) – who later claimed their tenants had forced them to do so – and by Thomas Metcalfe of Knappa, Edward Franke of Knighton, Sir Robert Percy of Scotton, Sir Ralph Assheton of Fritton-in-Redesdale, and Sir

Edmund Hastings of Pickering. Tenants of Jervaulx Abbey may also have been involved. They defeated a smaller Tudor loyalist force under Lord Clifford on the night of 10 June at Bramham Moor, scene of a crucial Lancastrian victory against rebel Percies in 1408, but failed to secure entry to York when the two Lords Scrope attacked a gate on the 12th. The loyalist Earl of Northumberland was nearby with his tenants, which may have stiffened resistance; but York's civic authorities had a record of caution and in 1471 had only admitted Edward IV on his return to England when he assured them that he was only seeking his legal rights as Duke of York, not to depose the current King Henry VI.

Overall, the rebels seem to have had around 8–10,000 men by the time they reached Yorkshire, a larger force than Edward IV had had in 1471 (until the Duke of Clarence defected to him) and twice what Henry had had in 1485. They failed to build up momentum, at least according to Bacon's assessment, and possibly the uncouth appearance and reputed savagery of their Irish contingent was partly to blame.[39] (Using 'uncivilized' troops from the 'Celtic fringes' had also harmed Queen Margaret's recruitment as she marched on London with a Scottish contingent early in 1461.) Apparently Schwartz, the most professional soldier in the invading army with experience of battles on the Continent, had expected – and relied on – a far larger body of recruits from England to bolster his troops and complained to Lincoln that the latter had tricked him about local enthusiasm. He was thus expecting to lose an encounter due to lack of men before he encountered the royal army.[40] The fact that Lincoln lacked the 'hard core' of dedicated and experienced veterans from the gentry class, plus veteran aristocrats, which Edward and Henry had had in 1471 and 1485 was a problem too – men such as Broughton and Percy were hardly the potential 'inner core' of a future regime such as Lord Hastings had been for Edward and Bray and Giles Daubeny for Henry. Their absence may also have put off potential recruits from the gentry class, as implying that the invasion was not thought likely to succeed; though Henry's French mercenaries of 1485 had not had the reputed experience and skill of Schwartz's men. It was also useful when a major magnate went over to the invaders, as Clarence had done and as Lord Montague had done for his invading brother Warwick 'the Kingmaker' in 1470 – or stood back, as Derby and his brother had done from joining Richard's camp in 1485.

The invaders, however, had the advantage of speed, as the Swabian/Swiss mercenaries and presumably most of the few local landed gentry recruits had horses and the Irish infantry were used to long-distance 'jogging' in attendance to their lords' campaigns at home. They could thus maintain momentum towards the waiting royal army, and had the better of three days of clashes with a smaller waiting royal force under Lord Scales south of Doncaster on 12–14 June. The latter were probably only meant to delay their advance and give the King time to choose his battlefield and receive reinforcements. As they retreated through Sherwood Forest they left the road to the River Trent open, and later on 14 June Lincoln's army crossed the unguarded river at Fiskerton to camp for the night near the village of East Stoke.[41] In the meantime, Henry and the royal army had left Kenilworth on news of the rebel landing to march north-east via Leicester and Loughborough, but surprisingly got lost en route to Nottingham in woods on 12 June. On the 14th they arrived in Nottingham to join up with 6000 reinforcements sent by Henry's stepfather, the Earl of Derby (the crucial Ricardian defector at Bosworth), commanded by his son Lord Strange (who Richard had threatened to execute before Bosworth).[42] The royal army then marched along the ridge beside the Trent to face the rebels outside Stoke the following day. According to the 1548 chronicler Hall the King was aware of all that the rebels were doing and intended to do via his spies,[43] and thus knew how large and (in)experienced an army he faced.

### The Battle of Stoke: a close-run thing?
The resultant Battle of Stoke has been reassessed as the real last armed encounter of the 'Wars of the Roses', as mentioned earlier, and had similarities to Bosworth. But little is known of precise events, or of the exact size of the armies. The King had around 12,000 men, the main contingents being from the Earl of Oxford, his commander-in-chief at Bosworth and a veteran of Barnet (where he had defeated the opposing section of Edward IV's army); Derby; the Earls of Shrewsbury and Devon; and his uncle the Duke of Bedford with his Welshmen. All were reliable, with Derby the only well-known 'turncoat' and unlikely to desert his own son-in-law; no repeat of Bosworth was thus likely. Lincoln had around 9000 men, and relied heavily on the 2000 experienced and well-armed Continentals; by past precedent the Irish would have been badly-armed and without much protective clothing, enthusiastic in the charge but very vulnerable to the better-armed English knights and tenantry. Henry sent Oxford and the vanguard – around 6000 men – ahead of him towards the foe while he hung back, evidently keen to avoid being exposed to a charge of the enemy cavalry intent on winning the battle by killing him as seen at Bosworth. Thus Lincoln could not repeat his uncle Richard's tactic at Bosworth, and had to carve his way through Oxford's compact body of well-armed troops first. Apparently, Henry's main army had not yet formed up when Lincoln launched a headlong attack on Oxford's vanguard, hoping to use the disciplined German/ Swiss pikemen with their famous long javelins plus

the ferocious Irishmen to smash through the enemy line. This combined the 'phalanx' tactic of a compact, bristling 'hedgehog' square of infantry, which enemy cavalry could not penetrate and less-well-trained infantry could not push back, with the 'Highland' charge. The 'phalanx' tactic had worked well for the Swiss when facing the Burgundian feudal cavalry in 1477, smashing Duke Charles' army and leaving their general dead, and was to achieve further victories into the sixteenth century – but did Lincoln have enough men?

In the event, the Yorkist charge unnerved part of the royal vanguard who fled, but most held firm and Oxford was able to use his archers to wreak havoc on the poorly-protected Irish. As seen at Barnet and Bosworth, Oxford had plenty of experience in handling a determined attack by a large body of men. Nevertheless, it took around two hours for the royal army to prevail over the determined enemy assault, and as the Irish casualty rate soared the Germans/ Swiss lost heart too. Finally, after around three hours the Irish broke, the Continentals followed them, and the rebel army began running back down the ridge towards the River Trent to get away from the pursuit. A substantial body was caught and massacred in a narrow lane (duly named the 'Red Gutter') en route, and many more were drowned in the river or picked off as they tried to swim across. Around 4000, that is up to half the Yorkist force, were killed – including almost all their leadership such as Lincoln, Schwartz, Kildare's brother Sir Thomas Fitzgerald of Lackagh, and Sir Robert Percy.[44] Hastings was pardoned, the two Lords Scrope were arrested and imprisoned but released after paying fines, and Broughton escaped to Scotland.[45]

Lovell was last seen trying to swim his horse across the Trent, and his complete disappearance led to him entering legend; he was supposed to have fled into hiding at his house in Minster Lovell, Oxfordshire, and two centuries later a body was allegedly found in a sealed-up room there. Did he accidentally become shut in his subterranean hideout and starve to death? Romantic writers and the novelist John Buchan (in *The Blanket of the Dark*) made the most of the lurid Gothic tale, but it is unproven.[46] More prosaically, Lovell was granted a permit to enter Scotland as a refugee in 1488,[47] though apparently he never took it up so it is likely that he was known to be alive months after the battle and then failed to make it to Scotland as originally planned. Symonds and the pretender were taken alive; as the meddling priest had 'benefit of clergy' he could not be executed but was imprisoned for life. As recorded by Polydore Vergil, Henry used a sense of humour and mild contempt in employing the captured but harmless Simnel as a turnspit in the royal kitchens and twenty years later he was still in his service as a falconer.[48] Apparently, a few years later when Henry was entertaining some of the pardoned Irish lords who had backed Simnel he called on their ex-king to serve them wine and told them that they would be crowning apes next.[49] More to the point, Kildare was so powerful in Dublin and Henry so short of resources that he had to be pardoned when a – small – royal army under Sir Richard Edgcumbe arrived in Ireland in summer 1488.[50] He held onto his post as Lord Lieutenant for several more years, his pro-Lancastrian rival the Earl of Desmond not having adequate armed tenants or allied lords to be risked as his replacement. The bishops who had backed Simnel were, however, excommunicated by the Pope at Henry's request.[51]

### And had Henry lost the battle of Stoke...?

Lincoln's tactics at Stoke failed, as much due to the experienced nature of the opposing commander – Oxford – as to his lack of numbers. He had had a larger army than the previous insurgent to take on a king on the battlefield, Henry, had had, and unlike him had been a veteran of at least one major battle (Bosworth). However, the crucial facts were that Oxford's disciplined vanguard failed to break either in the first impetus of Lincoln's attack – though some of it did flee – or during the next two hours of close combat. Had the vanguard broken in the first impetus of the enemy's charge it would probably have doomed Henry's army, as the rest of his troops were not yet ready to engage and panic would have been infectious. The cautious Henry was not the sort of general to try to reverse a losing battle by charging into the enemy leadership as Richard III had done; nor did he have the experience to keep his nerve as one 'wing' fled as Edward IV and Richard had done at Barnet. It is unlikely that his senior commanders would have defected to Lincoln in order to save their skins, or that they were deliberately hanging back from engaging, as some historians have suggested[52] – men such as Jasper Tudor, Derby, and the Earl of Devon could expect no mercy from their long-time foes in the Yorkist ranks. There is a difficulty over the fact that Henry did not order the rest of his army to back Oxford up and/or to advance around the flanks and take Lincoln in the rear, but left Oxford to fight on alone;[53] did he fear desertions or did Oxford assure that he could handle the attack himself? Also, the full strength of the royal army at around 12,000 was far from the potential total of troops that all senior royal 'tenants-in-chief' within reach of Kenilworth as of early June 1487 could provide. Many senior peers did not join the royal army, either while waiting at Kenilworth in May or after the rebel landing on 4 June – although Lincoln advanced so fast that some who were summoned may have been unable to reach Henry in time. The question arises – did Henry not summon his full strength for fear of defections as Richard had suffered in 1485? Did he prefer to rely on a few trustable vassals than a large, unwieldy and potentially treacherous gathering?

If Henry relied on a smaller army than he could have summoned in order to be sure of its loyalty, the tactic nearly ended in disaster. If the entire vanguard had fled at the first attack by the Continentals and Irish, Henry does not seem to have had the rest of his army drawn up and would probably have had to retreat. The royal army could have disintegrated as it was perceived to be losing, and the loyal Jasper Tudor, Derby, and Devon had retained too small a body of experienced tenants to withstand the advancing Yorkists. It is extremely unlikely, however, that Henry would have got himself killed in a heroic last stand – he was too cautious a man for that and was apparently about a mile behind Oxford's vanguard as the enemy attacked them, giving him time to withdraw if necessary. As in 1471 after Tewkesbury, he would have been likely to flee abroad – again, with Jasper Tudor as his principal supporter. The probability is that Margaret Beaufort would have seen to it that Queen Elizabeth was forcibly evacuated to friendly France with Prince Arthur, rather than risking her joining up with ex-partisans of her late father and uncle to be divorced and then remarried to a Yorkist king. As the Yorkist heiress, Elizabeth was a valuable prize and was more likely to have been married off to Lincoln (two years her senior) than to Warwick (nine years her junior). No doubt Elizabeth Woodville would have changed sides again to return to her Yorkist allegiance, and if the Queen had left for France it is possible that the latter's next sister, Cecily, would have been chosen as replacement 'prize' and Yorkist heiress to be married off to either Lincoln or Warwick.

The question cannot be answered definitively as to whether Lincoln would have allowed the 'crowned King Edward', i.e. Warwick (real or fake?) to assume the throne of England or reclaimed it for himself as 'John II'. He was adult, aged around twenty-three, and the coronation of 'Warwick' (i.e. Simnel) in Dublin would not have been definitive for the latter's claim as his Irish partisans had less politico-military weight than the German/ Swiss 'landsknechts' and the English Yorkist gentry. If Henry VII had fled the country and both Lincoln and Lovell had agreed that Lincoln should be king, the Irish peers present in the Yorkist camp – who did not include Kildare himself – would have had to accept it, however unwillingly. If Henry's partisans in London had murdered the genuine Warwick to deny him to the victors, a Machiavellian tactic that men like Sir Reginald Bray (or even Archbishop Morton?) were capable of, the fake 'Warwick' would have had a problem if Lincoln and Lovell, knowing that he was not genuine, had pointed out that he could easily be exposed and ruined. If the real Warwick had been released as the captive Henry VI had been released by Archbishop

Neville as his rival fled in 1470, then probably he would have been substituted for Simnel by the victors. Could some ex-Yorkist senior Churchman such as Bishop Alcock, recently Chancellor and formerly Edward V's tutor, be relied upon to persuade the panicking Henrican Council to release Warwick so as to obtain the advancing rebels' gratitude and pardon if Henry had already fled the country – or would Morton have insisted on carrying off Warwick into exile as a hostage?

'King Edward VI', i.e. the real or possibly fake Warwick, would have been twelve in 1487 and so needed a 'governor' (personal guardian) or even a 'Protector' – if memories of Richard III's behaviour had not doomed that office for a few decades. The senior royal male kinsman available was the usual choice for this role, and so it would have gone to Lincoln. Archbishop Morton would have been sacked as Chancellor as he was so closely tied to the Lancastrian cause on account of his activities in 1483–7, despite his loyalty to Edward IV in 1471–83. Possibly a move would have been made to confiscate his archbishopric too, and either Alcock or Bishop John Russell would have been the probable new Chancellor. Rotherham, now in his late sixties and already superseded as Chancellor so possibly declining in capability, would have remained Archbishop of York. If Warwick had been on the throne the role of principal female 'power-broker' would have gone to Elizabeth Woodville – an irony if she had been responsible for having his father, Clarence, killed. She may have regained her role as 'Queen Mother' if either Elizabeth or Cecily of York was married off to Lincoln or Warwick, and in any case would have regained all her property, which Henry had recently confiscated. If Lincoln was king, he was less likely than Warwick to have been amenable to her advice and power-broking activities.

All the acts of attainder passed on Richard III's partisans after Bosworth would have been overturned, though some Henricans who were politically invaluable such as the Earl of Northumberland (not present at Stoke) would have been likely to retain all their lands and posts. Lord Derby, as Richard's betrayer at Bosworth and the husband of the ex-King's mother, would have been the main 'loser' and if not killed at Stoke would have had to flee the country; his brother Sir William Stanley, as Henry's Lord Chamberlain and another Bosworth defector, would have faced similar Yorkist enmity. (As events turned out, he was not entirely lost to the Yorkist cause and apparently offered support to 'Perkin Warbeck' a few years later.) Lacking senior Yorkist peers, Lincoln or Warwick would have probably called on the son of Richard's late commander-in-chief, the Duke of Norfolk – Thomas Howard, Earl of Surrey (b. 1443), a veteran of Barnet and Bosworth and put in the Tower by Henry in 1487. In real life Henry only slowly restored some of the extensive Norfolk (ex-Mowbray) lands given to him by Richard; he became Lord Treasurer in 1501, and the Dukedom was finally restored by Henry VIII after he had won the battle of Flodden in 1513. He could have expected a quicker restoration to favour from a new Yorkist regime – and his son Thomas, given Edward IV's younger daughter Anne by Henry VII, could still have expected this sort of prestigious match. Lincoln would have brought his father's de la Pole Suffolk lands into the royal fisc if he was king when the latter died (in real life, in 1491). The Tudor-confiscated lands of the Dukedoms of York and Gloucester would have been the King's, plus the Dukedom of Lancaster and Margaret Beaufort's lands – and would York have gone to his next brother Edmund? The question of whether Warwick was mentally sub-normal and thus would have been as much of a 'figurehead' as King 'Edward VI' as Henry VI was in the 1450s cannot be answered, given that his naivety and ignorance as a Tower prisoner in the 1499 plot to free him was possibly due to his being kept incommunicado for so long.[54] Being kept away from political activities or the senior court figures for many years as a hostage had also been the fate of Henry VII in 1471–83, without effect on his political skills once he had had opportunities to learn and to take action.

It is apparent that King 'John II', i.e. Lincoln, would have been a more active ruler in his first years as king after 1487, possibly facing a hostile French government harbouring Henry VII and having to rely on the Burgundian alliance to stop another French-backed invasion. It is unlikely that Henry would have had the nerve to invade again for years, with or without French troops, given his habitual caution; and his expected power-base of Wales would have had to be removed from Jasper Tudor and given back to a Yorkist magnate. Unfortunately, the Herberts, on whom Edward IV and Richard III had relied, were extinct in the senior line; possibly the late Duke of Buckingham's son Edward (b. 1478), as Elizabeth Woodville's nephew, would have been raised up as a 'figurehead' for the Stafford/Bohun tenantry to rally round. Elizabeth's younger brothers Sir Edward Woodville and Sir Richard Woodville could have expected more rewards than they had obtained from Henry, as could her son by her first marriage, the Marquis of Dorset (who had tried to desert Henry in 1484–5). In the aftermath of yet another spin of the royal 'wheel of fortune' and deposition of another king in 1487 – the sixth in thirty years – England would have seemed even more unstable than it did in the real-life 1490s, and either 'Edward VI' or 'John II' would have had to rely on a narrow base of committed and partisan peers to hold off another attack from Continent-based opponents. At least John/Lincoln could have relied heavily on his next brother Edmund de la Pole, already adult by 1488 as he was born in 1470/1 and able to share the burdens of military campaigning, though he would have been short of reliable senior pro-Yorkist peers experienced in battle due to the losses of 1483–5. There were also two younger brothers, Richard and Geoffrey – and though the latter proved a weak character in real life, betraying his brothers to Henry VIII in return for his life after his arrest as a 'plotter', Richard was a determined opponent of Henry in exile as the 'White Rose' pretender and died in battle at Pavia in 1525.[55] Richard at least would have proved a valuable henchman to John or to Warwick as king, and John as king would logically have given him a major bloc of lands plus a duchy (perhaps the confiscated Dukedom of Bedford or of Lancaster). Assuming John as king to have married one of Edward IV's older daughters, born by 1475, they should have had a son and heir in the 1490s and if John had died before the boy reached his majority Edmund or Richard would have wielded power as regent or 'Protector'.

### Perkin Warbeck: the second chance to depose Henry VII

*(i) The background*
The Simnel/ Lincoln/ Lovell revolt of 1487 was a straightforward provincial revolt plus foreign invasion by an 'excluded' royal relative against a hopefully weak King, in the tradition of 1460, 1470, 1471, 1483 and 1485. But the next case of a Yorkist pretender, the enigmatic 'Perkin Warbeck', was more unusual – and his real identity was even more contentious than that of Simnel. For one thing, he or his backers, decided that he would assume the identity of Edward IV's younger son, Duke Richard of York, last seen in the Tower of London and never conclusively proved to be dead – and Henry VII's cancellation of *Titulus Regius* put Richard back in the line of succession should he turn up, ahead of Henry's wife. Unlike the case of Warwick, Henry could not produce the genuine Duke to prove the pretender to be a fraud – though he made a show of treating Warbeck with as much contempt as he had done to Simnel, calling him a 'feigned lad'[56] and boasting to foreign visitors that his agents had discovered that he was the son of a Flemish boatman.[57] After Warbeck's appearance at Cork in 1491 he was apparently taken in hand by a Devon merchant called John Taylor, ex-servant of the Duke of Clarence and mastermind of the plot to smuggle the latter's son abroad in 1477/8, and deputy Mayor of Cork John Atwater, aided by local Yorkist merchants and Irish lords. Taylor had already been involved in a nebulous plot in September 1491 to rescue Warwick from the Tower, concerning which Taylor had written an encouraging letter to a fellow-Devonian ex-employee of Clarence's, John Hayes, speaking of aid from two places abroad (possibly France and Flanders).[58] The King was now at war with Charles VIII's regency in France over control of Brittany, where his ex-

host Duke Francis II had died in 1488, and the French had seized hold of his heiress, Anne of Brittany, to marry their King and forcibly taken over the state. As a result, the French despatched a small army to Ireland in autumn 1491 to raise a second rebellion in Warwick's name, but achieved little – and unlike in 1487 the invaders did not even have a pretender in tow. Therefore, the discovery by Taylor and his local supporter Atwater of a 'Yorkist prince lookalike' in Cork, visiting merchant Pregent Meno's servant, was a godsend. They considered who to pass Warbeck off as, and apparently thought of Warwick and of an illegitimate son of Richard III before settling on Prince Richard. But was this merely coincidence, or was Warbeck's presence in Ireland not as much of a whim as he claimed in his 1497 'confession'? Had his previous employer Brampton put him up to it? And as Brampton had been pardoned, did Henry order his role to be 'forgotten'?

The timing of the French expedition to Ireland and the first thoughts of Taylor and Atwater about another 'fake Warwick' imply that the King's problems would have been worse in 1491 if a mysterious plan to rescue the real Warwick in January 1490 had succeeded – there would have been a better pretender available. As with so much of the murky world of 1490s plots, we only know about this conspiracy from the subsequent legal documentation of it on the government side – in this case the indictments of the alleged plotters for treason. Edward Franke, former Sheriff of Berkshire and a Yorkist veteran of Bosworth and Stoke who had been put in the Tower after the latter but had escaped, was apparently lurking in London and he and a priest, Thomas Rothwell, met a fellow-enthusiast from Abingdon called John Mayne in the capital on 1 December 1489 to plan the escape. The latter then went to his home town to contact the sympathetic Abbot Sante, host of the sanctuary-seeking Stafford brothers in 1486, who promised them a sum of money and suggested laying a false trail to lure the authorities to Colchester (where Lovell had hidden in 1485–6) when the Earl was rescued. The so-called 'Sante Plot' got no further as someone informed the regime and all the above were arrested; Mayne and Franke were executed but Sante (after a large fine) and the monk who had brought his money to the London plotters were pardoned.[59] We cannot tell how far advanced the plot was, but certain facts recur in other plots too – circles of conspirators in London, the Abingdon area (not far from Minster Lovell and Lincoln's old home at Ewelme), and the presumption of subverting guards in the Tower to rescue Warwick. The latter was to recur in 1499. Had the plot succeeded and Warwick been spirited away, he could then have been available for Taylor and the French to use in Ireland in 1491 and for Maximilian to use as a pawn in 1493–4 as he was to do with Warbeck. A genuine Warwick would have been of more import than a dubious 'Prince Richard', but still would have had difficulty in securing the throne unless he had substantial foreign military aid – which Maximilian did not give Warbeck.

Despite aid from the principal local Anglo-Irish magnate, the Earl of Desmond (limited due to his lameness), the Yorkists and French could not make any military headway in Ireland in 1491, though contact was made with King James IV of Scotland. This time Kildare, wary of his narrow escape from ruin in 1487–8 and his kinsmen's deaths at Stoke, held aloof; so if he had not already learnt his lesson by a previous failure would he have been more willing to revolt? Without a Simnel expedition to Ireland in 1486–7, would Kildare have joined Desmond (a rival for power) and secured Dublin for the fake 'Richard IV'? In due course French ships arrived to evacuate the expedition, and Warbeck and his sponsors were taken to France where he was recognized as 'Richard IV'. On board the ships was the Tudor defector, Etienne Fryon, recently Henry's French secretary, and he and Taylor between them probably knew enough about court life to transform and coach Warbeck into a convincing 'prince' with appropriately detailed 'memories' of his 'past life at court'.[60] As with the equally convincing 'Grand Duchess Anastasia', aka Anna Anderson, in the 1920s–1980s and her alleged memories of the Romanov court and ability to recognize 'old friends' and 'relatives', the pretender was not short of allies experienced at the courts of their 'father' who could have filled in any gaps in their 'memories'. At any rate, that was what their detractors could point out.

The Treaty of Etaples between Henry and the French government in December 1492 meant that the latter had to expel Warbeck, and he moved on to the Low Countries. As Duchess Margaret had sent troops to aid Simnel, so both she and her stepson-in-law Maximilian of Habsburg recognized Warbeck as the rightful King of England; and when Henry's relationship with Maximilian deteriorated due to his rapprochement with France the latter invited Warbeck to his court and paraded him as 'King Richard IV' with a bodyguard decked out in Yorkist livery.[61] Warbeck was received as rightful king at the State funeral of Maximilian's father, Emperor Frederick III, and was given a royal residence at Malines where exiled Yorkist plotters congregated under the noses of Henry's diplomats and spies.[62] (In fact, the hard-headed Maximilian was not acting totally altruistically, as he had made the childless Warbeck sign a document recognizing him as his heir to England.[63])

Ferdinand of Aragon and Isabella of Castile, co-rulers of Spain and supposed allies of Henry VII under the Treaty of Medino del Campo (1489), referred to Warbeck in their coded letters in the manner normally reserved for genuine royals.[64] Unlike Simnel, Warbeck had a regal manner and a marked resemblance to Edward IV, and could pass himself off as a prince and as the son of his supposed father[65] – and even senior courtiers of Henry's were exposed in the mid-1490s for saying privately that if he was really the Duke of York they would not oppose him.[66] Like Simnel, he had substantial support from the traditionally pro-Yorkist lords in areas of semi-Anglicized Ireland remote from the 'reach' of the weak government in Dublin. Unlike Simnel, he was able to secure support from the King of Scotland (now James IV, more warlike than his controversial father James III) and received not only a high-born bride, Katherine Gordon, but Scottish troops and James' personal company for his abortive invasion of Northumberland in 1496. This was, however, not an unqualified bonus, given the locals' loathing of the Scots and the inevitability of the pretender being seen as a Scottish puppet and receiving no local support – and the gauche Warbeck was so horrified at the blatant terrorizing of his future subjects by the unruly Scots Borderers that he complained to the unimpressed James.[67] An invasion of Northumberland by her Scots allies had not worked for Queen Margaret in 1462 or 1463, despite the useful defection of local pro-Lancastrian castle commanders, and she had had the advantages of her husband being the 'rightful' and long-ruling, recently-deposed King not an unknown pretender, and having support from senior members of the local Percy dynasty. The Scots war only aided Warbeck indirectly, by requiring Henry to impose harsh new taxes to raise troops and antagonizing the distant and independent-minded Cornishmen so much that they launched their own rebellion. As we shall see, Warbeck's best hope would have been to hasten to Cornwall and join this expedition, which was able to march all the way to Kent unopposed – though given fifteenth-century communications he would have needed luck rather than a Cornish Yorkist messenger sailing to Scotland to be sure of arriving in time for this unexpected outbreak.

### (ii) Fake or real scion of the House of York?

The question of who exactly Warbeck was in reality was unresolved at the time, and has never been cleared up despite the best efforts of Henry's spies and 'spin-doctors' to dismiss him as a fake. There are still novelists and historians who think that he was the genuine Prince Richard, and in the absence of a 'DNA' test on the bones of the supposed Prince in Westminster Abbey this cannot be disproved. As mentioned earlier, his own story – which varied in detail from time to time – was that an unknown 'lord' commissioned to murder him in the Tower had decided to spare him, smuggled him abroad, and given him a new identity but required him to keep quiet about his real identity for a number of years.[68] There was no comment on the fate of Edward V – had he been murdered or had he died naturally after being smuggled abroad? Or what about the story that at least one boy had been drowned at sea (convenient for explaining the absence of a body).[69] The presumed location of Prince Richard's hiding place was Tournai, where ' Perkin Warbeck' (or Osbeck) was supposed to have been born and raised; it was part of the Burgundian dominions so Duchess Margaret, Richard III's sister, could have placed him there under her secret protection. The local Bishop was a close ally of Margaret's – and Tudor 'smear-mongers' later suggested that he was Warbeck's real father and Margaret was his mother.[70] Payments have been discovered to an unknown small boy who was being brought up at Margaret's court in the mid-1480s – was this 'Prince Richard' before he was sent to Tournai?[71] Given the payments by Richard III to Sir James Tyrrell, could these have been for smuggling the Prince abroad and settling him at Tournai? And was it significant that Warbeck's first employer in 1489–90 was the international Anglo-Portuguese Jewish sea-captain and adventurer Sir Edward Brampton (Duarte Brandao), who could thus have smuggled Richard to the Low Countries on board a ship from London?[72] Did Tyrrell and/or Brampton take Richard abroad, and know his real identity? Was this why Henry gave Tyrrell an extra pardon for past misdeeds in 1486 (on finding out what he had done) and made him reside overseas, so he could not spread the story that the rightful King of England was still alive? Was this why Tyrrell was 'selected' to be accused of murdering the Princes once Warbeck was safely dead and Tyrrell had 'betrayed' Henry by entering into a new Yorkist plot – but Henry had him executed in private and did not give public and specific details of the alleged murders as the story was full of holes?[73] Or did Richard III genuinely want the boys dead, and it was the Duke of Buckingham – their aunt Catherine's husband – who saved the Prince but, as the usurper's loyal subject or intended betrayer, wanted the boy out of the reckoning during a future power-struggle over the Crown?[74]

The theory that Warbeck was really Prince Richard is plausible, and the pretender allegedly was able to show Yorkist visitors to his 'court' in the Low Countries 'secret marks' on his body that proved to veterans of Edward IV's court that he was genuine.[75] This may, however, have been propaganda spread about by people committed to his cause and seeking to make it seem more plausible. His resemblance to Edward IV may be explainable by him being an illegitimate son of Clarence, who appears to have been at large (possibly in the Low Countries) in the years after the Duke's arrest in 1477 – and one of Warbeck's first backers at Cork in 1490, John Taylor, was a member of Clarence's household who was accused of trying to smuggle Clarence's legitimate son, Warwick, abroad at that time.[76] Taylor was capable of taking Clarence's illegitimate son abroad as a potential pretender in 1477/8 and hiding him with the Warbeck family, and Duchess Margaret could have given sanctuary to her brother Clarence's son then and after 1485 decided to use him as 'Prince Richard' to depose Henry. Does this explain why Warbeck was said by Brampton in 1496 not to have spoken English when he first knew him, in 1489–90?[77] Prince Richard, born in 1473, would hardly have forgotten English if he left England as a ten-year-old in 1483; a son of Clarence's, born before 1477, could have done so if he had left England as a baby. The possibility that Warbeck was an illegitimate son of one of the senior males of the House of York must focus on Clarence, given his location as of 1490 and his age – he was supposed to have been born around 1474/5.[78] He was too young to have been a son of Edward IV or Richard III, born during their exile in the Low Countries in winter 1471–2; and Edward and Richard both acknowledged at least one illegitimate son born in England (Arthur and John) so it is unlikely that a discarded mistress of theirs would have been unable to secure money for her son's upbringing in England (or faced hostility from their wives) and so moved abroad.

Two more points can be raised about Warbeck's real identity and the possibility that he was not just the son of a Flemish boatman with a coincidental resemblance to Edward IV. This is not to say that he was Prince Richard – merely that the 'official' Tudor version of events put about at the time of his capture in 1497 has problems. Firstly, the 'confession' that Warbeck signed up to and was quickly distributed across England and Europe shows signs of having been prepared by the government beforehand, not dictated by Warbeck himself. It was sent out so quickly that the logistics of printing it 'from scratch' in the time available were difficult.[79] There were two versions, one in English for Henry's subjects to read of the pretender's lowly origins, presumption, and sinister foreign sponsors and one in French to disabuse his foreign backers about his real identity. The terminology used in the French version's – inaccurate – account of events in and around Tournai is that of 'literary' French as would have been used by an English-speaker (a Tudor court writer?) rather than the local Picardy patois that Warbeck himself would have spoken and written.[80] It made two crucial mistakes – it gave the wrong Christian name for Warbeck's mother, Nicaise (called Catherine in the text), and it gave the wrong professions for Warbeck's father and grandfather. His godfather, Pierre Flan, was described as his grandfather. There were also mistakes concerning local geography and customs in Tournai, which a long-term resident would have known were wrong.[81] The same mistakes were made in a rather odd and forced-sounding letter that Warbeck allegedly wrote to his mother after his arrest, which does not read naturally and has the same idiosyncratic spelling as the 'confession' – it seems to have been written or composed by the same, non-local author.[82] The question arises of whether Warbeck knew these details were wrong but was too scared or depressed to correct them, whether his interrogators did not bother to correct them when he pointed this out as it would mean re-writing the text, or whether Warbeck let the mistakes pass as a deliberate sign to his backers that he had been forced to sign up to a pack of lies.[83] Another point worth noting is that his account of his early years refers to his having been 'ill' for a long time in 1483–4. This would imply that he was not seen in public by the locals in Tournai – so was this when he was introduced to the Warbeck household as replacement for the 'real' Pierre Warbeck and was coached in his new identity by his sponsors?

### (iii) Could Warbeck have overthrown Henry? And when?

#### (a) The plots of 1492–5

The thorny question of Warbeck's real identity is less important than the perceived 'fact' that he could have been Prince Richard, as accepted by a number of the new King's courtiers in the early to mid 1490s, and there was no way of proving that he was not the Prince without producing the latter's body. There may have been secret searches of the Tower of London for the missing boys' remains, but if so they were unsuccessful; nor did the alleged murderer who 'confessed' in 1502, Sir James Tyrrell, oblige Henry by giving details of where to look or at least provide a coherent anonymous story of Ricardian villainy that could be circulated. For that matter, if Sir Thomas More was able to state in c. 1510 that at least one of the alleged killers was still at large (presumably in London) and could end up hanged for his (further?) crimes it should not have been beyond Henry's intelligence service's resources to track the man down in the early-mid 1490s and force him to confess.[84] A confession would seem 'forced' and might not be believed – but the same could apply to Warbeck's confession. As Henry had not even specifically named Richard III as the killer in 1485–6 or held a Requiem Mass for his 'late' brothers-in-law it would seem that he had little idea what had happened and preferred to avoid stirring up more debate by poking around in the mystery when he could not produce answers. There was one odd incident in spring 1495 when Henry's Captain of the Guard, visiting Duchess Margaret and meeting Warbeck, blustered that the real Prince was dead and he could show anyone the chapel where he was buried (possibly one of the two in the Tower); but in that case why had Henry not revealed this 'fact' and held a public memorial service? The most useful time to publicize a confession to regicide by Tyrrell (or someone else) was while Warbeck the 'fake Prince' was still at large, not 1502 when he was safely dead – and even in 1502 Henry only apparently showed Tyrrell's account around the court and it was not printed.[85] But this gave Warbeck a major advantage throughout his period at liberty, and his backers made the most of it. Notoriously, even Henry's stepfather's brother, Lord Chamberlain Sir William Stanley, apparently seriously considered that Warbeck might be genuine in 1494–5 and pledged that he could – or would? – support him.[86] This was 'treason' at the very heart of the court, or at least chronic insecurity by 'fence-sitting' nobles fearing another invasion, and its committers could even argue that as *Titulus Regius* had been repealed Prince Richard was the rightful king so it was not treason. The belief that Warbeck could be genuine extended widely across the senior ranks of society, according to Polydore Vergil[87] – and this sort of commitment could have had a 'snowball effect'.

Believing that Warbeck could be the rightful king was not the same thing as actively plotting his 'restoration', and a question mark remains over how dangerous the actual 'plot' of 1494–5 was. As named in the later 'official' version of events, the plotters at court included Stanley, his brother-in-law Sir Humphrey Strange, Steward of the Household Lord Fitzwalter, and Sir Giles Debenham. The crucial evidence to arrest the activists was provided by Sir Robert Clifford, son of a Lancastrian peer killed in the second battle of St Albans in 1460 and a veteran of Stoke in 1487; he apparently masterminded the initial grouping of conspirators in spring 1493 and then crossed over to Flanders with his father-in-law, William Barley, to contact Duchess Margaret at Malines.[88] He then took up residence at Warbeck's 'court', where the leading Yorkist figures were the shady John Taylor and John Atwater who had masterminded (or just taken advantage of?) Warbeck's first appearance at Cork in 1491. Duchess Margaret wrote to Ferdinand and Isabella of Spain to assure them that he was genuine.[89] It seems that Henry expected an invasion of England in summer 1493 as he set up his headquarters at Kenilworth and put a watch on the coasts as in 1487, but none materialized; Maximilian had other priorities across central Europe, and his father Emperor Frederick (aged 78) was to die that autumn so logically he was waiting to secure his succession to the latter's title and lands before acting. He invited Warbeck to Vienna – as 'Richard IV' – for the funeral, but only arrived in person in the Low Countries with his guest in summer 1494. There, Maximilian's son and heir Philip was invested as the local Duke of Brabant in October, with Warbeck in attendance – a shield was put up in public proclaiming his heraldic arms as King of England but was pulled down by Henry's supporters, leading to scuffles.[90] Crucially, no invasion took place, although Charles VIII offered Warbeck ships too[91] – the first time that both France and the Empire were simultaneously hostile to England, though (as in the next case of this in 1538) they were unlikely to co-ordinate an invasion.

Crucially, at the end of 1494 Henry's agents persuaded Sir Robert Clifford to defect back to England via Calais. He allegedly provided 'proof' that Warbeck was a fake, and a vital list of the pretender's court and Church sympathizers.[92] They were supposed to be planning the assassinate the King, how effectively is impossible to judge. Arrests followed early in 1495, an impressive list including not only Stanley and Lord Fitzwalter but a number of top Churchmen – Dean Worsley of St Paul's Cathedral, Friar William Richford the leader ('Provincial') of the Dominican Order in England, another senior Dominican friar (the Prior of King's Langley, Hertfordshire), John Kendall the Prior of the Knights of St John of Jerusalem, and William Sutton (priest at St Stephen's Wallbrook in London, a famous preacher). Dr William Hussey, Archdeacon of London, and James Keating (prior of Kilmainham and head of the Knights of St John in Ireland) were also involved, and possibly Bishop Thomas Langton of Winchester. Kendall was the most dangerous of them, as a senior figure in a semi-autonomous Knightly Order who handled their funds and correspondence across Europe and could use both to benefit Warbeck. He was also on Henry's Council and ironically helped to negotiate the Anglo-French treaty in 1492, which removed Warbeck's first foreign patron – and unlike with Stanley, there is evidence of his active ill-will towards the King. According to the 1496 confession of his agent Bernard de Vignolles, during a trip to Rome in 1492 Kendall (who could travel abroad on Order business without arousing Tudor suspicion) asked him to hire a poisoner to murder the King and his family, and a bizarre episode resulted with an astrologer promising him a box of poisonous ointment, which he could smear on a doorpost in Henry's apartments and so incite anyone who came into contact with it (smell or touch?) to regicide. It was allegedly so toxic that exposing it to open air was dangerous to its carrier, so the question of how safe its user would be helped to put de Vignolles off and he threw it away and substituted a fake.[93] Assuming the whole episode was not invented, it indicates Kendall's determination to be rid of the King if not his commonsense; and his network of Hospitaller links made him very useful to avoid detection.

Laymen included Thomas Cressener, son of a relative and legatee of Edward IV's elderly mother Duchess Cecily of York, and two of the Brampton family who lived near her residence at Berkhamsted Castle – also close to the priory at King's Langley. William Daubeny, clerk of the Jewel House, and Warwickshire military veteran Sir Simon Mountford of Coleshill (who sent £30 via his son to Warbeck) took part too. Sir Thomas Thwaites, treasurer of the garrison at Calais (and former Chancellor of the Exchequer to Edward IV) and military official Sir Robert Radcliffe represented a dangerous 'Yorkist cell' at Calais. In these circumstances, Henry's choice of the secure Tower of London for his residence over Christmas 1494 and New Year 1495 was clearly not only to enable him to be on hand to interrogate suspects. Stanley ended up executed for treason on 16 February after a round of executions of the lesser lay suspects, the clergy escaping this fate by reason of legal immunity. But Fitzwalter was not sentenced until the autumn, was reprieved and deported to prison at Calais, and was finally executed in 1496 for plotting to escape.[94]

The extent and identities of the conspirators made the plot sound like a serious threat and it was portrayed as such, though it should be remembered that no attempt at a coup by regicide and domestic revolt succeeded in medieval or Tudor England. A plot plus foreign invasion would have been far more dangerous, and to that extent Henry was lucky in that 1494 had seen Charles VIII of France take his army off to Italy to overrun both assorted North Italian states (principally Milan) and then the distant Kingdom of Naples. He and his geo-strategic rival Maximilian were thus otherwise preoccupied at the time of maximum danger for England, and the new Emperor could not follow up his provocative parading of 'Richard IV' in Flanders in autumn 1494 with an expedition to aid him, though he apparently asked the rulers of Saxony to provide troops. Duchess Margaret promised an expedition for February 1495, which never materialized.

When did the possibility of English aid to an invasion become serious? This mattered more than the apparent flood of letters that Warbeck received from minor gentry and ex-soldiers promising to help him as their late King's son.[95] Whether the full list of plotters arraigned in January 1495 had been ready for action and properly co-ordinated back in 1493 too is unknown. According to Clifford's later testimony it was in January 1493 that he first discussed Warbeck with Lord Fitzwater (who promised to raise 500 men to fight for him) and in March that he first discussed him with the sympathetic Sir William Stanley.[96] At what date this trio and Kendall's 'ecclesiastical' group of plotters linked up is unclear. But it is significant that Henry's intelligencers were 'on top of' Yorkist activity in London well before the arrests, as well as managing to investigate 'Prince Richard's background enough in Flanders for Henry to name his 'real' identity as Warbeck the boatman's son that summer.[97] In February 1493 London plotters Humphrey Savage (coincidentally or not, Stanley's nephew) and Sir Gilbert Debenham had to flee into sanctuary at Westminster Abbey, where they were kept under surveillance, and executions of unknown persons for treason followed that summer; another London Yorkist group who pinned up inflammatory pamphlets on church doors in February 1494 were quickly identified, chased into sanctuary at St Martin's-le-Grand, dragged out by the King's men, and tried and executed.[98] Dean Worsley, Richford, Fitzwater, Radcliffe, Daubeny, Mountford, Thwaites, and Cressener were all in custody well before the arrests of January 1495. The crucial moment may have been when, according to French chronicler Molinet, three double-agent 'Tudor defectors' who had secured places in Warbeck's entourage persuaded a large group of senior English figures to send letters under their personal seals to the 'Prince', then seized the evidence and defected back to England with it. (The Calais records show that these men travelled back to England in October 1494.[99]) They were followed in December by Clifford himself, according to Polydore Vergil of his own free will after months of bribes and threats from Henry's agents.[100] Some analysts think that Clifford had been a double agent all along; he was given an official pardon on 22 December, soon after he landed, but was still being escorted around by Henry's close henchman Bray as a 'prisoner' in January (to cover up his defection or because he could not be trusted?).[101] Given all that Clifford knew, this question is important – if he was a Tudor agent all along, the King was in less danger of overthrow as Clifford should have been able to alert him of any planned immanent coup or invasion. It is, however, apparent that Warbeck kept 'open house' for defectors at his 'court' at Malines in 1493–4 and does not seem to have been cautious in keeping secrets to a few close and trustable allies, so the chances of Henry discovering who his court sympathizers were in time were always high.

*(b) Invasions, 1496–7*
The first armed incursion by Warbeck's motley fleet finally occurred in July 1495, over four months late; in the interim his patron Maximilian had failed to interest the Imperial Diet in loaning the expedition money to replace the hostile Henry VII with a pro-German Yorkist king. There was minimal support to be expected in England due to the arrests, though if Stanley and other senior lay figures had been at liberty undetected they might have been able to meet the rebels as they landed or raised a diversionary attack elsewhere. The only major plotter still at liberty, in the south-east Midlands, was Kendall who appears to have been equipping his tenants ready to fight but not to have done more.[102] Leaving Flushing in Holland on 2 July, Warbeck's expedition arrived offshore at Deal next day; around 300 men landed to erect 'Richard IV's banner and were assured of support by the locals. The latter invited their new king ashore, but he wisely stayed on his ship and a short time later armed loyalists who had evidently been waiting for him emerged to ambush the invaders. About half of them were killed; those who were taken captive were swiftly tried and executed, and Warbeck had no option but to head for more promising territory.[103] The Kentishmen had been notorious for pro-Yorkist revolts since 1450 and had taken part in seemingly desperate (and unsuccessful) attacks on London in 1471 and 1483, but were apparently wary of involvement this time. Henry – away at

Worcester so not expecting the attack to come then or there – wrote that he had not even needed to use his troops and the Kentishmen had spontaneously showed their loyalty, though the delay in attacking the landing party may indicate hesitation and 'prodding' from loyal gentry as one commentator claimed.[104] Once the attack had been driven off, it would have disheartened any hesitating partisans in England; it also seems that Maximilian's son Philip, as governor of Flanders, washed his hands of the rebels and by the autumn even Maximilian was considering an anti-French international alliance that would include Henry as a member (with a 'get-out' clause just in case Warbeck won).[105] Warbeck, shadowed by royal ships so he could not land in Devon or Cornwall away from immediate Tudor military reprisal, sailed on to Southern Ireland and joined his old ally the Earl of Desmond for an attack on Waterford. He had the backing of Cork, thanks to his ally Atwater, and assorted magnates including the northerners O'Neill of Clandeboye and O'Donnell, but the central government in Dublin had been strengthened by new Lord Lieutenant Sir Edward Poynings in 1494 so a repeat of Simnel's triumphant takeover in 1487 was not on the cards. Instead of marching on Dublin and forcing Kildare to choose sides he wasted nearly two weeks besieging the strongly-walled Waterford, was driven off and lost some of his ships, and wandered around western-central Ireland with his supporters to no good purpose for several months.[106] In November he arrived in Scotland to a warmer welcome from King James IV and was recognized as king and given a high-born wife, Lady Katherine Gordon, but the resulting invasion of Northumberland in September 1496 was another fiasco. Quite apart from it arousing local antagonism to a pretender now seen as a puppet of the traditional enemy and leading to Warbeck complaining at the terrorizing of his 'subjects', all it achieved was the usual burning, raping, and looting over a small area plus the sack of Heton Castle by King James. The Scots were only in England for four days,[107] and after their return home Warbeck stayed inactive at his host's court for the best part of a year. He had been stymied in Ireland and had no obvious hope of a rising in England, but it should have been clear that James was of no practical military use to him; presumably the thrill of actually being treated as an honoured fellow-sovereign at a hospitable court made him unwilling to move on and go back to Desmond's lands around Cork or to Flanders. In either location he would have been closer to any unexpected revolt in England – though in Flanders he would probably have had difficulty in getting a ship or any troops out of Duke Philip for any more adventures. As events were to show, he was to miss his best chance of leading a large army on London by his staying in Scotland, well away from southern England.

The most serious revolt to shake Henry VII's throne since 1497 was ironically not a Yorkist conspiracy but a 'bona fide' popular uprising in the tradition of the revolts of 1381 and 1450, seemingly unplanned, unpredicted, sparked off by a particular local incident, and reflecting the underlying grievances of people with no particular adherence to a rival candidate to the throne. Unlike in 1381 or 1450 there was no background of recent 'misrule', fiscal oppression, social unrest, or favouritism at court to explain it, and it was made more complicated than the more usual outbursts nearer London by being centred in a notoriously independent-minded county far from London – Cornwall. The area had a distinct ethnic and cultural identity as a centre of surviving Romano-British society during the Anglo-Saxon 'conquest', having been part of the ancient British kingdom of Dumnonia and survived under its own non-Saxon kings until conquest by the West Saxon king Egbert in 825 and final annexation by Athelstan in the 920s. It still remained a separate 'duchy' with its own legal and administrative institutions, the title of Duke having been held by the Prince of Wales since the fourteenth century, and the fiercely autonomist Cornish tin-mining communities were largely self-governed by their own body, the 'Stannaries', under a royally-appointed 'Lord Warden'. It also had its own language and distinct customs, and was so far from London that it could be as promising as Northumberland as a centre for revolt if the local gentry chose to act – as Yorkist Sir Henry Bodrugan had been intending in 1486–7 until he was forced to flee. It had not been particularly involved in the struggles for the Crown since 1453 apart from a half-hearted rising in favour of Henry Tudor against the usurping Richard III in autumn 1483 and the Bodrugan plot – though the support for Henry (unknown locally) may well have indicated indignation at the usurpation and a desire for 'justice'. Now, however, a revolt broke out in summer 1497 due to resentment at the high level of taxes demanded in the January 1497 Parliament to pay for the King's war in faraway Scotland – apparently the opinion was that the war was nothing to do with the Cornish.[108] The Scots did not threaten them so they should not have to pay for it. There was a parallel with the 'poll tax' revolt of 1381, with 'unjust' financial demands from London as the background to popular violence directed at the court. As with the Wat Tyler revolt in Kent in 1381, a local incident sparked off a wider revolt – Michael Gof, a blacksmith at the village of St Keverne on the isolated Lizard peninsula, killed a visiting tax collector and an angry gathering of locals demanding the repeal of the war-taxes followed. Once the King's men had been attacked, retribution and executions could be expected so the chances of the fearful protesters taking things further and seeking outside support was high; a riot could thus 'snowball' into a formidable protest, which in the absence of modern law-enforcement methods could outnumber the men who the local sheriff and gentry could collect to stop them. A lawyer who could articulate the popular demands in legal terms, Thomas Flamank, took charge of the demonstration and persuaded the rioters that they should march on the county capital, Bodmin, and more villagers joined them en route. The gentry who would normally have acted to halt such protests seem to have been taken by surprise by the size of the crowds and no doubt feared that their servants and tenants would sooner desert than fight the protesters. As a result the 'army' of around 15,000 of the 'commons' were able to decide to march on London and did so without hindrance. They had no obvious leaders apart from Flamank and Joseph, although they soon persuaded one local peer – James Touchet, Lord Audley, son of Richard III's Treasurer – to join them. Despite Touchet's probable Yorkism they had no apparent dynastic agenda to remove the King, though antipathy was expressed to ministers such as Cardinal Morton; the rebellion was thus in line with 1381 and 1450. Noticeably, there was no move made to intercept them by loyal nobles in the counties en route, though more local volunteers protesting at the King's taxes joined them.[109] Instead, the King's senior commander, Lord Daubeny, hurried back from Newcastle with his army to London. It was later wondered why he had not marched out to intercept the rebels before they reached the vicinity. Was this just caution as he had to rest his men and had little information on the rebels' capacity, or was it potential treason?[110] Henry was supposed to have been annoyed at the delay. The rebels did not head directly to the capital but swerved away east to Blackheath in western Kent, probably in the hope of attracting support from that notoriously restless county. Blackheath was also the scene of the Duke of York's encampment as he challenged Henry VI's government in 1452, and was a 'high-profile' and well-known site, close to London, for sympathizers from south-east England or the capital to assemble to join the rebellion. Probably the leadership expected to be invited into the City by a spontaneous rising there, which would overwhelm the King's men, as had occurred in 1381 and 1450; though unlike then the government was headed by a determined adult monarch with no compunction about drastic measures.

Nor was there any obvious current network of anti-Tudor plotters at large ready to turn out with weapons and 'White Rose' banners to divert the rebellion into Yorkist paths and argue to Flamank and Joseph that the current King would inevitably execute them but 'Richard IV' would grant full tax-remission. The last of the Stanley group, John Kendall the national head of the Knights of St John of Jerusalem, had been detected and arrested in spring 1496. His group's centre of operations had been southern Bedfordshire (i.e. to Henry's army's 'rear'), with his Hospitaller connections meaning that he could call on men and money from a national organization subject to the Pope not the King; if he had still been at large he would have been a major recruit to the rebel army. He had had clerical allies in London, including the Dean of St Paul's – men whom could have preached to the populace to join in the rebellion and seize the City's gates? As it turned out, the network had been broken up in 1496, thanks to the confession of Kendall's ally de Vignolles about the 1492 poison plot. The presence of a substantial and well-armed royal army in the vicinity dissuaded any large-scale reinforcements for the rebels from the south-east; and on 16 June Daubeny stormed the rebel encampment and massacred the ill-armed peasants. The inevitable round of grisly executions and exhibitions of body parts across the rebel area to dissuade future rebels followed.[111] Had there been more uprisings across the south-east and Midlands against the current level of taxation, as in 1381, the King would have been less able to concentrate reinforcements in London and the rebellion might have had more chances of success. The fact that Daubeny and the main body of troops had to come from Northumberland accounts for the rebels managing to reach the vicinity of the capital easily; presumably most militarily experienced pro-Tudor gentry en route had taken their men off north to fight the Scots.

Crucially, the rebellion had lacked any candidate to replace the King and so did not pose an immediate dynastic challenge to him. The best potential candidate to act had been Edmund de la Pole, Lincoln's younger brother and future Yorkist pretender; but as of 1497 he had had not broken with the King. Indeed, when he was sent a royal summons to join the army to defeat the rebels one of his friends suggested that he should join the rebels instead, and proposed to do so himself. Edmund not only refused but stole his friend's breeches and took his horse's saddle before he left, in order to hinder him from carrying out his plan.[112] Nor was Warbeck able to support the rebels, as he left Scotland by sea in early July 1497 on board the ironically nicknamed *Cuckoo*, purchased for him the previous autumn by James (which may imply that James had hoped to be rid of him earlier.) Henry had mustered a large army at Newcastle under Lord Daubeny that spring, with an advance force ready in Berwick and artillery from the Tower being moved north too; if James did not abandon Warbeck an invasion was intended. If James agreed to peace, on the other hand, he could marry Henry's elder daughter, Margaret (which he eventually did in 1503). The sheer size of resources committed by England meant that it was not possible for James to help Warbeck by distracting Henry with another invasion, even if he had wished to – though that summer the surprise Cornish revolt meant that the English had to send most troops south so James briefly attacked Norham Castle.

Warbeck headed back to Cork to join his supporter Atwater and renew his campaign in Ireland. Having only one ship and no Scots recruits, weapons, or money on board, he was reliant on Irish lordly reinforcements for his next move, and these failed to materialize (again). The Earl of Desmond had changed sides to back the King since Poynings' reassertion of royal power in Dublin in 1494, Kildare had learnt his lesson and would not risk ruin, and the pro-Yorkist Sir Thomas Ormond (one of the senior Anglo-Irish lords of central Munster, from the local Butler dynasty) was killed a few days before Warbeck arrived by his dynastic rival, Sir Piers Butler. As Desmond and Kildare led a pro-royal force on Cork and royal ships from Waterford patrolled the coast, Warbeck had to leave Cork and lurked around the rugged Munster coast where Spanish ships picked him up. Their ambassador in England, Pedro de Ayala, apparently told Warbeck where to go to meet them; it would seem that the Spanish sovereigns (who used the diplomatic code for a genuine prince in their written references to him) hoped to use him as a pawn now that the Habsburgs had dropped him. But instead of sailing off to Spain Warbeck ended up in Cornwall – after a royal ship had intercepted his vessel and the captain had led his men aboard and asked the sailors if the pretender was there. They denied it, and he was unable to identify Warbeck who either pretended to be an ordinary sailor or hid in a barrel.[113]

The King's savage repression of the rebellion had failed to stamp out resentment or terrorize his Cornish subjects into obedience, and belatedly his surviving local detractors had thought of enlisting gentry and noble support – an essential prerequisite of any revolt attracting serious outside backing. The few gentry involved now decided to link their cause to Warbeck's and sent representatives to track him down (before or after he arrived in Ireland?) and invite him to Cornwall to lead a second rebellion. The rebel leaders named later by the government were John Nankivell of St Morgan, Walter Tripcony of St Columb, and Humphrey Cawodely of Helland, plus assorted yeomen of Cornwall and western Devon; none of any great standing.[114] On 7 September Warbeck landed at Whitesand Bay near Land's End – a place as far away from the King's forces as he could find so it gave him time to raise an army, albeit a badly-armed one of local miners, farmers, and labourers.[115] Even Polydore Vergil admitted that he was able by his charisma, appearance, and promises to enthuse the locals and raise a substantial force, taking Penzance and placing his wife, Katherine Gordon, in the safety of St Michael's Mount after it surrendered. (It had also been the stronghold of a pro-Tudor invader, the Earl of Oxford, in 1474.) He then moved on east to Bodmin with up to 8000 men, and had the sense to take over and fortify the ancient earthworks at Castle Canyke nearby; the Sheriff of Cornwall, Sir Piers Edgcumbe (from the main gentry dynasty in East

Cornwall), arrived with up to 20,000 men but could not storm it as his troops lacked enthusiasm or military discipline. Instead they turned and fled,[116] and Warbeck could march on into Devon unhindered – which would have been unlikely had Edgcumbe had the luck or determination to arrive at Bodmin first, block the road east, and challenge him to do the attacking. Edgcumbe's army was larger, and so could hold a defensive position provided that discipline held; and Warbeck's rural recruits would not have had large amounts of arrows to drive the royal forces back from a distance. Given the reliance of both armies on non-professional county levies, morale, weapons, and trust in a competent leader were vital and a strong defensive position even more so. Anybody but a professional commander with skilled and well-armed troops would have difficulty in attacking a fortified position and a popular revolt frequently 'broke' against a defended town. In this case, the setback of desertions meant that Edgcumbe could not fall back to hold the Tamar and Warbeck was able to enter Launceston and cross the river into Devon, ignoring Plymouth and taking the more direct route north of Dartmoor to Exeter. In the meantime, Henry (at Woodstock near Oxford, centrally-placed as in 1487 and 1493) sent out orders to his principal subjects to collect troops and head south-west on 12 September; Daubeny was to command again, with his army reinforced by the Tower of London artillery.[117] While the royal army assembled, the principal peer in Devon, the county's titular Earl (who had proclaimed Henry as King in Bodmin in the 1483 rebellion), took his levies to Okehampton to meet Warbeck but, fearing he was outnumbered, withdrew to the safety of walled Exeter to meet Edgcumbe and various senior loyalist Devon gentry. The 'showdown' of the rebellion thus occurred at the county capital of Devon as Warbeck arrived on 17 September, with around 8000 badly-armed but enthusiastic rebels trying to storm a walled city full of well-armed royal levies without cannon or any officer with serious military experience. The townsmen seem to have been understandably nervous, though, and it only took a few 'traitors' to open a gate while guards were distracted, asleep, or drunk.

Henry apparently expected the rebels to avoid attacking the city and march on, and ordered Courtenay to pursue and harass them so that they could be trapped between his Devon forces and Daubeny's army, now in Somerset advancing west. Logically, it was unlikely that the rebels could take the defended walled city and not much use if they did as they had no cannon to defend it and would only lose time and men in doing so. Instead the rebels made a first attack on Exeter from the north and east sides on the afternoon of the 17th, and in a determined second attack next morning broke in through the east gate and fought the King's men in the main street. Eventually, Courtenay in person led his men to drive them out, but the royal troops were too tired to take the offensive and a truce was agreed. The rebels, who had lost around 3–500 men in a few hours, marched off east.[118] Their intention was to tackle Daubeny's advancing army – as of 20 September the King was still at Woodstock – though their losses and lack of weapons or training made it unlikely that they could prevail against a larger and better-disciplined force under an experienced commander in open battle (except by a lucky ambush). Daubeny also had a large number of nobles and gentry in his force and Courtenay had the latter; all were more used to fighting than Warbeck's army of commoners from knightly training. Warbeck managed to reach Taunton, where ironically the 1493–5 'plotter' Bishop Langton was the local lord of the castle, but his men were starting to desert – the King was able to allege that his advance was in reality a panicking retreat after his failure at Exeter.[119] He was heading into the path of a foe he could not hope to defeat without substantial reinforcements (which a losing cause would not obtain), and some of his men may have decided that slipping away home was the safest option. How much of this desertion was propaganda by the relieved King's writers is unclear, but Warbeck was bold enough to hold a review of his men outside Taunton on the 21st.

Daubeny sent a formal challenge to battle, which was expected to take place at Glastonbury,[120] but that night Warbeck deserted his army. With around sixty horsemen he headed south-east for the south coast, apparently intending to find a ship and set sail for Flanders. Polydore Vergil thought that he panicked and reckoned that he was bound to lose a battle.[121] He moved fast enough to elude pursuit for two days, and was presumably heading for Southampton Water – as refugee King Charles I was to do in autumn 1647 – as he ended up taking sanctuary at nearby Beaulieu Abbey.[122] Most of his entourage seem to have split up, and a few hid in London. Warbeck, however, was quickly located, surrounded by royal troops, and induced to surrender a fortnight later;[123] if he had not done so he would have been dragged out of the Abbey by force. The town levies of Southampton under the Mayor took him into custody and escorted him to Taunton to be interrogated by the King, who had arrived there on 30 September. Most of Warbeck's army, in fact, stayed loyally in their camp at Taunton for a few days expecting him to reappear, showing their determination, but even if their leader had stayed with them they would have been in as serious a position as the other Cornish army had been at Blackheath. Instead, the captive 'boatman's son' had to confess his alleged fraud to Henry's court, his own wife, and in print to the whole of Europe and was taken off to London as a prisoner – initially to court for reasonable treatment but later to the Tower.

## Could Warbeck have won?

The ranks of medieval or Renaissance era pretenders who achieved their goals are limited, particularly those who were not even plausibly the people whose identity they assumed. The only obscure pretender of dubious origins to seize a major throne by rebellion was the 'False Dmitri' in Russia in 1605 – a probable runaway serf who claimed the identity of the last male heir of the extinct 'House of Rurik' Prince Dmitri, killed in an apparent accident with a knife in a remote provincial town in 1591. On his elder half-brother Czar Feodor's death in 1598 the latter's powerful, capable and ruthless brother-in-law Boris Godunov secured the vacant throne, but was believed to have murdered Dmitri; only his death in 1605 saved him from overthrow by the pretender, backed by Russia's foe Poland with troops and leading an army of rebellious peasants and brigands. The pretender was then crowned, but was regarded as a Polish agent and was lynched a year later by his ambitious nobles. There are similarities between the situations of Dmitri with Edward V and Prince Richard and between Boris Godunov and Richard III, though Dmitri's death is more certain than the Princes'; and the 'False Dmitri' was as personally ambitious and charming an opportunist as Warbeck. But would Warbeck have been as insecure on his throne as 'Dmitri' and ended up in a similar way? Unless he had secured the throne without the 1494–5 conspiracy being detected he would have had a very narrow band of active support, and lacked any major magnates coming out openly on his side – and there would have been 'genuine' Yorkist princes at hand who would justifiably feel that they had a better right to the throne, led by Edmund de la Pole. In Russia in 1606 the great nobles of remote but genuine Rurykid blood led the coup that removed Dmitri and one of them, Vassily Shuisky, then took the throne; once Warbeck's foreign (Flemish? German?) troops had gone home he could have faced a similar fate from his local rivals.

Warbeck had the advantages that he looked and sounded like a Yorkist prince, and in his 1496 proclamation (repeated at Exeter in September 1497) he presented himself as the restorer of the natural order in place of a usurper who had promoted greedy and presumptuous 'caitiffs and villains of simple birth' such as Bishops Fox (of Winchester) and King (of Bath), Lord Daubeny, Sir Reginald Bray, Sir Thomas Lovell (Lord Treasurer), and the Beaufort bastard Sir Charles Somerset (Captain of the King's Guard).[124] This propaganda about low-born favourites always hit a raw nerve and was used by Henry IV to denounce Richard II's 'duketti' and other close allies in 1399 and by Warwick to denounce the Woodvilles in 1469. It was also implied in the Tudor rhyme about 'the Rat, the Cat and Lovell our dog' against Richard III in 1485, and the Duke of Norfolk allegedly abused the low birth of Cardinal Wolsey under Henry VIII. The Duke of Buckingham then also resented low-born ministers.[125] Kings had always promoted 'new men' so this was not a special failing of Henry VII's, and indeed Warbeck's target Bishop King had been his own 'father' Edward IV's secretary. Moreover, the practice of using upwardly-mobile clerical ministers as royal advisers was normal practice, the Church having both social mobility and literate, trained bureaucrats – the Lord Chancellor in late medieval England was normally a cleric and so was the King's secretary. Even Edward III, the admired 'courtly' paragon of chivalric leadership for his nobles, had relied on humbly-born clerical 'self-made man' Bishop William of Wykeham (of Winchester). Nor had Henry ennobled or enfeoffed large numbers of 'upstarts' as Richard II had done; he only created five peerages in his twenty-four-year reign, one of them being Daubeny's. It was thus a fitting fate that Henry was to use the same propaganda weapon against Warbeck, spreading the story about him being a boatman's son from Tournai.

The notion that the 'old nobility' would rally to this obscure pretender to be rid of their usurping sovereign was naïve, though the 'spark' that touched off the 1497 Cornish revolt – financial extortion – was to be one that led to more grumblings later in Henry's reign. Then, with less excuse, he was noted for demanding huge bonds for good behaviour from his nobles, and keeping them on a tight rein with confiscations at the slightest excuse. The instruments of his exactions were again to be 'self-made men' of relatively low birth, this time two lay careerists – Sir Edmund Dudley and Sir Richard Empson. Once Henry was dead his son Henry VIII made his new regime popular by arresting and executing them,[126] the first of many callous sacrifices of ministers and intimates that marked the career of the 'Tudor Stalin'. Would Warbeck have had more of a response to his propaganda about extortionate 'new men' if he had been rebelling in the mid-1500s, when Henry became noticeably more venal and allegedly miserly after his wife's death in 1503?[127] Was his timing wrong – and would he have had more luck if the Cornish envoys had missed him in August 1497 and he had gone back from Ireland to Flanders to wait for a better chance later? Would he have been able to call on angry regional magnates suffering from royal extortion by c. 1505, or would the flight of Edmund de la Pole to the Continent in 1501 have sidelined him permanently as a credible pretender?

The hard facts of military campaigning meant that Warbeck would need both a reasonably-sized foreign force (as provided by France for Henry in 1485 or by Duchess Margaret for Simnel in 1487) and English defections or neutrality to succeed. Edward IV had not had any significant foreign help from Burgundy as he returned to challenge Henry VI and Warwick 'the Kingmaker' in 1471, but had a ready 'power-base' as a past, competent ruler and was known to his ex-subjects; and he duly benefited from defections led by his brother Clarence. Similarly, Warwick was a known and popular senior magnate and political actor when he invaded England on Richard of York's behalf in 1460 and on his own behalf in 1470. The Duke of Buckingham was the principal local magnate in South Wales as he revolted against Richard III in 1483, though lacking known allies outside the region. Henry Tudor was as unknown in 1483 and 1485 as Warbeck was to be in the 1490s, but his genealogical provenance was known; as of December 1483 he had promised to marry the 'legitimate' heiress Elizabeth of York, and he faced a murdering usurper and possible regicide. He also benefited from having his stepfather, Stanley, in charge of one of his opponents' main military contingents. Even Simnel, of uncertain provenance, had military veterans and senior ex-Yorkists Lincoln and Lovell at his side and a body of Continental mercenaries fighting for him. By contrast Warbeck – whoever he really was – lacked support in England after the arrests of January 1495, or at the latest the arrests of Kendall's Hospitaller-Church circle in spring 1496, and had no foreign troops to make up for it.

Had Charles VIII or Maximilian and Philip provided him with as many experienced men to attack Kent in 1495 as Margaret had given Simnel in 1487 (or preferably more), Henry might at least have faced a hard-fought battle. Warbeck's main backer after 1492 was Maximilian, who even set him up as a 'genuine' exiled King of England in Flanders, but the prospect of a large army of German 'landsknechts' marching on London for him was remote despite this support. Maximilian was only regent of the Flemish duchies for his son Philip, who achieved full control in 1494, and the prospect of Flemish funds for Warbeck's cause would depend on the local elected assemblies of cautious, thrifty burgers who needed a friendly regime in England for trade. Maximilian was not Emperor until his miserly father Frederick III died late in 1493 so had no Austrian lands or funds from the German princes until then, and in 1493 he 'bought out' his cousin Sigismund, Duke of the Tyrol and Styria, to secure their revenues (especially the lucrative local mines). Until this double windfall he was reliant on loans from the Fugger banking family, agreed on in 1491 to save him from bankruptcy. 1494 also secured him a rich wife, Bianca Sforza of Milan, with a huge dowry; but this brought him into Italian politics to oppose French ambitions there as a greater priority than invading England.[128] Thenceforward he was usually resident in Innsbruck, and had diminished interest in Flanders, where Philip was now ruling and did next to nothing for Warbeck. The Habsburg family developments of 1491–9 thus served to minimalize the chances that Warbeck would get serious aid from them, and Duchess Margaret was a widow living on a fixed income on her jointure lands. Warbeck, and later the refugee Edmund de la Pole, were useful threats to hold over Henry VII but not objects of urgent consideration – and when Duke Philip and his wife Queen Juana of Castile were shipwrecked in Dorset in 1506 Henry was to 'invite' them to Windsor and not let them leave until Edmund was handed over. Would this have been Warbeck's fate too?

What of Warbeck's English support? The Cornish rebels of September 1497 suffered from their recent losses in the June rebellion, though in neither case were experienced commanders or well-armed military veterans with adequate artillery involved. Many had billhooks or spears. The best hope Warbeck would have had in 1497 would be if he had happened to leave Scotland for southern Ireland sooner (April or May?) so luck would have had it that he could hasten to Cornwall when the first revolt broke out. He lacked senior gentry backers in the county who would have had the resources to send messengers to him in time once they heard of the revolt at St Keverne gathering pace, so it would have depended on Lord Audley deciding to send for him and him arriving quickly. This would rely on luck, as a royal ship could easily intercept him en route; and even if he reached the rebels in time and they accepted him as their leader the expedition would still have been outclassed militarily by Daubeny. Lacking major defectors, he would have faced defeat in Kent in June 1497 as he did in reality in Somerset in September. But he might still have been able to flee safely to a ship at a Channel port and return to Flanders to eke out a frustrating existence as Margaret's pensioner until she died in 1503 and Maximilian or Philip expelled him. His decision to take sanctuary at Beaulieu – probably as there was no ship available in Southampton Water – meant that he would fall into royal hands and end up having to confirm that he was a fake. But his eventual imprisonment in the Tower and execution followed a failed attempt to 'run for it' from honourable detention at Court at Westminster, which ended with him floundering about in the reeds of the Thames somewhere near Sheen.[129] If he had had sympathizers ready to find him a ship then, instead of bolting without a clear plan, he could still have ended his days safe on the Continent. Instead, he was put in the Tower and later lured into a 'plan to escape' for which he was tried and executed – probably at least partly a 'put-up job' by the King to ensnare the unfortunate Earl of Warwick in the cell beneath him and secure enough of a legal excuse to execute both of them. Ferdinand and Isabella seem to have been behind this, insisting that Warwick be executed to ensure that the English throne was secure before they would send their daughter Catherine of Aragon to England to marry Prince Arthur.

At best, a genuine 'cell' of Yorkist plotters in London – a site of earlier plots to free Warwick in the early 1490s – was infiltrated and used by the King, and the 'coincidence' that Warbeck was put in the next cell to Warwick and allowed to make a hole in his floor and contact him was clearly no such thing. Henry, to his credit, seems to have been aware of the injustice of executing the innocent Warwick – and in 1497–8 he had treated Warbeck with considerable leniency given his proven offences. Was this just a ploy, or did he believe that he might be a genuine prince after all? The involvement of Warwick in the 'escape plot' and his subsequent trial and execution also brings in another 'what if?' possibility, as the injustice of the punishment was widely felt in England. Subsequent rumour had it that the sudden death of Henry's eldest son, Arthur, in April 1502 was divine vengeance on him for the 'murder'[130] – and a king who was believed to have incurred God's wrath could be at greater risk of revolt. Luckily for Henry, the only likely potential beneficiary in 1502–6 was Suffolk, in exile and with no great chance of his host Archduke Philip lending him an army as Charles VIII had loaned one to Henry against another 'royal murderer' in 1485. Warwick's own sister and the 'legitimist' Yorkist claimant, Margaret, was safely married off to a regime loyalist and Beaufort relative, Sir Richard Pole.[131] What if she had been at large on the Continent too and available to marry Suffolk? Instead, the last senior member of the House of York ended up arrested for an alleged plot in 1538 and on the execution block in a 'clear-out' of potential threats by Henry VIII in 1541. She was chased round Tower Green by the King's henchmen as she refused to submit quietly – tragedy combined with farce.

# Notes

## Chapter 1

1. For the 1320s, see Ian Mortimer, *The Greatest Traitor: the Life of Roger Mortimer, First Earl of March, Ruler of England 1327–30* (Pimlico 2004) pp. 100–01, 109–10, 126–8. For the mid-1380s: Anthony Tuck, *Richard II and the Nobility* (Edward Arnold 1971), pp. 66–7; Nigel Saul, *Richard II* (Yale UP 1997) pp. 120–1. For the 1440s, see Bertram Wolffe, *Henry VI* (Methuen 1981) pp. 106–34.

2. See *The Brut*, ed. F T de Brie (London 1906–8) pp. 511–13 on the popular view of Humphrey's victimization by the 'peace party'. Also: J A Giles, *Chronicles of the White Rose of York* (London 1845), pp. 33–4; *Historical Collections of a Citizen of London: Gregory's Chronicle, 1189-1469*, ed. James Gairdner (Camden Society 1876) pp. 187–8, John Benet, 'Chronicle for the years 1400 to 1462', ed. G and M Harriss in *Camden Miscellany*, vol xxiv (Royal Historical Society 1972) pp. 192–3, *Davies' Chronicle* pp. 62–5, *Chronicles of London*, ed. H Kingsford (Oxford 1905) pp. 157–8; also *English Historical Review*, vol xxix (1914) p. 513.

3. Juliet Barker, *Conquest: the English Kingdom of France 1415–50* (Abacus 2009), pp. 247–9.

4. Wolffe, pp. 162–5.

5. Ibid, pp. 110–11.

6. See also 'Articles of the Duke of York against the Bishop of Chichester', *B L Harleian Mss*. 543, ff. 161r–163r.

7. Wolffe, p. 221.

8. Roger Virgoe, 'The Death of William de la Pole, Duke of Suffolk', in *Bulletin of the John Rylands Library*, vol xlvii (1965) pp. 489–502.

9. Wolffe, p. 224.

10. The claim of Humphrey's murder by the King or court was not widely believed in 1447 (Wolffe, p. 131) so it was probably exacerbated by York's propagandists later; a few individuals did, however, blame Henry that early, see PRO King's Bench 9/256/12 indictment.

11. *Davies' Chronicle*, pp. 79–80; but as above, the story of Prince Edward's illegitimacy was only widespread in the later 1450s.

12. *Giles' Chronicle*, p. 39; *The Brut*, p. 517.

13. Wolffe, pp. 240–1.

14. *Benet's Chronicle*, pp. 205–6; *Bale's Chronicle*, p. 139. See also J Roskell, 'Sir William Oldhall, Speaker in the Parliament of 1450–1' in *Nottingham Medieval Studies* vol v (1961) pp. 87–112.

15. *Benet's Chronicle*, pp. 206–7; Wheathampstead, *Registrum*, vol I p. 162; *Rotuli Parliamentarum*, vol v p. 346; H Kingsford, *English Historical Literature in the Fifteenth Century* (Oxford 1913) pp. 297–8.
16. *Rotuli Parliamentarum*, vol v, pp. 147–8; *Benet's Chronicle*, p. 195.
17. *Rotuli Parliamentarum*, vol v, p. 148.
18. Quoted in Joseph Stevenson, *The English Wars in France in the Fifteenth Century*, vol ii part ii (Record Society 1861–4) pp. 639–42.
19. Capgrave, quoted by Wolffe p. 16. Also: PRO King's Bench 9/260/85; 9/256/12; 9/262/1; 9/262/78; 9/122/28; and see RF Heinesett, 'Treason by Words' in *Sussex Notes and Queries*, vol xiv (Lewes 1954–7) pp. 116–20.
20. Wolffe, pp. 137 and 139–41, 143–4.
21. Ibid pp. 5–8 and 10–11.
22. Ibid pp. 119–26, and Sir J Ramsay, *Lancaster and York* (Oxford 1892) vol ii pp. 49–53. On a local level in a region with a pro-regime 'favourite' as the local 'strongman', see *Documents Illustrative of Medieval Kentish Society*, ed. F H Du Boulay (Kent Archaeological Society 1964), pp. 220–43. For Fortescue's complaints, see his *The Governance of England* (Oxford 1885) p. 134.
23. See R A Griffiths, 'The Trial of Eleanor Cobham: an episode in the fall of Duke Humphrey of Gloucester', in *BJRL*, vol li (1968–9) pp. 381–99.
24. Wolffe, p. 39.
25. Bertram Wolffe, *The Royal Demesne*, pp. 124–30; Wolffe, *Henry VI*, pp. 230–1; see also *The Paston Letters*, ed. James Gairdner (6 vols, 1904).
26. See Bertram Wolffe, *Henry VI*, chapter 7.
27. As n. 18.
28. Wolffe, p. 234. See also *Giles' Chronicle* p. 33 for Henry's fear of Duke Humphrey and resort to armed guards from c. 1445.

## Chapter 2

1. See the first documentary reference to York as a potential challenger in PRO King's Bench 9/265/12–29, an indictment of January 1451. J Stevenson, *Wars*, vol ii (Record Society 1861–4) p. 750 for the 1451 formal Parliamentary proposal that York be named as heir.
2. *Rotuli Parliamentarum*, vol v, pp. 228–33.
3. K B MacFarlane, 'William Worcester: a preliminary survey' in *Studies Presented to Sir Hilary Jenkinson*, ed. J Conway Davies (Oxford 1957) pp. 211–15; and p. 5 for the expectation that Henry would lead the expedition.
4. Wolffe, *Henry VI* (Methuen 1981) pp. 263–4.
5. *Paston Letters*, introduction: p. cxi.
6. *Calendar of Patent Rolls 1446–52*, pp. 537, 577.
7. *Rotuli Parliamentarum*, vol v, p. 346.
8. Wheathampstead, *Registrum* vol I, p. 162; *Benet's Chronicle*, p. 206; *Davies' Chronicle* p. 70.
9. *Benet's Chronicle*, p. 207.
10. *Giles' Chronicle*, p. 43; *A Short English Chronicle*, p. 69; *Rotuli Parliamentarum*, vol v, pp. 346–7.
11. PRO E 101/ 410/ 9; for the 'rebels' grovelling in halters in the snow, see *Six Town Chronicles*, ed. R Flenley (Oxford 1911) p. 107.

12. *Calendar of Patent Rolls 1446–52*, pp. 111, 162; ibid 1452–61, pp. 34–5; PRO E 28/83/41.
13. D Wilkins, *Concilia*, vol iii, p. 560.
14. Robert Knecht, *The Valois: Kings of France 1328-1589* (Hambledon and London 2004) p. 47.
15. See Wolffe, *Henry VI*, pp. 270–1 for plausible reasons for Henry's collapse. For Heworth Moor, see R A Griffiths, 'Local rivalries and national politics: the Nevilles and the Duke of Exeter, 1452-61' in *Speculum* xliii (1968) pp. 589–632.
16. *Cambridge Medieval History*, vol vii, pp. 372–3.
17. *Paston Letters*, vol I pp. 259–61 and 403–6.
18. *Rotuli Parliamentarum*, vol v, pp. 242–4; Wolffe, *Henry VI*, pp. 278–81.
19. *Benet's Chronicle*, p. 211.
20. C A J Armstrong, 'Politics and the Battle of St Albans, 1455' in *Bulletin of the Institute of Historical Research*, vol xxxiii (1960) pp. 8–9.
21. Armstrong, pp. 8–9.
22. Griffiths in *Speculum*, vol xliii, pp. 606–8; *Benet's Chronicle*, p. 210; *Paston Letters*, vol I p. 264.
23. Wolffe, *Henry VI*, p. 285.
24. *Proceedings of the Privy Council*, ed. Nicholas (1834–7) vol vi, pp. 339–42.
25. PRO E 404/70/3/ 2, 71: orders for arms for the King's entourage.
26. Wolffe, *Henry VI*, p. 291.
27. Ibid pp. 291–2.
28. Ibid p. 292.
29. *Paston Letters*, vol I, pp. 328–9 and Wolffe, *Henry VI*, pp. 292–3.
30. Armstrong, pp. 42–8; Wolffe, *Henry VI*, pp. 293–5.
31. *Rotuli Parliamentarum*, vol v, pp. 321–2.
32. Ibid, pp. 289–90; and pp. 284–9 on provision for the Prince of Wales to succeed as regent.
33. See J Roskell in *BIHR*, vol xxix (1956) pp. 193–5.
34. *Rotuli Parliamentarum*, vol v ,pp. 300–03, 335a; Armstrong, pp. 58–62.
35. Wolffe, *Henry VI*, p. 299; PRO E 28/87/ 29A.
36. Wolffe, *Henry VI*, pp. 297–8.
37. *Rotuli Parliamentarum*, vol v, pp. 321–2.
38. Wolffe, *Henry VI*, p. 306. See also Thomas Gascoigne, *Loci et Libra Veritatum*, ed. J E Thorold Rogers (Oxford 1881) p. 214; *Croyland Chronicle*, p. 454 on Henry's weak-mindedness by 1460. See also R L Storey, *The End of the House of Lancaster* (Cambridge University Press 1966), pp. 178–82 and 228–30 on politico-military reasons for the King's progresses.
39. Wolffe, *Henry VI*, p. 309; *Calendar of Patent Rolls 1452-61*, pp. 371, 400, 405, 410.
40. Storey, p. 179.
41. PRO E 404/70/3/44, C. 81/ 1546/89c.
42. Gascoigne, op. cit., and *Paston Letters*, vol I, pp. 407–9 for the Queen's involvement in these changes of personnel.
43. *Proceedings of the Privy Council*, vol vi, pp. 333–4; *Rotuli Parliamentarum*, vol v p. 347.
44. PRO King's Bench 9/35/24, 44, 60, 70, 71, 72; *Calendar of the Patent Rolls 1452–61*, pp. 348, 353.
45. *Benet's Chronicle*, p. 221; *Davies' Chronicle*, p. 77; *Six Town Chronicles*, pp. 145, 160; *Chronicle of London*, ed. Nicholas, pp. 251–4 on the 'Love-Day' ceremony.

46. John Gillingham, *The Wars of the Roses* (Weidenfeld and Nicolson 2001) p. 72.
47. Gaston du Fresne de Beaucourt, *Histoire de Charles VII* (Paris 1881–91, 6 vols) vol vi pp. 52, 55, 137.
48. Beaucourt, vol vi, pp. 144–5.
49. *Memoires du Philippe de Commignes*, ed. D Godefroy and L de Fresnoy (Paris 1747) vol ii pp. 110–11.
50. Wheathampstead, *Registrum*, vol I, pp. 336–7.
51. *Six Town Chronicles*, p. 113; *The Brut*, p. 526; *Davies' Chronicle*, p. 77; Kingsford's *London Chronicles*, p. 169.
52. For the story of the Prince's 'real' paternity circulating, see *Davies' Chronicle*, pp. 78–9, *Benet's Chronicle*, p. 216; *Rotuli Parliamentarum*, vol v, p. 348. Order for weaponry spring 1459: PRO E 404/71/3/343.
53. *Benet's Chronicle*, p. 223.
54. *Davies' Chronicle*, pp. 80–3.
55. *Gregory's Chronicle*, p. 205.
56. See n. 32 for the formal statement of this plan in Parliament 1459. This was made in the aftermath of Margaret's triumph at Ludlow and accompanied the attainder of her enemies so it was clearly a major 'plank' of her intentions.
57. *Rotuli Parliamentarum*, vol v, pp. 349, 366; *Calendar of the Patent Rolls 1452–60*, pp. 536–614; *Foedera*, vol xi, pp. 446–8. See also propaganda against York at this point, e.g. the 'Somnia Vigilante', ed. J Gilson, in *E H R* vol xxvi (1911) pp. 512–25.
58. *Benet's Chronicle*, pp. 150–2.
59. Ramsay, *Lancaster and York*, pp. 227–9.
60. De Wauvrin, *Chroniques*, eds. W and E Hardy (Rolls Series 1891) vol v, pp. 312–18.
61. *Gregory's Chronicle*, p. 208; Wheathampstead, *Registrum* pp. 376–80 for the nobles' dismay at York claiming the throne. Discussion in J Lander, 'Marriage and Politics in the Fifteenth Century: the Nevills and the Wydvills' in *BIHR*, vol xxxvi (1967) pp. 126–8.
62. *Gregory's Chronicle*, p. 208. For papal involvement, see Constance Head, 'Pius II and the Wars of the Roses' in *Archivum Historiae Pontificiae*, vol viii (1970) pp. 160–1. Pius, as papal diplomat Aeneas Sylvius Piccolomini, had visited Britain himself so had personal knowledge of some of the contenders.
63. *Gregory's Chronicle*, p. 207.
64. *Hall's Chronicle*, quoted by Alison Weir, *The Union of the Two Noble Illustre Houses of Lancaster and York*, 1547, reprinted and edited by H Ellis (London 1809) p. 257 for the episode of Margaret gloating over York's body and putting his head on Micklegate Bar, York. In fact, Hall's grandfather had been in York's entourage at Wakefield in 1460, so he may have used family tradition for this story. Clifford's psychopathic tendencies were already known, as he had led an armed posse to London earlier to demand that King Henry arrest York and Salisbury for killing his father in 1455 at St Albans.
65. *Benet's Chronicle*, p. 228; *Bale's Chronicle*, p. 152; *Three Fifteenth Century Chronicles*, pp. 154, 171–2; Ramsay, *Lancaster and York*, pp. 237–8. See analysis in P Haigh, *The Battle of Wakefield* (Stroud, 1996).
66. 'Short English Chronicle', in *Three English Chronicles*, ed. James Gairdner (Camden Society 1880) pp. 76–7; *Gregory's Chronicle*, p. 211.
67. See C A J Armstrong, 'The Inauguration Ceremonies of the Yorkist Kings, and their title to the throne' in *Transactions of the Royal Historical Society*, fourth series vol xxx (1948) pp. 51–73.

68. *Croyland Chronicle*, pp. 421–3.
69. *Gregory's Chronicle*, pp. 211–15; *Davies' Chronicle*, pp. 107–8; *Chronicles of London*, ed. Kingsford, p. 173; *Three Fifteenth Century Chronicles*, pp. 76, 155, 172. Also see Scofield, *The Life and Reign of Edward the Fourth* (London 1923), vol I, pp. 147–8.
70. So-called because annalist John Stow relied on it for his 1610 account of the battle.
71. See n. 52 for the significant timing of this story.
72. Wauvrin, vol v, pp. 312–18.
73. For 1327, when Parliament (or rather those peers and MPs carefully selected by the insurgent leader Mortimer) agreed to depose Edward II and the King was informed afterwards and 'voluntarily' concurred by abdicating: N Fryde, *The Tyranny and Fall of Edward II 1321–6* (Cambridge UP 1979) pp. 197–200, C Valente 'The deposition and abdication of Edward II' in *E H R*, vol cxiii (1998) pp. 880–1, and Ian Mortimer, *The Greatest Traitor*, pp. 166–70. For the abdication followed by Parliamentary approval in 1399, see *Chronicles of the Revolution 1397–1400*, ed. C Given-Wilson (Manchester UP 1997) pp. 160–1, 187.
74. *Rotuli Parliamentarum*, vol v, pp. 463–7.
75. Ibid.
76. See Wolffe p. 270 and Storey, p. 136n and p. 252n.
77. *Paston Letters*, vol v, pp. 40–52, 55–7.
78. Ibid, vol I pp,. 416–17.
79. Ibid, p. 403.
80. C Ross, *Richard III*, p. 4; Paul Murray Kendall, *Richard III* pp. 37 and 440n.
81. See n. 65.

## Chapter 3

1. See A. Allan, 'Yorkist propaganda: pedigree, prophecy and the "British History" in the reign of Edward IV' in C Ross (ed.), *Patronage, Pedigree and Power in Later Medieval England* (Gloucester, 1979).
2. For the battle of Towton: see *Gregory's Chronicle*, p. 217; *Paston Letters*, vol iii, pp. 267–8; John Sadler, *Towton: the Battle of Palm Sunday 1461* (Pen and Sword 2011).
3. Charles Ross, *Edward IV* (Methuen 1974) pp. 37–8.
4. See George Goodwin, *Fatal Colours*, pp. 214–17. The direction that the sleet-laden wind was blowing in was vital to this tactic succeeding.
5. Charles Ross, *Edward IV*, pp. 71, 131–2.
6. Ross pp. 66–7; J Lander, 'Attainder and Forfeiture 1453 – 1509' in *Historical Journal*, 1961, p. 124.
7. Ross, pp. 45–51, (Sir Ralph Percy's treason) 52–3 ; *Gregory's Chronicle*, p. 219; 'Annales Rerum Anglicanum' in *Letters and Papers Illustrative of the Wars of the English in France*, ed. Joseph Stevenson (Rolls Series 1864, 2 vols) vol ii, pp. 780–1; John Warkworth, *Chronicle of the First Thirteen Years of the Reign of King Edward the Fourth*, ed. J Haliwell (Camden Society 1839) pp. 2–3; *Three Fifteenth Century Chronicles*, p. 176; Jean de Wauvrin, *Anchiennes Chroniques d'Angleterre*, ed. E Dupont (Paris 1858–69) vol iii, pp. 159–60; C L Scofield, *The Life and Reign of Edward the Fourth* (1923) pp. 268–9. For early criticism of Edward IV, see: Philippe de Commignes, vol I p. 203; *Gregory's Chronicle*, p. 221; *Three Fifteenth Century Chronicles*, pp. 177–8.
8. *The Paston Letters*, vol iii, p. 292.
9. *Gregory's Chronicle*, pp. 223–4; *Three Fifteenth Century Chronicles*, p. 178; *Paston Letters*, vol iv, p. 25 and (siege of Caister Castle) vol v, pp. 40–52, 55–8.

10. Ross, *Edward IV*, pp. 43, 57–8.
11. Wauvrin, ed. Dupont, vol ii pp. 406–9; Warkworth, pp. 6–7; *Chronicles of the White Rose of York*, ed. J A Giles (1841): 'Hearne's Fragment' pp. 24–5. Edward Hall, *Chronicle* (ed. H Ellis, 1809) pp. 273–4; *The Croyland Chronicle*, p. 446.
12. Warkworth p. 10; Commines, vol I, pp. 200-01; J Calmette and G Perinelle, *Louis XI et l'Angleterre* (Paris 1930) pp. 317–18.
13. *Croyland Chronicle* p. 542.
14. Ross pp. 90–2 on the French marriage negotiations. For Council criticism of Edward's choice of wife: Wauvrin, ed. Dupont, vol ii, pp. 327–8. Was Warwick not really all that annoyed, and is it exaggerated to talk of a fatal breach between him and the King's new wife? See Lander, 'Marriage and Politics in the Fifteenth Century: the Nevills and the Wydvills' in *BIHR*, vol xxxvi (1963).p. 133. For Warwick's public contempt for the 'arriviste' Woodvilles in 1460, see *Paston Letters*, vol iii, pp. 203–4.
15. See Lander, 'Marriage and Politics', *B I H R*, pp. 119–52 for detailed discussion of the Woodville marriage. Fabyan, *New Chronicles of England and France*, ed. H Ellis (1854) – written c. 1500 so not contemporary, but within memory – on the details of the private ceremony at Grafton Regis. See also Scofield, vol I, p. 177.
16. Fabyan, as n. 15.
17. See Wauvrin, ed. Dupont, vol ii, pp. 326–8; Scofield, vol I, pp. 351–4; Calmette and Perinel, p. 61.
18. More, *Complete Works*, ed. R S Sylvester, vol ii (*History of Richard III*, 1963) pp. 60–1; Hall, *Chronicle*, p. 264. For an earlier, contemporary Italian version of this story see C Fahy, 'The marriage of Edward IV and Elizabeth Woodville: a new Italian source', in *E H R*, vol lxxvi (1961) pp. 660–72.
19. See John Ashdown-Hill, *Eleanor: the Secret Queen* (History Press 2009) and Muriel Smith, 'Reflections on the Lady Eleanor' in *The Ricardian*, September 1998.
20. See Ian Mortimer, *The Perfect King: the Life of Edward III, Father of the English Nation* (Pimlico 2007) p. 267. This papal ruling was in 1349.
21. E.g. Charles Ross in his *Richard III*, pp. 89–91, who also refers to 1483 witness Mancini calling the other party in the pre-contract an anonymous French princess not Eleanor or Elizabeth Lucy. But does this just reflect non-expert foreign visitor Mancini's reliance on confused second-hand reports of the City speeches?
22. *Paston Letters*, vol iii, pp. 203–4.
23. Warkworth, pp. 46–9.
24. Calmette and Perinel p. 108, citing a 1469 rumour that reached France.
25. Warkworth, pp. 6–7; 'Hearne's Fragment', p. 24.
26. *Calendar of the Close Rolls 1468–76*, pp. 85-7.
27. *Paston Letters*, vol v, p. 63.
28. Warkworth pp. 8–9; *Chronicle of the Lincolnshire Rebellion*, ed. J G Nicholls (Camden Society 1847) pp. 6–16; Kingsford, *Chronicles of London*, pp. 180–1; *Six Town Chronicles*, p. 164; Polydore Vergil, *Anglia Historia*, pp. 126–8. For historians' scepticism over Warwick being behind the rebellion, see Sir Charles Oman, *Warwick the Kingmaker*, pp. 189, 196–8. Discussion in Ross, *Edward IV*, pp. 141–2.
29. Ross, *Edward IV*, pp. 141–2.
30. Ibid p. 147; Calmette and Perinel pp. 139–40.
31. *Calendar of the Patent Rolls 1467–77*, pp. 214–16.
32. *Croyland Chronicle*, pp. 553–4; Wauvrin, ed. Dupont, vol iii, pp. 46–8; *Chronicles of the White Rose of York*, p. 28–9. For the Coventry records' testimony to popular enthusiasm

for Warwick, see *Coventry Court Leet Book vol ii* (Early English Text Society 1907–13) pp. 35–9.

33. J C Wedgwood, *The History of Parliament, 1439–1509: Register* (HMSO 1938), pp. 378–82. (The 'Register' for the period 1439–1509 is one of the volumes in the 'History of Parliament' series.)

34. Ross, *Edward IV,* p. 155.

35. *Calendar of the Patent Rolls 1467–77*, p. 233; *Calendar of the Fine Rolls: Edward IV, 1461–71*, pp. 293, 295.

36. Warkworth p. 13; *Chronicles of London*, pp. 182–3.

37. John Stow, *Annales or a General Chronicle of England (1631)*, p. 423.

38. *The Arrivall of Edward IV*, p. 10; J Lander, 'The treason and death of the Duke of Clarence: a Reinterpretation' in *Canadian Journal of History*, vol ii (1967) pp. 14–15. Clarence's seemingly self-defeating repeated treachery to all and sundry is more explicable if he had an idea – rightly or wrongly – that he had legal justice on his side.

39. Lander, pp. 14–15; Ross, pp. 146–7, 156–7.

40. Commignes, vol I, pp. 207–12.

41. Wauvrin, ed. Dupont, vol iii, p. 97; *The Arrivall*, p. 2.

42. *Calendar of the Patent Rolls 1467–77*, pp. 251–2.

43. *The Arrivall*, pp. 5–7; Wauvrin, ed. Dupont, vol iii, pp. 96–147; Warkworth, pp. 13–20; Polydore Vergil, *Anglia Histora*, pp. 136–54; *Croyland Chronicle*, pp. 554–6. See also J A Thomson, ' "The Arrivall of Edward IV" – The Development of the Text' in *Speculum*, vol xlvi (1971) pp. 84–93; and Alison Weir, *Lancaster and York*, p. 388.

44. *The Arrivall*, pp. 6–7.

45. Ibid, pp. 7–12; p. 17 (Edward's entry to London). Also *The Great Chronicle of London*, ed. Thomas and Thornley (privately printed 1938), pp. 215–16, and Wauvrin, ed. Dupont, vol iii, pp. 210–15.

46. *Paston Letters*, vol v, p. 137; Warkworth, pp. 24–6; *Calendar of the Patent Rolls 1467–77*, p. 346.

47. *The Arrivall*, pp. 18–21; Warkworth, pp. 15–17; *The Great Chronicle of London*, pp. 216–17; *Polydore Vergil* pp. 144–7; Wauvrin, ed. Dupont, vol iii, pp. 210–15; a reconstruction of the battle of Barnet in Paul Murray Kendall, *Richard III* (1955) pp. 93–9 and 449–50. On Margaret's delay, see Scofield, vol I, pp. 558–9, 563–4, and 582–3 and Calmette and Perinel, pp. 133–42.

48. *The Arrivall*, pp. 23–8.

49. Ibid, pp. 28–30; J D Blyth, 'The Battle of Tewkesbury' in *Transactions of the Bristol and Gloucestershire Archaeological Society*, vol lxxx (1961) pp. 99–120; reconstruction of the battle in Paul Murray Kendall, op. cit., pp. 101–3. The killing of Prince Edward – *The Arrivall*, p. 30; *Paston Letters*, vol v p. 104; *Three Fifteenth Century Chronicles*, p. 184; H Kingsford, *English Historical Literature in the Fifteenth Century* (Oxford 1913) pp. 374 and 377; *Croyland Chronicle*, p. 555; *Great Chronicle*, p. 218. Warkworth (p. 18) says he appealed to Clarence for help.

50. The killing of Henry VI – *The Arrivall*, p. 38 (which calls it a natural death, unlikely given its convenience); *Chronicle of London*, ed. Kingsford, p. 185; Fabyan, *Concordance*, p. 662 (murder by Richard, but this source is writing thirty years later); Commignes, vol I, p. 201, *Croyland Chronicle*, p. 468, *Three Books of Polydore Vergil's English History* Polydore Vergil, ed. H Ellis (Camden Society 1844). *Three Books* pp. 155–6 (all say murder by Richard, but non-contemporary); More, *History of Richard III*, pp. 9–10 (murder by Richard without Edward's authority, but non-contemporary and with dubious motives).

51. Colin Richmond, 'Fauconberg's Kentish Rising of May 1471' in *E H R*, vol lxxxv (1970) pp. 673–92; *The Arrivall*, pp. 33–9; *Great Chronicle*, pp. 218–20.
52. Fabyan, p. 654; and see David Baldwin, *Elizabeth Woodville: Mother of the Princes in the Tower*, pp. 9–11.
53. *Gregory's Chronicle*, p. 221; *Three Fifteenth Century Chronicles*, p. 127.
54. Commignes, vol ii, pp. 63–7; he and Louis XI were probably under a misapprehension about Warwick's real influence (as opposed to high public profile) in the early-mid 1460s.
55. Ian Mortimer, *The Fears of Henry IV: the Life of England's Self-Made King* (Jonathan Cape 2007) pp. 305–6.
56. *Rotuli Parliamentarum*, vol v, pp. 497–9.
57. See his *The English Nobility and the Wars of the Roses 1459–61* (Nottingham Medieval Studies, 1997).
58. Edward Hall, *Chronicle*, p. 251. But the surviving statements that this 'perihelion' was seen as a good omen were written in retrospect, once Edward was king.
59. Ross, pp. 124–5; Warkworth, pp. 11–12 (blaming Warwick for stirring up discontent); Commignes, vol I, pp. 214–15 (Warwick more popular than Edward in late 1460s).
60. *Great Chronicle*, pp. 204–8 (Cook case); see also PRO King's Bench 9/319/mm. 7, 35–7, 40, 49–51. See also Warkworth p. 6 and Ross pp. 122–3 on Henry Courtenay. Richard III later claimed in a 1484 letter to the Earl of Desmond's heirs that the Woodvilles had destroyed Clarence and assorted other relatives and friends of his, but was not specific so we cannot tell which cases he meant.
61. Ross, pp. 100–01.
62. See discussion in Ashdown-Hill, *Eleanor: the Secret Queen* (History Press 2009)on the link between Eleanor and the Mowbrays via her sister.
63. *Paston Letters*, vol v, p. 80.
64. Ross, pp. 54–5.
65. Bertram Wolffe, *Henry VI*, pp. 38–9.
66. Scofield, vol I, pp. 446–53.
67. Ibid, pp. 518–36, and Ross p. 118 for 1467–8 rumours that Warwick was already in touch with Margaret of Anjou (via Louis XI?). As Margaret had murdered his father and brother and he had not yet lost the power to influence events at the Yorkist court – as he had in 1470 – this seems unlikely.
68. Ross, pp. 112 and 118.
69. *Croyland Chronicle*, pp. 558, 559; *Great Chronicle*, p. 224; *Chronicles of London*, ed. Kingsford p. 187.
70. *Gregory's Chronicle*, p. 219; Scofield, vol I, pp. 273–4, 292.
71. Warkworth, pp. 46–9.
72. Scofield, vol I, p. 320, on the negotiations with Castile in 1464.
73. For Stillington's arrest, see Bertram Fields, *Royal Blood*, pp. 112–15; and Chapter 5, n. 6 for the original sources and modern historians' verdicts. For Edward's illegal seizure of the Mowbray estates, see *Rotuli Parliamentarum*, vol vi, pp. 205–7.
74. *Croyland Chronicle*, p. 446; Warkworth, pp. 6–7.

## Chapter 4

1. Polydore Vergil, *Anglia Historia*, p. 135.
2. *Croyland Chronicle*, p. 557.
3. Ibid, p. 561; *Rotuli Parliamentarum*, vol v, p. 173 and (bill of attainder) vol vi, pp. 193–5; pp. 172–3; Scofield, vol ii, p. 188; *Calendar of the Patent Rolls 1476–85*; Calmette and Perinel pp. 376–7.

4. Dominic Mancini, *History of the Usurpation of Richard the Third*, ed. C Armstrong (Oxford 1969) p. 63; *Croyland Chronicle*, p. 562 (manner of execution unknown) and Polydore Vergil p. 167 and More p. 7 (butt of Malmsey wine). See also J Lander, 'The treason and death of the Duke of Clarence: a Reinterpretation', *Canadian Journal of History*, vol ii (1967) especially pp. 27–8.

5. Mancini p. 63 and More p. 7. Analysis in M Levine, 'Richard III: Usurper or lawful King?' in *Speculum*, vol xxxiv (1959) pp. 391–401. Historians still argue over the relationship between Richard and the Queen pre-1483; but the fact that she fled into sanctuary sooner than appeal to his mercy after attempting to block his Protectorship in May 1483 argues for mutual ill-will.

6. *Paston Letters* vol v, pp. 135–6.

7. Mancini, pp. 74–7; *Croyland Chronicle*, p. 565.

8. Charles Ross, *Richard III* (Methuen 1981) p. 69; and see pp. 65–9 on the question of the Protectorship as envisaged by Edward IV.

9. Mancini, p. 126; *Great Chronicle*, p. 567.

10. Mancini, pp. 78–9 and 90–1; and see Annette Carson, *Richard III: the Maligned King* (History Press 2010) for the theory that Rivers and/or Dorset poisoned Edward IV.

11. Mancini, p. 63; expanded on dubious evidence by Paul Murray Kendall, op. cit., pp. 125–6 and 454–5.

12. Mancini, pp. 76–9 – presumably relying on one of Edward V's attendants at Stony Stratford, or on what the ex-King later told Dr Argentine.

13. Mancini pp. 92–3 for Dr Argentine's evidence; Molinet, vol ii, p. 402.

14. For the 'evidence' of the bodies discovered in 1674 and the question of osteomyelitis being present in the jaw of the elder child, see: L E Tanner and W Wright, 'Recent Investigations regarding the Fate of the Princes in the Tower', *Archaeologia*, vol lxxxiv (1934) pp. 1–26. P W Hammond and L J White, 'The Sons of Edward IV: a Re-Examination of the Evidence on their Death and the Bones in Westminster Abbey' in Hammond (ed.), *Richard III: Loyalty, Leadership and Law* (Richard III and Yorkist History Trust 1986) pp. 104–47. Helen Maurer, 'Bones in the Tower: a Discussion of Time, Place and Circumstance' in *The Ricardian* (December 1990), part 1. Annette Carson, *Richard III: the Maligned King* (History Press 2009) pp. 172–99; Bertram Fields, *Royal Blood*, (Sutton 1998) pp. 238–57.

15. Quoted by Fields, pp. 140–8. See also Ross, p. 97 and Fields, p. 247 on the discovery of two bodies in the Tower c. 1614, written up in 1647.

16. *Croyland Chronicle*, p. 564; Commignes, vol I, p. 203; Mancini, p. 67; More, p. 4; *Gregory's Chronicle*, p. 226.

17. Mancini, p. 59 (Edward caught a chill out fishing at Windsor); Commignes, vol ii, pp. 54–9; Vergil pp. 171–2; Hall p. 338.

18. *Rotuli Parliamentarum*, vol vi, pp. 240–2; discussion in Ross, pp. 90–1.

19. More, pp. 55–6; Ross, *Edward IV*, pp. 315–16. The play that invented much of the 'Jane Shore' story (and her inaccurate Christian name) was written by Thomas Rowe in 1714.

20. *Croyland Chronicle*, p. 562; Ross, *Edward IV*, pp. 308–41 and 388–413.

21. One possible author was Nicholas Harpisfield, Clerk of the Signet.

22. See Michael Bongiorno, 'Did Louis XI Have Edward IV Poisoned?' in *Ricardian Register*, vol xxii, no. 3 (Autumn 1992) pp. 23–4.

23. Mancini, pp. 78–81.

24. Ibid, pp. 76–8.

25. Ibid, pp. 78–9.

26. *Croyland Chronicle*, pp. 564–5 on Hastings warning Richard. For Morton and Buckingham, see More p. 91, Ross, *Richard III*, pp. 113–15, and S B Chrimes, *Henry VII*, pp. 20–6.
27. Chrimes, p. 28.
28. More, pp. 10–11; Mancini, pp. 67–9.
29. Anne Sutton and Livia Vissier-Fuchs, 'The "Retirement" of Elizabeth Woodville and her Sons', in *The Ricardian*, vol xi (1999) pp. 56–14; Baldwin, *Elizabeth Woodville*, pp. 111–15; Chrimes p. 76 and n. For the idea that Elizabeth was secretly backing 'Simnel' and/ or that the latter was really Edward V, see Fields, *Royal Blood*, pp. 203–4.
30. The 'Song of the Lady Bessey' is in *Bishop Percy's Folio Manuscripts*, ed. J W Hales and F J Furnivall (Frederick Warne 1863) pp. 319–63. For the Princess' letter to John Howard in 1485, which was extant in the early seventeenth century, see Alison Hanham 'Sir George Buck and Princess Elizabeth's Letter: a Problem in Detection' in *The Ricardian*, vol vii, no. 97 (June 1987) pp. 398–400. The letter may refer to the Princess' hopes of marrying Prince Manuel of Portugal rather than Richard.
31. *Rotuli Parliamentarum*, vol vi, pp. 204–5.
32. Vergil, *Anglia Historia*, pp. 206–8; Gairdner, *Richard III*, pp. 167–9; Chrimes, pp. 29–31.
33. See Christopher Williams, *The Last Knight-Errant: Sir Edward Woodville and the Age of Chivalry* (IB Tauris 2009). Woodville was killed in battle in August 1488; a plaque was erected to him at his 1470s captaincy, Carisbrooke Castle.
34. Fields, pp. 190–1.

## Chapter 5

1. Ross, *Richard III*, pp. 104–24, 157–69.
2. *Croyland Chronicle*, p. 567; More, quoted by Bertram Fields, *Royal Blood*, pp. 190–1.
3. See analysis by John Ashdown-Hill in *Eleanor: the Secret Queen* (History Press 2009).
4. Fabyan, p. 654; *Rotuli Parliamentarum*, vol vi, pp. 240–2, stressing that the private nature of the marriage and the failure to gain the peers' consent made it illegal.
5. John Ashdown-Hill, *Eleanor: the Secret Queen*, p. 105.
6. On Stillington and his role: Michael Hicks, 'The Middle Brother: False, Fleeting, Perjur'd Clarence' in *The Ricardian*, vol 72 (1981) pp. 302–10; I Wigram, 'Clarence still perjur'd' in *The Ricardian*, vol 73 (1981) pp. 352–5; M Hicks, 'Clarence's calumniator corrected' in ibid, vol 74 (1981), pp. 399–401; I Wigram, 'False, Fleeting, perjur'd Clarence: a further exchange', Clarence and Richard' in ibid, vol 76 (1982) pp. 17–20 and M Hicks 'A further exchange: Richard and Clarence' in ibid, pp. 20–1; Michael Smith, 'Edward, George and Richard' in ibid, vol 77 (1982), pp. 47–9; also P W Hammond, 'Stillington and the Pre-Contract' in *The Ricardian*, vol 54 (1976). Hammond states that a debate about *Titulus Regius* by the Exchequer Court judges in Hilary Term 1485/6 saw it affirmed that the Bishop of Bath (i.e. Stillington) was the origin of the story of the pre-contract, but Henry VII refused to allow him to be questioned about it. Stillington's involvement in the 1477–8 Clarence 'showdown' is doubted by Peter Hancock, in *Richard III and the Murder in the Tower* (i.e. of Hastings, not the Princes) (History Press, 2009) pp. 104–7. He suggests that Stillington's admission about the pre-contract in 1483 was forced by Richard after the latter's ally Catesby discovered it from his family links to Eleanor Butler. On the legal implications of the pre-contract for the legitimacy of the Princes, whoever exposed it and why: R M Helmholtz, 'The Sons of Edward IV: a Canonical Assessment of the Claim that they were Illegitimate' in *Richard III: Loyalty, Lordship and Law*, 1986.

7. Henry also used the argument of Divine support as shown by victory in battle, which was unanswerable given what had happened but reflects the legal doubt over his paternal descent being sufficient to claim via the Tudor line. The only other king who could use such 'proof' was William I.

8. See the letters of Imperial ambassador Chapuys to Emperor Charles V of December 1533 and November 1534, quoted in J Ashdown-Hill, p. 209.

9. Polydore Vergil, pp. 186–7; Fields p. 101 quoting Commignes.

10. Stated in a January 2004 Channel Four programme, 'Britain's Real Monarch', and based on the research of Dr Michael Jones.

11. Mancini pp. 94–5; *Great Chronicle*, p. 232.

12. *York City Records*, vol I pp. 73–4.

13. Ross, *Richard III*, pp. 81–6; *Croyland Chronicle*, p. 566; Vergil pp. 179–81; More, pp. 47–9 (probably derived from eye-witness Bishop Morton); Mancini pp. 90–1; also reconstruction of events favourably for Richard by Kendall, pp. 190–6.

14. See Alison Hanham, 'Richard III, Lord Hastings and the Historians' in *E H R*, vol lxxxvii (1972) pp. 235–48; Bertram Wolffe, 'When and Why did Hastings lose his head?' in *E H R*, vol lxxix (1974) pp. 835–41: J A Thomson 'Richard III and Lord Hastings: a problematical case reviewed' in *BIHR,* vol xlviii (1975) pp. 22–30; Alison Hanham, 'Hastings Redivivus' in *E H R*, vol xc (1975) pp. 82–7 and B Wolffe, 'Hastings Reinterred' in *E H R*, vol xci (1976) pp. 813–24 (on the potential dispute over the date of the execution as 20 not 13 June 1483, since explained). C H Coleman, 'The execution of Hastings: a neglected source' in *BIHR*, vol liiii (1980) pp. 244–7.

15. See W L Warren, *Henry II* (Methuen 1973) pp. 508–10.

16. *The Arrivall of Edward IV*, p. 30; *Three Fifteenth Century Chronicles*, p. 184; Kingsford, *English Historical Literature in the Fifteenth Century*, pp. 374, 377. The claim that Richard killed Prince Edward in cold blood in Shakespeare, *Henry VI Part Three*, act 5 scene 5, is based on Vergil p. 152 and Hall p. 301.

17. Suggested by Peter Hancock in his *Richard III and the Murder in the Tower* (History Press 2009). He also suggests that it was Catesby, not Stillington who 'tipped off' Richard about the 'pre-contract' – and that Hastings knew about it as a close friend of Edward IV and had done nothing, which enraged Richard.

18. Polydore Vergil, pp. 179–81; More, pp. 47–9.

19. Fields, pp. 282–5.

20. Ross, *Richard III*, pp. 141–2 on Von Poppelau.

21. See ibid, pp. xxi–xxii.

22. *Croyland Chronicle*, p. 557; *Paston Letters*, vol v, pp. 135–6.

23. Sir Clement Markham, *Richard III: His Life and Character* (London 1906).

24. Kendall, a Ricardian enthusiast, ignores the possibility that Richard's actions were as much about creating a good image for himself as due to sincerity.

25. *Croyland Chronicle* p. 572.

26. More, pp. 22–3; Annette Carson, *Richard III: the Maligned King* (History Press 2009), pp. 136–7 on the London plot to free them in late 1483, which gives Richard a plausible reason for their inaccessibility.

27. *Croyland Chronicle*, pp. 567–8.

28. Mancini, ibid; John Ashdown-Hill, 'The Death of Edward V: New Evidence from Colchester' in *Essex Archaeology and History*, vol xxxv (2006).

29. *Croyland Chronicle*, ed. N Pronay and J Cox (Gloucester 1986) pp. 162–3.

30. As stated by his confidant Commignes.

31. More, p. 91; Ross, p. 115.
32. A contemporary allegation against Buckingham: 'Divisie Chronicle' of Holland, Zeeland and Friesland, c. 1500, quoted in Anne Wroe, *Perkin: a Story of Deception* (Vintage 2004) p. 108. Commignes also blamed him. Discussion of this theory: Fields, pp. 291–9.
33. See Fields, pp. 292–3: what did the words 'by the advice of' mean in 1483, the modern sense or 'by the means/ intermediary of'?
34. See Warbeck's letter to Isabella of Castile in 1493, quoted by Wroe, pp. 106–8.
35. *Croyland Chronicle*, pp. 567–8. For Richard's oath to Elizabeth Woodville, see *BL Harleian Mss. 433*, ed. R Horrox and P W Hammond (Richard III and Yorkist History Trust 1979–83) vol 3 p. 190.
36. Audrey Williamson, *The Mystery of the Princes* (Alan Sutton 1981).
37. Horrox and Hammond (eds), vol 3, nos. 2050 and 2063.
38. Fields, pp. 230–7.
39. PRO King's Bench 441/9/6.
40. See n. 34.
41. Wroe, *Perkin*, pp. 16–17. Apparently Warbeck had first come into Brampton's service via his acting as Brampton's wife's 'relief' page while they were living in the Netherlands and then asked to be taken to Portugal to gain foreign experience.
42. *Chronicles of London*, ed. Kingsford, pp. 219–22; *Great Chronicle*, pp. 284–6; Warbeck's 1493 letter to Isabella of Castile, *BL Egerton Mss. 6/6/3*.
43. The inconstancies in the 'confession' in 1497: see Fields, pp. 213–16. For the pretender's letter to Catherine/ Nicaise, his 'mother', see Wroe, pp. 513–20.
44. *Calendar of State Papers Venetian*, vol I, p. 285.
45. Wroe, pp. 185–6.
46. Ibid, pp. 49–50.
47. Ibid, pp. 208–9, 468–9. The story was reported by Maximilian in 1494, as originating from Warbeck's adviser Sir Robert Clifford – a possible 'double agent' already in touch with Henry VII.
48. D M Kleyn, in *Richard of England* (Kensal Press 1990).
49. See n. 33.
50. Ross, pp. 104–18; A E Conway, 'The Maidstone Sector of Buckingham's Rebellion, October 18, 1483' in *Archaeologia Cantiana*, vol xxxvii (1925) pp. 106– 14.
51. *Croyland Chronicle*, pp. 567–8; Polydore Vergil, pp. 219–20; *Chronicles of London*, ed. Kingsford, p. 191.
52. Polydore Vergil, p. 195.
53. Ross, pp. 105–24; also a statement of Richard's over-reliance on northerners to keep the restive South down in *Croyland Chronicle*, p. 570.
54. Hall, p. 398.
55. Especially in 1471, when Warwick ordered them to aid him against Edward IV.
56. Bacon, *Reign of Henry VII*, pp. 137–42.
57. *Letters and Papers of Henry VII*, vol I, pp. 231–40.
58. See *Calendar of State Papers Spanish*, ed. C Bergenroth et al (Longmans 1862 ff), supplement to vols 1 and 2, pp. 8 and 39–40 for the Duke's dismissive attitude to the Tudors as parvenus.
59. On Bosworth: Polydore Vergil, pp. 221–4; *Croyland Chronicle*, pp. 574–5; E Nokes and G Wheeler, 'A Spanish Account of the Battle of Bosworth' in *The Ricardian*, vol 36 (1971) pp. 1–5; 'The Ballad of Bosworth Field' in *Bishop Percy's Folio Manuscripts*, ed.

Hales and Furnivall, vol iii (1868) pp. 233–59. D T Williams, *The Battle of Bosworth* (Bosworth Publications 1973) pp. 1–24; James Gairdner, 'The Battle of Bosworth', in *Archaeologia*, vol lv, part 1 (1896) pp. 159–78; Ross, Richard III, pp. 216–25.

60. Polydore Vergil, pp. 209–16.
61. S B Chrimes, *Henry VII*, p. 44.
62. *The Historie of the Arrivall of King Edward the Fourth in England and his Final Recoverye of his Kingdom from King Henry the Sixth, AD 1471*, ed. J. Bruce (Camden Society 1838) pp. 29–30.
63. Ross, p. 129; Pamela Tudor-Craig, *Richard III* (National Portrait Gallery, London 1973) pp. 126–9. For the York tribute: R Davies, *Municipal Records of the City of York during the Reigns of Edward IV, Edward V and Richard III* (London 1843) p. 218.
64. See Barrie Williams article, 'The Portuguese Marriage and the Significance of the Holy Princess' in *The Ricardian*, May 1983.
65. Ibid.
66. Ian Mortimer, *The Greatest Traitor*, pp. 188–95, 197–9, 244–52, and 259–63; and his 'The death of Edward II in Berkeley Castle' in *E H R*, vol cxx (2005) pp. 1175–1214.

**Chapter 6**
1. Ross, *Richard III*, pp. 158–9 on the question of whether Lincoln was ever formally named as heir.
2. Desmond Seward, *The Last White Rose* (Constable 2010) p. 13.
3. Ross, pp. 222–3.
4. Seward, pp. 27–32.
5. See Michael Jones and Malcolm Underwood, *The King's Mother: Lady Margaret Beaufort, Countess of Richmond and Derby* (Cambridge UP 1992) pp. 19–20 and 24–6.
6. Margaret allowing herself to be superseded in 1485 was first noted by Horace Walpole in his *Royal and Noble Authors of England* in 1796. It was explained as due to practical politics by John Britton in his unpublished biographical notice of Margaret in the 1830s, now in the Cambridge University Library.
7. See *Chronicles of the Revolution 1399–1403*, ed. C. Given-Wilson, (Manchester UP 1993) pp. 166–7 and *Archaeologia*, vol xx (1824) p. 203 (transcript of French ambassador Creton's 'Metrical History') for the method of Henry's accession in Parliament in September 1399. Significantly, it appears that Edmund Mortimer – underage and nearest heir to Richard II by female descent – was not put forward by Henry's 'cheerleaders' in Parliament as an alternative candidate when they asked for approval – only Henry's adult and genealogically junior rivals from the House of York, who had backed the deposed Richard.
8. Chrimes, *Henry VII* (Methuen 1972) pp. 50–1.
9. Ibid, pp. 65–6.
10. Ibid, pp. 59–60.
11. *Rotuli Parliamentarum*, vol vi, pp. 275–8.
12. Fields, pp. 190–1.
13. Ibid, pp. 191–2.
14. Seward, pp. 13–18.
15. See Chapter 5, note 63.
16. *Letters and Papers of Henry VII*, vol I, p. 234.
17. E H Fonblanque, *The Annals of the House of Percy*, 2 vols (London 1887) vol I p. 300.
18. C H Williams, 'The rebellion of Sir Humphrey Stafford in 1486' in *E H R*, vol xliii (1928).

19. Seward, p. 18.
20. Ibid, pp. 19, 38.
21. See David Baldwin, *The Lost Prince: the Survival of Richard of York* (History Press 2008) especially chapters 1, 6, and 8. The story of Richard Plantagenet of Eastwell, Kent, first appeared in a local memoir of the estate's owners, the Earls of Winchelsea, in 1735 and was publicized by Arthur Mee in his 1930s guidebooks, *The King's England*; it formed the basis of the plot for the children's novelist Barbara Willard's book *The Sprig of Broom*. The anonymous 'lord' who Richard claimed took him to see his father King Richard on the eve of Bosworth may have been Lord Lovell.
22. See P W Hammond, 'The Illegitimate Children of Richard III' in J Petre (ed.), *Richard III: Crown and People* (Sutton 1985).
23. See M. Bennett, *Lambert Simnel and the Battle of Stoke* (Sutton 1987).
24. *Calendar of the Carew Manuscripts*, 6 vols (London 1867) vol v, pp. 188–9.
25. Seward, p. 28.
26. Chrimes pp. 75–6.
27. Seward, p. 31.
28. Ibid, pp. 31–2.
29. Ibid, p. 27.
30. *Materials for a History of the Reign of Henry VII*, ed. W Campbell (Rolls Series 1873) vol ii p. 148.
31. D Baldwin, *Elizabeth Woodville*, (Sutton 2004) pp. 112–13.
32. Wolffe, *Henry VI*, pp. 6-7.
33. Baldwin, pp. 113–14.
34. Fields, pp. 203–4.
35. See Gordon Smith's article in *The Ricardian*, December 1996.
36. Polydore Vergil, pp. 12 ff.
37. Ibid, p. 23.
38. Vergil, p. 20 ff.
39. Seward, pp. 38–40.
40. *The Great Chronicle of London*, p. 241.
41. Ibid, pp. 241–2.
42. Seward, p. 41.
43. Hall, p. 434.
44. Polydore Vergil, pp. 12–26.
45. J M Thompson, J Paul et al. (eds), *Registrum Magni Sigilli Regnum Scotorum: Register of the Great Seal of Scotland* (Scottish Record Society Edinburgh, 1882–1914) vol ii, p. 370.
46. D Baldwin, 'What Happened to Lord Lovell?' in *The Ricardian*, vol 89 (June 1985).
47. As n. 45.
48. Polydore Vergil, p. 24.
49. Quotation from the *Calendar of the Carew Mss: The Book of Howth*. See also the *New Dictionary of National Biography* article on Simnel, vol 50, p. 630.
50. Chrimes, pp. 259–61.
51. Wroe, p. 82.
52. See D Roberts, *The Battle of Stoke Field* (Newark and Sherwood District Council 1987).
53. As n. 45.

54. PRO 53rd Report, appendix ii, pp. 30–6; *Third Report of the Deputy Keeper of Public Records* (1842), appendix ii, pp. 216–18.

55. Desmond Seward, *The Last White Rose* (Constable and Robinson 2010) pp. 223–4.

56. Henry's letter to Charles VIII, autumn 1494: in *Letters and Papers of Henry VII*, vol ii, pp. 292–7.

57. A F Pollard, *The Reign of Henry VII from Contemporary Sources*: Volume One, Narrative Extracts (Longmans, Green 1913) pp. 82–3.

58. D Luckett, 'The Thames Valley Conspiracies Against Henry VII' in *BIHR*, vol lxviii (1995) pp. 164–72; *The Plumpton Correspondence*, letter lxxi.

59. Francis Bacon, *History of the Reign of Henry VII and Selected Works*, ed. B Vickers (Cambridge UP 1998) p. 105.

60. Wroe, pp. 141–3 and 153–60.

61. Ibid, pp. 141 and 153–8.

62. Ibid, pp. 165–6.

63. As Chapter 5 n. 48.

64. Hall, p. 465; John Stow, *Annales*, p. 478.

65. Polydore Vergil, p. 77.

66. Ibid, pp. 88 and n, 89; and Ellis, *Letters*, vol I pp. 24, 29.

67. See Chapter 5 note 34.

68. See Fields, p. 143 for the emergence of this story – known to More's son-in-law Rastell by the time of his 1550s edition of More's (c. 1510) work. Also see *Great Chronicle*, pp. 209, 212 and 213 and Hammond and White, 'The Sons of Edward IV' p. 108 for other rumours.

69. See Chapter 5, note 47.

70. See Wroe, pp. 87–8 and 516–17 on the mysterious 'Jean Le Sage', adopted 'son' of Duchess Margaret, living near her court around 1480.

71. See Wroe on Brampton: pp. 17–22, 73, 91, 105, 109.

72. Fields, pp. 230–7 and 242–3.

73. See Chapter 5 note 34.

74. See Wroe pp. 527–8 on the testimony of a Portuguese Herald, Tanjar, on this in 1496.

75. *Rotuli Parliamentarum* vol vi p. 94.

76. Wroe, pp. 16–17, 526–7.

77. 'Warbeck' himself said vaguely in his letter to Isabella of Castile in 1493 that he had been 'about nine' at the time of the Tower episode in summer 1483; in fact the Prince's tenth birthday was in August 1483. By modern standards his lack of knowledge should count against his claim – but medieval accuracy about dates for junior royals was limited. Fabyan thought the Prince was seven in 1483, Mancini eight.

78. Wroe, pp. 379–81, and pp. 400–07 on Henry's search for the 'truth' before 1497.

79. Ibid, pp. 381–93.

80. Ibid, p. 383.

81. Ibid, pp. 414–18.

82. Ibid, pp. 417–18.

83. According to More's account – but why had Henry VII not used this man as a convenient scapegoat and forced him to 'confess', blaming Tyrrell, in 1502?

84. Molinet, *Chroniques* vol v, pp. 49–50.

85. W A J Archbold, 'Sir William Stanley and Perkin Warbeck' in *E H R*, vol xxix (1899) p. 533.

86. Polydore Vergil, p. 65.

87. Wroe, pp. 176–91; W Hampton, 'The White Rose under the first Tudors' in *The Ricardian*, vol vii, no. 97 (June 1987) pp. 414–17.

88. Seward, p. 66.
89. Wroe, p. 141.
90. Seward, p. 74.
91. Bacon, p. 202; Polydore Vergil, pp. 71–4; Molinet, vol v pp. 47–8.
92. Wroe, pp. 222–5; and pp. 186–8 on Kendall's bizarre poisoning plot. See also *Letters and Papers of Henry VII*, vol ii pp. 318–23 (deposition by de Vignolles).
93. Wroe, pp. 222–5.
94. Ian Arthurson, *The Perkin Warbeck Conspiracy* (Sutton 1994), pp. 187–91 and Polydore Vergil, *Anglia Historia*, p. 67.
95. Wroe, pp. 182–4.
96. See n. 55.
97. PRO E/404/81/2.
98. PRO DL 28/2/2, and Molinet, vol v, pp. 47–8.
99. Polydore Vergil, pp. 73–4.
100. *Excerpta Historia*, ed. Samuel Bentley (London 1831) pp. 100 and 101.
101. *Rotuli Parliamentarum*, vol vi, p. 504.
102. Molinet, vol v, pp. 50–1; *Memorials of Henry VII*, ed. James Gairdner (Rolls Series vol x, 1858): the *Historia Regis Henrici Septimi* of Bernard Andre, pp. 66–7.
103. See Vergil p. 84 on the locals' apparent hesitation as the rebels arrived. There were, however, no prominent local Yorkists to give a 'lead' in taking a risk to welcome the rebels; if the latter had sailed to Great Yarmouth as was rumoured they would have had more support. But such initial setbacks had met other, successful invaders e.g. Edward IV in 1471.
104. Wroe, pp. 243–5.
105. *Calendar of the Carew Manuscripts: Book of Howth*, p. 472; Rymer, *Foedera*, vol xii, p. 567.
106. Polydore Vergil, pp. 87–9.
107. J Arthurson, 'The Rising of 1497' in J Rosenthal and C Richmond (eds), *People, Politics and Community in the Later Middle Ages* (Sutton 1987) pp. 1–18; Chrimes, p. 90.
108. Seward, pp. 100–01.
109. See *Letters and Papers of Henry VII*, vol I, pp. 231–40 for the 1504 Calais discussions where the incident was remembered. Governor Sir Richard Nanfan said Henry had been furious with Daubeny for delaying his arrival.
110. As n. 108.
111. PRO King's Bench: 9/441/2.
112. Wroe, pp. 308–10, 323–4.
113. *Rotuli Parliamentarum*, vol vi, pp. 544–5.
114. Polydore Vergil, pp. 104–6; *Calendar of State Papers and Manuscripts Relating to Milan*, ed. Allen B Hindes (HMSO 1912) vol I pp. 325–7.
115. Wroe, p. 328.
116. *Letters and Papers of Henry VII*, vol I, p. 112; Ellis, *Letters*, vol I, pp. 32–3.
117. Polydore Vergil, pp. 105–7; Wroe, pp. 333–7.
118. Pollard, *The Reign of Henry VII*, vol I, pp. 167–8.
119. *Calendar of State Papers Venetian*, ed. R Brown, vol I (HMSO 1864) pp. 263, 265.
120. Polydore Vergil, *Three Books*, p.227; also *Calendar of State Papers Milan*, p. 328.
121. Wroe, pp. 341–2.
122. Pollard, vol I, pp. 173–6; *Calendar of State Papers Milan*, p. 329; *Chronicles of London*, ed. Kingsford, p. 218; PRO E 101/14/16 and 90v, E 36/426, f. 37v.

123. Polydore Vergil, pp. 142–4; CSP Milan p. 329; Bernard Andre, pp. 72–3; Wroe, pp. 365–70 (Warbeck at Taunton) and 373–9 (Katherine at Taunton).

124. Warbeck's 1496 proclamation attacking Henry's ministers: *BL Harleian Mss.* 283, f.

125. Buckingham's sneers at the Tudors: *Calendar of State Papers Spain*, ed. C Bergenroth et al.: supplement to vols 1 and 2 (HMSO 1862), pp. 8 and 39–40.

126. Thomas Penn, *Winter King: the Dawn of Tudor England* (Penguin 2011) pp. 367– 74.

127. Penn, pp. 167–70 and 261–332. The King's decline into paranoia and extortion notably worsened after Dudley's appointment in 1504, as the latter's foes alleged in 1509 – but the famous 'Morton's Fork' tax-policy and other instances of oppressive fiscal policies had already been invented by the King's long-term adviser Bishop Fox who was carefully exonerated as being more useful to Henry VIII.

128. J Berengar, *A History of the Habsburg Empire 1273–1700* (Longman 1994) p. 134.

129. Polydore Vergil, p. 115; *Excerpta Historia*, ed. Bentley, p. 118; *Great Chronicle*, p. 287; Molinet, vol v, p. 120. The indictments of Warbeck's 'negligent' guards are in PRO King's Bench 9/416/22. See PRO 53rd Report, appendix ii, pp. 30–6; *Third Report of the Deputy Keeper of Public Records* (1842) appendix ii, pp. 216–18; also Wroe, pp. 475–86. The trials: *Third Report*, pp. 216, 218, and 53rd Report pp. 30–1, 33, 35. The executions: *Chronicles of London*, ed. Kingsford, pp. 226–8.

130. Vergil pp. 118 and 119n; also Seward pp. 132–4; *Calendar of State Papers Spain* (from Simancas archive), volume 1, ed. G. Begenroth (HMSO 1862), p. 239.

131. H Pierce, *Margaret Pole, Countess of Salisbury 1473–1541* (University of Wales Press 2003) p. 114.

# Bibliography

**Primary sources**

*The Anglia Historia of Polydore Vergil AD 1485-1537*, ed. and tr. D Hay (Royal Historical Society, Camden Series, vol lxxiv (1950).

Andre, Bernard, *Historia Regis Henrici Septimi*, ed. James Gairdner (Rolls Series 1858).

'The Ballad of Bosworth Field', in *Bishop Percy's Folio Manuscripts*, vol iii, ed. J Hales and F Furnivall (Frederick Warne 1868).

Benet, John, *Chronicle for the Years 1400 to 1462*, ed. G and M Harriss in *Camden Miscellany*, vol xxiv (Royal Historical Society 1972).

*British Library Harleian Mss. 433*. eds. R Horrox and P Hammond (4 vols, Richard III Society 1979–83).

*The Brut or the Chronicles of England*, ed. F de Brie, EETS, original series, vols cxxxi – cxxxvi (London 1906–8).

*Calendar of the Carew Manuscripts: vol v, The Book of Howth* (HMSO 1867).

*Calendar of Close Rolls: Henry VI* (6 vols, HMSO 1933–47)

*Calendar of Close Rolls: Edward IV / Edward V / Richard III* (2 vols, HMSO 1949–54)

*Calendar of Close Rolls: Henry VII* (2 vols, HMSO 1955–63).

*Calendar of Fine Rolls: Henry VI* (5 vols, HMSO 1935–40)

*Calendar of Fine Rolls: Edward IV to 1471* (HMSO 1949)

*Calendar of Fine Rolls: Edward IV, 1471–83 / Richard III* (HMSO 1961).

*Calendar of Patent Rolls: Henry VI* (6 vols, HMSO 1933–47)

*Calendar of Patent Rolls: Edward IV to 1475* (2 vols, HMSO 1897–9)

*Calendar of Patent Rolls: Edward IV from 1476 Edward V / Richard III* (HMSO 1901).

*Calendar of State Papers and Manuscripts Existing in the Archives of Milan*, vol I, ed. Allen B Hindes (HMSO 1913).

*Calendar of State Papers and Manuscripts Relating to English Affairs in the Archives of Venice (Calendar of State Papers Venetian)*, vol I ed. R Brown (HMSO 1864).

*Calendar of State Papers Spain*, ed. C Bergenroth et al., supplement to vols 1 and 2 (HMSO 1862).

*A Chronicle of London*, ed. N H Nicholas (London 1827).

*Chronicles of London*, ed. C Kingsford (Oxford 1905).

*A Chronicle of the Rebellion in Lincolnshire 1470*, ed. J G Nicholas (Camden Society 1847).

*Chronicles of the Revolution 1397–1400*, ed. C. Given-Wilson (Manchester UP 1993).

*Chronicles of the White Rose of York*, ed. J A Giles (London 1845).

de Commynes/Commines/Commignes, Philippe, *Memoires*, ed., E Dupont (3 vols, Paris 1840–7).

de Commynes/Commines/Commignes, Philippe, *The Reign of Louis XI, 1461–83*, tr. Michael Jones (London 1972).

*Croyland Chronicle: Ingulph's Chronicle of the Abbey of Crowland with the Continuation*, tr. H T Riley (London 1854).

*Croyland Chronicle: Ingulph's Chronicle of the Abbey of Crowland with the Continuation* ed. and tr. N Pronay and J Cox (Sutton 1986).

Davies, J S, *An English Chronicle of the Reigns of Richard II, Henry IV, Henry V and Henry VI* (Camden Society 1856).

Ellis, H, (ed.) *Original Letters Illustrative of English History*, 11 vols (London 1824–46).

Fabyan, Robert, *The New Chronicles of England and France*, ed. H Ellis (London 1811).

Fortescue, Sir John, *Fortescue on the Governance of England*, ed. Charles Plummer (Oxford 1885).

*The Great Chronicle of London*, ed. A H Thomas and I D Thorne (London 1938).

Edmund, Hall, *The Union of the Two Noble Illustre Houses of Lancaster and York*, 1547, reprinted and edited by H. Ellis, (London 1809).

*Chronicle*, ed. H Ellis (London 1809).

Hardyng, John, *Chronicle*, ed. C Kingsford in *English Historical Review*, vol xxvii pp. 462–83, 740–53.

*Historie of the Arrivall of King Edward IV*, ed. J Bruce (Camden Society 1838).

*Historical Collections of a Citizen of London: Gregory's Chronicle, 1189–1469*, ed. James Gairdner (Camden Society 1876).

*Letters and Papers of Henry VII* (1863 HMSO).

Mancini, Dominic, *History of the Usurpation of Richard the Third*, ed. and tr. C A J Armstrong (Oxford University Press edition, 1969).

*Chroniques de Jean Molinet*, ed. G Doutrepont and O Jourdogne (3 vols, Brussels 1934–7).

More, Sir Thomas, *History of King Richard the Third*, in *The Complete Works*, ed. J S Sylvester, vol ii (Yale UP 1963).

*The Paston Letters 1422–1509*, ed. James Gairdner (6 vols, Chatto and Windus 1904).

*Rotuli Parliamentorum*, ed. J Strachey et al. (6 vols, London 1767–77).

*The Plumpton Correspondence*, ed. T Stapleton (Camden Society 1839).

Public Records Office, *53rd Report* (HMSO date unknown).

Public Records Office, *3rd Report of the Deputy Keeper of Public Records* (1842).

*Registrum Magni Sigilli Scotorum: the Register of the Great Seal of Scotland*, eds. J M Thompson, J Paul et al. (Scottish Record Society 1882–1914): vol ii.

*The Reign of Henry VII from Contemporary Sources: vol I, Narrative Extracts*, ed. A F Pollard (Longmans Green 1913).

Rous, John, *Joannis Rossi Antiquarii Warwickensis Historia Regum Angliae*, ed. T Hearne (Oxford 1745).

*Six Town Chronicles of England*, ed. Ralph Flenley (Oxford 1911).

The 'Somnia Vigilante', ed. J Gilson. In *E H R*, vol xxvi (1911) pp. 512–25.

Stow, John, *Annales or a Generall Chronicle of England* (London 1631).

*Three Books of Polydore Vergil's English History*, ed. H Ellis (Camden Society 1844).

*Three Fifteenth Century Chronicles*, ed. James Gairdner (Camden Society 1880).

Warkworth, John, *A Chronicle of the First Thirteen Years of the Reign of King Edward the Fourth*, ed. J O Halliwell (Camden Society 1839).

Wauvrin/Waurin, Jean, *Anchiennes Chroniques d'Angleterre*, ed. E Dupont (3 vols, Paris 1858–63).

*York Civic Records*, ed. A Raine, vol I (Yorkshire Archaeological Society, Record Series, 1939).

## Secondary sources

*Books*
Arthurson, I, *The Perkin Warbeck Conspiracy 1491–1499* (Alan Sutton 1994).
Ashdown-Hill, John, *Eleanor, the Secret Queen* (2009).
Ashdown-Hill, John, Richard III's 'Beloved Cousin': John Howard and the House of York *(History Press 2009)*.
Bacon, Francis, Works, *ed. J Spedding: vol vi*, The History of the Reign of King Henry the Seventh *(10 vols, London 1858)*.
Bagley, *J J*, Margaret of Anjou *(London 1948)*.
*Baldwin, David*, Elizabeth Woodville: Mother of the Princes in the Tower *(Sutton 2004)*.
*Baldwin, David*, Stoke Field: the Last Battle of the Wars of the Roses (Sutton 2006).
Baldwin, David, The Lost Prince: the Suruval of Richard of York (History Press 2008).
Barker, Juliet, *Conquest: the English Kingdom of France 1415–50* (Abacus 2009).
Basin, T, *Histoire des regnes du Charles VII et Louis XI*, ed. J Quichereau (4 vols, Paris 1855–9).
de Beaucourt, Gaston du Fresne, *Histoire de Charles VII* (4 vols, Paris 1881–91).
Bennett, M J, *Lambert Simnel and the Battle of Stoke* (Alan Sutton 1987).
Boardman, Andrew, *The Battle of Towton 1461* (Stroud 1994).
Du Boulay, F H (ed.) *Documents Illustrative of Medieval Kentish Society*, (Kent Archaeological Society 1964).
Brooks, F W, *The Council of the North* (Historical Association, 1966).
Buck, Sir George, *The History of King Richard the Third*, ed. A N Kincaid (Alan Sutton 1979).
Calmette, J and G Perinel, *Louis XI et d'Angleterre* (Paris 1930).
Campbell, W (ed.) *Materials for a History of the Reign of Henry VII*, (Rolls Series 1873).
Carson, Annette, *Richard III: the Maligned King* (History Press 2010).
Chrimes, S B, *Henry VII* (Methuen 1972).
*Coventry Court Leet Book vol ii* (Early English Text Society 1907–13).
Conway Davies, J (ed) *Studies Presented to Sir Hilary Jenkinson* (Oxford 1957).
Dockray, K, *Henry VI, Margaret of Anou and the Wars of the Roses* (Stroud 2000).
Fields, Bertram, *Royal Blood: Richard III and the Mystery of the Princes* (Sutton 1998).
de Fonblanque, E B, *Annals of the House of Percy* (2 vols, London 1887).
Foss, P J, *The Field of Redmore Plain: the Battle of Bosworth* (Stroud 1990).
Gairdner, James, *History of the life and reign of Richard III* (Cambridge 1898).
Gairdner, James (ed.) 'Short English Chronicle', in *Three English Chronicles*, (Camden Society 1880).
Gillingham, John, *The Wars of the Roses* (Weidenfeld and Nicolson 2001).
Goodwin, George, *Fatal Colours: Towton 1461, England's Bloodiest Battle* (Phoenix 2011).
Haigh, P A, *The Battle of Wakefield* (Stroud 1996).
Hammond, P W, *The Battles of Barnet and Tewkesbury* (Sutton 1990).
Hancock, Peter, *Richard III and the Murder in the Tower* (History Press 2009).
Hanham, Alison *Richard III and his Early Historians* (Oxford UP 1975).
Harvey, I M, *Jack Cade's Rebellion of 1450* (London 1991).
Hicks, Michael, *False, Fleeting, Perjur'd Clarence* (Sutton 1980).
Hicks, Michael, *Anne Neville: Queen to Richard III* (London 2006).
Horrox, Rosemary, *Richard III: a Study of Service* (Cambridge 1989).
Jones, M K and M G Underwood, *The King's Mother: Lady Margaret Beaufort, Countess of Richmond and Derby* (Cambridge UP 1992).

Kendall, Paul Murray, *Louis XI* (London 1971)
Kendall, Paul Murray, *Richard III* (1955).
Kendall, Paul Murray, *Warwick the Kingmaker* (London 1957).
Kingsford, C, *English Historical Literature in the Fifteenth Century* (Oxford 1913).
Kleyn, D M, *Richard of England* (Kensal Press 1990).
Knecht, R, *The Valois: Kings of France 1328–1589* (Hambledon and London 2004).
Lander, J R, *The Wars of the Roses* (London 1965).
Lander, J R, *Crown and Nobility 1450–1509* (London 1976).
Markham, Sir Clement, *Richard III: His Life and Character* (London 1906).
Mortimer, Ian, *The Fears of Henry IV: the Life of England's Self-Made King* (Jonathan Cape 2007).
Mortimer, Ian, *The Greatest Traitor: the Life of Roger Mortimer, Earl of March, Ruler of England 1327–1330* (Pimlico 2004).
Mortimer, Ian, *The Perfect King: the Life of Edward III, Father of the English Nation* (Pimlico 2007).
Oman, Sir Charles, *Warwick the Kingmaker* (Clarendon Press 1891).
Petre, J, (ed.) *Richard III: Crown and People* (Richard III Society, 1975–81).
Pierce, H, *Margaret Pole, Countess of Salisbury 1473–1541* (University of Wales Press 2009).
Ramsay, J H, *Lancaster and York* (2 vols, Oxford 1892).
Rawcliffe, C, *The Staffords, Earls of Stafford and Dukes of Buckingham 1394–1521* (Cambridge 1978).
Roberts, D E, *The Battle of Stoke Field* (Newark 1987).
Ross, Charles, *Edward IV* (Methuen 1974)
Ross, Charles, *Richard III* (Methuen 1981).
Ross, Charles, *Patronage, Pedigree and Power in Later Medieval England* (Alan Sutton 1979).
Sadler, John, *Towton: the Battle of Palm Sunday 1461* (Pen and Sword 2011).
Saul, Nigel, *Richard II* (Yale UP 1997).
Scofield, C L, *The Life and Reign of Edward the Fourth* (2 vols, London 1923).
Seward, Desmond, *The Last White Rose: the Secret Wars of the Tudors* (Constable 2010).
Stevenson, J (ed.) *The Wars of the English in France during the Reign of Henry VI: Letters and Papers* (2 vols, Record Society 1861–4).
Storey, R L, *The End of the House of Lancaster* (Cambridge University Press 1966).
Tuck, Anthony, *Richard II and the Nobility* (Edward Arnold 1971).
Tudor-Craig, Pamela, *Richard III* (National Portrait Gallery 1973).
Warren, W L, *Henry II* (Methuen 1973).
Weir, Alison, *Lancaster and York* (Vintage 2009).
Williams, D T, *The Battle of Bosworth* (Bosworth Publications 1973).
Wolffe, Bertram, *Henry VI* (Methuen 1981).
Wroe, Anne, *Perkin: a Story of Deception* (Vintage 2004).

*Articles*
Allan, A, 'Yorkist Propaganda: Pedigree, Prophecy and the "British History" in the Reign of Edward IV' in C. Ross (ed.), *Patronage, Pedigree and Power in Later Medieval England* (Alan Sutton 1979).
Archbold, W A, 'Sir William Stanley and Perkin Warbeck' in *E H R*, vol xiv (1899).
Armstrong, C A J, 'The Inauguration Ceremonies of the Yorkist Kings, and their Title to the Throne', *Transactions of the Royal Historical Society*, 4th series, vol xxx (1948).
Armstrong, C A J, 'Politics and the Battle of St Albans, 1455' in *Bulletin of the Institute of Historical Research*, xxxiii (1960).

Arthurson, I, 'The Rising of 1497' in J Rosenthal and C Richmond, eds., *People, Politics and Community in the Later Middle Ages* (Sutton 1987).

Ashdown-Hill, John, 'Edward IV's Uncrowned Queen: the Lady Eleanor Talbot, Lady Butler' in *The Ricardian*, no. 11 (1997–9) pp. 166–90.

Ashdown-Hill, John, 'Lady Eleanor Talbot: New Evidence, New Answers, New Questions' in *The Ricardian* (2006).

Ashdown-Hill, John, 'The Death of Edward V: New Evidence from Colchester' in *Essex Archaeological History*, vol xxxv (2006).

Baldwin, David, 'What Happened to Lord Lovell?' in *The Richardian*, no. 89 (June 1985).

Barker, Nicholas and R Birley, 'Jane Shore' in *Etoniana*, nos. 125 and 126 (June and December 1972).

Bentley, Samuel (ed.) *Excerpta Historia* (London 1831).

Bongiorno, Michael, 'Did Louis XI Have Edward IV Assassinated?' in *The Ricardian Register*, vol xxii no. 3 (autumn 1997).

Blyth, J D, 'The Battle of Tewkesbury' in *Transactions of the Bristol and Gloucestershire Archaeological Society*, vol lxx (1961).

Cavell, E, 'Henry VII, the North of England and the First Provincial Progress of 1486' in *Northern History*, vol xxxix (Sept 2002).

Coleman, C H, 'The Execution of Hastings: a neglected source' in *BIHR* vol liii (1980).

Conway, A, 'The Maidstone Sector of Buckingham's Rebellion, October 18th 1483' in *Archaeologia Cantiana*, vol xxxvii (1925).

Crawford, Anne, 'John Howard, Duke of Norfolk: a Possible Murderer of the Princes?' in *The Ricardian*, vol v (1980).

Dockray, K, 'The Yorkshire Rebellion of 1469' in *The Ricardian*, no. 83 (1983) pp. 249–52.

Dockray, K, 'Edward IV: Playboy or Politician?' in *The Ricardian*, vol 10 (1995).

Edwards, J G, 'The second continuation of the Croyland Chronicle: was it written in ten days?' in *BIHR*, vol xxix (1966).

Fahy, C, 'The marriage of Edward IV and Elizabeth Woodville: a new Italian source' in *E H R* vol lxxvi (1961).

Gairdner, James, 'The Battle of Bosworth' in *Archaeologia*, vol lv, part 1 (1896).

Griffiths, R A, 'Local rivalries and national politics: the Percies, the Nevilles and the Duke of Exeter 1452–3' in *Speculum*, vil xliii (1968).

Griffiths, R A, 'The trial of Eleanor Cobham: an episode in the fall of Duke Humphrey of Gloucester' in *BJRL* vol li (1968-9) pp. 381-99.

Griffiths, R A, 'Duke Richard of York's intentions in 1450 and the origins of the War of the Roses' in *Journal of Medieval History*, vol I (1975).

Hammond, P W, 'Stillington and the Pre-Contract' in *The Ricardian*, no. 54 (1976).

Hammond, P W and W J White, 'The Sons of Edward IV: a Re-examination of the Evidence on their Deaths and the Bones in Westminster Abbey' in C. Ross (ed.), *Loyalty, Lordship and Law* (Richard III and Yorkist History Trust 1979).

Hanham, Alison, 'Richard III, Lord Hastings and the Historians' in *E H R*, vol lxxxviii (1972).

Hanham, Alison, 'Hastings Redivivus' in *E H R*, vol cxi (1975).

Hanham, Alison, 'Sir George Buck and Princess Elizabeth's Letter: a Problem in Detection' in *The Ricardian*, vol vii (1987).

Harriss, G L, 'The Struggle for Calais: an Aspect of the Rivalry between Lancaster and York' in *E H R*, vol lxxv (1960).

Head, Constance, 'Pius II and the Wars of the Roses' in *Archivum Historiae Pontificiae*, vol viii (1970).

Helmholtz, R M, 'The Sons of Edward IV: a Canonical Assessment of the Claim that they were Illegitimate' in *Richard III: Loyalty, Lordship and Law* (Richard III and Yorkist History Trust 1986).

Hicks, Michael, 'The Middle Brother: False, Fleeting, Perjur'd Clarence' in *The Ricardian*, no. 72 (1981) pp. 302-10.

Hicks, Michael, 'Clarence's Calumniator Corrected' in *The Ricardian*, no. 74 (1981).

Hicks, Michael, 'False, Fleeting, Perjur'd Clarence: a Further Exchange' in *The Ricardian*, no. 76 (1982) pp. 20-1.

Hicks, Michael, 'Edward IV, the Duke of Somerset and Lancastrian Loyalism in the North' in *Northern History*, vol xxii (1984).

Hicks, Michael, 'Warwick the Reluctant Kingmaker' in *Medieval History*, vol I (1991).

Hicks, Michael, 'Unweaving the Web: the Plot of July 1483 against Richard III and its Wider Significance' in *The Ricardian* (Sept 1991).

Holland, P, 'Cook's case in History and Myth' in *Historical Review*, vol lxi (1988).

R F Hunnisett, 'Treason by Words' in *Sussex Notes and Queries*, vol xiv (Lewes 1954-7).

Jack, R I, 'A Quincentenary: the Battle of Northampton, July the 10th, 1460' in *Northamptonshire Past and Present*, vol iii, no. 1 (1960).

Jones, M K, 'Edward IV, the Earl of Warwick and the Yorkist Claim to the Throne' in *Historical Resarch*, vol lxx (1997).

Knecht, J, 'The Episcopate and the Wars of the Roses' in *University of Birmingham Historical Journal*, vol vi (1957).

Lander, J R, 'Edward IV: the Modern Legend and a Revision' in *History*, vol xli (1956).

Lander, J R, 'Henry VI and the Duke of York's Second Protectorate' in *Bulletin of the John Rylands Library*, vol xliii (1960).

Lander, J R, 'Attainder and Forfeiture 1453–1509', *Historical Journal*, vol iv (1961).

Lander, J R, 'Marriage and Politics in the Fifteenth Century: the Nevills and the Wydvills' in *BIHR*, vol xxxvi (1963).

Lander, J R, 'The Treason and Death of the Duke of Clarence: a Reinterpretation' in *Canadian Journal of History*, vol ii (1967).

Leslau, J, 'Did the Sons of Edward IV Outlive Henry VII?' in *The Ricardian*, vol iv (1978).

Levine, M, 'Richard III: Usurper or Lawful King?' in *Speculum*, vol xxiv (1959).

Luckett, D, 'The Thames Valley Conspiracies Against Henry VII' in *BIHR*, vol lxviii (1995) pp. 164–92.

Madden, Frederick, 'Documents relating to Perkin Warbeck, with Remarks on his History' in *Archaeologia*, vol xxvii (1838), appendix 2.

Maurer, Helen, 'Bones in the Tower: a Discussion of Time, Place and Circumstance' in *The Ricardian*, December 1990, part 1.

Morehen, W E, 'The Career of John de la Pole, Earl of Lincoln' in *The Ricardian*, vol xiii (2003).

Morgan, D A L, 'The King's Affinity in the Polity of Yorkist England', in *TRHS*, 5th series vol xxii (1973).

Mortimer, P, 'York or Lancaster: Who was the Rightful Heir to the Throne in 1460?' in *The Ricardian Bulletin* (autumn 2008).

Myers, A R, 'The Household of Queen Margaret of Anjou' in *BJRL*, vol xl (1957–8).

Myers, A R, 'The Outbreak of War between England and Burgundy in February 1471' in *BIHR* vol xxiii (1960).

Myers, A R, 'Richard III and Historical Tradition' in *History*, vol liii (1968).

Nokes, E and G Wheeler, 'A Spanish Account of the Battle of Bosworth' in *The Ricardian*, no. 36 (1972).

O'Regan, Mary, 'The pre-contract and its effect on the succession in 1483' in *The Ricardian* (Sept 1976).

Pollard, A J, 'The Tyranny of Richard III' in *Journal of Medieval History*, vol ii (1977).

Richmond, Colin, 'Fauconberg's Kentish Rising of May 1471' in *E H R*, vol lxxxv (1970).

Roskell, J S, 'The Office and Dignity of Protector of England' in *EHR* vol lviii (1953).

Roskell, J S, 'William Catesby, Councillor to Richard III' in *BJRL*, vol xlii 1959).

Roskell, J S, 'Sir William Oldhall, Speaker in the Parliament of 1450–1' in *Nottingham Medieval Studies*, vol v (1961).

Roth, C, 'Perkin Warbeck and his Jewish Master' (i.e. Sir Edward Brampton), in *Transactions of the Jewish Historical Society of England*, vol ix (1922) pp. 143–62.

Rowse, A L, 'The Turbulent Career of Sir Henry de Bodrugan' in *History*, vol xxix (1944).

Scofield, C L, 'Henry, Duke of Somerset and Edward IV' in *E H R*, vol xxi (1906).

Smith, G, 'Lambert Simnel and the King from Dublin' in *The Ricardian*, vol x (1994–6) pp. 498–536.

Smith, M, 'Edward, George and Richard' in *The Ricardian*, no. 77 (1982) pp. 47–9.

Smith, M, 'Reflections on the Lady Eleanor' in *The Ricardian* (Sept 1998).

Sutton, Anne and Livia Vissier-Fuchs, 'The "Retirement" of Elizabeth Woodville and her Sons' in *The Ricardian*, vol xi (1999) pp. 561–4.

Tanner, L S and W Wright, 'Recent Investigations Regarding the Fate of the Princes in the Tower', in *Archaeologia*, vol lxxxiv (1934).

Thomson, J A F, ' "The Arrivall of Edward IV" – the Development of the Text' in *Speculum*, vol xlvi (1971).

Thomson, J A F, 'The Courtenay Family in the Yorkist Period' in *BIHR*, vol xlv (1972).

Thomson, J A F, 'Richard III and Lord Hastings' in *BIHR*, vol xlviii (1975).

Virgoe, Roger, 'The death of William de la Pole, Duke of Suffolk' in *BJRL,* vol xlvii (1965) pp. 489–502.

Williams, B, 'The Portuguese Marriage and the Significance of the "Holy Princess"', *The Ricardian* (May 1983).

Wigram, Isolde, 'The death of Hastings' in *The Ricardian*, no. 50 (1975) pp. 7–9.

Wigram, Isolde, 'False, Fleeting, perjur'd Clarence: a further exchange, Clarence and Richard', in *The Ricardian*, no. 76 (1982) pp. 17–20.

Williams, B, 'Lambert Simnel's rebellion: How Reliable is Polydore Vergil?' in *The Ricardian*, no. 6 (1982).

Williams, C H, 'The Rebellion of Sir Humphrey Stafford in 1486' in *E H R*, vol xliii (1928).

Williams, J M, 'The Political Career of Francis, Lord Lovell' in *The Ricardian*, vol. 8 (1990).

Wolffe, Bertram, 'When and Why did Hastings Lose His Head?' in *E H R* vol lxxix (1974) pp. 835–44.

# Index